COTTAGE BY THE SEA

Rocked by tragedy, Annie Marlow returns to the one place she knows she can heal: the cottage by the sea where she spent many happy childhood holidays with her family. There, Annie meets Keaton, a local painter with a big heart; Mellie, the reclusive landlord she is determined to befriend; and Britt, a teenager with a terrible secret. With them, her broken spirit starts to heal. Then events threaten Annie's new idyll. And when the opportunity of a lifetime lands in her lap, she is torn between the excitement of a new journey and the pull of the haven — and the man — she has come to call home. Will she be able to make her new-found happiness last?

SPECIAL MESSAGE TO READERS

THE ULVERSCROFT FOUNDATION
(registered UK charity number 264873)
was established in 1972 to provide funds for
research, diagnosis and treatment of eye diseases.
Examples of major projects funded by
the Ulverscroft Foundation are:-

- The Children's Eye Unit at Moorfields Eye Hospital, London
- The Ulverscroft Children's Eye Unit at Great Ormond Street Hospital for Sick Children
- Funding research into eye diseases and treatment at the Department of Ophthalmology, University of Leicester
- The Ulverscroft Vision Research Group, Institute of Child Health
- Twin operating theatres at the Western Ophthalmic Hospital, London
- The Chair of Ophthalmology at the Royal Australian College of Ophthalmologists

You can help further the work of the Foundation
by making a donation or leaving a legacy.
Every contribution is gratefully received. If you
would like to help support the Foundation or
require further information, please contact:

THE ULVERSCROFT FOUNDATION
The Green, Bradgate Road, Anstey
Leicester LE7 7FU, England
Tel: (0116) 236 4325

website: www.foundation.ulverscroft.com

COTTAGE BY THE SEA

DEBBIE MACOMBER

LARGE
PRINT

First published in Great Britain 2018
by
Arrow Books

First Isis Edition
published 2019
by arrangement with
Arrow Books
Penguin Random House

A catalogue record for this book is available
from the British Library.

ISBN 978–1–78541–728–3 (hb)
ISBN 978–1–78541–734–4 (pb)

Published by
F. A. Thorpe (Publishing)
Anstey, Leicestershire

Set by Words & Graphics Ltd.
Anstey, Leicestershire
Printed and bound in Great Britain by
T. J. International Ltd., Padstow, Cornwall

This book is printed on acid-free paper

To Candi and Tom,
dearest of friends
(and I'd say that even without
drinking Tom's wonderful wine)

A LETTER FROM
Debbie

Summer 2018

Dear Friends,

It actually happened. Without warning or any indication of what was about to take place, an entire hillside collapsed near Oso, Washington. The March 22, 2014, mudslide took with it forty-nine homes and claimed forty-three lives. The Oso mudslide is part of history now, but the tragedy will long be remembered in the Pacific Northwest. The suddenness of it, the shock that such a thing could happen.

As a writer, I couldn't help wondering about family members who weren't at home at the time — those who escaped death only to be left behind. In this germ of an idea the plot premise for *Cottage by the Sea* was born. My heroine lost her entire family and is now alone in the world, seeking out a place she can call home. And isn't that what we are all searching for — home?

I work with a remarkable group of publishing professionals. My editors, Shauna Summers and Jennifer Hershey, strive to bring out the best in me as an author. Although I'd like to think every word that flows from my computer keys is perfect in every way, it's not. There are rewrites and edits, more rewrites and more edits. I am blessed every single day for the privilege of being their author.

As always, hearing from my readers is vitally important to me. I look forward to reading your comments, suggestions, and corrections. Yes, even after several reads by any number of people, mistakes still sometimes get through. Don't ever be shy about letting me know. And of course you can tell me how much you enjoyed the book, too. That's always appreciated. You can reach me at debbiemacomber.com or write me at P.O. Box 1458, Port Orchard, WA 98366. You can also find me on social media such as Facebook or Twitter, etc.

Warmest regards,
Debbie Macomber

Prologue

Thirteen years earlier

Keaton had noticed the beautiful teenage girl on the beach earlier in the week. Once he saw her playing volleyball with a group of other teens, he hadn't been able to take his eyes off her. Her family had rented the Munson cottage and arrived Saturday morning. As soon as the car was unpacked, the girl and her older brother had made their way to the beach. They'd been there every day, laughing, swimming, and making friends. The girl was vivacious and full of life, and her laugh carried with the wind and made him smile every time he heard it. She couldn't be more than fourteen or fifteen years old, and her brother was a year or two older. Keaton noticed how people were naturally drawn to her and wanted to be around her. He felt it himself, even though he watched from afar.

Oceanside was a small, out-of-the-way town, but when summer arrived all the hotel rooms and rentals were filled. The shops were busy with tourists, eager to spend their vacation dollars. The scent of the ocean mingled with that of fried clams and fish and chips. Children jockeyed at the window of the candy shop for a view to watch Mr. Buster pull saltwater taffy or pour fudge onto large cookie sheets. The kite shop was a favorite to both the locals and tourists. The sky was filled with every imaginable shape, with children and adults alike running up and down the beach. It was like this every summer.

The beach was crowded, bustling with activity, and yet this one girl had caught Keaton's attention to the point he found himself looking for even a glimpse of her.

From the moment she arrived in Oceanside, Keaton found it hard not to think about her. He liked her hair, which was auburn, tinted by the sun, and long. She wore it in a single braid that bounced against her back as she raced down the beach, her bare feet kicking up the sand. She didn't lack for attention, he noticed; he could tell plenty of boys were interested in her. Keaton couldn't blame them.

More than anything, he wanted to talk to her. The problem was that he didn't know how to approach her, or what to say when he did. He didn't know how to tell her that he thought she was pretty. On the best of days, he rarely spoke. Girls left him tongue-tied and red in the face. His heart pounded so hard he felt his pulse in his head every time he thought about approaching the girl on the beach. For the first time in his life, Keaton thought about ways to overcome his aversion to speaking just so he could talk to her. He never had been good with words, and being naturally shy worked against him. Preston, his best friend, encouraged him to try to meet this girl who had taken up so much of his thoughts.

"Nothing ventured, nothing gained," Preston had advised.

Keaton wanted to throw those words right back at him; after all, Preston had had a thing for Mellie Johnson all through high school, and despite being nearly lovesick over the girl, Preston hadn't done more than greet her in the halls for four years. Not that it would have done him any good — Mellie had run off with some guy she'd met in Aberdeen the day after graduation. No one had seen or heard from her since.

That didn't stop Preston from hounding Keaton about the beach girl, though. It took Keaton nearly the entire week to find the nerve to approach her. It was now or never, but still, he fretted and stewed. His inability to carry a conversation was one problem, but then there was another *bigger* problem.

His size.

Keaton's biggest fear was that she'd be intimidated or frightened by him the way most people were. The girls in school had avoided him because he came across as aggressive and mean. He didn't intend to appear that way; it was simply the way he'd always looked, because he rarely smiled. The truth was there was little in Keaton's life to smile about. If he had his way, he'd have been invisible, but his height and size made that impossible. He'd grown to six-six while a junior, and another two inches his senior year. His shoulders were broad to the point that he barely made it through a doorway. His hands and feet were huge. He'd become used to the names people called him, making fun of his size.

Ox.

Moose.

These were only two of several commonly used to taunt him. He was an easy target because he chose to ignore the mocking and didn't respond. The names had never really bothered him.

With his heart pounding like a thunderbolt inside his massive chest, Keaton slowly approached the girl.

"Hey, look, it's the Jolly Green Giant," one of the teenagers observed.

Keaton ignored him, and smiled. "Hi," he muttered, staring intently at her. Up close, she was even prettier than she was at a distance. Her eyes were a hazel/green and her thick braid lay across her bare shoulder. She wore a sundress with a pattern of red poppies and her swimsuit underneath it. He wanted in the worst way to reach out and touch her cheek, to make certain she wasn't a figment of his imagination.

"It's the Abominable Snowman," cried another teenage boy in mock horror.

Keaton didn't recognize him, and assumed he was a tourist.

"No, it's Sasquatch."

"It does have big feet."

"Yeah. He's Big Foot."

"Stop it," the girl said, whirling around and confronting the group of teens with her. She turned to Keaton, smiling back. "Hi," she returned.

"Come on, Annie," her brother urged, grabbing her hand. "We need to get back."

Annie. Her name was Annie. Keaton ran it through his mind, liking the way it echoed there.

She continued to focus on him, her eyes inquisitive, wide, and warm.

"King Kong, you got something to say?" Devon Anderson taunted.

Keaton knew Devon from high school. He was a jerk. It didn't surprise him that Devon had noticed Annie and tried to get her attention.

"Don't call him that," Annie charged angrily, confronting Devon.

"He doesn't talk."

"Well, he just did," she countered, annoyed with Devon and not bothering to hide it. "He said 'hi,' in case you didn't hear."

"Bet he won't say anything else," Devon challenged, glaring at Keaton with a know-it-all look.

Annie waited expectantly, but for the life of him, Keaton couldn't manage to get out a single word. He wanted to tell her she was pretty and that he'd noticed her running along the beach. It was on the tip of his tongue to mention how much he liked her braid and the color of her hair, but he couldn't get that out, either.

"See what I mean?" Devon taunted.

"Don't do that," she snapped. "That's mean."

Her brother jerked at her hand. "Come on, Annie, Mom and Dad are waiting."

"Sorry," she told Keaton, her eyes becoming gentle as she spoke. "We have to go. It was nice meeting you."

Keaton nodded and attempted a smile, wanting to let her know he felt the same.

"We'll be back next summer," she said, walking backward, with her brother pulling her along.

A year. He could wait that long. By then, Keaton hoped, he'd find the words to tell her all the things he'd stored up in his head.

Annie, though, never returned.

Keaton waited, year after year, and never forgot the beautiful auburn-haired girl he'd seen on the beach that summer. The picture of Annie running along the sand stayed with him. Countless times he sketched scenes of the beach with her in them, using pencil and charcoal. Pictures no one saw. He carried on lengthy conversations with her in his head — just the thought of her brought him a rare taste of happiness.

Maybe one day, he thought, looking over the ocean as the waves crashed against the shore.

Maybe one day . . .

CHAPTER
ONE

Annie Marlow hated to disappoint her parents, but she simply wasn't going to fly home to Seattle for Thanksgiving. She'd already made the arrangements for Christmas and it was too late to change everything now. She had plans.

Working as a physician assistant, Annie didn't get many four-day weekends, and Trevor was cooking a turkey and had invited her over for the day. Steph would be there, too, and they were both anxious to meet a cute young doctor who had recently joined the clinic at another site.

What her mother really wanted, Annie realized, was a family photo for the Christmas card her parents routinely sent out each year. For all she cared, they could photoshop her in. There wasn't any need for her to change her plans, especially now, less than a week before Thanksgiving.

Gabby, her cousin, was flying to Los Angeles to join them. Giving up time with Gabby for a Christmas-card photo? Not happening. Besides, Annie had a new pair of four-inch designer heels and a dress she intended to use for a girls' night out on the town.

Her mother tried again, laying on the guilt. "Annie, *please?*"

"Mom, you can't change everything at the last minute like this." She glanced at the time and inwardly groaned. Much more of this conversation and she'd be late meeting Steph for their yoga class.

"Your brother is coming with Kelly and the baby."

This was her mom's best inducement? Her *brother?* The favored son? She had already seen Mike and his family twice this year. "He was planning to be there for Christmas, too, remember." Mike was the one who needed to change everything around. It was unfair that she should rearrange her entire life to suit her brother's schedule.

"We haven't been together as a family since August."

Pressing the phone to her ear, Annie became impatient as her mother continued speaking.

"You haven't seen the baby in a while. Did you know Bella is walking already?"

"I'll see Bella when I drive up this Christmas. I'll make sure to stop in Portland on my way through," Annie protested. "Mom, please. We've been through this already."

Her phone dinged, indicating she had a text message. Putting her phone on speaker, she checked the text to see that Steph had sent her a selfie. Her friend was gorgeous, with her purple-tinged hair. She'd made a pouty face and looked like she was kissing through the phone.

Annie laughed.

"Annie? Are you laughing at me?"

"No, sorry, Mom," she said, squelching her amusement. "Steph just sent me a text."

"I'd so hoped you would change your mind."

"Sorry, Mom, really I wish I could, but I simply can't." Well, she *could*, but not without ruining her own plans. "You won't miss me," she said, trying to soothe her mother's disappointment. "You'll be involved with Kelly and the baby, and Dad will spend all of his time with Mike." Bella would command all their attention; they cherished this first grandchild. To be fair, Bella was adorable. It was hard to believe she was walking already.

"Promise me you won't change your mind about Christmas, then, will you?" her mother asked. Annie had been given the chance to work last Christmas, and with money so tight, she'd jumped at the chance at double-time. Her parents had no idea what the cost of living was like in southern California, and how hard it was to make ends meet.

"I'll be home for Christmas, Mom, I promise." She hated it when her mother doubted her. One time, one measly time when she didn't get home for the holidays, and her mother refused to forgive her.

"I'm sorry to harp on you," her mother said. "It's a disappointment is all."

"I know. I'm sorry, too, but Gabby and I have the entire weekend planned. If I'd known sooner I could have made other arrangements, but it's too late now. It's only a few weeks and I'll be home for Christmas. I have my own life, you know."

Her mother's frustrated sigh came through the line. "Don't be like that, honey."

"Like what?"

"Stubborn," her mother countered. "Family is what's important. I know you have a lot going on, but your father and I are getting up in age. We won't be around forever, you know."

Annie couldn't believe her mother. This was a new low when it came to making her feel bad, reminding Annie that at some point in the future her parents would die. It was ridiculous, seeing that they were both healthy and in the prime of their lives. Biting down on her lower lip, she resisted the urge to tell her mom that she was being absurd.

Her mother seemed to sense that she'd gone too far with the guilt. "I have an idea," she quickly rebounded. "Invite Trevor."

What her mother didn't understand was that she wasn't romantically interested in Trevor. She'd happened to mention his name a time or two, and she had yet to hear the end of it ever since then. Inviting him to Seattle would only perpetuate the idea that they were involved. He was a friend, and besides, Steph had set her sights on him. There'd never been any sparks between him and Annie. She liked him, though, and he was fun to hang out with. It didn't hurt that he was a terrific dancer and being on the floor with him generated her a lot of attention.

"You like him, right?"

"He's a friend, Mom, nothing more. Besides, you're forgetting about Gabby. She's already purchased her ticket. I'm picking her up at LAX early Wednesday afternoon." Annie had already mentioned her cousin's visit a dozen times or more.

"Oh, right."

Her mother had yet to recognize how unreasonable she was being. "I'm genuinely sorry to disappoint you, Mom, but this whole family Thanksgiving just isn't going to work this year."

"Okay, honey, I understand. We'll miss you."

"Mom, I really need to go."

"Okay. Just one more thing. I wasn't going to tell you since I thought you'd be home for Thanksgiving, because I wanted to surprise you."

Time was ticking away. Grabbing her yoga mat and her bag, Annie headed for the front door of her condo.

"Dad and I remodeled the kitchen. We bought all new appliances and countertops. You won't recognize it!" Her parents loved their home and had saved thirty years to build it. It was on a hillside that overlooked Puget Sound. The views were stunning. Her parents had purchased the property years earlier and then diligently saved and sacrificed to build the home of their dreams.

"That's great, Mom. I'll see it at Christmas. Love you."

"Love you, too."

"Before you go, your dad wants to say hi."

"He's not going to pressure me about Thanksgiving, is he?"

"No, silly." She must have handed off the phone because the next voice Annie heard was her father's.

11

"How's my daughter, the doctor?" her father asked. He'd wanted Annie to continue on to medical school.

"I'm not a doctor, Dad." Annie had grown tired of school. The breakup with her college boyfriend had devastated her, and she'd been eager to be done. Instead of continuing school to get a medical degree, she'd opted to become a physician assistant.

"Someday," her dad said. He never seemed to lose a chance to remind Annie of her dream of working in medicine. What he didn't understand nor seem to appreciate was that she *did* work in medicine, just not as a physician.

They spoke, and Annie found herself glancing at the time. "Dad, I'd love to chat more, but I'm meeting a friend."

"Bye, sweetheart."

"Bye, Dad."

Annie pulled into the gym at the last minute and found Steph impatiently waiting outside. Together they rushed into their class. Afterward, Annie felt worlds better, relaxed and in good spirits.

They stopped for a smoothie at the juice bar, and while Steph wasn't looking, Annie snapped a selfie of the two of them and tweeted it.

"Let me see, let me see," Steph protested and then laughed. "You're bad."

"Hey, we both look great."

"Is it Gram-worthy?"

Annie laughed. "Looks like it to me," she confirmed, and posted the photo on Instagram, so Gabby would see it. She couldn't wait for Gabby to arrive on Wednesday; Annie had looked forward to cousin time for weeks. The two were close in age and had been best friends nearly their entire lives. Gabby had recently ended a six-month relationship, and Annie intended to do everything she could to make her forget Geoff, starting off with a pre-Thanksgiving party with friends from the clinic at a popular night spot.

Thanksgiving morning, Annie woke with a killer hangover. Her head felt like someone was inside swinging a sledgehammer, and her mouth was as dry as an Arizona riverbed. The incessant ringing of her phone, which was sitting on the nightstand by her bed, made it even worse. Caller ID showed that it was her aunt Sherry, Gabby's mother. Why, in the name of all that was decent, was she calling Annie at this time of the morning? Gabby had checked in with her mom when she landed. She was more than ready to hand the phone off to her cousin, who rolled over and grumbled at the interruption.

"Hello," Annie barely managed to say, holding her hand firmly against her forehead, hoping that this would appease the tiny men inside her brain, so they'd stop hammering.

"Annie." Aunt Sherry's voice was breathless, as if someone had knocked the wind out of her. "Oh Annie . . . Annie."

Sitting up in her bed at the sound of tears in her aunt's voice, Annie asked, "Aunt Sherry, do you need Gabby? She's here."

"No . . . no. I need to tell you."

"Tell me what?"

A gasping sob escaped her aunt.

Annie tensed and keeping her voice steady and low, asked, "Are you okay, Aunt Sherry?" Seeing how serious the conversation was sounding, Annie put the call on speaker for Gabby to listen in.

By this time, her cousin had sat up and was rubbing the sleep from her eyes. The two exchanged looks and Annie shrugged, unable to decipher what was happening.

"Do you . . . Do you . . . television . . . Is it on?" her aunt asked, barely getting the words out.

"No. Aunt Sherry, for the love of heaven, just tell me what's happened." As Annie spoke, she reached for the remote and turned on the television, switching channels to the twenty-four-hour news station. She tuned in, and the first thing that popped onto the screen was a Thanksgiving Day advertisement from Macy's, which told her nothing.

Instead of answering, her aunt started sobbing. "It's horrible, Annie. I . . . I don't even know how . . . I don't know . . . how to tell you."

As a physician assistant, Annie had often dealt with people in crisis mode. "Take a deep breath, count to five, then take another breath, and start at the beginning," she advised her aunt in a calm, soothing voice. Her immediate suspicion was that something had happened to Lyle, the man her aunt had been dating for the last fifteen years. That didn't make sense, though. She would have called Gabby if that had been the case.

"I'm . . . trying." Aunt Sherry counted softly, out loud, and sucked in another breath, just as Annie had recommended. "Your mom . . . and dad . . ."

Annie tensed. "My mom and dad?"

"They . . . invited me to breakfast."

Her mother had always made a big deal about breakfast on Thanksgiving, inviting family and friends over.

"I . . . wanted to see . . . the baby . . . Bella." Her words were staccato-like between sobs; she was having trouble even getting the words out.

"Aunt Sherry," Annie said softly. "Has something happened to my parents?"

Her aunt ignored the question. "When I got . . . close . . . just . . . two blocks away . . ." She continued in the same jerky speech. "The police . . . they . . . stopped me."

"The police?" Annie repeated, her mind whirling. "What were the police doing there?"

"They . . . had . . . It was barricaded."

"A barricade?" Annie hated that she sounded like an echo, but her aunt wasn't making a whole lot of sense.

"It's . . . been raining . . . and raining."

"Well, that happens in Seattle quite a bit." Annie impatiently added, "Especially around this time of year." The Seattle area was known for its rainfall, which was another reason Annie chose to live in California.

"Annie," her aunt said, sobbing hysterically, while sucking in deep breaths between her words. "You . . .

You . . . don't understand, the entire hillside . . . is gone. It . . . simply . . . gave way, taking . . . taking everything with . . . it."

Gabby gasped at the news.

Annie slowly rose out of her bed, standing with one hand pressing against her forehead while the other pressed the phone to her ear. "Are you telling me Mom and Dad's house slid off the hillside?"

"Yes," Aunt Sherry said and gasped. "Their house . . . and . . . twenty . . . other homes."

Annie froze and glanced at the television screen. Breaking news had just interrupted the newscast. A helicopter was flying over the water, identified on the screen below as Puget Sound. A single home was breaking apart in the mud-caked waters below the helicopter and sinking into the water.

"Mom and Dad?" Annie pleaded, as her heart pounded at the seriousness of what had happened. "Did they get out?"

"I . . . I don't know . . . I don't know how they could have. Everyone said it happened so fast, and so early . . ."

Annie fell back onto her bed, her legs shaking so hard they wouldn't hold her up any longer. Her entire body began to tremble. "How early this morning?"

"The officer said . . . it happened around four . . . They think . . . most everyone was still in bed. No . . . notice. No . . . warning."

The tightness in Annie's chest made it impossible to speak. It was highly likely that her entire family had just been wiped out in a mudslide.

Her mother.

Her father.

Her brother.

Her sister-in-law.

And her baby niece.

Annie's mind couldn't absorb what she was hearing and seeing on the television. Her aunt's sobs echoed in her ear and seemed to be reverberating against the walls of her head.

"Annie?" her aunt sobbed. "Are . . . Are you there? Say . . . something."

"I'm here," Annie managed to whisper. She inhaled and followed her own advice, counting to five and then breathing in again, hoping the technique would calm the rising sense of panic that threatened to overcome her. "I . . . I need . . . I'll get there as soon as I can."

"Good. Have Gabby . . . make . . . Have her do . . . the flight arrangements."

"I will." How calm she sounded, Annie thought to herself, but her voice wasn't her own. It seemed to come from across the room somewhere. Her cousin placed her arms around her, hugging her closely. "Find out what you can before I get there."

"I'll . . . do what . . . I'll see what I can learn."

"There must be survivors," Annie insisted, doing her best to think positively, convinced her parents had somehow found a way to escape. She had to believe they were alive, because anything else would be impossible to accept.

"I'll do . . . what I can. I promise, but . . ."

"But what?" Annie demanded, her voice gaining in strength.

"But . . . Annie . . . there's little hope for survivors. I'm so sorry, so very sorry."

Annie and Gabby sat on the edge of the bed, sobbing and holding each other. The television showed the result of the entire hillside that had broken away. The only home visible was the one still slowly sinking into the water. Every other home was either completely buried by the slide or had gone before the others into the sound.

CHAPTER
TWO

Sixteen months later

Annie had never felt more alone. Fitting, she supposed, because she *was* alone. Her entire family had been wiped out in a single day. Even now, all these months later, she continued to find it hard to believe. Countless times she'd reached for the phone to call home, only to remember that her mother was dead, buried in a deluge of mud, debris, and seawater, killed in what was called an unforeseeable tragedy.

The news of the mudslide had filled the airwaves, getting both local and national coverage. Crews from all the major news networks descended on the area to do their reporting. But then, a few days later, there was another catastrophe in another part of the country that commanded media attention, and the mudslide became old news and was forgotten.

But not by Annie and the others who had lost family and friends. Their lives had been forever marked, forever changed.

In the aftermath, Annie sold her condo and left her job in L.A., moving back to Seattle to deal with the horrific consequences. Waiting for rescuers to locate the bodies, identifying her family, planning the funerals, settling the estate, or what was left of it. Then there were the attorneys, determined to find who best to blame: the city, the state, the builders. Someone needed to accept responsibility, to pay the price for this awful tragedy and to compensate those who had been left behind.

Left behind.

This was exactly the way Annie felt. *She* should have been with her family that day. *She* should have died with them. As the months wore on, she wished she had died. But instead, Annie was alive, thrust into the complicated legal issues and ugliness that followed. It was more than she could mentally handle, and she spiraled into a deep, dark hole. The grief and regret weighed her down until she wasn't convinced she could resurface. How could she possibly ever be the same again?

A counselor she'd started to see claimed Annie suffered from survivor's guilt. Perhaps she did. Annie didn't know. It demanded too much of her emotionally to give any thought to it, as her endless days were filled with so much else. Support came in the form of the counselor and group sessions with other people who had lost loved ones. All of this stood in stark contrast to the countless meetings with attorneys and city officials.

The first year passed by in a fog. Friends, and what was left of her extended family, Aunt Sherry and Gabby, gave her books to read: books on grief and dealing with the death of a loved one . . . so many books that Annie found it impossible for the words to hold her attention. It wasn't that she didn't try to move forward. She made a gallant effort but found it impossible. Instead, she spent countless hours working Sudoku puzzles. Hour upon hour she'd buried herself in numbers because numbers made sense. Everything fit neatly together in a small square on the page with tidiness and logic, the way her life once had.

Only her life felt out of control, lost in the mire of grief as she struggled to dig her way out, trapped as she felt in this void of darkness.

The next four months were no better. Gabby did her best to encourage and support her, but even she was at a loss on how to give Annie what she needed. That was the crux of the matter.

What Annie needed was her family back. But that wasn't going to happen.

Her friends from Los Angeles had kept in touch. Trevor and Steph would call every now and then, and she was pleased to learn they were now dating. They flew up to Seattle to spend time with her on the one-year anniversary of the mudslide. They wanted to offer their love and support but left early. Annie was even more depressed after their visit than she'd been before they arrived. It didn't take them long to realize that the mudslide and losing her family had changed her. They seemed to think that after twelve months — a single year — she would return to the same Annie she'd once been. What they didn't understand, what no one did, not even Gabby, was that burying her family wasn't something she would ever "get over."

Through her counselor, Annie learned that, she had to accept that she would grieve for the rest of her life.

Her counselor had assured her that what she felt was normal. The pain of loss would be with her forever, but *with time*, she would eventually learn to live with it.

With time, she would gradually learn to rebuild her life around this horrific loss.

With time, she would be whole again, but with the knowledge that she would never be the same. Annie was willing to accept that reality. The truth was she wouldn't want to be the same person she'd been.

At night, when she was most vulnerable and when thoughts and regrets bombarded her, Annie recalled the last conversation she'd had with her mother. It was as if her mother had had a premonition of what was about to happen when she'd mentioned that Annie should take the time to be with them because they were both going to die one day. Little did either of them realize how quickly that day would come.

In the months since the mudslide, it seemed like someone had been holding Annie by her feet in the air, dangling her over the edge of a high-rise, asking her to make sense of it all. The days spun past in a whirl, and before she realized it, sixteen months were gone. *Sixteen months* — four hundred and eighty-six days — had passed by in one fell swoop, and Annie didn't remember a one of them. They all blurred together in her mind.

A settlement was said to be coming. A settlement. Apparently, that was supposed to replace her family. A check she would deposit in the bank that would compensate for her loss. That was a joke, right? How do you replace your parents, your only sibling, your sister-in-law, and your baby niece? It wasn't possible. No amount of cash, no matter the agreed-upon number, would ever make up for her entire family.

"Annie?" Gabby sat across the table from her at Starbucks, trying to bring her back into their conversation.

Looking up from her coffee, Annie attempted a smile, but even that demanded more resolve than she could muster.

"You're depressed."

No kidding, Sherlock. Even during the daytime, not just at night, Annie was unable to get that last conversation with her mother out of her mind. It haunted her. Annie had been stubborn, self-absorbed, and so wrapped up in herself that she'd shuffled her family aside. It hadn't seemed unreasonable at the time to refuse to change her plans and head home for Thanksgiving instead of Christmas. In retrospect, Annie would have given anything to have been with her family that day. At least she would have escaped the horror and emptiness that had since become her life.

"I'm on antidepressants, Gabby, you know that." She wasn't sure what more could be done to get her through this. Perhaps subconsciously, she didn't *want* her spirits lifted. It was doubtful she would ever smile again. That sounded melodramatic, she realized, worthy of a soap opera. But joy, real joy, was forever lost to her. It had been buried in the mud and in the sea, along with her family. Annie felt as if her entire life had slid down that hillside, trapping her as well. She would have rather died with them than live in this void.

"What advice did the counselor give you today?" Gabby asked.

"She wanted me to think about some thing or some place that made me happy before this all happened."

"You used to love to dance!" Gabby tossed her arms into the air and let out a shriek that caused everyone in Starbucks to glance their way.

"At one time I did." Annie sipped on her Frappuccino and tried to smile. The counseling sessions had gone on all these months, yet Annie didn't feel any better. She listened, took notes, and tried, but nothing had seemed to help.

Gabby stared at her, shaking her head. "Annie. You need to dig yourself out of this place that you are in. You're alive. You know I love you. I'd do anything for you, anything in the world to help you, but I don't know what to say anymore."

"You want me to move on." This wasn't the first time Annie had heard that.

Let go.

Pretend.

It sounded good in theory, but if she let go, then what and who was she going to hold on to? Her family had died. No one seemed to get that. She had no one left except her aunt and cousin, and they had their own lives and interests. While they genuinely cared, they weren't her parents.

When she didn't respond, Gabby tried again. "That's not a bad idea, you know."

"What?" she asked quizzically.

24

"What your counselor said about finding a happy place," her cousin said. "Someplace you can go to mentally, or even physically, that makes you happy."

Annie frowned. "A happy place," she whispered. It wasn't the dance floor, she thought. Perhaps at one time, but no longer.

"Disneyland?" Gabby asked flippantly. "We both went there when we were ten. Well, you were ten, I was nine."

"No." Annie shook her head. The trip had been fun, but it wasn't what came to mind when she thought of a happy place. In fact, she'd completely forgotten about that trip.

"Well, think about it. What were the things you did with your family, the places you went where you were happy?" Gabby asked, clearly wanting to be helpful.

Annie's mind was blank.

"What about when you graduated from college? You were happy that day, right?"

"Right." She understood what Gabby was trying to do, but at this point Annie was afraid that she was beyond help. It was far too easy to slip back into the darkness that filled her heart. That lack of light, of joy, had become almost comfortable. That space seemed to be where she belonged now.

"What about when Bella was born?"

Bella. Immediate tears filled Annie's eyes. That precious baby had to die in such a horrible way.

"Okay, mentioning Bella wasn't a great idea," Gabby conceded, immediately regretful.

Annie smeared the moisture across her cheeks.

Her cousin tried again. "What's one of your favorite memories?"

"From when?"

"From your life. Your first kiss, your first crush, anything you remember that stirs you."

Despite how she was feeling, a weak smile grew across Annie's face. "My first kiss happened when I was twelve."

"Who was it?"

"His name was Adam, and we met at the beach." Every August, her family had rented a cottage by the sea, and they spent seven glorious days there. They were the happiest days of the year, the happiest of her childhood.

"Tell me about him."

"Adam." She hadn't thought about him in years, and she didn't remember his last name. "He was Mike's friend."

"And you kissed."

Annie nodded. "We were running along the beach, flying kites and laughing so hard we could barely remain on our feet. Mike had to go back to the cottage for something and it was just Adam and me. We plopped down on the sand, exhausted, and held on to the kite strings while we waited for Mike to return. Then, without warning, Adam asked me a question, and when I turned to answer him he kissed me." It was more like bumping his mouth against hers from what she remembered, but it'd been her first kiss and one she would remember. Her heart had swooned.

"And?" Gabby pried.

"And nothing. It was my first kiss. I think it might have been his, too, because he turned beet red afterward."

"Did he kiss you again?"

"No. I suspect that kiss was a big disappointment to him, because he never tried it again, at least not with me. Neither one of us spoke about it again, either." Caught up in the memories of that summer, Annie let her mind drift to other summers and the times she'd spent with her family in that cottage across from the beach. It was one week out of the year when Mike and Annie barely squabbled, the lone week of every year when her entire family was free of all worries and responsibilities.

After Gabby and Annie parted ways, she returned to the Seattle apartment she'd rented, yet the conversation with her cousin lingered in her mind. She'd always loved the beach. The sound of the waves roaring onto the sand, leaving a foam trail . . . the feel of wet sand between her toes, laughing with her brother, exploring tide pools with her father, and roasting marshmallows next to her mom over a driftwood campfire. She could almost smell the scent of the burning fire as she replayed those scenes in her mind.

They were at the beach every summer for years until Mike graduated from high school and took a summer job. They hadn't returned as a family after that. Annie had briefly gone back by herself to the same beach town during her junior year of college when she'd broken up with her boyfriend.

To be more accurate, Davis was the one who'd broken up with *her*.

Annie had been crushed, truly devastated. He'd been her first love, her first everything, and she'd assumed they'd always be together. She'd thought that they would marry after they graduated from college and live happily ever after. It'd come as a complete shock when Davis casually announced that he didn't think their relationship was working.

Not *working?* Since when? Annie had been oblivious and totally content, taken aback by Davis's declaration.

She'd wept buckets over the breakup. It didn't help that within only one week, she'd learned he was dating someone else. At the time, it made no sense that he could move on so quickly. She refused to believe that he had been cheating on her, but then she'd been forced to face the ugly truth, as it was the only possible explanation. Looking back, she was humiliated by the way she'd pleaded with him to reconsider, to work on their relationship. She'd been willing to do whatever it took to be the woman he wanted her to be. How foolish she'd been. How blind. Davis had taught her valuable things about herself, lessons that she had learned well and had taken to heart. She wasn't nearly as trusting any longer, nor was she naïve. She hadn't given her heart away since then, although she'd casually dated . . . at least until the tragedy happened.

After Davis broke her heart, the one place Annie found comfort had been the beach at Oceanside. It wasn't where she had intended to go when she got in her car. She'd started driving with no destination in mind, weeping and emotional, convinced she would never fall in love again and that all was lost.

Somehow, Annie had ended up at the beach that day. For hours afterward, she reclined on a log that had drifted onto the shore. With tears clouding her vision, she stared at the open expanse of the ocean and cried until no more tears were left in her to shed.

The lull of the ocean had eventually calmed her. She breathed in the scent of the salt and sea, and peace began to steal over her. Perhaps it was the rhythm of the waves, slapping against the shore. Or the cries of the seagulls circling overhead, drifting on the wind. Children raced past her and teens zipped by on motor scooters. Those hours had soothed her as nothing else had.

She'd sat until dark, leaning against that log. As night descended, she stared up at the sky, startled by the vast array of stars, so many that they were impossible to count. As a kid, she didn't ever remember there being such a multitude of stars.

Eventually, she'd drifted off to sleep and woke a couple hours later, chilled. She went back to her car and drove home in the middle of the night. From that point forward, she put Davis and their broken relationship behind her. She'd decided against medical school, and became a physician assistant instead.

The sea had worked its magic.

Annie straightened, as a sudden realization came to her. Perhaps the sea could do the same thing again.

Perhaps she could find peace by the ocean. Losing her family was different from breaking up with Davis, though. She knew that it would take more than the lull of the waves to soothe her now. Still, the cottage by the sea was the one place she could remember where she'd been completely happy. She didn't know if she would ever find that sense of peace again, but Annie was determined to try.

CHAPTER
THREE

The following morning, Annie packed an overnight bag, and with a sense of purpose she hadn't felt since that fateful Thanksgiving Day, she walked to her car. On the off-chance that Gabby or her aunt would worry about her being gone, she sent her cousin a text.

Heading to my happy place.

It didn't take long for her to get a response.

And where would that be?

The ocean.

The drive took about three hours in light traffic. Annie arrived and parked on the beach. Climbing out of her vehicle, she wrapped her arms around her torso and filled her lungs with the fresh salt air. It didn't take long before a sense of calm settled over her. At first she didn't recognize. what it was.

Calm felt strange.

Different.

Unfamiliar.

Closing her eyes, she inhaled tranquility, holding her breath until her lungs cried out for relief. Slowly, she exhaled and listened to the steady pounding of the surf that synchronized with her pulse. Her stomach growled and she realized she hadn't eaten all day. Over the last sixteen months, Annie had lost weight, her appetite gone.

Her cell pinged with a text message. It was her Aunt Sherry. Gabby must have told her what she'd done.

You okay?

Yup. Staying the night in Oceanside.

Her aunt worried too much.

Walking back toward her car, Annie saw a large dog racing toward her with a stick in its mouth. Seeing him, she bent down on one knee and the dog dropped the stick onto the sand at her feet. She petted his head and he looked up at her with his bright brown eyes, making her grin. The mutt looked like he'd waited all day for just this moment.

"I bet you want me to throw this stick, don't you?" she asked him.

The dog's eyes filled with adoration.

Annie's smile broadened. She grabbed ahold of the stick and stood, preparing to toss it, when she noticed a man standing off in the distance. He was tall. Taller than anyone she knew, close to seven feet, from what she could tell. He wore a jacket, jeans, and work boots. His hair appeared to be dark, but he was too far away to see his features. What she did notice was the way he intently stared at her, his head cocked at an angle, trying to figure out who she was and where she belonged.

He made no move toward her, and she had to assume the dog belonged to him. She threw the stick back in the direction of the man. Eagerly, the dog chased after it, his tongue lolling out of the side of his mouth as he eagerly tore down the beach, kicking up sand.

As she suspected, the canine returned to the man in the distance.

They continued to stare at each other across the expanse of beach for several moments until Annie grew uncomfortable, turned away, and walked back to her car.

Instead of looking for a restaurant, she found a little coffeehouse named Bean There, and ordered a latte. A teenager behind the counter took her order and smiled shyly at her. Her nametag read BRITT.

Taking the latte with her, Annie strolled down the street, looking in the shop windows. The store that made saltwater taffy was still in business, she noticed. She remembered that Mike would dig out the licorice pieces, stuffing two or three into his mouth until black liquid drooled out the sides and down his chin. He'd taken great pleasure in grossing out his sister, she recalled. She missed her brother dreadfully and forced herself to walk away from the candy store.

The kite shop was still in business, too, she saw. The space was larger than she remembered, with even more elaborate kites. The young man behind the counter glanced up and smiled as she strolled past. Annie smiled back as she recalled the fun times she'd had with her family assembling and flying the kites.

The ice-cream stand was in the same place, and it had always done a robust business. Every night of their vacation her dad would take the family down for ice-cream cones. Annie had chosen a different flavor every night, determined to try each one. She never achieved her goal because she loved the caramel-pecan flavor the best and couldn't resist ordering it along with the scoop of another flavor.

Behind the stand was a large stone wall entirely covered by a huge mural. The focus of the mural was the oceanfront, with waves so real-looking, it felt as if they would come crashing down on her at any second. Multicolored kites flew overhead in a blue sky covered with popcorn-shaped clouds. The scene was so inviting that Annie had a hard time looking away. Whoever had done the painting was wildly talented. As she studied the mural, Annie saw a teenage girl on it with a single auburn braid lying over her shoulder. It was the same shade as her own and the style was the way she'd once worn her hair at that age. Strangely, it was like looking at a picture of herself. She stared at that carefree girl for a long time.

Annie searched but couldn't find the artist's name. She'd like to see if it was someone she'd once met during her summers here. After a minute or two she turned away, wondering if the mural was some sort of sign, some indication that Oceanside was where she was meant to be, that given the chance, she might find solace and peace in this small town. Her chest swelled with a small glimmer of hope.

As she continued to walk, she came to the street that was most familiar to her: the street with the cottage her family had once rented. Without thinking, she turned and headed in that direction.

Ten minutes later, her steps paused and her pulse quickened. The cottage was still there. It was much smaller than she remembered. At one time, it might have even been a garage, a part of the main house behind it, which was a large two-story structure with a wide central porch and shutters. The exterior paint had faded on both the cottage and the main house, and the small porch on the cottage slouched unevenly with the toll the years had taken on it.

Cottage by the sea.

The one place where she'd spent the happiest days of her life with her family. She had found her way back. She had found her happy place.

CHAPTER
FOUR

As Annie made the return drive to Seattle, she felt the grief gradually seep back in and surround her soul. Her speed decreased until car horns blasted her as they sped past, and she realized she was driving forty miles an hour on a road where the speed limit was sixty. She could feel herself becoming surrounded by the darkness again. The closer she came to her apartment, the more difficult it became to breathe.

Annie had spent the night in a motel in Oceanside, and for the first time since the accident, the very first time in sixteen months, she'd slept straight through until morning. When she woke, she was shocked to find it was daylight. Nightmares had continually plagued her, but she woke rested, in stark contrast to nearly every other night since the disaster.

Because it was raining, she had quickly loaded up the car, checked out, and returned to Seattle. That was when she figured it out. As she neared the city, she could distinctly feel her heart grow heavy as the sadness slipped back into place. It wasn't her imagination. She'd only been half kidding that she'd found her happy place when she texted Gabby, but the joke was on her. She knew where she belonged now.

Once back in Seattle, Annie was restless and at loose ends. She hadn't worked as a PA since the tragedy. She couldn't, not with all the demands on her time, the legal issues, and the counseling sessions. Agitated, she paced the small living room, unsure of what was wrong. All she could think about was the beach, and the need — no, the urgency — to return there, if for no other reason than to escape the dark cloud that hung over her head.

The mural she'd seen of the girl who resembled her had to be a sign. It started to make perfect sense: Oceanside was more than a place to visit; this was where she needed to be. After all these months of not working, she felt the first stirrings of desire to get back to work, back to the career she'd once loved.

Logging on to her computer, she looked at available jobs in the area, scrolling down the list. She nearly gasped aloud when she saw a posting in Oceanside's only medical clinic. They were looking to hire a PA.

This couldn't be a coincidence. This job listing had God's fingerprints all over it. This was her fate, as much a miracle as the parting of the Red Sea. First the girl in the mural who looked identical to her as a teenager, and now this — an opening for a physician assistant in Oceanside. To Annie, it felt like this move was meant to be.

She completed the application form and submitted it via email, attaching certifications for both Washington state and California. It came as no surprise that she didn't have long to wait for a response. Within twenty-four hours, she had an interview scheduled.

Twice within one week, she packed an overnight bag and drove to Oceanside. As she neared the ocean, she felt the weight lifting from her shoulders and light descending upon her. That single ray of sunshine was narrow and small, but she could feel it, as tiny as it was. She supposed what she felt was something like a reprieve, someone or something giving her a break from all the dark, with a tiny bit of hope that she could pull herself through that hole and back into the light.

Annie drove directly to the medical clinic without stopping for a meal or a bathroom break. The interview was scheduled for right after lunch with the only doctor at the clinic. Not having held a job for sixteen months now, Annie should have been more nervous than she was. Before she'd arrived, she had decided not to mention the tragedy, desperately wanting to put it behind her and move forward. Once people found out about her connection to the mudslide, the inevitable sympathy followed, the knowing looks and the quiet whispers. These were all things Annie had hoped to avoid. She desperately needed a fresh start, away from it all.

As soon as she introduced herself, the receptionist glanced up and welcomed her with a ready smile. "Oh, you're the PA. I'm so pleased to meet you. I'm Candi Olsen."

"Hi, Candi."

"Dr. Bainbridge is eager to meet you. Would you mind waiting a moment while I let him know you're here?"

"Of course." She returned to the waiting room, took a seat, and reached for a six-month-old issue of *People* magazine. She hadn't finished reading the front cover headlines when Candi returned.

"Dr. Bainbridge will see you now."

Annie had the feeling Candi said those exact words to nearly every person who walked into the clinic. She followed the receptionist down a long, narrow hallway to the last room on the right. When she entered the office, Dr. Bainbridge stood from behind his desk. He was older than she'd expected, retirement age, if not beyond. He had a full head of thick white hair and bushy eyebrows, which were badly in need of trimming. His blue eyes were kind, and tired.

Extending his hand, he introduced himself: "Marcus Bainbridge."

"Annie Marlow," she said, shaking his hand.

He gestured for her to take a seat. Reaching for a file on top of his cluttered desk, he said, "I checked your references. Your previous employer gave you a glowing recommendation."

Annie had expected nothing less.

He regarded her for a moment, then commented, "I noticed it's been sixteen months since you've worked in your field?"

Shifting in the chair, Annie met his look head-on. "It was a family situation." He didn't ask her to explain, but seeing that he'd left the comment hanging, she realized he was asking without saying the words.

Annie remained silent, choosing not to fill the silence. She wanted to keep the mudslide and its aftermath separate. This job, this community, would be a new beginning for her, and if that meant building a protective shield around herself, then so be it. Part of the healing process was to move forward with her life and not dwell in the past, in the might-have-beens and the mire of regrets. She wouldn't be able to do that if others were aware of the tragedy. There would be speculation, questions, sympathy — all of which she was looking to avoid.

"Ah, yes . . . a family situation. Say no more." He flipped through a couple of the sheets, silently reviewing her application. "What the community really needs is a doctor, but unfortunately we haven't been able to find one with the credentials who is willing to serve in this community. It's difficult, as we don't get many applicants who are willing to live and work this far off the beaten path."

He paused and looked up. "I don't mind telling you that I need a break. I'm tired. I originally came on as part-time staff until someone else could be hired for the full-time position. As I mentioned, that hasn't happened. When I was hired, I was looking to work one or two days a week at the most, and this has evolved into far more hours than I'd like.

"I had a family practice for thirty-five years," he continued. "My wife and I wanted to leave city life behind and relax; instead, I'm trapped into working ten-hour days. I need help. We'd hoped to do a bit of traveling — to see the world, that sort of thing. As soon as another doctor is hired, I plan to retire, pack my bags, and head out with the wife in our RV."

"You mean to say you haven't had a chance to travel?"

"Not lately. Even finding a PA has proven to be a challenge. The one who was here prior to my arrival left within the first month. Finding a replacement hasn't been easy. The two others who applied had a change of heart once they saw how small the town is."

"I'm not going to change my mind, Dr. Bainbridge. I *want* to live in Oceanside," Annie assured him. Shortly after the disaster, she had briefly considered returning to medical school, but she hadn't been in a good place mentally and decided against it. Perhaps one day in the future. The interview continued for the next hour, until Dr. Bainbridge once again reminded Annie about the nature of Oceanside.

"Annie, you understand that the economy here is mostly tourist-driven. In the winter, this becomes something of a ghost town. Before the clinic agrees to hire you, I will need a solid one-year commitment. Can you give me that?" His eyes narrowed and focused on her with laser-beam intensity.

"I will promise you one full year."

Dr. Bainbridge nodded with what seemed to be relief. "Wonderful. When can you start?"

"When would you like me to start?"

"I'd like you here as soon as you can make the arrangements. Next week, if possible."

"Next week." It was crazy to think she could move in that short amount of time. Nevertheless, Annie was determined to do whatever it took to make it happen.

Dr. Bainbridge and Annie discussed her hours and pay. Before she left, he gave her a tour of the facility and introduced her to the nurse, Julia James. Both Julia and Candi seemed professional and knowledgeable and as anxious to have Annie join the staff as Marcus Bainbridge was to work with her.

Annie left the clinic in good spirits and drove directly to the cottage her family had rented all those years ago. The cottage and main house weren't directly on the beach but across the street from it. She assumed it wasn't rented, as it appeared unkempt. The lawn was badly in need of mowing and the windows were so dirty and dusty, it was impossible to see inside. In the past, the cottage had been well maintained, as she recalled. Seeing its current condition saddened her. And while it obviously needed a little TLC, Annie didn't care. This was where she wanted to live, where she hoped to recapture the memories of those carefree days of her youth, the happy times with her parents and brother.

From the time she was young, Annie remembered that the small house was rented by the week. She hoped that she could persuade the owner to give her a full year's lease. She didn't care what the cost was; whatever was asked, she'd agree to the price, willing to pay what was necessary for the memories alone.

An older couple had owned the cottage back when her family rented it. They had a teenage granddaughter living with them, close to Mike's age. Her brother had a huge crush on her. Annie couldn't remember her name — what she did remember was how goofy Mike got around her. She was a couple years older, with long blond hair and blue eyes. Funny, Annie hadn't thought about her in years. Darn, she wished she could remember her name. The older couple must have passed on by now, and judging by the exterior, the new owner had let the property go downhill. Annie couldn't help wondering what had happened to the girl.

Parking in the allotted space by the cottage, Annie walked up to the main house and rang the doorbell. A white Siamese cat appeared on the large living room windowsill, casting her a curious look.

Annie waited, but no one answered.

She tried again, and when she didn't hear anything, she was left to assume that like so much else about the house, the doorbell no longer worked. This time, she knocked.

Nothing.

Hearing a sound on the other side of the door, Annie knocked again, harder this time, so hard her knuckles hurt.

No response.

She had the oddest sensation that someone was standing on the other side of the door, someone who refused to answer.

"Hello," she called out. When she didn't hear anything back, she tried again. "I'm here to ask about renting the cottage."

After waiting several moments longer, Annie had no choice but to walk away. Well, at least she'd tried.

Because she hoped to move as quickly as it could be arranged, she stopped off at a real estate office that advertised rentals. A middle-aged woman with horn-rimmed glasses perched at the end of her nose manned the front desk. The office was undergoing some renovations, she could tell. Two desks were pushed aside and the far wall was half painted.

"May I help you?" the agent asked, standing to greet her.

"Yes, please." Annie was about to explain that she was looking for a place to rent, when the painter returned to finish the job. Although she'd seen the man on the beach only that one time recently, she immediately recognized that he was the same man she'd seen that day with the dog.

He was massive, easily the largest man she'd ever seen. With shoulders so broad she had to wonder if he could buy clothes off the rack or if he had to special-order them. His arms were long and muscular. His hair and eyes were a deep, dark brown. His nose was slightly bent, appearing to have been broken and never properly set. He took note of Annie and paused, his eyes widening briefly, obviously recognizing her from that rainy, windy day. For one embarrassing, long moment, they continued to stare at each other.

As though to draw Annie's attention, the agent cleared her throat.

Feeling foolish, she broke eye contact and asked, "You're the man with the dog on the beach, aren't you?"

After a moment's pause, he gruffly acknowledged the question with a simple nod.

Annie took a step closer to him. "What's your dog's name?"

"Lennon."

"After John Lennon?"

He nodded abruptly.

"What kind of dog is he?"

He ignored the question and turned his back to her, quickly reaching for his paintbrush and getting to work.

The agent leaned toward Annie and whispered, "Don't mind Keaton; he isn't much of a talker. He doesn't mean to be rude."

"That's okay." Annie wasn't offended by his lack of friendliness. If anything, he intrigued her. She imagined people must view him as something of an oddity, being as big as he was.

Focusing her attention away from Keaton, Annie said, "I stopped by the cottage on Seaside Lane. My parents rented it years ago when I was young. A nice older couple owned it back then, but I'm guessing someone else does now. Is there any chance the cottage is available for rent?"

"That's Melody Johnson's place," the agent explained, frowning. "After her grandparents passed, she inherited the property. It sat vacant for a few years until she returned, what must be four or five years ago now. Unfortunately, she hasn't done much in the way of upkeep."

Melody Johnson. Melody. Annie let the name, which was vaguely familiar, run through her mind several times. The teenage girl she remembered had a different name. "I stopped by and knocked on the door, but no one answered. I felt certain someone was home," Annie shared.

"Yes, well . . . That's not unusual. Melody is something of an agoraphobe. She doesn't answer the door unless she knows the person knocking."

Annie blinked hard twice, knowing that this disorder caused people to be anxious in public and to retreat into their homes for security. Hopefully it wouldn't keep the owner from renting to her. "Do you think she'd consider renting me the cottage? I'd be more than willing to take a one-year lease and pay whatever she felt was fair. Do you know how I could contact her?"

The agent shook her head. "I doubt she'd be interested . . . Now, if you're looking for a rental house, I have a few I can show —"

"I'd like to find out if Ms. Johnson would be willing to rent me the cottage before I look at anything else." Annie had her heart set on it. She didn't care about the condition. If repairs were needed, she'd take care of them herself.

"Yes, well, you could always ask. You can slip a note under the door and she'll respond . . . eventually. I've tried to speak to her about using it as a rental myself, with no success. From what I understand, other agents have tried, too. Ms. Johnson doesn't appear to be interested, which is a shame. She could make a pretty penny in season, seeing how close the cottage is to the ocean."

Keaton, who had apparently been listening to the conversation, laid aside his paintbrush. "I'll ask."

"*You'll* ask Melody?" The agent sounded more than mildly surprised.

"Wait here." He shot a glance at Annie, his look intense. She supposed she should be daunted by him, because of the strange, abrupt way he spoke to her. But for whatever reason, she wasn't. He seemed to want to help get her the cottage, which was more than the agent was willing to do.

The agent didn't take kindly to his interference. "Keaton, you should know it's a waste of time," she said, shuffling papers around on her desk.

Annie didn't want to discourage him. "I don't mind waiting. Thank you, Keaton."

He nodded, slipped past her, and left. Annie's eyes followed him, wondering about this giant of few words.

The woman offered Annie an apologetic smile. "I wouldn't get your hopes up. Melody is difficult, and Keaton, well, he's a bit intimidating, but perfectly harmless, you understand."

Annie wasn't concerned in the least, although he had been a bit gruff. If anything, this bear of a man intrigued her, especially his willingness to approach the landowner to inquire about the cottage on her behalf.

"Like I said," the agent continued, "Melody is problematic. As far as I know, she doesn't have any contact with the outside world. Heaven knows how she survives in that house all by her lonesome self."

"It sounds like Keaton might know her," Annie volunteered.

"That's possible," the agent agreed. "If I remember correctly, Keaton and Melody graduated from high school around the same time. Just remember Melody Johnson is an odd duck, if you know what I mean."

Annie let the comment drop. If by some miracle the woman agreed to rent her the cottage, Annie would be forever grateful.

The agent grew restless. "While you're waiting, perhaps you'd care to look at a few of our listings?"

Annie hoped it wouldn't be necessary but complied. "All right."

"Would you prefer a home or an apartment?"

"A home." After living in an apartment from the time she was a junior in college, and having had a condo in L.A., Annie was looking forward to moving into a house.

"We have several apartments that are available for rent, but only two homes." She handed Annie the listings for her review. Both houses were larger than what she would need, with multiple bedrooms. The cottage would be perfect, if only the owner would agree.

Twenty minutes passed before Keaton returned. He handed Annie a folded slip of paper.

Annie's heart raced as she opened the slip and read the words.

Cottage rents as is. Don't come to me with complaints.
Keep to yourself and don't bother me.
One-year lease, with six months' rent up front.
I'm doing this against my better judgment, so don't make me regret it.

Annie glanced at Keaton, who had taken up his brush and continued painting. Instinctively, she knew that he'd been the one to convince Ms. Johnson to agree to renting the cottage.

"Keaton," she said, "thank you."

Without looking her way, he acknowledged her appreciation with a single nod and continued with his painting.

CHAPTER
FIVE

It was *her*. Annie. After all these years.

Keaton had never forgotten the girl whose family had rented the cottage by the sea.

A few days earlier, he'd seen her while walking Lennon on the beach and had recognized her immediately. Stunned at finding Annie again, he'd stopped, afraid if he moved closer she would disappear. Even now, after all this time, she still had the power to mesmerize him.

She was just as beautiful as she'd been that summer all those years ago. Annie had never left his mind, and the sound of her laughter had stayed with him. When life had seemed harsh and he'd had to deal with his father's hate, he would remember Annie. His mind would go back to that summer when he first saw her, running along the beach, her hair flying behind her, her laughter carried on the wind. Thinking of her had given him the power to look past the ugliness that surrounded him.

That one day they'd met, she'd been kind and gentle, refusing to join in the teasing. She'd insisted Devon stop calling him names. Devon had made mocking him a job while in high school, but Keaton had never let it bother him. All he had to do, if he wanted, was look at his tormentor, take one step in Devon's direction, and it was sure to stop. No one dared to rile the beast.

Since the first glimpse of her, Keaton had sketched Annie countless times, on paper and in his mind. He viewed her as the beauty to his beast — perfection against his flawed, miserable life. After all these years, he'd never expected to see her again. He'd built her up in his mind to the point that reality would never live up to his fantasy, and yet here she was, as beautiful and wonderful as he remembered. Perhaps more so.

Just seeing her had taken his breath away. He'd stood immobile, unable to move, uncertain whether she was real or a figment of his imagination. Lennon, however, had instantly raced to her side as if he'd known her all his life. She leaned down and petted him, while Keaton was unable to do anything more than stare.

The next day, she was gone, and he wondered if he'd ever see her again. Keaton was filled with instant regret, certain he'd missed his chance. He felt like that awkward young man all over again, afraid to speak to the beautiful girl on the beach.

When he returned from his errand to get more paint and found her in the realtor's office, his heart felt like it was about to explode. Taken aback, all he seemed capable of doing was gazing at her in disbelief. She was real, and she was in Oceanside.

Annie had come back, and it'd caught him completely off guard.

And even more shocking, she was looking to rent the cottage. Mellie's cottage. Keaton knew he could convince Mellie to rent it out, although it wouldn't be easy. Mellie Johnson was one stubborn woman. Nevertheless, Keaton had been prepared to do whatever was necessary to get her to agree. He sensed that Annie needed that cottage, but he didn't know why. He'd heard the yearning in her voice and was determined to do this for her, seeing that he had nothing else to offer her.

Mellie had been unwilling to rent out the cottage, but eventually she'd relented. Mellie depended on him. He'd never asked for anything in return for supplying her with groceries, collecting her mail, and doing other errands. He was asking now, and he wasn't taking no for an answer. He made sure she understood renting Annie the cottage was important to him. Naturally, being Mellie, she had a list of requirements. He didn't have a problem with any of her demands, and he figured Annie wouldn't, either.

Keaton didn't know what had brought Annie to Oceanside. All he cared about was that she was back. He'd been given a second chance, and by all that was right, he intended to put this new opportunity to good use.

CHAPTER
SIX

Annie was thrilled when she learned that she would be able to rent the cottage. She didn't know what had convinced Melody Johnson to agree but sensed that Keaton had somehow made it possible. Unwilling to question her good fortune, Annie quickly agreed to the woman's demands.

As she drove to the cottage, a sense that this was all meant to be washed over her. A sense of rightness. After sixteen angst-filled months, she was convinced she was on the right path at last. The one she'd been traveling on had been filled with ruts, potholes, self-pity, grief, and loss so profound that she had often lost her way.

She felt like she was finally back on track now, ready to move forward, to start her life over again in a town filled with happy memories from her childhood. She would do it in that same cottage by the sea, the very one she'd once shared with her brother and parents. Annie was certain her parents had sent her to Oceanside, knowing that this was the one place where her wounded heart would heal.

Keaton had given her the key to the rental. Annie held it in her hand as she stood in front of the cottage with its sagging porch and uneven steps. Holding her breath, she opened the door and peeked inside. She'd been right in her assumption; no one had rented this place in years. The living room was filled with cobwebs and layer upon layer of dust. It came fully furnished, and thankfully someone had placed sheets over the furniture.

Taking a tentative step inside, she inspected the kitchen. The table was the same one where her family had sat and played board games and cards, where they'd eaten their meals. Closing her eyes, Annie heard the echo of their fun as a smile came to her lips.

The grime was thick on the windows, something she'd noticed earlier. One of her first tasks would be to wash them on the inside and outside to let in the light. After living in the dark for all these months, light was important to her.

When she tested the water, the faucet had creaked and burped from lack of use before rust-colored water gushed from the spout. Annie left it running for several minutes while she inspected the two bedrooms and the bath. She remembered that she always got the bedroom, while her brother, Mike, had to sleep on the sofa bed. He complained every year. Annie would give anything to hear him complain again. The bathroom had the same shower curtain as it had the last time they'd rented. Funny that she would recognize it. She flushed the toilet and was pleased to note that the plumbing was in working order.

All the cottage needed was a thorough cleaning and a bit of paint. With a week of hard work, two at the most,

Annie would have it back as it had once been, the way she remembered it.

While compiling a list of cleaning supplies, Annie heard a dog barking. She immediately thought of Lennon, the friendly mutt she'd met on the beach. She'd left the front door open to air out the cottage, and when she glanced outside she saw the large canine standing outside the front door, his tail wagging so hard it slapped against the sides of his body. His big brown eyes looked up adoringly at her.

"Hello, Lennon," she said, and, bending down, she ran her hands through his thick, slightly matted fur. Glancing up, she noticed Keaton was standing on the street still, watching her in that gruff way of his. He was large and intimidating, just as the real estate agent had mentioned, but in a beautiful sort of way. That sounded odd, she realized, but his size didn't frighten her as it might others. She felt herself drawn to him, almost to the point of attraction. She straightened and smiled.

"I know I have you to thank for this," she said, raising her voice so he could hear her. "I don't know what you said to convince the owner to rent me the cottage, but whatever it was, I'm grateful."

He shrugged, seemingly embarrassed by her appreciation.

"My family rented this very cottage for several summers when I was a teenager," she explained, feeling self-conscious.

Walking across the unwieldy, overgrown grass to the front door of the cottage, Keaton handed her a slip of paper with a phone number scribbled in large numbers and Melody Johnson's name written below it.

"Mellie wants you to sign a lease."

"Mellie?" That was the name. The girl her brother had a crush on that last summer. "Is this the same . . . the Munsons' granddaughter?"

Keaton nodded. "You'll sign the lease?"

"Yes, of course. I remember her. She was older than me, and my brother, Mike, had a crush on her."

Keaton grinned. "Most guys did."

"As I recall, she tolerated his silly attempts to get her attention." She smiled at the memory of her brother quoting Mellie poetry, and all the fun Annie had razzing him about how ridiculous he sounded. From that last summer at the beach, Annie remembered Mellie as outgoing and friendly. The years had apparently changed her. But then they'd changed Annie, too.

Keaton handed her a set of papers. Annie went inside and read over the standard lease form before she penned her name on the bottom line. She'd already written the check. Keaton waited outside for her. When Annie returned, she gave him the signed documents and the check, grateful that Mellie had given her the key before she had the money.

"Thank you, again," she said, and she was thankful, more than he would ever guess.

He nodded and whistled. Immediately Lennon scampered off to join Keaton, who left.

With her landlord's contact information in hand, Annie programmed the number in her phone and hoped that they could be on good terms. She doubted Mellie would remember her or Mike. The cottage had a lot of guests over the summer and her family was one of many. Annie understood that Mellie was a private person, but she hoped that in time they could be friends. It would be a small connection to the brother she'd lost, and that was what Annie needed.

Connection.

Almost against her better judgment, Annie pushed the button on her phone that would ring to Mellie's phone line. It rang five times before her landlord answered.

"What?" Mellie demanded gruffly.

Annie blinked twice as the greeting assaulted her as sharp as a slap.

Annie recovered quickly. "Mellie, hi. I thought I should introduce myself," she said in her softest, most cordial voice. "I'm your new renter."

"You call me again and I'm canceling your lease."

"But why —"

"What part of leaving me alone don't you understand?" her landlord demanded coldly.

"I promise I won't be a pest," Annie assured her, ignoring the question. "I'm calling to let you know that I remember you from when my family —"

"You think I care if you remember me? Because I don't. What I want," Mellie said pointedly, "is to be left alone."

Wow, this was hardly the girl Annie remembered. She sucked in a breath. "Sure. I can do that. I won't bother you again . . . well, unless it's something important."

"Good. Remember that, seeing that you're already making a nuisance of yourself."

"Okay. Got it. I called to thank you for allowing me to rent —"

"Don't thank me," she interrupted. "Keaton bullied me into agreeing to this madness."

Just as Annie thought. "But you did agree, and I'm grateful."

"Then show your appreciation by sticking to your own business and staying out of mine. I don't expect to hear from you again unless it's something dire, in which case you can contact Keaton."

"I understand."

"I hope you do."

The phone was slammed down, and the sound was so loud that Annie had to quickly pull her phone away from her ear. Exhaling a long sigh, she couldn't help wondering what had happened to change Mellie from the happy-go-lucky teenager she remembered.

Annie fondly remembered Mellie's grandparents. Each year when Annie's family returned to the beach, the Munsons had greeted them with warmth and enthusiasm. A vivid image came to mind of her father sitting with Mr. Munson on the wraparound porch, the two men smoking cigars. Mrs. Munson had often invited the family to the big house for lemonade. They'd come in August when Mrs. Munson was busy canning produce. The property had an abundance of blueberry and raspberry plants, plus several apple trees.

Annie and Mike had enjoyed picking the berries, stuffing their mouths with the sweetness while the colorful juice coated their lips and stained their hands. If the bushes had survived, they were buried in the twisted invasive blackberry vines that choked nearly half of the property.

It shocked Annie to hear how troubled and unfriendly the Munsons' granddaughter seemed to be. Annie remembered her as fun and outgoing. And gauging by the condition of the house and yard, Mellie revealed no love or appreciation for the house or for the acreage. The home had once been a showcase in town. Now it sat sad and neglected, beaten down by the weather and years. Gone were the man and woman who had lovingly cared for it, only to be replaced by a disturbed and seemingly ungrateful granddaughter.

Annie worked, scrubbing and cleaning the cottage until eight, quitting only when she grew too exhausted to continue. She returned to the hotel room, which was across from the city park. A notice was up about Concert in the Park on Thursday evenings, being held at a small outdoor community stage. Tired as she was, Annie decided to attend. She found a seat on the makeshift bleachers facing the band under the gazebo and listened to the jazz band. The music soothed her spirit. After the concert finished, Annie returned to the hotel and fell into bed, sleeping straight through until eight the following morning.

Straight through.

It felt incredibly good to sleep. Marvelously good. Annie hadn't realized how sleep-deprived she'd become until she managed eight hours of uninterrupted sleep in a single night.

First thing the next morning, she drove back to Seattle to make the arrangements to move to Oceanside. With so much to do, she put her phone on speaker and started packing boxes at her apartment while chatting with Gabby.

"You're doing what?" her cousin demanded. "You're not seriously moving to Oceanside? This is a joke, right?"

"It's not a joke. I have a job and a place to live. Do you remember Melody Johnson?"

"Who?" Gabby asked, frowning.

Annie shook her head. There wasn't any reason her cousin would remember Mike's heartthrob from all those years ago. "Never mind, it isn't important. What is wonderful is how everything fell into place like it'd all been planned in advance."

"Annie. Surely you realize Oceanside is a ghost town most of the year. What kind of shopping do they have? Is there even a mall? Is this town even big enough for a Walmart or a theater?"

"It has a theater." She didn't mention that the town's lone theater had only one screen, unlike the multiplexes they were accustomed to in Seattle.

Gabby did nothing to disguise her feelings. "This isn't like you, Annie. It's crazy; I don't understand what's happening. One minute you're deeply depressed, and then a day later you're over-the-moon excited. It's like you're on drugs or something."

Annie hadn't anticipated her cousin's negative reaction. She'd assumed Gabby would be happy for her, excited that Annie was showing interest in something for the first time in a long time. She'd hoped her best friend in all the world would cheer her on.

"Remember, you're the one who gave me the idea."

"Yes, but I didn't think you'd pack up and move."

Annie realized her cousin was worried about her. Gabby was afraid Annie was looking for a geographical cure. That wasn't it at all. "You don't understand," Annie explained patiently, "I slept eight hours through the night, twice now." Of anyone, Gabby was aware of how poorly Annie had slept since the mudslide.

"I get that, Annie, but you moving away on the spur of the moment like this concerns me."

"I'm fine, Gabby. I feel better than I have in a long time. This feels right. The way everything fell into place makes me think Mom and Dad somehow arranged this."

Her cousin sighed in exasperation. "You'll be hours away. Mom and I will worry." Gabby and her aunt had treated Annie with kid gloves and she had let them. She needed to break away, otherwise she might never get over the loss. It was time to stand up and take care of herself. Move forward instead of getting trapped in the thick tightness of loss that consumed her night and day.

"I could always move back to L.A.," Annie teased, wanting to lighten the mood. Returning to her life in southern California had been her original intention: Once she'd settled her family's affairs, Annie had assumed she'd return to her life there. Dealing with the

61

legal issues, not to mention the emotional toll, hadn't turned out to be as simple as she'd thought it would be.

The class-action lawsuit had yet to be settled. Annie had wanted no part of it, yearning to escape all the drama and angst of reliving that horrible Thanksgiving morning. Unfortunately, the legal ramifications were unavoidable; she was part of the lawsuit. Aunt Sherry had insisted that Annie owed that much to her parents, and she was right. As hesitant as she was to deal with the legal aspects of the tragedy, it was necessary. And it hadn't been easy to go on as before. Her life was different now. She'd been emotionally cast adrift, alone in an ocean of personal pain. Nothing felt the same. Nor would it. It'd taken her months to fully understand and accept the ramifications of having lost her family. That feeling of being empty and alone never seemed to end. Just when she assumed all was settled and she could breathe again she'd get hit with something more, some issue, some forgotten detail that required attention. Soon her California life became a distant memory and she had to accept that there was no going back.

"I hate that you're moving away," Gabby admitted. "I guess I'm being selfish. Having you close has been great. I'm going to miss you something awful. You're good for me."

"It goes both ways." Annie had relied heavily on Gabby and her aunt, probably more than she should. "I need this, Gab. Oceanside soothes my spirit; I don't know how to explain it. From the moment I arrived,

I've felt more at peace than I have since I lost my family."

"You sound different, Annie," Gabby reluctantly acknowledged. "If living in Oceanside is what you need, then go for it. Get your head on straight, and then move back to Seattle. I've been telling you all along to take care of yourself, but I didn't expect you to move away."

Annie exhaled, relieved. She needed Gabby's support. "You can always visit, and you know I'll be coming back to Seattle someday."

After packing up her apartment, Annie returned to Oceanside and to the cottage. Once she arrived, she was surprised to find that the lawn had been mowed and the front door had been freshly painted. It wasn't until she started unpacking her car that she realized the steps were new wood and that the porch had been leveled, with several of the planks replaced and painted. Other improvements had been made as well, but those were the first that Annie noticed. The difference was night and day. It went without saying that only one person would have done this.

Keaton.

With so much to accomplish before she started her new job, Annie decided she would seek him out later to thank him. But first things first, and that included unpacking her SUV. She'd stuffed as much as she could into her vehicle, taking only what she would need right away.

Without bothering to unpack her clothes, Annie headed to the grocery store for the basics, and then went about setting up her kitchen. It didn't take her long to realize she would need new pots and pans. She started making a list that grew to two full pages as the afternoon progressed. After multiple trips to the closest Walmart in Aberdeen, Annie felt like the cottage had become her home.

On Monday, Annie was ready to start work at the Oceanside Walk-in Medical Clinic and hit the ground running.

Her first patient was a fifty-year-old who complained of a sharp, constant pain in her shoulder and back. She was traveling with her husband in their motorhome and had been on the road for two weeks. She'd recently received word that her father had suffered a heart attack. It became clear that the woman was under a lot of stress, worrying about her parents and their health issues.

Annie swallowed hard as she listened to the woman talk. This was an issue that she would never need to face, as her parents didn't have the luxury of growing old. After taking her vitals and examining her, Annie realized her patient had developed a case of shingles. She prescribed an antiviral medication and pain pills and advised the woman to check with her family physician once she was home.

The next patient was a local woman named Rebecca Calder. Her eyes lit up when Annie entered the exam room.

"I'm pregnant!" Rebecca exclaimed. "I've been feeling ill every morning for two weeks. Morning sickness," she announced proudly. "I skipped my period, too. That means I'm pregnant, right?"

"The urine test will confirm a pregnancy," Annie said, enjoying the excitement that she saw in the young woman.

"Lucas and I have been trying for four years to have a baby and it's been one disappointment after another. Lucas has good health insurance from his work, but it doesn't cover infertility treatments, and we can't afford them out of pocket. My husband is going to be a wonderful father." Her eyes glowed with pride and love.

Annie handed Rebecca a small plastic jar to collect her urine.

The joy and excitement drained from Rebecca's eyes as she reluctantly took hold of the plastic cup. "I've taken three of those drugstore pregnancy tests already," she admitted softly, "and they all say negative, but that can't be right. I mean, not with me skipping my period and the sickness every morning. They're all false readings, right?"

"We'll find out and put your mind at rest."

"Shouldn't you take blood instead?" she asked, as if having her blood drawn would change the outcome.

"No, the urine test is ninety-nine percent accurate."

"Oh." Rebecca slid off the table. "Then don't bother, because I know I'm pregnant. Those tests are all wrong."

"Rebecca," Annie said gently, "let's do the test."

"No," she insisted, her eyes snapping with defiance. "They're wrong; those tests mean nothing to me. I'm pregnant. I know I am. I can feel this baby growing inside of me. It's different this time." She flattened her hand against her stomach. "Our baby is right here," she declared. "He can feel my love and I'm not going to let you or any of those worthless drugstore strips tell me otherwise."

Annie sympathized with the young woman.

"I can see that this visit was a waste of time and money. I took time off work for this, you know." Grabbing her sweater and purse, Rebecca flew out the door of the examination room.

Annie's heart ached for her. She keenly felt Rebecca's desperation for a baby. Her need to give her husband a child was so strong that she'd mentally convinced herself and her body that she was pregnant.

Rebecca stomped out of the clinic, startling those in the waiting area. The door slammed in her wake.

Candi approached Annie. "Poor Becca," she whispered. "She's been in before."

"Who's next?" Annie asked, doing her best not to let the young woman's disappointment upset her.

"The man in room three is in for a cut. He's going to need stitches. Julia has everything ready for you."

Before she entered the room, Julia, the nurse, handed Annie the file. Annie flipped it open and read it as she entered the room. Looking up, her smile froze in place when she recognized the man who sat waiting.

Keaton.

CHAPTER
SEVEN

Keaton didn't know who was more surprised, him or Annie.

She stood inside the small exam room where the nurse had placed him, and simply stared at him. Keaton was equally shocked. He'd heard the scuttlebutt around town that a new physician assistant had recently been hired, but he'd had no idea it was Annie.

Not that a lot of people talked to him, or would have even told him, other than Preston and Mellie, but it wasn't anyone's fault. He wasn't much of a talker, never had been, and probably never would be. Before Keaton was comfortable enough to carry on a conversation with someone, he liked to observe that person and get to know them on his terms. Then, and only then, was he willing to engage in conversation. Folks around town accepted him, and for that he was grateful. They knew he was the one who painted the murals and they seemed to appreciate his efforts to add color and texture to their small beach town.

His lack of connection with others had never bothered him; he didn't much care what people thought. He'd stuck to his business and left others to tend to their own. He had a nodding acquaintance with most everyone in town.

It would help if he could be more comfortable with speaking. For as long as he remembered, words had been nothing but trouble. If he spoke as a kid, it often resulted in his father's hand on the back of his head. It'd been drilled into him from a young age to keep his thoughts to himself, and that tendency had followed him into his teen years and adulthood. Silence suited him. He was a large man, and intimidating. At six-eight, he towered over most everyone. He'd grown accustomed to his size as a big-boned, muscular man.

Annie stood in the examination room, her eyes rounded with surprise, and she, too, seemed to have lost the ability to speak.

"Keaton," she whispered, doing her best to hide her reaction.

He acknowledged her with a sharp nod.

Glancing down at the chart, her gaze bounced back to his. "It says here your first name is Seth. Seth Keaton."

He held her look.

"But you go by Keaton?"

His thoughts ran together in his head. "Yeah." It frustrated him that he couldn't tell her what he wanted to, that he'd been named after his father, who had never loved him or wanted him. It seemed inappropriate to carry the name of the man who detested his very existence.

"All right, Keaton, let me look at that cut." She sat on the rolling stool and carefully removed the bandage he'd wrapped around his hand. Thankfully, it was his left one, as he was right-handed. He had several projects scheduled and he'd hate to get behind because of the injury.

Her touch was soft and gentle as she tentatively explored the wound. It hurt like hell, but he didn't let her see his pain. Her eyes lifted to his and she frowned. "This is a defensive wound."

He didn't disagree.

"Keaton, were you in a knife fight?"

Again, he didn't respond.

"Okay . . . so you don't want to tell me."

He grinned, grateful she wasn't going to ply him with more questions.

She frowned slightly, concerned. "This is a nasty cut; you're going to need stitches."

He figured as much; he wouldn't have wasted time coming to the clinic if he thought a butterfly bandage would suffice.

"I'm happy to see you," she commented, as she carefully cleaned the wound. Reaching for the needle, she proceeded to numb the area. Her touch was confident and caring. The feel of her skin against his, even in a professional way, caused him to be even more aware of her. He held his breath tight inside his chest. He resisted reaching out with his free hand and taking hold of hers, intertwining their fingers. Yearning for her touch — anyone's touch, for that matter — was foreign to him, and he found it unsettling. Unusual. He'd never experienced this sort of attraction to anyone before and it flustered him.

He accepted that she hadn't remembered him from their teen years. No reason she should, he supposed. He wasn't offended or surprised, simply grateful that she was back, and this time for longer than a few days.

She looked up, expecting him to talk. This happened on occasion — someone would make a comment and his mind would take off on a different course, and he couldn't remember what he was going to say.

The last thing he'd heard her say, he recalled, was that she was happy to see him.

Him? He arched his brows in question.

Her smile broadened as she held his gaze. "I never realized how much a person can communicate without words. You're looking shocked because I'm happy to see you."

"Yes." He yearned to say more but faltered, unable to find words.

"When I returned to the cottage I found the lawn had been mowed and several repairs made. I might not be much of a detective, but I suspect you're the one respbnsible. Thank you, Keaton."

With all she had to do setting up the cottage, he didn't want Annie to deal with the yardwork. The other repairs he'd made were minor and had taken him only the better part of a day. It was important to him that she feel welcome. It was his way of telling her how much it meant to him that she'd returned to Oceanside. Heaven knew she wouldn't get any warm fuzzies from Mellie.

Mellie didn't hide the fact that she was curious as to why Keaton had insisted she rent the cottage to Annie.

He had no intention of explaining it, either. Mellie didn't need to know that Keaton had tender feelings for this woman. He'd never forgotten her beauty from that summer all those years ago. He wasn't one for premonitions or even for hunches. All he could say was that deep down in a part of him that he couldn't explain, he believed Annie Marlow needed to be in Oceanside. It was where she was meant to be. Furthermore, it was important that she live in that cottage.

Mellie's problem was that she didn't want anyone, man or woman, close. He didn't know what had happened to her in the years after she'd run away. All he knew was that she'd returned a changed woman, crippled by her fears, hiding inside the house she'd inherited from her grandparents. To the best of his knowledge, from the moment Mellie showed up back in town, she'd holed up and never once set foot outside. In all the years they'd been in school together, Mellie hadn't said more than a handful of words to Keaton. Once she was back, she reached out to him. He guessed she figured he would be safe, seeing how rarely he spoke. She'd hired him to run errands on her behalf, to take care of things she couldn't from inside the confines of those four walls. In the beginning, Keaton figured, it was his size that had prompted her to hire him — that she'd been looking for protection. But as far as he knew, no one had ever come looking for her. He'd assumed that after a few months, Mellie would feel secure enough to leave the house, but she never did, and he had never asked. Whatever it was that kept her locked behind those doors was her business and not his.

Keaton was lost in his thoughts until he felt a sting. He looked down and realized that while he'd been mulling over Mellie and the cottage, Annie had been busy stitching his hand. By the time he noticed, she was nearly finished. Seemed she'd been chatting, too, and he'd completely tuned her out, lost in his thoughts. He was guilty of that far too often. He should have paid attention, uncertain now what he'd missed.

"You didn't hear me, did you?" she asked, looking up at him.

He shook his head. "Sorry."

"That's all right. It wasn't anything important. I mentioned how much I was enjoying living in the cottage and that I'd spoken briefly to Mellie. She didn't take kindly to my call."

"Don't take offense."

"I didn't."

He silently wished her luck and had to smile, knowing Mellie wouldn't make it easy.

Once she'd finished with the bandage, Annie glanced up, her eyes connecting with his, and immediately Keaton felt it again — that connection, that peculiar fluttering deep inside his chest. The same sensation he'd experienced years earlier when he'd first caught sight of Annie on the beach. He felt a longing, a need to know her, to protect her, and to be with her. These feelings were completely alien to him, and he wasn't sure what to do with them. Part of him wanted to leave until he could understand what it was about this woman that affected him this way. And yet at the same time he found it impossible to pull away from her. Being around her was like getting trapped ankle-deep in wet sand, finding it impossible to move in any direction.

"Are you in trouble?" she asked, her words gentle as she held his injured hand in her own.

Keaton grinned. Trouble? Him?

"That didn't come out the way I meant it. Is someone trying to hurt you?"

"No," he said with a shrug. Explaining the circumstances of how he'd been cut would only lead to more questions, and they were ones he'd rather not answer or explain, especially to Annie.

Now that she'd finished tending to his wound, she rattled off a list of care instructions. He listened while intently staring at her, lost in her beauty. It demanded every bit of mental strength he possessed not to lean forward and wrap her hair around her ear. He'd always loved her auburn color, and regretted that it wasn't long enough for the braid she once had.

"I'll need to see you in a week to remove those stitches. Candi will make you an appointment."

If it were anyone else, he would've taken out those stitches on his own. He didn't need Annie to do it, but because it was her, he'd return for the opportunity to see her again.

CHAPTER
EIGHT

The lights in the cottage were on when Keaton walked past on his way to see Mellie. Lennon paused as they neared Annie's place, and Keaton smiled. His dog wanted to visit. He whistled, and Lennon reluctantly followed him, although he stopped once and looked back over his shoulder toward the cottage.

"Another time," he whispered to his dog.

Lennon took him at his word and bounded ahead to the main house.

Keaton didn't bother to knock. Mellie had given him keys, and he let himself in. From the day she'd returned, Mellie'd had the house locked up tighter than an armory. In addition to the deadbolt, she had three other locks. The windows were sealed shut. Houdini couldn't have broken into this house with all the safeguards Mellie had put in place. The woman was beyond paranoid.

"That better be you, Keaton." She looked up expectantly and he could tell she was hoping it was Preston, not him. Heaven forbid that she'd admit it. Not to Keaton, and certainly not to Preston. His best friend, Preston, was in love with Mellie, and was completely tongue-tied around her. He sometimes accompanied Keaton, especially when he brought her an injured animal. Preston managed the local animal shelter and worked to find good homes for mistreated and abused dogs and cats.

She was in the kitchen, where she was most often, sitting at the dinette, surrounded by stacks of miscellaneous boxes of papers and magazines, which she had stored all over the house. Mellie had managed to accumulate mountains of what most people would consider garbage. He doubted she'd discarded a single newspaper in the five years since she'd moved back to town.

"I suppose you're here to check on the dog."

Preston had heard a rumor about an abused dog being kept in the woods. With no time to search himself, he'd asked Keaton to investigate. It'd taken him two weeks to locate the dog. The cabin was in an obscure location, ten miles outside of town. Sure enough, Keaton found a badly mistreated brown Labrador chained to a tree without food or water. The owner was a deadbeat who lived in the area. Keaton didn't know the man, and didn't care to. It didn't take much for him to realize the pitiful dog had been nearly starved to death, so thin his ribs showed through. By the time Keaton found him, the dog was too weak to stand.

Anger filled him that anyone would mistreat an animal this way. Keaton held his temper and brought the dog a small amount of food and a bowl of water, feeding him out of his hand. While the dog eagerly lapped up the water, Keaton removed the chain. It was tight around the Lab's neck, leaving open sores. It sickened him to imagine the abuse this poor dog had suffered.

That was when the cabin door flew open and the owner came barreling outside, shouting obscenities, claiming Keaton was trespassing on his property. The man was drunk and belligerent, too far gone to recognize that Keaton was easily double his size. When he saw that Keaton had removed the chain around the dog's neck, he'd swung wildly at Keaton. Avoiding the man's feeble attempts to hit him was a simple matter. With one fist to the man's stomach, the drunk fell to the ground, cursing and throwing out empty threats about gutting Keaton. Ignoring him, Keaton bundled up the dog and carried it to his truck, laying the half-dead animal down in the bed on a blanket he kept there.

To Keaton's surprise, the man recovered enough to chase after him.

"You can't take my dog."

Keaton had laughed.

"That dog is my property."

Ignoring the fool, Keaton had walked around the vehicle to the driver's side when the dog's owner suddenly lunged at him with a knife. Thankfully, he'd caught the reflection of the weapon in his side mirror and turned around in time to avoid a more serious injury, but the knife caught him on the side of his hand, slicing through the meaty part. Because he was so enraged, Keaton hadn't felt any pain until later. He'd reacted on instinct, disarming the homeowner and taking the man down.

In Keaton's mind, cruelty to a helpless animal shouldn't go unpunished. He dragged the man to the very tree where he'd chained the poor dog and wrapped the chain around him, securing him to the tree. That wouldn't be the only penalty the drunkard would pay. Keaton knew that Preston would contact the authorities and see to it that this monster was prosecuted. That, however, would take time.

After delivering the half-dead Labrador to Mellie that day, he'd fed him a mixture of milk and bread. Mellie fussed over Keaton about the cut, insisting on looking at it and wrapping it in a dressing. That hadn't stopped the bleeding, and she'd demanded he head over to the clinic as soon as it opened in the morning. Mellie could be stubborn and bossy, which made it even more difficult for Preston to express his feelings to her. If Keaton didn't follow through and get to the clinic, she would likely go into a rant. And if there was anything he wanted to avoid it was one of Mellie's rants.

"I gave the dog a bath," Mellie said, beginning to update Keaton on the dog's progress after his trip to the clinic. "Poor thing had fleas and has a severe infection in both ears. I've put him on antibiotics and vitamins. I fed him again, and he ate a little more this time. How could anyone treat an animal like this? I hope this bastard pays for what he's done."

Keaton grinned. He hadn't returned to check on the drunk and sincerely hoped that the man had spent a miserable night out in the cold. One thing was clear, he'd have sobered up by now.

Before he left Mellie's, Keaton checked on the Lab himself. Bending down, he stroked his head. The sickly dog looked at him with big brown eyes and gratefully licked his hand.

Like Keaton and Preston, Mellie had an affinity for animals. He often brought those he found to her. He suspected that at one time she might have worked for a veterinarian. She was far too knowledgeable for a novice, and he'd watch her perform countless procedures. She seemed capable of handling just about any injury, short of surgery. Keaton was grateful to partner with her on behalf of these animals, and he knew Preston appreciated her help since the closest veterinary clinic was more than fifty miles away.

Over the years, Preston had trusted her with just about every kind of beast one could imagine. Working at the shelter, Preston had brought her stray dogs and cats, several birds, a baby raccoon, and even a bear cub with a broken leg. Not once had Mellie complained.

After checking on the dog and Mellie, Keaton returned home and figured it was time to unchain the dog's owner. It took him twenty minutes driving down country roads to return to the cabin where he'd found the Labrador. As he knew he would be, the man remained chained to the tree.

The cabin owner looked up when Keaton parked his truck. His eyes filled with fear.

Keaton walked toward him, a menacing frown on his face.

"Unchain me. I'm no animal. You can't do this to me."

Keaton snickered.

"You think I don't know who you are? You're that freak who doesn't talk." Sober now, he spit the words out at Keaton. "You'll pay for this. I swear I'll make you pay for what you done to me."

Fine by him. Keaton felt no obligation to release a man who was threatening him. He returned to his truck, prepared to drive away.

"Don't leave me!" the man shouted. "You can't just leave me here. I could die."

Keaton hesitated. As far as he was concerned, that was exactly what the dog owner deserved. Slowly, he turned back. Squatting down so he was at eye level with the dog abuser, he spoke softly. "You ever treat another dog or any animal the way you did that brown Lab, I will find you and make you regret you were ever born."

The threat wasn't an idle one. The other man's eyes widened with fear.

"You hear me?" Keaton asked.

Again, the man nodded.

"Say it," Keaton demanded.

"I'll do what you said . . . no animals. Nothing but a damn nuisance anyway."

Keaton unchained him and watched as the man staggered toward the house before heading back to his truck. He was confident he wouldn't be seeing the drunk again.

CHAPTER
NINE

After her first week working at the clinic, Annie had fallen into a routine. She hadn't realized how much she'd missed her work in the medical community. This was a fresh start for her and it felt good. That didn't mean she'd forgotten her family — the reminders were everywhere, especially living in the cottage. What she held on to, though, were the memories of the happy times, of the laughter and fun they'd shared the weeks they'd vacationed at the beach.

Living and working in Oceanside was different from vacationing because this was now her home, the place where she was determined to find the strength to be happy again.

Annie enjoyed working with Dr. Bainbridge, Candi, and Julia. Within only a few days, she could tell they would make a great team. For the first time in nearly a year and a half, Annie's days had purpose. She had a reason to set the alarm and get out of bed in the morning. She was needed in that little community, and each day, broken as she was, Annie felt like she had a positive impact on peoples' lives. It was good to have a role in something that didn't involve the tragedy that had swallowed up her life.

On her way to the clinic, as part of her normal morning routine, Annie stopped off at Bean There for a caramel latte. Most mornings she was greeted by the young, shy barista named Britt.

"Mornin', Britt," Annie said when it came to her turn at the counter.

Britt offered her a bashful smile. "The usual?" she asked, recognizing Annie after only a week.

"Please." As she came closer to Britt, Annie could see a bruise on the side of her face, one the teenager had taken great care to conceal with cosmetics. At first Annie was tempted to say something, but she didn't want to embarrass or call attention to the girl in front of her peers.

"You're working on Saturday?" Britt asked as she wrote the coded instructions on the paper cup and handed it off to her coworker.

"It's my weekend. I work at the medical clinic," Annie explained.

"I know. Not much new happens in this town that goes unnoticed," she said before turning to the next person in line. Looking back to Annie, she added, "Have a nice day."

"You too," Annie returned, and frowned slightly as she glanced at the bruise again. Once she'd collected her drink, Annie continued walking to the clinic. If the weather cooperated, she could easily walk, making her way along the beach, and then past the shops and that intriguing mural. It was a little less than a mile between the cottage and the clinic, and it took her thirty minutes with a stop for her latte at the halfway point.

By the time she arrived at the clinic, she'd finished her drink and was eager to start her day.

The exercise was good for her. Her mother had always kept fit and found it important to get at least thirty minutes of moderate exercise a day. Annie found herself thinking more and more about her mother. The sadness remained, of course, but adapting part of her mother's daily routine helped Annie fill in the hole her mother's absence had created. Now that Annie had made this walk a habit, she had to admit it felt good. The fresh air, heavy with the scent of the ocean, invigorated her. She enjoyed picking up seashells along the way and had a small collection she kept on her kitchen windowsill. In some obscure way, Annie felt her mother would be pleased by the treasures she'd collected.

When she arrived at the clinic, Annie found Candi sitting at her desk. The receptionist glanced up and smiled. They were on the same weekend rotation, which suited Annie. She liked Candi, who made it her responsibility to familiarize Annie with the community. It seemed she had a story to tell about every local who visited the clinic.

Annie waited until Candi had disconnected the answering service and collected the messages before she asked the question.

"Do you happen to know Britt? I have no idea what her last name is. She works mornings at Bean There?"

Candi frowned and bit into her lower lip. "Britt?" she repeated.

"She's a teenager, possibly still in high school?"

Candi's eyes widened as she recognized the name. "Oh yes, that's Britt McDuffee."

Annie leaned against the counter and folded her arms. "What can you tell me about her home life?"

Candi sadly shook her head. "It's not the best; her mother's a hard worker, cleaning houses. Britt works mornings at Bean There and attends classes in the afternoons. She's a senior this year, finishing up her last few credits."

"Is her father in the picture?"

"Not that I know of. Her stepfather worked in the lumber industry but has been out of work for as long as I can remember. Between you and me, I think he has a drinking problem."

Annie mulled over the information as the clinic officially opened. Soon the teenager slipped her mind as the day quickly filled with those in need of medical attention. As it had been when she worked in California, people tended to wait until the weekend for help, to avoid missing work. Saturdays were often the busiest days of the summer at the clinic; Candi and Annie had to work hard to support each other.

By closing time, Annie was physically and mentally drained. She walked out with Candi, who offered her a ride home. Annie was about to accept when her phone rang. Caller ID told her it was Trevor. They hadn't talked in a while and she didn't want to put him off.

"I'll walk, but thanks anyway; I have to take this call," she told Candi before sliding her finger across her phone to accept the call.

"I haven't talked to you in forever," she said, happy to hear his voice.

"What's this I hear?" he asked, sounding upbeat and a little amused. "You've left Seattle and moved to some obscure beach community?"

"Gabby told you? It's not a secret or anything. I've been busy moving and —"

"Excuses, excuses," Trevor interrupted.

Annie grinned as she started walking toward the cottage, chatting with him at the same time. "True, that is a weak excuse. I'm sorry, Trevor, I've been meaning to reach out." Consumed with her grief and dealing with the aftermath of the tragedy had stymied her. As a result, Annie hadn't made the effort to maintain friendships. Trevor had been the one who consistently kept trying, and Steph too, of course, now that they were a couple.

"Seeing that you're so curious to find out how I knew, then you should know it wasn't Gabby. Steph told me."

"And Gabby was the one who told her."

Gabby and Steph had been college roommates, and later, when Annie moved to Los Angeles, Steph had become her friend, too.

"If you were going to move," Trevor continued, "I'd have thought you'd come back to California. We miss you, girl."

"And I miss you guys." It was the truth, but California seemed like a distant memory, an entirely different lifetime. It was hard to fathom that it had been seventeen months ago that she'd been fun-loving and carefree. She was not the same person now; she was far more serious, more focused and committed to her career.

While she wouldn't want to admit it, especially to Gabby or to her aunt, until the move to Oceanside, Annie had been floundering badly. Being able to rent the cottage had given fresh breath to her lungs, and in some ambiguous way, it had freed her.

"I understand you're working. How long is your contract?" Trevor asked.

"A year." She felt better now than she had for a long time, and if it worked out the way she hoped, Annie wasn't opposed to extending the contract beyond that.

"A year," Trevor repeated slowly. "Hopefully you'll find time to visit every now and again. We miss you. Everyone does."

"Same here," she said automatically, and while it was true, what she really missed was the devil-may-care lifestyle she'd experienced living in southern California. Back then, she hadn't given more than a fleeting thought to the future, bouncing from paycheck to paycheck, running up her credit cards. With few responsibilities, she lived for the weekends when she wasn't scheduled to work at the clinic. Those lighthearted days were gone. The woman she'd once been was no more. Annie didn't think it was possible to be that person again.

Trevor was full of gossip about their mutual L.A. friends. As she walked, Annie listened and smiled, commenting now and again. Chatting with him did her heart good. She could almost forget . . .

Almost.

"I'm glad you called."

"Your arm isn't broken, you know. You can stay in touch, too, Annie."

"Yes, I can," she agreed.

He hesitated, as if there was something more he wanted to say but wasn't certain if he should.

Annie suspected that he was about to tell her that he'd proposed to Stephanie. She sincerely hoped that was the case. Early on, Annie and Trevor had dated and enjoyed each other's company. For Annie it had always been about friendship. It became awkward when she realized he was far more serious than she. After her broken relationship from college, Annie was leery of becoming romantically involved with anyone. She found it hard to trust.

"Okay, Trev, what's on your mind?"

"How . . . What?"

"Give it up. I know you. You're holding something back; I can hear it in your voice."

"Am not."

"Trevor!" she said, smiling broadly. She walked past Bean There and looked inside, half expecting to see Britt even though the teen had worked the morning shift.

"Does this involve Steph?" Her friend had fallen hard for him and done her best to hide her feelings while he and Annie dated. As soon as Annie realized Steph had a thing for him, she stepped aside, giving the other woman her chance. And seeing that he was a man, Trevor seemed completely oblivious to Steph's feelings until a year or so ago.

"In a way, it does involve Steph."

Annie knew it, and she was happy for her friends. "What aren't you telling me? Come on, spill," she chided good-naturedly.

Again, the hesitation, and then finally: "I ran into Steph this morning and she said she'd been talking with Gabby . . . Listen, Annie," Trevor blurted out, sounding concerned and anxious. "I need to know that you're okay."

"Okay? Of course I'm okay. What do you mean?"

"With the date?"

Date? What did any of this have to do with the date? It was April seventh, she thought to herself. Then she abruptly stopped walking.

Her mother's birthday. Today. April seventh.

Annie had forgotten. The date had completely slipped her mind.

"Annie? Are you there?" Trevor asked desperately. "Talk to me."

"I forgot," she whispered.

"Damn. And I had to remind you. I'm so sorry, Annie."

"No . . . No, it's fine. I would have remembered at some point." No wonder her mother had been on her mind all day.

"Damn," he said, cussing himself out again. "I should have kept my mouth shut."

Annie's throat was growing tight as she struggled to hold back the surge of emotion. "I . . . need to go.

Trevor, I appreciate the call. I promise I'll be better about staying in touch."

"Don't hang up, Annie, please. I feel terrible. I shouldn't have said anything. I'm a jerk."

"Trevor, I'm fine, but I need to get off the phone."

"You'll call me back?"

"Yes. Not today, but soon; I promise." Trevor was sensitive, and he would need that reassurance.

Standing in the middle of the sidewalk, Annie disconnected and remained frozen as tightness enveloped her chest, making it difficult to breathe. How could she have forgotten her mother's birthday? The guilt ate at her like acid.

In the months that followed the loss of her family, Annie had gone over that last conversation with her mother a thousand times. She'd been a brat, insensitive and selfish. She'd refused to change her plans for Thanksgiving because she wanted a four-day weekend to herself.

She could have made it work, but spending time with her family had been low on her priority list. Annie had refused to give in, not even when her mother had practically begged her to come. While it was true that her refusal had saved her life, she felt dead in other ways. After the mudslide, Annie wished she had been killed rather than facing the future so utterly alone.

Lost in her thoughts and in her renewed grief, Annie made the turn to the beach. Walking along the shore with the wind buffeting against her would hide her from curious stares. She needed to be alone.

The weather was gloomy, cloudy and cold. Rain was predicted for later in the evening. The wind off the ocean chilled her, but Annie ignored it as she walked, her arms tucked around her middle. Her pace was fast and furious, in an attempt to outrun the terrible memories.

"Happy birthday, Mom," she whispered, tilting her chin toward the heavens. At that moment, Annie would have given anything to talk to her mother one last time, to be able to tell her how sorry she was and how much she regretted her stubbornness. A sob tore through her. She wanted her mother. She needed her mother, especially now, when she was alone. Being a daddy's girl, Annie had no idea how much she would miss her mother.

After a while, continuing at a clipped pace, she was breathless. Sinking to her knees in the sand, she covered her mouth with one hand in a useless effort to hold back the sobs. Her shoulders shook as she gave in to her heartache. Soon she was hiccupping and struggling to breathe. It took several minutes to regain control of herself.

Exhausted by the effort to pull herself together, Annie sat back in the sand and wrapped her arms around her knees, rocking back and forth gently. Before she continued on to the cottage, she needed to calm herself and find her center. She didn't know how long that would take. An hour? Two? An eternity?

With her eyes closed, she sat listening to the wind and the pounding surf, seagulls crying overhead. The tide was coming in, so the waves surging toward the shore grew in intensity. Drained, she couldn't find the energy to get up and move. Sitting there, wrapped in the familiar beach sounds, she was desperate for solace.

What she wanted, she supposed, was some sign from the beyond that her mother was close, if not in body, then in spirit. Annie and her mother had often clashed, especially in her teen years. To her discredit, Annie hadn't appreciated her mother nearly as much as she should have. Now that her mother was forever stripped from her life, Annie missed her every single minute. Some days, the need to connect with her mom felt overwhelming. She'd always been closer to her dad, but now, for reasons she couldn't explain, it was her mother she missed most. Perhaps it was because her last conversation with her family had been with her.

From out of the corner of her eye, a movement captured Annie's attention. She turned her head and noticed Keaton and his dog walking along the beach. She assumed this was part of his daily routine, as she often saw him and Lennon; usually they simply waved to each other, but they never stopped to talk. She would have enjoyed getting to know him better, but Keaton was the one who showed no interest.

When the big dog caught sight of her, Lennon sprinted ahead, kicking up sand in his wake, heading straight to her. If she didn't know the dog, she would have been alarmed. He stopped directly in front of her, panting hard. Annie circled her arms around his neck and buried her face in his fur.

Keaton was several feet behind his companion but caught up to Lennon in short order.

90

Annie looked up at him as he approached, certain her red eyes spoke of her anguish.

Without speaking, Keaton sank down on the sand, sitting next to her, his presence surrounding her, reminding her that he was a giant of a man.

He didn't ask questions.

Didn't strike up a conversation.

Didn't comment.

He simply sat at her side, giving Annie the comfort of his silent strength. His warmth seeped into her, chasing away the chill. Lennon went to the opposite side of Annie and sank down, resting his head in her lap.

Annie petted his thick fur, gliding her splayed fingers through his coat.

After a few minutes, Keaton surprised her and reached for her free hand, entwining their fingers.

Annie thought for a minute that she should explain what had caused this emotional breakdown, but she couldn't find the words. To say it was her mother's birthday explained nothing. Offering excuses was beyond her.

Keaton was a man of few words. Until they'd met she hadn't realized how much could be said through silence. He didn't need words to communicate, and in the moment, Annie discovered that she didn't, either.

They sat on the beach as storm clouds gathered overhead. Only when she felt the first sprinkles of rain did Annie experience an inclination to leave.

As she went to stand, Keaton released her hand. Once upright, Annie brushed the sand from her backside.

Again, Keaton had nothing to say.

But Annie did.

"Thank you," she whispered.

Keaton's eyes gentled, silently indicating that he would do anything to help her.

Annie left him and Lennon on the beach and headed back to her home, to the cottage by the sea.

CHAPTER
TEN

Keaton had never felt about a woman the way he did about Annie Marlow. She was constantly on his mind.

It had nearly gutted him when he found her on the beach, caught up in some deep emotional agony. He didn't know who or what had broken her heart. Although he'd grown up with a brutal father, Keaton wasn't a violent man. He'd learned at age fifteen that by losing his temper he could badly hurt someone. His strength was beyond that of a normal kid his age. He'd put a bully in the hospital by losing his temper protecting Preston. Keaton was fortunate not to serve time in juvie. Because he refused to fight from that point forward, kids soon learned they could say and do what they liked to him, which was fine. Keaton could take it. As a result, he internalized a lot of his feelings. He didn't instigate fights and he used his fists only when attacked. He was a strong man and could easily do physical harm. Although it was often difficult, he was careful to restrain himself, unless the option was taken away from him.

Annie's eyes had been swollen and red, struggling to hide the pain deep inside. It had deeply affected him. It'd taken every ounce of restraint he possessed not to demand who was responsible, and then to hunt that person down and make them pay. His own reaction shocked him. Lennon had immediately raced to her side, happy as always to see Annie. Until he could control his unfamiliar emotions, Keaton had hunkered down.

With everything in him, he regretted his inability to express himself. If he was a better communicator, he might have been able to offer her words of comfort. And even if he had managed to talk to her, he feared his anger toward whoever had hurt her would upset Annie even more. All he could think to do was sit silently by her side, hold her hand, and pray that human touch would ease her torment.

He half expected her to draw away from him, as others had. He'd been relieved when her fingers had curled around his, squeezing his hand, holding on to him, as though his sitting at her side was exactly what she'd needed.

After the incident on the beach, Keaton kept close tabs on her. The following day they met accidentally-on-purpose at the library sale and walked to Bean There for coffee. Annie's mood was lighter, and she talked animatedly about the recent book she'd read. Keaton enjoyed hearing the sound of her voice, and if anyone had asked him the title of the book she'd mentioned he would have been at a loss.

"Did you hear anything I said?" she asked, chiding him.

He grinned and nodded. "Most everything."

Seeing that she walked to and from the clinic, Keaton watched over Annie from a distance to be sure she made it home safely. He rested easier when he saw the lights were on at the cottage. He came to know her routine, so on two days the following week, he stopped by Bean There at the same time she did. He never had been overly fond of those fancy coffee drinks, but he ordered an overpriced Americano.

"We seem to be on the same schedule," Annie commented when he walked the rest of the way to the clinic with her.

He shrugged rather than explain that he had gone out of his way for the pleasure of spending time with her.

Annie left him at the door of the clinic with "Have a good day" and a bright smile. He lived on that smile for the rest of the day.

Keaton was scheduled to have the stitches removed on Thursday morning. Never had he been more eager for a medical appointment. He'd never been prone to nervousness, but he was now as he sat, waiting for Annie. Eager. Anxious. Flustered.

All morning he'd been toying with ideas of what he should possibly say to her. Every thought he entertained sounded forced or stilted. In the end, he fell back on what was most comfortable: silence. Simply being close to her left him tongue-tied and ill-at-ease.

The door to the exam room opened and Annie entered.

Keaton straightened, and his heart started to race. He locked his jaw for fear he might blurt out something stupid.

"Hello again," she said, smiling at him, seemingly unaware of the tension in him.

A man could drown in that smile of hers, Keaton mused, as the tension eased from his shoulders. She wore her hair pulled away from her face in a sloppy ponytail. She sat on the stool and rolled over to where he sat.

"I was running late this morning and didn't have time to deal with my hair." She raised her hand to her head, seeming to need reassurance that it was still there. Confident that it was intact, she washed her hands, reached for her gloves, and then carefully started to cut away the bandage on his left hand.

He enjoyed watching her, treasuring her touch.

She glanced up and their eyes met as she grinned back. Keaton swore his heart could melt, lost in her smiles.

Annie returned her attention to his wound. The cut had healed nicely. She seemed pleased with her stitchwork as she gently checked the area for any sign of infection. Once satisfied, she reached toward the tray that held the scissors to remove the stitches.

"I have something I wanted to run by you," she said, briefly glancing up to see if she had his attention.

The fact was, Keaton found it impossible to look away.

"I enjoy living in the cottage," she commented, and again looked up, anticipating a response from him.

He grinned, wanting her to know how pleased he was to have her in Oceanside. He would have spoken, but the words tangled on the end of his tongue, and so he left them unsaid.

"What I wanted to talk to you about has to do with Mellie. I'd like to plant a garden. My mother always had one, and I'd enjoy growing my own." She looked away for a moment. "There's a good space for one on the south side of the cottage," she said, continuing to work on his hand. "Do you think Mellie would let me do that?"

He shrugged, not wanting to discourage her, although secretly he had his doubts.

"I'd do all the work myself, and I'd be willing to share any produce with her." She finished removing the last stitch and rolled back a couple feet. Her eyes were filled with questions, and she looked to him for the answers.

Keaton silently cursed that he had none to give her.

"I plan on asking her, but I thought . . . you know, after our last conversation, I don't know what to expect. When I called her before, she nearly bit off my head."

Keaton barked a laugh, as that was typical of Mellie.

"I haven't tried to contact her since, although I've thought about it plenty."

"She's not friendly," he said.

"Yes, I got that. What happened? She didn't used to be that way."

Annie glanced up at him, her eyes intense.

"Don't know." And that was the truth.

Annie leaned forward enough to place her hand over his uninjured one. "Keaton, I've seen you several times and enjoyed those times. But you rarely have anything to say. I end up doing all the talking. I realize you're not much of a conversationalist, but is there a reason you avoid talking to me?"

She had no idea how desperately he wanted to do exactly that. His shoulders sagged with regret. She'd completely misread him. He looked away and debated how close to the truth he should get. "I'm afraid."

Her eyes widened. "Afraid of what?"

"You."

Her head came back in shock. "You're afraid of *me*? Why?"

That made him sound weak and pathetic. He needed to explain. "Of saying the wrong thing."

"Keaton, if we're friends, and I certainly hope that we are, then you don't need to worry that I'll take offense. Okay?"

All he could do was stare at her, completely shocked. Annie saw him as a friend. It was more than he dared hope for with her.

"Okay?" she repeated.

"Okay." His friends were few. His heart swelled with appreciation that she considered him one. "Is there anything you'd like me to say?" he asked, and he was serious.

Her face had the same stunned look he'd had seconds earlier. After a short pause, Annie burst out laughing. She doubled over and held her stomach as the laughter rolled over her.

Keaton had no idea what was so funny. He might have taken offense, but he knew that wasn't her intention.

"That was hilarious," she said, wiping a tear from her eye. "Thanks. I needed that."

He grinned then, loving the sound of her laughter, the way he had the first time he'd heard it all those years ago. Soon they were smiling at each other.

"I'll talk to Mellie," he offered.

"I'd appreciate it," Annie replied. "Don't say too much, though. Just mention that I have something I need to ask her and that I'd appreciate it if she didn't hang up on me."

"Got it." Keaton would do almost anything she asked of him.

"I'd like to get to know Mellie. I have the feeling you might be the key to that."

"Mellie's different than she was in high school."

"I know. My brother had a huge crush on her back then."

"She lived with her grandparents — ran away with some guy she met as soon as she was eighteen."

Annie mulled that over. "I wish I'd known her better. She gave me the impression that she doesn't remember me, but I think she might. I've met a few women in town now, but I was hoping that Mellie and I could be friends. Seeing that we live close to each other, it only makes sense."

"Mellie doesn't have friends."

"So I gathered," Annie murmured, frowning.

Soon after Mellie had returned, a few of the girls she'd run with in high school that still lived in town had reached out to her. Mellie made it clear she wasn't interested in re-establishing any connection with her former friends. After a while they stopped coming around. Keaton didn't blame them.

Her high school friends weren't the only ones Mellie shied away from, unfortunately. Keaton had hoped Mellie would recognize Preston's feelings for her. He'd given up urging his closest friend to try to make a connection. Keaton had the feeling that Mellie needed Preston, although she'd never admit to it. The two had a lot in common, but Mellie refused to see it. Preston claimed he'd made a fool of himself over her once, and he wasn't looking for a repeat performance. Keaton had no idea his best friend could be so stubborn, or what had happened. Neither spoke of it. Apparently, it was soon after she'd returned to town.

Sighing, Annie said, "Mellie made it clear she isn't in the market for friends. My brother and I loved the Munsons. They were good people. I don't know what happened in Mellie's life to make her the way she is. She needs a friend, and I could use one myself."

Keaton hated to discourage her.

"Are you her friend?" she asked, hopefully.

Rather than explain their relationship, he didn't answer. "I'll tell her you'll be calling."

"Thank you," she said, and hesitated. "It seems I'm always needing to thank you for one thing or another." She squeezed his forearm and then looked mildly embarrassed, thinking she might have overstepped her bounds.

She quickly gave him a list of care instructions for the cut and then stood, ready to attend to her next patient. "You're good to go. Nice seeing you, Keaton."

"Thanks, Annie," he said, as she started to leave the room.

"You're most welcome."

Again, her smile took his breath away. He struggled to hide the effect she had on him, and left the clinic wearing a big grin.

On the pretense of checking on the Lab, who continued to need almost constant care, Keaton headed directly to Mellie's after leaving the clinic.

As he expected, he found Mellie gently caring for the dog, rubbing salve into the open sores around his neck left from the chain. She looked up when she saw Keaton standing in the doorway to the room where she treated the animals he brought into the house. As far as he could tell, this room was the only one in the entire house that wasn't stacked to the ceiling with enough stuff to fill a garbage dump.

"You worried about John-Boy?"

Mellie tended to name the helpless creatures he brought to her. Keaton thought it was harmless, unless they were already named.

"He's healing?"

"Amazing how quickly he's rebounded. He's going to make a good family pet if he isn't too psychologically damaged."

"Good." Keaton had spoken with Preston about the brown Lab. They'd discussed a possible home. John-Boy would need a loving and patient family. Preston was good at finding homes for these abused animals. Keaton was certain it was Preston's way of showing Mellie how he felt about her. He made sure the dogs and cats she nursed went to homes where they would be loved and cared for with understanding and patience. Preston also handled the legal work; guilty parties needed to be prosecuted. Keaton and Mellie provided the photos as evidence, and Preston would contact the authorities.

"Talked to Annie today," Keaton said.

Mellie frowned. "You sweet on her or something?"

"Something," Keaton replied. "She's going to be calling you later."

Stiffening, Mellie shook her head. "Told her if I rented her the cottage, then she'd need to not bother me. I didn't want her living there in the first place. Don't give me a reason to get rid of her, Keaton, because I will."

"You won't," he said in a firm voice. He wouldn't allow it, although he really had no say in what Mellie did or didn't do.

The woman glared back at him. "What does she want?"

"A garden."

"What?"

"She wants to plant a garden."

Scratching the side of her neck, Mellie met his determined look and seemed unwilling to back down. "Not happening."

102

"Happening," Keaton countered. "Can't see that it would hurt. Yard's a mess. Your grandmother used to have more flowers growing than a floral shop. This home was once a showplace, and look at it now. A garden will be an improvement." This was probably the most words he'd spoken since he'd convinced Mellie to rent Annie the cottage.

Her shoulders lowered as the defiance left her. "My grandmother had a well-known gift when it came to coaxing things to grow."

"You ever try?"

She snickered. "I kill houseplants."

"Not the same," he argued.

Mellie laughed, which was a rare occurrence. It sounded more like a dog barking than any form of amusement. "In case you hadn't noticed, I haven't set foot outside this house in five years."

"I've noticed."

"Then it's not likely I'll be inclined to plant flowerbeds, now, is it?"

Keaton couldn't argue.

Mellie leaned back on her haunches. "Never knew you to do much talking, and certainly not on behalf of anyone else, especially a woman."

He chose to ignore the comment. "Annie's going to call you."

"So, what are you? The advance artillery?"

He cocked a grin. "Something like that. She mentioned it, and I don't want you scaring her off."

Mellie didn't take kindly to his comment. "If I scare her off, then she deserves to be gone."

No way was Keaton going to let that happen.

Mellie's eyes brightened, as though she had something on him. "You *like* her, don't you?"

He crossed his arms, unwilling to admit his feelings.

"I've seen you, Keaton."

He didn't know what she could have seen.

"You stop by nearly every night to check on her. I might prefer to stay in this house, but I'm not blind to what's going on around me. I keep an eye out. You stay in the shadows."

Keaton refused to confirm or deny it.

"News flash. Big guy like you has a hard time being inconspicuous."

True enough.

"What's with you and this girl?" Mellie asked.

"Nothing."

She wasn't letting up. "You talk to her?"

"Some." Mellie knew there were only a few people Keaton spoke to on a regular basis.

She paused, processing this information. "That tells me everything I want to know."

Keaton refused to make eye contact.

"What's her story?" Mellie asked next.

"Don't know."

"Yet you're drawn to her more strongly than any other woman in town?" This was a question of disbelief rather than a statement of fact. Mellie seemed eager for him to disclose his interest in Annie, but he wasn't about to put up with her prying.

Mellie grew suspicious at his silence. "She in trouble?"

Keaton shrugged. He doubted it, but he couldn't say for sure.

"You think she's in danger? Is that why you come by after dark to check on her?"

"No."

"Then why?"

Another good question. He wasn't stalking her, just looking out for her. Watching over her. All he knew was that she carried a heavy burden, a pain. And if he could ease this load on her heart, then he would gladly find a way to do it. As for Annie being attracted to him, Keaton had no illusions. It would take a miracle for a woman as beautiful and caring as Annie to be interested in him.

CHAPTER
ELEVEN

Annie shouldn't have been this nervous about making a simple phone call. But this call was to Mellie. Mellie, who had made it clear Annie wasn't to bother her. Her landlord, who wanted to be left alone. The longer Annie thought about that garden, the stronger the appeal became. Her mother had had a garden, one she proudly showed to anyone who happened to visit. She took pictures of it to send to Annie in California. She'd loved her garden. Annie had never grown one herself, but the desire to try refused to go away. All she needed was to get her landlord's verbal permission. It shouldn't be this difficult.

Annie hadn't seen Keaton since Thursday. He'd said he would talk to Mellie for her. She didn't want to use their friendship to her own advantage. That seemed wrong, but she needed his help. Keaton would put the idea in Mellie's head and smooth the way for her. She was afraid Mellie would immediately refuse if she came at her cold.

A good feeling came over Annie as she remembered their brief conversation. Although she'd seen him several times, he never used more than a casual greeting. From what the real estate agent had said,

Keaton rarely talked to anyone, and when he did, it was generally only a few words at a time. He'd intrigued her from the beginning. She could say, in all honesty, that she'd never met anyone quite like him. He was one of the largest men she'd ever seen, ungainly, and at the same time, totally comfortable in his own skin. Big, yet gentle. Tenderhearted and thoughtful.

Okay, enough.

She was letting her thoughts get all tangled up in Keaton when she should be calling Mellie. Thinking about him was a delay tactic to put off making that call to her brusque landlord.

Braving it, she sucked in a deep breath and called Mellie Johnson's number.

Three rings later, Mellie answered in the same gruff manner she had the first time Annie had called. "What?"

"It's Annie Marlow."

"Know that. And I know why you're pestering me. You want to talk to me about tearing up my yard?"

"I don't want to tear up anything. I want to grow a few vegetables is all, if . . . you don't . . . mind," she faltered, stumbling over the words, letting the woman intimidate her, when she'd promised herself she wouldn't.

"Talk," she demanded.

"What do you want me to say?" Annie asked.

"You're the one who called me. Tell me what you want to do to my property and I'll tell you if you can or can't. Now talk."

"Oh, of course. Okay. A garden. A small one on the south side of the cottage, because that area gets the most sun. If you're okay with it. Like I said, it would be just a small patch, maybe eight feet by eight feet. No bigger than that. I doubt I could handle anything larger. Oh, and I'd be happy to share whatever I grow with you."

"Not interested."

Annie pretended not to hear. "I'll order some tomato plants, and I thought I'd put in leaf lettuce and a cucumber plant. Just one. Cucumber plants can grow like crazy. Zucchini, too. Do you like jalapeños? From what I understand, they grow well in this area, so I thought I'd put in one or two jalapeño seedlings."

"Are you finished yet?"

The woman was both rude *and* cranky. It surprised Annie that Mellie could be related to the Munsons. Mike and Annie had thought of them as an extra set of grandparents that one week each summer. The couple had spoiled them with homemade desserts and attention.

"Yes, I'm done," Annie said, waiting impatiently for Mellie to agree.

"Good."

Annie could see that the landlord was about to disconnect, so she rushed to ask, "Does this mean I can go ahead, then?"

She heard Mellie exhale impatiently. "Do you want me to mail you a certified letter? Fine, do what you want."

"Thank you."

"Don't thank me. Thank your advocate. If it wasn't for Keaton, I wouldn't have to deal with you. Now leave me alone."

Annie had one more request, one she'd nearly forgotten. "Mellie," she said hurriedly. "I'm so sorry . . . there's something else . . ."

"Now what?" She exhaled, exasperated.

"The bushes," Annie blurted out. "When my family rented the cottage, and I admit that was several years ago, there used to be blueberry and raspberry bushes on the property."

"What about them?"

"Are they still there? The area where they used to be is overgrown now. Are they still alive, or have the vines choked them?"

Mellie sighed deeply, her patience at an end. "Now, how on earth would I know?"

"Right. Good point." Because Mellie felt unsafe outside the doors of her home, she wouldn't have been able to investigate. Forging ahead, Annie asked, "Would you mind if I pulled the overgrowth away and looked for them?"

Silence greeted her question. Annie's shoulders sagged in defeat. However, she was mildly surprised Mellie hadn't slammed the phone down on her ear.

"Do you want to start up a farmer's market in my front yard as well?" Mellie demanded. "Set up a booth and hawk your wares?"

"What?" The question was ridiculous. "No!"

"Good."

"Like I said, I'll be happy to share with you, and Keaton." She hadn't told him that, but it was part of her plan. It was the least she could do, after all the help he'd given her.

"Fine. Whatever. Dig away. I've been meaning to hire someone to clear away those vines for a couple years now. Have at it."

"Thank you," Annie said, relieved.

Mellie hesitated, and her voice softened, leaving Annie a bit shocked. "So, Keaton talks to you."

"Some. Not much. We're friends."

Mellie paused, carefully gauging her words. "I hope you know his heart is as big as he is. Don't you hurt him. I swear if you do, you'll regret it."

"I wouldn't —"

"Heard that before. Just know, if you hurt him, you'll be sorry. You got me?"

"Of course . . . I understand . . ."

"Make sure you do." Some of the gruffness had left her voice, mellowing it to a softer tone.

"I appreciate everything, Mellie. If there's anything I can do for you, please let me know."

Without hesitating, Mellie said, "Don't call me again. How does that sound?" And with that, she disconnected the call.

So much for having made a connection with her less-than-friendly landlord.

Saturday morning, excited to be working on her garden project, Annie drove an hour to a nursery to pick up the special heritage tomato plants she'd found while searching on the Internet. Because she couldn't resist, she bought a few other seedlings as well. She'd need to nurse these fragile plants until she could get them in the ground. She'd thought to run a few other errands but decided instead to head back to Oceanside, eager to get started on the project.

Of course, she'd need to dig up the land and prepare the soil for her little patch of green. That would be hard physical labor, but she was willing. This would be her first effort. All she could do was hope that she'd inherited her mother's green thumb.

She'd never felt the urge to do anything like this before. When she'd lived in Los Angeles she hadn't had a single houseplant. It wasn't her thing back then, but she was drawn to gardening now. She didn't need a counselor to tell her why she had this desire.

It was about connecting with her mom, with the earth, and with the basics of sustaining life. Maybe this garden could help her understand the meaning of life. To plant the seeds, to bury them in the rich, sandy earth, to let them die and then produce life, produce meaning. In Annie's mind it was more than a way to connect with her family, it was a means of proving that life could come from death, and that she could continue for them, honoring each one, never letting them fade from her heart.

When she returned to the cottage, Annie was surprised to find Keaton hard at work rototilling up a garden space on the south side of her yard. She hadn't asked for his help. Sweat ran down the sides of his face. He wore faded overalls and boots. His shirt was sleeveless, giving her a view of his thick, muscular arms. Seeing how much Keaton struggled to plow through the tangled weeds, she realized that cutting out a garden space on her own would have been close to impossible.

He didn't seem to notice she'd returned. Either that or his lack of attention was intentional. She suspected he would rather have finished it anonymously. Her early return had ruined that.

Annie removed all the gardening equipment she'd purchased and set it on the small front porch, leaning it against the short railing. She paused when she saw the seashell on the top step, close to the door.

Keaton. She knew it was him. She'd found several such items on her small porch since moving in. She didn't mention it, because she knew it would fluster him.

Smiling to herself, she collected the seashell and brought the seedlings into the house, setting them on the windowsill in the kitchen, where the morning sun would encourage growth.

Next, she poured Keaton a tall glass of her special lavender iced tea and carried it outside. Then she waited until he was sure to see her. When he did, she held out the glass, silently inviting him to take a break.

He turned off the machine and walked over to where she stood. "Hey," he said, and wiped the sweat from his brow with his forearm. His gaze intently rested on her, as if she were the sun he rotated around. In all her life, Annie had never had a man look at her the way Keaton did. His eyes revealed more than words could express.

She read longing in him, a craving for human contact, for a purpose. She had yet to fully understand this man. To this point, she'd only scratched the surface in uncovering who he was. With that came the knowledge that she wanted to know more.

"Where's Lennon?" she asked, breaking the spell by deliberately pulling her eyes away from him. It would be too easy to get lost in those dark eyes of his. Annie was convinced that wouldn't be good for either of them.

"Home."

"I miss him."

"I'll bring him next time."

Before she could mention him clearing her garden space, he took the iced tea from her hand and drank the entire glassful without stopping. His Adam's apple moving up and down in his throat mesmerized her.

"You were thirsty," she commented, stating the obvious.

"I was. This is great. What is it?"

"Lavender iced tea. Would you like more?"

"Please."

He waited while she returned to the cottage and refilled the glass. The second glassful disappeared as quickly as the first had.

"You didn't need to do this, you know." She gestured toward the half-tilled garden space.

"Mellie said you'd share with me. I want to do my part."

"Thank you," she said, and then flopped her hands against her sides. "See, I've done it again. I'm forever thanking you. What can I ever do to show you how much I appreciate everything you've done for me?"

He continued to stare at her, almost in a daze.

"Keaton?"

"Smile," he said. "Just smile."

She couldn't have held one back for anything. She beamed her biggest, brightest smile at him, and he grinned back. For the longest moment, all they did was stare at each other. He leaned forward slightly, as if he intended to kiss her, but stopped and shook his head, attempting to clear his thoughts.

"How long have you been working here?" she asked, wanting to continue their conversation. She hoped he'd keep talking, so she could learn more about him.

"A while."

"You're going to spoil me with all the nice things you do for me," she said.

"Want to."

"But why?" she asked.

He lowered his face, trying to keep her from reading his eyes. "You smiled. You didn't judge me, you stitched up my hand, and you're smiling again now."

Impulsively, she wrapped her arms around him and gave him a big hug.

"What was that for?" he asked, once she'd finished. He was clearly flustered and red in the face.

Annie shrugged. "Because I felt like it. If you'd rather I didn't touch you, you need to let me know."

In what was an obvious attempt to change the subject, he shifted his feet and said, "Mellie said you asked about those overgrown vines."

"I want to get rid of them. That's next on my list after I plant the garden," she confirmed. "At one time, there were blueberry and raspberry bushes growing there. There still might be if the vines haven't completely smothered them."

"You can't do that."

"Why not?" she asked, frowning now. Those bushes brought back good memories, and they were all Annie had to hold on to now.

"Tearing them out would be far too strenuous for you. Vines have thorns. I'll do it."

"Keaton, no. I can't let you do that."

"You plant. I'll pull vines. Deal?"

Despite herself, she laughed. "I'm not going to be able to talk you out of this, am I?"

"Nope."

"That's what I thought."

"Don't want to argue," he said with a grin. "You know too many words."

She laughed. Annie did know a lot of words, but they certainly didn't make her any wiser than Keaton. "Guess that means I win the argument," she teased.

Keaton shook his head. "Nope. Just means I won't listen."

Annie chuckled again. "You're a stubborn man, Seth Keaton."

He grinned. "I get what I want." Returning the empty glass to her, he went back to tilling the land. While he was busy, she planted a small potted herb garden and filled the area around the porch with the flowers she'd purchased. The marigolds and impatiens added color and life to what had once been barren and dark.

When they were both finished, Annie poured them each a glass of her lavender iced tea. Tired, they sat together on the top step of her porch, which creaked under his weight. When Annie looked up she noticed Mellie watching out her kitchen window. It almost seemed like she was smiling.

CHAPTER
TWELVE

When Annie stopped by Bean There on Monday morning, Britt wasn't there.

"Where's Britt?" she asked, after giving her order to the young man at the counter, whose nametag read JIMMY.

"She called in sick," he explained with a worried frown. "That isn't like Britt. She isn't answering her phone, either."

Annie was concerned, too. A new bruise had appeared on Britt's shoulder earlier in the week. That was the second one Annie had noticed since she'd met the teenager. "Has anyone talked to her recently?"

"I saw her yesterday and everything was fine — at least I thought it was. Sometimes Britt hides —" He stopped abruptly, regretting saying that much.

He looked at the line forming behind her, and Annie realized she was holding everyone up. Unsure what to do, if anything, she decided that if Britt was "sick" the following day, then she'd personally check on the teenager. Candi was a warehouse of information, and she'd be able to tell Annie where Britt lived.

Annie wasn't left to wonder about Britt for long. When she arrived at the clinic, Britt and a young boy were sitting in the waiting room, along with several others. A quick glance in her direction assured Annie that the girl was fine. She could only assume the boy was her younger brother.

Her first patient of the day was a woman with bronchitis. Annie prescribed rest, antibiotics, and a cough medication. In the second exam room, Britt sat with her arm protectively around the boy. The name in the file read LOGAN HOFFERT, and it indicated that he was ten years old. Annie noticed he was small for his age. He held his right arm close to his body and leaned in to his sister's side, apparently terrified. He carefully watched Annie, his eyes following her as she stepped into the small room.

"Hi, Logan," she said, sitting on the stool in front of him. "I'm Annie."

Logan buried his face in Britt's side.

"Can you tell me why you're here today?" she asked.

"I think his arm is broken," Britt answered for him. Tears filled her eyes, which she tried to hide by blinking several times. "We don't have insurance, so I'll need to make payments for Logan's care."

"You?" Annie asked. "What about his parents?"

Logan shared an anxious look with his sister. "They . . . They needed me to bring Logan in today."

Reading between the lines, Annie had to assume both of his parents were at work, although Candi seemed to think Britt's stepfather was unemployed. "We won't worry about that right now," Annie said reassuringly. Her job was to help Logan.

118

Britt's shoulders stiffened. "You might not worry about it, but I do. I need to know if the clinic will take installments."

"Of course we will, Britt. What's important is making sure Logan isn't in any more pain than necessary."

"I know . . . He couldn't sleep last night. His arm hurt too much, and he won't let me touch it. I . . . I didn't know what to do. Every time he tries to move it, he screams in pain. Mom didn't know what to do. She cleans for Mr. Johnson from the bank and she doesn't dare miss because Mrs. Johnson is real picky and . . ." She shook her head and continued. "It isn't important. I said I knew you and you'd help Logan, so she said I should bring him to the clinic. She wanted to check if she could pay for his care in installments, though."

"You know I'll do whatever I can." Annie eased her stool closer. "Logan," she said softly, "will you look at me?"

Slowly, the boy lifted his head away from his sister's side and peeked out enough to look at Annie. He had a smattering of freckles across his nose and brown eyes, dull now with pain. He needed a haircut, and a mop of hair fell over his left eye.

Smiling to make him feel comfortable, she asked, "Can you show me where it hurts?"

"My whole arm hurts." His pulled it closer against his body, afraid she was going to reach for it.

"What happened?"

Logan looked to his sister, unsure of what to say.

"He fell," Britt blurted out. "Off his bike. He took a bad spill." Her words were jerky, almost rehearsed.

119

It was clear to Annie that she was not telling the truth. After seeing Britt's bruises, and learning what she had about Britt's stepfather, Annie had her suspicions. But mentioning those suspicions might be all the excuse Britt needed to bolt and run. Annie was determined not to make that happen.

"That must have hurt a lot," Annie said, looking to Logan, hoping to get a read from him. He leaned back against his sister, and she protectively tightened her arm around him.

"Did it hurt when you fell?" Annie pressed Logan. She noticed he didn't have any scrapes or bruises to indicate he'd taken a tumble off his bicycle.

He nodded. "It hurt bad. Really bad."

"Did the pain come right away?"

Once more he looked to Britt, who nodded.

"He said it did," Britt answered for him.

"Who was there to help him?" she asked, pressing for more information.

"Dad," Logan said. "Mom was working."

"His arm is swollen, too," Britt added. "That's why we think it might be broken. He's been in a lot of pain."

Annie had already noticed the swelling.

"Would you let me take a picture of your arm, Logan?" she asked.

"An x-ray?" he asked.

Britt smiled. "I already told him that was what you'd need to do."

"Yes, an x-ray," Annie said. "But I'm going to need you to let Julia, the nurse, touch your arm so she can take the x-ray. Will you do that for me?"

120

Again, Logan looked at his sister, who silently encouraged him. "I think I can, if you let Britt stay with me."

"I promise, Julia will be as gentle as can be. You tell her if it hurts too much."

"Okay."

Annie gave instructions to the nurse, who led Logan and Britt into the x-ray room.

It wasn't long before Annie had the results. When she returned to the room, she had the film with her.

"Is his arm broken?" Britt asked anxiously.

"Yes, it's broken, all right; thankfully, it's only a hairline fracture." She clipped the x-ray to the lighted board and pointed out the spindly line.

"That little line makes it hurt so bad?" Logan asked, aghast.

"Bone pain is the worst," Annie explained. "Looks like you're going to need a cast. That's cool, isn't it? You can have all your friends write their names on it. What color cast would you like?"

"Red," he said automatically.

"Then red it is."

After Annie finished casting Logan's arm, she asked Candi to look after Logan while she spoke privately to Britt.

"Sure thing," Candi said.

Bringing the teenager into her office, Annie closed the door and had Britt take a seat.

"Is something wrong?" Britt asked, glancing nervously around the room. "If it's about the money —"

"It isn't," Annie said, interrupting her. "I want to know what really happened to your brother."

Her shoulders tightened. "I already told you, he fell."

"Tell me again."

Britt squirmed in the chair and broke eye contact. "He fell off his bike. He took a corner too fast and lost control. If you don't believe me, ask Logan. He'll tell you the same thing." She scooted back the chair. "I should be going. I have classes this afternoon, and I need to be there so I can graduate."

"Britt, please, anything you tell me —"

"I'm sorry," Britt said, rushing to her feet. "But I really need to leave. Thank you for taking care of Logan. I knew you would. I told Mom we could trust you. She didn't know what to do. Nothing like this has happened before, and —"

"Britt, I can help."

Her eyes flashed with anger. "You can't . . . No one can. I need to go."

Before Annie could stop her, Britt had the door open and was gone.

Because she'd frightened the teenager away, Annie mulled over their conversation. It was abundantly clear that Britt was afraid to tell her the truth. Annie suspected that the stepfather was responsible for Logan's injury. But unless Britt admitted to what had happened, Annie had no proof.

She waited until it was time for a lunch break to talk to Candi. The receptionist was familiar with the community and could advise her.

"Something on your mind?" Candi asked, as they sat down together in the breakroom. "You've been quiet all morning."

"It's Logan Hoffert."

"Ah yes, Logan. I wonder if you were thinking what I'm thinking."

"And what's that?" Annie asked.

"That fracture of his. I doubt it came from a fall off his bike."

Annie mulled over the fact that she wasn't alone in her suspicions. "I don't think that's what happened, either."

Candi reached for her turkey sandwich but didn't take a bite. "Do you know what you're going to do?"

"Not really." It wasn't an easy decision. She didn't want to jump to conclusions, report the incident, and then discover she'd been entirely wrong. Having the community's faith was important. One wrong accusation could ruin her chances of gaining the trustworthiness she would need to make Oceanside her home. But at the same time, she had a responsibility to report any suspected abuse.

"Are you going to contact Child Protective Services?" Candi asked.

That was the correct protocol, but Annie only had her suspicions. "I don't know. I don't want to make matters worse for Britt, either." She reached for her own sandwich, but like Candi, she seemed to have lost her appetite. "What do you know about the mom?"

"Teresa? Not much. She mostly keeps to herself. Don't think she has any friends. Far as I know, she works every housecleaning job she can get. Between her and Britt, they hold that family together."

"From what I understand, Britt isn't Carl's daughter?"

"No. Teresa was a single mom. She got pregnant in high school and raised Britt on her own until she met Carl. They seemed happy when Carl had steady work at the lumber mill. Then he was laid off for being drunk on the job. A short while later the mill closed completely. Far as I know, Carl hasn't had steady employment since."

"What does Carl do with himself if he isn't working?"

"Nothing that I know of. I've seen him in town a few times, hanging out in a tavern with his drinking buddies."

Annie was afraid of that.

"I think it might be best if you have Child Protective Services check out the home situation."

Annie was considering doing exactly that; however, she wanted to think it over to be sure she would be helping the situation more than hurting the family and her own standing in the community. The best person to ask would be Dr. Bainbridge. If Logan had his arm broken at the hands of an abusive father, then something needed to be done. It was clear to Annie that Britt was afraid to tell her the truth.

"Give it some thought," Candi advised her.

At the end of the day, Annie conferred with Dr. Bainbridge, who agreed that she needed to contact the

124

authorities and ask that the state do an investigation. With her stomach in knots, she sat at her desk for several minutes before she reached for the phone and made the call to the state hotline. The woman on the other end took down the pertinent details, asking questions as Annie relayed her concerns.

"Unfortunately, we're short-staffed and nearly everyone is pulling double shifts to keep current."

"But you *will* investigate?" Annie pressed, her heart pounding.

"Yes, but it could take up to forty-eight hours. We appreciate your concern. I promise we'll send someone out as soon as possible."

"Thank you," Annie said, sensing that the social worker was already stretched to her limit. She knew there had been budget cuts in Washington state and that social services had been hit hard by the cutbacks.

As she walked home, Annie's thoughts repeatedly wandered to Britt and Logan. To distract herself, she decided to spend time in her garden. Her mother had always claimed that it calmed her, and Annie was hoping for the same results. Although she'd spent most of the weekend working in the yard, a lot remained that needed to be done. Before she could plant the seedlings she'd purchased, she would need to spread the fertilizer. Annie thought how lucky she was to live along the coast where she could begin planting so early without a fear of frost.

Once home, she changed clothes and went outside, unwilling to waste a sunny afternoon indoors. After spreading the fertilizer, she carted the tomato and jalapeño plants to the tilled ground, grateful again for Keaton's help.

Keaton.

She found that he was on her mind a lot lately. Not since her college days had any man affected her the way he did. She was drawn to his intensity, his brute strength, and his honesty. One thing was certain: She'd never met anyone like him. Saturday afternoon was the last time she'd seen Keaton, and she found she missed him. She couldn't talk to him about Britt and Logan because of the privacy laws, but she could mention the incident without names and get his opinion.

Getting down on her knees in the freshly tilled earth, Annie prepared the land and buried the seedlings in the rich soil before tenderly dribbling water over the infant plants. When she glanced up, she noticed Mellie Johnson intently watching her from the kitchen window in the big house.

Annie stood, brushed the dirt from her knees, and removed her garden gloves before waving. Not surprisingly, Mellie abruptly turned away from the window. The woman's attention proved that Mellie wasn't as disinterested as she wanted Annie to believe.

To her surprise, Annie's phone rang. When she tugged it out of her jeans, she was taken aback to see that the call came from her landlord.

"Hello," Annie answered skeptically, uncertain what to expect.

"What are you planting out there?"

Annie told her. "Is there anything you'd like me to plant?"

"No."

"I have plenty of space if you had something in mind."

"Grams grew green beans. She used to make me snap them for her. Peas, too."

"I can do that." Annie was delighted at Mellie's request and was eager to comply. This was exactly the opening she'd been looking for.

"I'm not asking you to plant anything, understand?"

Guess Mellie was too prideful to ask for anything.

"If you grow green beans, you're going to need poles," Mellie said.

"I can get them at the nursery. I saw some there on Saturday and —"

"Keaton can make them," Mellie said, cutting her off. "Doubt there's much he can't do. Preston, either."

"Preston?" Annie couldn't remember anyone named Preston.

"A friend."

"A boyfriend?"

"No," she snapped. "Like I said, Keaton can make what you need to grow those beans."

"I won't ask him to do that for me," Annie countered. Keaton had been more than generous with her already, even if she would welcome an excuse to contact him.

"Fine, then *I* will."

Annie could see arguing would do her little good.

"He's good at that sort of thing. Besides, he likes you. Don't understand it myself, but then I'm not good at relationships."

127

"I'd like to be friends with you, if you'd let me," Annie said.

"I don't need friends."

"What about Keaton?" Annie asked. "Isn't he your friend? And Preston, too?" If Mellie mentioned him, then he must have some connection to her.

It took her a few stilted moments before she was ready to answer. "I suppose you could call them friends."

"Perhaps I could come for tea one day at the house. I loved your grandparents; they were wonderful to my brother and me."

"They were good people," Mellie agreed. "I'll invite you when I'm ready. Should be sometime before the next century, so don't sit at your phone waiting for me to call."

"If you say so," Annie said, holding back a smile.

"I'm serious. Don't hold your breath."

Annie laughed. One step forward and two steps back was how it seemed to go with Mellie.

CHAPTER
THIRTEEN

Keaton had never learned what had upset Annie the day he found her weeping on the beach, sitting and looking lost and staring soulfully at the ocean. If he was a betting man, he'd lay odds it had to do with a broken relationship. Her heart had been broken. The depth and intensity of his feelings for her rattled him to the point that he'd avoided her as much as he could. Keeping away hadn't helped. If anything, it made him want to see her even more.

Because he kept his own hours and worked on his own schedule, he'd been able to stop by the cottage and Mellie's property. He spent an hour or longer every day that week pulling out the wild blackberry vines, purposefully choosing times when he knew Annie would be at the clinic. Battling the thicket helped ease the internal battle raging within. Until Annie, Keaton had been comfortable being by himself and with who he was. Now he discovered he wanted to be more for her. What he couldn't figure out was how he could be more of *anything*.

Mellie knew Keaton was coming to the property on a regular basis, and why. The woman couldn't leave well enough alone and had taken to constantly pestering him with calls. She quizzed him with questions about Annie that he didn't want to answer. She repeatedly warned him to guard his heart. Her concerns weren't necessary. Keaton already knew that he was treading water where Annie was concerned. On more than one occasion he'd been tempted to ask Mellie about her non-relationship with Preston. That would hurt his friend far more than it would silence her, and so he did what he always did and said nothing.

Irritated with Mellie and with himself, Keaton quit answering his phone. He refused to let her pessimism sway him. If what she had to tell him was that important, then she could come outside and say it to his face. Like that would ever happen!

The last time they spoke, Mellie declared that Keaton was a fool for giving his heart away to Annie Marlow. She was convinced Annie would leave him high and dry. Keaton didn't need her telling him what he already knew. At the end of her contracted year, Annie would pull up stakes and move. No one stayed in Oceanside who hadn't been born and raised in the area. The population had always been transient. Folks came and went with a regularity that was as changing as the timing of the tides.

With his head full of thoughts of Annie, Keaton tugged on a twisted, thorny vine. If he never saw another blackberry vine again, he'd die a happy man. There wasn't anyone in the world he would do this for other than Annie. He was determined to find those raspberry and blueberry bushes for her. He couldn't bear the thought of her dealing with these barbed vines.

130

Even with gloves, the thorns had a way of poking through the fabric and piercing his hands. If the fruit bushes had survived the last five years, it would be miraculous.

When he finished for the day, he decided it was time to confront Mellie and check on John-Boy. The Labrador's physical wounds were almost completely healed now, thanks to Mellie's and Preston's care. Emotional wounds were a different story. The poor dog cringed at every loud noise and trembled uncontrollably whenever anyone came close. Mellie had worked hours with him, earning his trust, and John-Boy had come to accept her. Not so with Keaton, even though he'd been the one to rescue him. Keaton suspected John-Boy would react the same to any man after the treatment he'd received from his previous owner.

Lennon followed him up the porch steps. His own dog had taken to lying at John-Boy's side whenever he was allowed in the house. John-Boy trusted Lennon and was less frightened whenever Keaton's sidekick was there.

Keaton let himself inside the house and was braced for Mellie's harangue. He didn't need words when Mellie used twice as many as he ever would.

Sure enough, she was waiting for him. From her pinched lips, he could tell she had a lot to say. Mellie had once been a real natural beauty. They were close to the same age, born within a few months of each other, although she looked older now. He never understood what it was that had led to her refusal to step outside the doors of her grandparents' home. She'd returned after being gone for ten years, moved back into the family home, and refused to leave even for the most mundane of reasons. He hadn't asked, figuring she wouldn't tell him even if he did.

"About time," she huffed, arms akimbo. "I've been trying to get your attention all week."

"I know."

"You could have returned my calls!" she barked, none too pleased with him.

He wasn't inclined to argue. Like he told Annie, he didn't have the talent to win with words. "What did you want?"

"Well, first off, I told Annie you could build her poles for the beans she planted. I don't need you making a fool out of me."

"You and Annie talked?" This was an interesting development. It appeared that Mellie's stance against her tenant had softened.

Afraid to admit she might be wrong about Annie, Mellie lowered her eyes. "She's not so bad."

"What changed your mind?"

"You," she admitted sheepishly.

This was an even bigger surprise. "Me?"

"You're a good judge of character, and you like her."

He nodded, because he did like Annie, way more than he should.

"You going to make those beanpoles or not?"

"Okay."

"I want you to know — I didn't ask her to plant those green beans," she insisted.

132

Naturally, Mellie wouldn't want him to think she'd asked for anything; her pride wouldn't allow it.

"All I said was that my grandmother grew green beans, and the next thing I knew, Annie is telling me that she'll plant them. I figured, being good with your hands, that you could help her."

"I will."

He couldn't help wondering if Mellie had a hidden agenda in this.

Following their conversation, Keaton went into the first room off the hallway to check on John-Boy. As soon as the dog heard heavy footsteps, he curled up and started to shake. Keaton feared Mellie was going to need to do a lot of work with him if he was ever going to get adopted. At this point, it looked doubtful. His previous owner deserved everything the law threw at him. The last Keaton had heard from Preston, the man had been arrested for animal cruelty.

When it was time to leave, Keaton had to whistle to get Lennon to leave his friend's side.

"You heading out already?"

He nodded.

"Did Preston tell you about the deaf kitten he found?"

Keaton shook his head. "Hurt?"

"Abandoned. Tossed on the side of the road. He mentioned it to me. The shelter is at full capacity and Preston felt it was unlikely anyone would want a less-than-perfect kitten. I already have one cat, and with me taking in the dogs, I don't need another."

"I'll take it," Keaton said quickly. He knew someone who needed a kitten, and who would cherish one that wasn't perfect. "I'll stop by the shelter and collect it later."

"You going to tell Preston, or do you want me to do it?"

"You let him know."

A small smile came over Mellie. Keaton wasn't fooled. Mellie welcomed the opportunity to have a reason to get in touch with Preston.

After leaving Mellie's, Keaton finished painting the inside of a home that was being prepared for the real estate market. He'd worked a ten-hour day, starting early that morning. By the time he returned to his small house, he was hungry and tired. Lennon was, too.

Keaton fed his dog while he heated up a can of chili in the microwave. He ate standing at the kitchen countertop while he sorted through the mail, the usual advertising flyers and bills. He needed to check on his father and dreaded the visit, putting it off another day. He should let the old man fend for himself, the way he had done to Keaton. His conscience wouldn't let him do it, though.

Lennon ate, did his business outside, and then promptly curled up in his bed. Keaton intended to make a short night of it himself. He'd been up early and on the go since before dawn.

After washing his dinner dishes, he took a long, hot shower. He'd dressed and combed his hair when he heard a knock on his door. He stiffened; he didn't get company. Preston on rare occasions, but that was about it. If he was dropping off the kitten, he would have called first.

Tossing open the door, he stood at his full height, hoping to intimidate anyone who would dare to disturb him.

Annie gasped and stepped back.

"Annie?" He was instantly alert, fearing she had come to him for help. Looking past her, he scanned the area. If anyone dared threaten or intimidate her, then Keaton would handle it.

"I know it's last-minute . . ." she blurted out, speaking so fast the words nearly ran together. "You weren't home earlier. I was wondering if you'd like to attend the high school play with me."

"A play?"

She nodded so hard he was afraid she would hurt her neck.

"Candi's daughter has a small part and I told her I'd go, and then I thought that maybe you'd like . . . you know . . . to go with me?"

She was asking him out? Like a date?

"I should have said something earlier," she continued, clearly flustered, "but I haven't seen you in a few days and . . . time got away from me. We used to meet up at Bean There, but you haven't been around lately and . . ." She let the rest fade.

Keaton was too shocked to respond. He'd stayed away on purpose and never guessed that she'd even notice.

Looking down at her feet, Annie whispered, "I've missed seeing you." Then, to his utter shock, before he could say anything, Annie reached up and pressed her mouth to his in the most fleeting of kisses.

He stared at her, dumbfounded, not knowing what to say. When he found his voice, he raised his fingers to his lips. "You kissed me."

She mimicked his action, her fingertips against her lips. She looked more than a little shocked at herself. "I did, didn't I?"

"Why?"

"I . . . don't know. I'm sorry."

He blinked at her several times and felt she should know. "Women don't kiss me."

He remained confused, as she obviously was.

"I feel like an idiot. Forget I was here. I'll go, and we can both pretend this never happened." She started to back away from him toward the porch steps. Keaton knew he couldn't let her leave. Not like this.

"No," he demanded, not wanting her to go and finding it necessary to stop her. Lost with what to do, Keaton splayed his fingers through his hair. He didn't know what to say, and as so often happened, the words twisted around his tongue, making it difficult, if not impossible, to speak.

"There's a play at the high school?" he asked when he was finally able to get the words out.

"It's *Billy Budd*. Candi didn't think it would draw a big audience."

Keaton had to agree with her. "A Herman Melville book; I remember reading it my junior year."

"I guess we should be grateful they didn't decide to do a play based on *Moby-Dick*," Annie said and chuckled weakly. She continued to look uneasy. "It isn't important. I just thought, you know, that you might be interested." She made a show of looking at the time. "I should go now, otherwise I'll be late."

Having her leave was the last thing Keaton wanted. He was hungry for the sight of her, starving for a chance to be with her. Depriving himself of her company had been hard and, yes, he'd admit it, painful. Annie had become like a drug to him. An addiction. Not knowing any other way to stop her, he captured her face between his huge hands. Looking down at her, he saw more than he dared dream in her eyes. For a long moment, all he could do was stare at her. She'd kissed him. He'd thought about kissing her a thousand times a day and feared her reaction.

"Keaton," she whispered, moistening her lips.

Slowly, half expecting her to stop him, he lowered his mouth to hers. Annie's hand curled around the top of his shoulder as she gave herself to him. Keaton felt her light touch, and it was unlike anything he'd ever experienced. Her lips were soft and malleable, and she tasted like what he was convinced must be heaven. With his arms wrapped around her, he had to resist crushing her against him. Compared to him, Annie was petite and fragile, and he feared unintentionally hurting her.

He broke away and looked at her, needing to read her reaction. He'd wanted to kiss her from the moment he saw her on the beach right before she'd moved to Oceanside. He hadn't dared to hope that she would want his touch.

His eyes captured hers once more. Annie blinked up at him. Her face eased into a soft smile. He smiled back. Life hadn't given him a lot of reasons to be happy, but unprecedented joy flooded his soul just for the opportunity to hold her.

After several seconds of doing nothing more than looking at her, Keaton brushed the hair away from her cheek and ran his fingers down the side of her face, loving the feel of her skin against his own. Then, because he couldn't resist, he kissed her again and again, each kiss becoming more involved and lengthy. If it were humanly possible, Keaton would find a way to keep her in his arms for all eternity. Arousal coursed through him. He sucked in a breath at the tingling sensation. Because most everyone avoided him, physical contact was at a minimum. Her touch was like fire braising his skin.

Easing away from his kisses, Annie braced her forehead against his chest. He instantly felt the loss.

"Say something," he pleaded after a few moments. He needed to know what she was thinking, to hear her say that she had wanted this as much as he did. His inability to express himself with words had never haunted him more than it did at that moment.

Annie raised her head, sighed deeply, and maintained eye contact. "Does this mean you'll attend the play with me?"

He chuckled. Little did Annie realize he'd gladly sit through *Moby-Dick* if it meant she would be at his side. "Be happy to."

Annie braced her forehead against his chest. "You should know. The play is an excuse. Not seeing you didn't feel right."

At her confession, he moved her head up and met her gaze as he struggled to express his feelings. "Missed you, too. Joy."

"Joy?" she repeated, as if he'd forgotten her name. "I'm Annie."

"Yes, I know. Joy." He swallowed hard, trying to express himself. "You bring me joy."

"You," Annie whispered in response. "You help me forget."

He frowned, and figured his guess was right. Annie had come to Oceanside to recover from a broken heart.

CHAPTER
FOURTEEN

Annie was scheduled to work Saturday, as it was her turn for the weekend rotation. Keeping to her morning habit, she stopped for her latte on her way to the clinic. Her brain didn't function at full capacity without her morning shot of java.

Britt was back behind the counter. Annie continued to keep a close eye on the teenager. She was deeply concerned about the girl and her family. When she'd discussed Logan's broken arm and her suspicions with Dr. Bainbridge before reporting the incident to the state agency, he'd mentioned that unless it was a high priority, government agencies often moved at a snail's pace. Because it was a suspicion rather than a firm case of abuse, it might take the full time allotted by law before the home would be investigated. She hadn't heard anything back and had to assume no one, had been out to interview the family.

Annie was further concerned because Logan had missed his follow-up appointment. The rumors she'd heard about Carl Hoffert raised Annie's fears up a notch. People around town said that since losing his job at the mill, Carl had become mean and lazy. He

140

depended entirely on his wife and stepdaughter to support the family.

Everyone said he drank too much, his temper was well known, and he wasn't someone to cross. The more time that passed after Logan's missed appointment, the more concerned Annie grew. She hadn't seen Britt for a few days, either, which troubled her even more.

As she neared the counter to place her coffee order, Annie groaned inwardly when she noticed a fresh bruise around Britt's wrist. The teenager had done her best to disguise the purplish hue with a long-sleeve shirt, but it showed when she reached for a cup to fulfill the order of the woman in front of Annie. Others probably wouldn't have noticed it, but Annie did.

"Morning, Britt," she said. "I'll have my usual."

Avoiding eye contact, Britt reached for the paper cup and wrote out the code for Annie's latte without making eye contact.

"I haven't seen you in a couple days," she said, hoping to draw the teenager into conversation. "Doesn't seem the same when you aren't here to take my order."

A hint of a smile touched the edges of Britt's mouth. "I have a big paper due this week. I needed to stay home and finish it."

"I figured it was something like that. Is Logan doing okay? He missed his follow-up appointment."

"He's fine," Britt said quickly. Too quickly. "He had his friends write on his cast. Thanks again for your help."

Annie was deliberately slow in removing the cash from her purse. Although she was nervous venturing into this topic, she felt she needed to ask. "Is everything okay at home?" She handed over the ten-dollar bill instead of using the app on her phone. This way, Britt had to make change, delaying the transaction a bit longer.

"Sure. Home is fine," Britt said, counting out the returned cash by hand.

Reluctantly, Annie moved aside to wait for the barista to complete her order. She recognized the young man behind the counter as Britt's friend . . . Jimmy, if she remembered correctly. When he finished, he handed her the hot drink. She reached for it, but he didn't release it until she looked up. "Britt isn't okay," he whispered, leaning forward over the counter, his look troubled. "I don't know how to help her."

"I was afraid of that," Annie said with a sigh. "I saw the bruise on her wrist."

"She keeps telling me she's clumsy," Jimmy continued. "I know she's lying. I believe her stepfather is hurting her."

"I think so, too," Annie confessed.

The rest of the way to the clinic, Annie's head was swimming with troubled thoughts about Britt and Logan.

"Did you get home late after the play?" Candi asked, standing in front of the coffee machine, waiting for it to finish brewing. "I really appreciated you coming."

"I enjoyed it," Annie assured her coworker, and she had, but mostly because she was with Keaton.

Candi laughed. "You're a true friend to suffer through that play. I appreciated it, and I know Amanda did, too."

It took a moment for her friend's comment to register. When it did, Annie struggled to hold back a smile. "Actually, I had a wonderful night." When she'd left for work that morning, she'd found another one of Keaton's gifts on the step leading into the cottage.

They were little signs that he left for her, she'd realized, to let her know he was thinking of her. It was easier for him to leave her small gifts than to say it with words. Recently, she'd found a worn piece of green sea glass. By far, Seth Keaton was the most thoughtful man she'd ever known.

In California, her Friday nights would have been spent dancing and having fun. Other than a few financial concerns, Annie hadn't a care in the world. She wore the proverbial pair of rose-colored glasses back then. It took losing everyone who was important to her for her to appreciate her family and what she'd once had. Her life had been forever changed. It would never be the same again, and she was okay with that. She was no longer that person. Her priorities were different. The way she looked at life and its meaning had been altered. The girl she once was had completely vanished.

"There's a message for you on your desk," Candi told her.

Taking her latte with her, she went back to her office and found the report from the state. The social worker had completed the home visit and concluded that nothing was amiss. Annie read the report twice and was shocked. She didn't know what had persuaded the state to overlook what in her mind was abuse. Leaning back in her chair, she released a slow sigh. Well, that was that. She'd done what she could and she had no further recourse.

The clinic on Saturday was busy, as usual. Annie barely had time for lunch. By the end of her day, she felt dead on her feet. Finishing up all of her paperwork, she reread the report from the state. Annie didn't feel right about the conclusion. Britt's bruises and Logan's missed appointment were telltale signs that there was more to what was happening than others knew.

With Britt and Logan heavy on her mind, she decided to make a friendly visit to the Hofferts' home to check to see if Logan's broken arm was healing properly. She found the address from his paperwork. If anyone was to question her, she had a ready excuse. Britt's mother cleaned houses, and Annie was looking to hire a housekeeper.

Once she was finished with the last of her documentation for the day, Annie walked back to the cottage to get her SUV. She noticed Mellie watching her out of the window. Annie paused and waved, and was delighted when Mellie waved back. This was progress. Annie was elated with each small sign of a budding friendship with her landlord.

Using her navigational guide, Annie found the Hoffert home about a mile off the beach. Knowing Britt didn't drive and had the early shift at Bean There, she suspected the teen either walked into town or caught a ride with Jimmy, who seemed to care about her.

Annie parked on the curb by the tilting fence. The lawn was overgrown and filled with weeds. Flowerbeds were nonexistent. The house was small; the outside paint looked like it might have been a light shade of yellow at one time but had since faded to a patchy, bleached white. The roof was covered with a blue plastic tarp.

"Dr. Annie, Dr. Annie!" Logan called out, racing his bicycle toward her, his thin legs pumping with all his strength.

"Hi, Logan." She didn't bother to explain that she wasn't an actual doctor. "How's your arm doing? You missed coming back to see me."

"I know. But I'm good." He proudly displayed his red cast. "It doesn't even hurt anymore. It itches, though."

Annie smiled. "There are ways to help that."

"I know. Mom gave me a chopstick to scratch with and that works."

The screen door opened, and Britt stepped onto the porch. Her gaze went from her brother to Annie and then back again.

"Hi, Britt," Annie said. "I hope I haven't come at a bad time. I wanted to check to see how Logan's doing."

She crossed her arms over her stomach. "I told you this morning that he's doing great."

"He missed his appointment."

"Dad said I didn't need to go back because it would only cost more money."

"I wish you'd said something. The money isn't an issue."

Britt continued to stare at Annie in the most unwelcoming way. Annie straightened. "I came for another reason, too."

"Oh?"

"I heard your mom cleans homes and I was hoping to talk to her."

Britt looked back over her shoulder. "Mom's busy right now. You could talk to her next week . . ."

"Mom's home," Logan disputed. "She said she wanted to meet Dr. Annie to thank her. Remember, Britt? You heard her."

"It won't take more than a few minutes," Annie promised, ignoring the nonverbal message Britt sent her younger brother. "Britt," she repeated, when the teenager didn't answer. "I'd like to meet your mother."

A tall, slender woman came out of the house and joined her daughter on the porch. She had a dishcloth slung over her shoulder; her look was weary.

"I'm sorry to disturb you, Mrs. Hoffert," Annie said, stepping toward the gate leading to the steps into the house.

"Mom, this is Annie Marlow," Britt gestured toward Annie. "She's the one I was telling you about who fixed Logan's arm."

The woman's face showed immediate gratitude. "You're Dr. Annie, from the clinic."

"That's me, but I'm a physician assistant, not a medical doctor."

"Thank you for everything you did for my son. And, please, call me Teresa." The woman smiled shyly.

"Annie needs a housekeeper," Logan said, kicking over his bike and running to the porch to join his mother and sister. "Dad said you needed to clean more houses."

"How often would you need me?" Teresa asked, bringing Logan close to her side.

Britt defiantly shook her head. "Mom, no," she insisted, and then sent a pleading look to Annie and said, "Mom can't clean any more houses. She's works all the time as it is."

Teresa pretended her daughter hadn't spoken and repeated her earlier question. "How many times a week are you thinking?"

"Mom," Britt protested. It looked like she was about to pull her mother back into the house.

As Britt's mother had done, Annie disregarded her complaints. "Just one day a week. Once every other week would work, too. I live in the cottage on Seaside Lane."

"Mom . . ."

Teresa studied Britt, and it seemed she was about to give in.

Losing interest in the conversation, Logan yawned and looked longingly toward his bike.

Annie didn't want to lose this opportunity, so, thinking quickly, she blurted out, "I'll pay you double your going rate."

Teresa's eyes shot back to her. She bit into her lower lip. "Double?"

Annie assured her she would. "From what I heard, you're worth it."

"Does it matter what day?" Teresa asked.

Annie shook her head. "Whenever you can fit me in would be great."

"Mom," Britt said under her breath. "You work every day already. You can't take on another house."

Logan disagreed. "But Dad said —"

Britt cut him off with a fierce glare.

"How about Monday afternoons?" Teresa asked.

"That would be perfect." It didn't escape Annie's notice that Teresa and Britt stood on the porch while she was on the other side of the fence.

"Thank you."

For the first time Teresa appeared to notice they had been virtually shouting across the yard. "Forgive my manners," she said as she opened the screen door. "Please come inside for coffee or tea. I've been thoughtless and rude."

"But . . . Dad?" Britt whispered, barely loud enough for Annie to make out the words.

"Unfortunately, my husband is out for the afternoon," Teresa explained, glaring at her daughter. Annie had the impression the information was more for Britt's sake than for her own. In other words, Carl Hoffert wouldn't be back anytime soon.

Logan skipped down the porch steps and opened the gate for her. "It's a little tricky," he said, as the gate scraped the broken concrete sidewalk, swinging inward.

Taking Annie's hand, he proudly led her to the house. "Watch out for the second step," he warned. "There's a weak spot."

Annie followed his advice. The inside of the house was what she had expected. The walls needed painting and the floors were cracked and badly worn, and yet, from what she could see, it was meticulously clean. Annie was certain Teresa had done everything within her power to make a good home for her children.

Annie followed Britt and her mother into the kitchen. "Britt," she said, hoping she wasn't being too obvious, "is that a bruise on your wrist?"

The teenager glared at her and didn't answer.

"Please sit," Teresa said, pulling out a chair at the kitchen table. "Would you like coffee or tea?"

"Either is fine," Annie said, hiding her disappointment that Carl was away. The entire purpose of her visit had been to meet the man she suspected of abusing his family.

Thirty minutes later, the two women were at the table talking when the door opened and Carl Hoffert staggered in. Discomfort filled Teresa's eyes when her husband entered the kitchen.

"Carl," she said cautiously, "we have company. This is Annie. She's come to inquire about me cleaning for her."

He immediately looked at Annie and grinned appreciatively. "Don't often have visitors."

Annie forced a smile.

Bracing his hands against the back of a chair to steady himself, Carl narrowed his gaze on her, suspecting something was amiss. "Do I know you?" he asked. "You ever been to The Pirate's Den?"

"No, I can't say that I have." She'd heard of it, though. The tavern was in the roughest part of town, where she'd been warned not to go alone. "I'm looking to hire your wife. I met your son and heard about his accident," she said, playing it cool, unwilling to give herself away.

Carl's expression hardened. "A broken arm. That's a crock of —"

"Carl, don't get all worked up about it," Teresa said, sending an apologetic look Annie's way.

"Damn busybodies."

"Carl, please," Teresa whispered, sounding almost desperate.

Her husband refused to listen. "The boy's mother is turning him into a spoiled brat. No way was Logan's arm broken. Britt should never have taken him to that clinic. We don't have that kind of money to be wasting on foolishness."

Annie noticed he seemed to have all the funds necessary to buy booze, but he was unwilling to allow his son the proper medical treatment. She didn't dare mention it, but the thought went through her head at lightning speed.

Sipping her coffee, she focused her attention on Carl. "How did Logan hurt his arm?"

"Fell out of bed," Carl said, without a moment's hesitation. "Damn boy is clumsy."

Just as she suspected, the story of the bike accident was as bogus as Carl's version.

150

"Given a day or two, he would have been right as rain. The boy's nothing more than a sissy. Time for him to man up. No need to rush him to that clinic."

"I'm sorry you feel that way, Mr. Hoffert. Logan's arm was broken. I can show you the x-ray if you like." The minute the words were out of her mouth, Annie recognized her mistake.

"You from that clinic?" he demanded.

Annie couldn't lie. "Yes. I was the PA who saw Logan."

Right away Carl stiffened, and his eyes narrowed to thin slits. "What the hell are you doing in my house?"

Teresa moved closer to Annie. "I invited her in, Carl."

"I know why you're here," he snapped, ignoring his wife. "You're looking to make more trouble for me. You take me for a fool? You're the one who sent those people from the state to check on me." His gaze narrowed and focused on Annie. His anger seemed to be brewing, and Annie feared it would soon reach the boiling point.

"Annie came to hire me and check on Logan," Teresa explained, keeping her voice calm, although Annie heard the slight tremble.

"Like hell she did."

Teresa slowly released her breath. "We'll talk about it later, Carl."

Carl looked at his wife, his eyes flashing fire. "No way did this busybody come to hire you. She came looking for trouble. Well, I have news for you. The guy

151

the state sent is an old school friend of mine. Harvey knows me from way back and he let it slide."

Teresa looked even more stunned. "Someone was here from the state?"

That explained what had happened and why Carl hadn't been charged. Annie's shoulders sagged. "I apologize for any trouble I caused," she said to Teresa and Britt. They both knew she wasn't referring to her phone call to the state. "I think it might be best if I left now."

"Damn straight you're leaving. Get the hell out of my house and don't come back." Carl Hoffert walked over to the door and held it open for her.

"Carl. Stop," Teresa demanded, although it did no good.

His head swerved toward his wife, his eyes narrowing menacingly. "I'd think by now you'd know better than to talk back to me, woman."

Annie could see that Teresa wasn't backing down. She feared that the minute she left, Teresa and the kids would pay the price for her visit, and she couldn't allow that to happen. The last thing she wanted was to be responsible for more harm done to this family.

"I need to explain something," Annie said calmly, hoping to smooth matters over. "Because I work at the clinic, I am obligated by law to report any suspicious injuries to Child Protective Services."

Her words fell like stones dropped from a ten-story building, landing with a violent crash.

"I told you to get out of my house," Carl shouted a second time. Grabbing hold of Annie's shoulder, he shoved her forward, his grip hard and tight. Annie knew she would have bruises to show for the rough treatment.

"Carl, don't!" Teresa screamed. "Leave her alone. Or do you intend to hurt her, too?"

"Shut up. You're to have nothing more to do with this troublemaker, understand?"

Teresa cast an apologetic look at Annie. "I'm so sorry my husband —"

"Are you apologizing to her because of me?" Carl demanded.

"You're being belligerent and rude."

"She deserves it," he shouted, and then whirled around and faced Annie. "Get out," he bellowed, "before I make you sorry you ever showed your face on my property."

Britt appeared in the doorway to the kitchen, her face tight with embarrassment and pain. "Go," she whispered urgently.

Heeding the teenager's words, Annie walked onto the porch but turned to face Carl Hoffert. "I'll leave, but I want you to know I will report any suspicious injuries to the sheriff." That was all she could do at this point.

Carl snickered, finding her threat little more than a joke.

Annie walked back to her car and was shocked when Carl followed her outside. Standing on his porch, he pointed at her.

"You want to make trouble for me? You don't know what trouble is. If I were you, I'd watch my back."

CHAPTER
FIFTEEN

When she returned to the cottage, Annie found a starfish on her porch.

Keaton again.

Bending down, she reached for it and held it close to her heart. Finding the starfish helped ease the unpleasantness of her encounter with Carl Hoffert. She'd never meant for her visit to go to such ugly extremes. Even now, Annie trembled in the aftermath of Carl's anger. Her biggest concern was that by confronting him, she'd done more harm than good. The thought of what Carl might do upset her so much that her hand tightened around the starfish to the point of pain.

Once inside the house, Annie set the starfish in the round bowl with the small collection of seashells she'd found on her walks, along with the ones Keaton had left for her. Regrets weighed down her shoulders. If the social worker who'd made the visit knew Carl, then he was likely to believe his story. She'd wondered what had gone wrong after the reassurances she'd received from CPS, and now she knew.

Collapsing onto the sofa, she grabbed her phone and reached out to her cousin. Gabby was her best friend and the person she most often spoke to when upset.

Gabby answered almost immediately. "Annie, I was just thinking about you — I hope you're calling to tell me you're coming to visit. I miss you, girlfriend!"

"No . . . I had a rough afternoon and needed to hear a friendly voice."

"What's going on?" Gabby asked.

Annie told her, condensing the story as much as she could, explaining her fears without using any names.

When she finished, Gabby was quiet. "What about you, Annie? He threatened you."

She hadn't taken Carl seriously. "Don't worry. I told him plain as day I would report him to the sheriff, and I meant it."

"Annie," Gabby said and groaned. "He could hurt you."

"He wouldn't dare. Besides, I took a self-defense class a few years back, remember?"

"The key words in that statement are 'a few years back.'"

"I'll be fine." Maybe she should be concerned, but she didn't believe Carl Hoffert would try anything. Perhaps she was being foolish, but deep down she believed the man was too much of a coward to attack her.

"I'd feel better if you came to Seattle for a couple days."

"Gabs, I can't. I need to be at the clinic on Monday morning. Stop fretting. I'm a big girl. I can take care of myself."

"I'll come to you, then."

"Gabby, no. I'm okay, really. I needed to vent, and I feel better already."

She felt her cousin's hesitation. "You'd better call me every day for a week."

"What? Why?"

"Because I'll worry unless you do."

Annie laughed.

"What's so funny?"

"I call, text, or email you nearly every day as it is."

Gabby laughed, too. "Okay, so you do. But I want a phone call. Otherwise I'm packing up my car and heading your way. Deal?"

"Deal," Annie agreed.

The mood lightened. "I'm surprised, you know. You're really enjoying living on the beach in your little cottage by the sea."

"I'm loving it."

"You haven't mentioned meeting any cute, shirtless guys playing volleyball."

"Not yet. Give it a month or two and the beach will be full of guys eager to show off their athletic skills." Not that Annie would be interested, although Gabby might.

"Anyone I should know about?"

She wanted to tell Gabby more about Keaton. She'd talked about him plenty in past conversations. She looked toward the starfish, sea glass, and other small gifts he'd left for her and her heart swelled. There'd been a subtle shift in their relationship since they'd kissed. Well, perhaps it hadn't been that subtle. He already occupied a good deal of her life, and . . .

"Annie?" Gabby said, breaking into her thoughts. "You're not saying anything, which tells me you're holding out on me. Start talking."

"It's Keaton."

"The guy who doesn't speak?"

"He talks plenty, but only when he starts getting comfortable around a person. He's a man of few words until then," Annie explained. "I'm serious, Gabby. I really like him. He's kind and caring and . . ."

"You're describing a Saint Bernard."

Annie laughed. "Wait until you meet him, and then you'll know what I mean. I think the reason I'm not afraid of Carl Hoffert is because I have Keaton in my life. He'd never let anything happen to me."

"I like him already. If you're that into him, then I don't need to know anything more about him."

They talked for another thirty minutes, and by the time Annie was off the phone she felt worlds better.

She moved into the kitchen to search out something for dinner, and again her attention went to the small collection from Keaton. Other than a few shattered seashells when she'd walked along the beach, Annie had never come across the kind of treasures that Keaton routinely gave her. She'd searched, but often her thoughts were wrapped around memories of her family instead. She found comfort in the wind buffeting against her, flinging her hair about her face. She'd felt closer to the family she'd lost with the sound of the surf humming in her ears, whispering memories of happier times and shared joys. The grief didn't seem quite as heavy.

Annie's musings were interrupted by a quiet knock against her front door. She stood to answer, intuitively knowing it was Keaton. He found no need to announce himself with brash clamor. He was a quiet man, strong and solid. An immediate smile settled over her when she saw him standing on the other side of the door. He wore his work clothes, paint-smeared overalls and work boots. It was clear he'd come directly from a job site.

"Keaton," she said, more than pleased to see him. "Come in!"

He shook his head. "Sorry, I can't stay."

She hid her disappointment. "I found the starfish. I love it. Thank you, as always."

He grinned. It usually took him a while to work his way up to a real conversation. Annie was patient. He'd loop more than two or three words together when he was ready.

"I have another gift."

"Did you leave it on the porch?" Annie had seen only the one.

"I have it with me." Reaching into the bib of his overalls, he scooped up a tiny gray-and-white kitten that was little more than a ball of fur.

"A kitten?" she asked incredulously. She'd never owned one. Her family had always been dog people. Annie and Mike had grown up with a series of small dogs they'd loved as fiercely as any member of the family. The closest she'd been to a cat was when Mellie's cat would peer out the window at her.

Keaton kissed the top of the small creature's head. "This is a special one." He handed her the kitten and his eyes held hers looking for her reaction. "He's deaf and Mellie thinks he's only four to five weeks old by his size."

"Deaf," she repeated, bringing the ball of fur close to her body and gently petting his soft fur.

"Preston found him on the side of the road, discarded like garbage."

"No," she cried, appalled that anyone would do anything so cruel and unfeeling.

"The shelter is full, and he was looking for a good home."

"And, naturally, you took him." Caring for defenseless animals was one of the reasons she was so strongly attracted to Keaton.

"I got him for you. He belongs with you."

"Oh? And why is that?" She couldn't help being curious.

He looked away. "Because you are willing to accept those who are less than perfect. You have a good heart . . . and I thought that maybe you needed this kitten as much as he needs you."

He must have read the question in her eyes, because he continued.

"I've seen you on the beach, Annie," he said, his voice gentle. "I know you carry a heavy pain. Your eyes speak of loss."

"I . . ."

"It's all right. You don't need to tell me who broke your heart. I thought giving you this kitten to love would help."

She blinked up at him as the moisture unexpectedly filled her eyes. "Thank you," she whispered and held the kitten gently below her chin. "I'll give him a good home."

"I know you will. When he's asleep, blow on his face," Keaton instructed, running his index finger over the kitten's head, gently petting him as he slept in Annie's arms.

"Why would I do that?"

"To let him know you're there."

"Okay." Her mind was working fast. She'd need to get all the things required for a cat, and not just any cat, but this special little guy. Thankfully, she had milk in the refrigerator. First thing Monday she'd make an appointment with the vet's office and have him checked out. She hoped to learn if the cat's deafness had been caused by an injury or if it was genetic.

"You don't need to worry about caring for him. Just give him food and water and plenty of love and the two of you will be fine."

It was spooky the way he could read her mind.

"Remember, he needs you," Keaton said, looking more serious than she could ever remember him looking before.

It was almost as if he was telling Annie that he needed her, too, and how important she had become to him.

"I won't forget," she said, and kissed the top of the kitten's head in the same way he had.

Keaton wrapped his arms around her and then, to her disappointment, quickly released her. "I don't want to get paint on you."

"I don't care if you do or not," she said, standing on the tips of her toes to kiss him.

It didn't take much for them to become fully involved in kissing. She felt his reluctance as he broke contact. "I need to go."

"Okay."

Still he hesitated. "You picked out a name for him?"

Mulling over a short list that immediately came to mind, she hit upon one she felt would be perfect. "Ringo."

"Ringo," he repeated.

"Yes, I want Lennon and Ringo to be friends."

"Good name."

"I'm glad you approve."

He retreated, his eyes holding hers. She read his regret. "I really hate to go."

Not nearly as much as she hated seeing him leave.

"I have to work," he explained.

"Another time, then." Annie remained in the doorway and watched Keaton walk away. When he was out of sight, she closed the door. Not more than a minute passed before her phone rang. Annie smiled when she saw that the caller was Mellie.

"Did he give you that deaf cat?" she blurted out.

"Yup." Annie set Ringo down next to her on the sofa. The kitten curled up in a minuscule ball, content to be close to her side.

"You keeping it?"

"Yup. Named him Ringo."

"Ringo," Mellie repeated, acting like the name was the most ridiculous thing she'd ever heard.

"I think it's cute."

"You two are starting to get on my nerves," Mellie muttered.

"Why's that?" She wouldn't dare to guess. From everything Mellie had said, Annie had always been a thorn in her side.

"Never mind."

"No, please, I want to know."

Mellie huffed. "It's like the two of you are characters in a romance novel. Kissing and staring at each other with stars in your eyes."

"You read romances?" Annie asked, refusing to take offense at her comments.

The question went unanswered. Then, "You want to make something of it?"

"I read them, too, on occasion," Annie confessed, enjoying the way Mellie had bristled as if she was ready to defend to the death her choice in reading material.

"You?" she questioned, doubtfully.

"I have a few here that I'd be happy to share," Annie said.

"If you want, I'll take them off your hands."

This was exactly the in that Annie had been waiting for. "Let me know when you're ready and I'll be happy to bring them over. We can have tea the way I mentioned a while back."

Mellie answered with a snicker. "I'm not that desperate."

Annie grinned. "Mellie, please, you're hurting my feelings."

Her almost-friend made a grumbling sound and cut off the call, but not before Annie heard what she could only believe was a chuckle.

CHAPTER
SIXTEEN

Sunday morning, when Annie woke, Ringo was asleep on the pillow next to her. He was adorable, and her heart melted as she gently blew in his face, afraid if she petted him it would startle the kitten. This had been Keaton's suggestion, and it seemed to work well. Ringo opened his eyes and stretched his legs and meowed in a small voice, telling her that he was hungry. That was how Annie interpreted it, anyway. Carrying him into the kitchen, she set a bowl of milk on the floor. Ringo immediately started lapping it up.

"I'm heading to church," she said, knowing that even if Ringo could hear, he wouldn't understand a word of what she said. "I'll stop off at the store on the way home." She had a short grocery list, plus items she would need to properly care for Ringo. He hadn't been with her even twenty-four hours and already he felt like a part of her. She suspected it was because Keaton had given her the kitten. She continued with her monologue. "Candi is stopping by and we're going to lunch later."

Ringo stared up at her before chasing after a dust ball. Annie laughed as she watched him and knew she was going to enjoy having a pet. She mulled over how

Keaton had sensed the comfort this tiny kitten would give her. It was obvious that he needed her. But then he'd added that she needed him, too. Although Keaton knew nothing about the tragedy — no one in Oceanside did — he had intuitively understood that she carried a searing pain within her soul.

Finishing the milk, the kitten looked up at her lovingly. She found a box and placed a folded fleece blanket in it and set him inside, hoping he would be content until she returned.

"Be good while I'm away," she whispered, and she gently petted his back with her index finger. He was incredibly small and fragile, and in many ways, so was she. She hesitated, looking down on this tiny creature, and felt a tug in her heart. She was going to love this kitten.

She left the house and headed around the side of the cottage to where she'd parked her SUV. Because she usually walked to the clinic, she rarely drove the vehicle, as everything she needed was within walking distance. At some point, she planned on buying a bicycle.

Right away she noticed something was wrong. It took her a moment to realize what it was.

All four of her tires had been slashed.

"No," she breathed, cupping her hand over her mouth. No one needed to tell her who was responsible. Annie knew.

Carl Hoffert.

He'd warned her that there was a price to pay for interfering, for contacting the authorities about him, for causing him the humiliation of undergoing an interview with a former classmate of his.

Bunching her fists at her sides, Annie closed her eyes to hold back an angry outburst. On the inside, she was stomping her foot and screaming in frustration. Annie refused to give Carl Hoffert the satisfaction of losing her temper.

Unable to attend church without a car, she returned to the house and reached for Ringo, knowing that holding him would help her relax. She'd wait until later to walk to the store. The shopping area was less than a mile away.

Going online, she found a tire shop, but because it was Sunday, she wouldn't be able to contact them until Monday morning. The frustration was maddening.

To deal with her irritation, she decided to clean house, scrubbing at every available surface with a vengeance until she was panting with exhaustion. She worked for more than an hour, sweat beading her forehead. Her tank top was sticking to her body. A scarf held back her hair. She was convinced she looked utterly pitiful when a loud knock came from her front door. Her heart leapt, afraid it might be Carl. Squaring her shoulders, she was determined not to show him any fear.

Only it wasn't Carl. It was Keaton. His eyes were like fire, anger burning as he shouted a demand.

"Who?" In his fury, he had trouble getting out any more than a single word. He'd seen her tires.

"Come inside." She reached for his hand and led him into the cottage.

"Who?" he demanded again, louder this time, his massive fists clenched at his sides.

"Keaton, please, sit down." The last thing she wanted was for him to take matters into his own hands.

"No," he insisted, shaking his head. Annie had reacted the same way when she'd first seen her ruined tires. All he needed was a few minutes to calm himself and then she'd explain.

"I brought this on myself," she said, expelling a sigh.

At her words, he whirled around and faced her. "Don't believe that. Tell me who."

She took in a deep breath, hoping that would calm her, and him, too. "I can't say for sure, but I have my suspicions."

Keaton continued to pace her small living room, growing more agitated by the minute.

"Getting angry isn't going to help the situation. Besides, I'm upset enough for the both of us."

He rammed his fingers through his hair and clenched his jaw. "Tell me."

"Would you like some coffee to settle your nerves?" she asked instead. She'd never seen Keaton angry before, and it was something to behold. He was terrifying. If she didn't already know and trust him, seeing his red face and clenched fists as he loomed over her would have stopped her heart. She could only imagine how someone who didn't know him would feel, seeing him this enraged.

"No coffee. Talk to me," he insisted.

166

From time spent with Keaton, Annie had noticed when he became frustrated or emotional, he spoke in incomplete sentences. His words were jerky and disconnected, almost as if he had trouble forming a coherent thought.

"How did you know about my tires?" she asked. Despite his refusal, she poured him a mug of coffee.

"Saw them . . . when I brought Mellie's groceries. Who?" he demanded again, leaving the hot coffee on the counter untouched.

Putting him off clearly wasn't working. "My guess is that it was Carl Hoffert."

His face became inquisitive, as though he found it inconceivable that she would have anything to do with the man. "You know Carl?"

She braced her hands against the kitchen counter that separated them. "By default." Because of privacy laws, she couldn't mention the situation with Logan's broken arm. "I heard his wife cleans houses and I wanted to hire her. I had a run-in with her husband." As much as she wanted to, she couldn't give him any other information.

"What do you mean by a run-in?" His look was skeptical. "What happened?" he demanded.

"He doesn't take too kindly to uninvited company, I found out."

"I know Carl. He has a temper. I'm not letting him anywhere near you." Keaton abruptly headed for the door, nearly throwing it off its hinges in his rush to leave.

"Keaton," she said forcefully, compelling him to look at her. She went to him and grabbed hold of his arm, her eyes pleading with him. "Don't. Please."

He hesitated. "There's more. You're not telling me everything."

"I can't."

"He . . . He . . . threatened you?" Keaton struggled to get the words out.

Afraid of what he might do, Annie wrapped her arms around his middle and hugged him with all her strength, hoping to waylay him before he did something foolish. Keaton remained as stiff as an oak tree for several moments before he released a ragged sigh and hugged her back.

"I won't . . . have you hurt."

"I'm fine. Yes, the tires are an inconvenience and an expense. I was angry when I saw them, too, but it isn't the end of the world." Compared to other losses she'd experienced, four slashed tires were barely a blip on the map of life.

"I should never have gone to the house, so the blame is on me. I didn't take his threats seriously, but I probably should have. It's fine now. He took it out on the tires; the worst is over."

Annie could feel Keaton's anger easing as his body relaxed. "He should pay," he muttered.

"I'm convinced he will eventually." She'd done what she could. Her hope was that Teresa would take the position as housekeeper, even against her husband's wishes. That would give Annie the chance to talk to the other woman about her situation. Perhaps then Teresa would find the courage to leave him.

Keaton wasn't willing to drop it. "Not good enough."

"No, please. If you have any feelings for me, then don't take matters into your own hands. No good will come of that."

His frown darkened.

"Promise me you won't do anything foolish. Promise me," she repeated.

He stubbornly refused, until she pressed the side of her head against his chest. His heart beat strong and steady in her ear, calming her. Gradually his arms came around her and he pressed his lips against the top of her head, holding her close with a tenderness that left her feeling cherished.

Although Annie didn't dare admit it, she loved the quick way in which Keaton had come to her defense. She'd never had anyone do that — well, other than her father, who had been as fiercely protective of her as Keaton was. Certainly no man she'd ever dated. Not that she'd been in situations like this before. This was new territory.

Keaton's phone hummed in his pocket, indicating that he had a call. He'd apparently put it on vibrate.

Reluctantly, Annie broke away from him. He reached for his phone, read the screen, and let the call go to voicemail. Within seconds her phone rang.

"It's Mellie," he explained. "Ignore it."

She did as he asked. "I imagine she wants her groceries."

Cupping the sides of Annie's face with his large hands, Keaton exhaled deeply, not wanting to leave her. "Probably," he agreed.

Annie wondered if Mellie had seen the damage done to her car. Progress had been made in their up-and-down relationship. The woman wasn't going to win any congeniality awards. But Annie was willing to overlook her landlord's gruffness in the hope of eventually becoming friends. If she could manage that, then at the end of her lease perhaps Mellie would be willing to let her renew for another year.

"I think Mellie might be warming up to me," she proudly told Keaton.

"Oh?" Keaton grinned, believing there wasn't anyone her smile couldn't win over.

"I have a few books that I thought she'd enjoy reading," Annie told him. "I invited myself over for tea and conversation."

His smile started to fade, and he looked skeptical.

"I'm patient. Before the year's up I intend for Mellie and me to be the very best of friends."

Keaton barked a laugh in disbelief.

"I honestly think she likes me," Annie said, and then clarified, "Only she's afraid to let me know. What's her story, anyway? How can she afford to live, when she doesn't work?"

Keaton shrugged. "She came to her grandparents' home when she was ten, after her parents were killed. She has a trust fund."

Annie mulled over the information, knowing that Mellie had left Oceanside when she was eighteen.

170

Losing their granddaughter like that must have broken the Munsons' hearts. Perhaps one day Mellie would feel comfortable enough to tell Annie her story, but that would mean that *she* would need to open up to Mellie regarding her own secrets.

CHAPTER
SEVENTEEN

If Annie's day had started out badly, it quickly went from bad to worse when Mellie's call came later that afternoon.

"I want you packed up and out of the cottage by the end of the week."

Stunned, Annie found herself unable to respond. "What? Why?" she finally managed.

"You heard me."

Pushing the hair away from her forehead and holding her hand there, a dozen responses battled themselves out in her brain. "Can you tell me what I did wrong?" Perhaps Mellie had some connection with Carl Hoffert. Carl obviously wanted her gone, and maybe he had somehow convinced Mellie to kick her out of the cottage.

"I don't need to give you a reason. I want you gone before the end of this week."

"I . . . can't. I don't have anyplace else to go."

"Not my problem."

Annie was too shocked to think. "Can we talk about this?"

"No." Mellie's voice was flat and sharp.

"Give me one good reason," Annie insisted, moving from disbelief to anger. This was grossly unfair. Just that morning she'd told Keaton she felt she was making progress with Mellie. She loved living in the cottage. Just being here with all the happy memories from her childhood summer vacations had helped her immeasurably. Moving now would set her back emotionally. Annie had to have some rights as a tenant.

Then she remembered they had both signed a contract. "What about my lease?"

Mellie hesitated, and then continued with the same angry edge. "I'm canceling it."

"It's legally binding, Mellie. I'll take you to court and I'll win. I haven't done anything to deserve this. I've paid my rent six months in advance. I've tried my best to —"

"It's because of Keaton," Mellie insisted. "He doesn't get upset like that unless provoked. What did you say to him?"

"Say? When?"

"This morning. He was furious. I don't know what you did to upset him, but I'm not having it. Keaton is good people. I warned you once before, and you didn't take me seriously. I told you if you do anything to hurt him, you'll regret it."

Composing herself, Annie took in several deep breaths and slowly let them out. "Did you happen to see me talking to the sheriff earlier?"

"Yes. Another reason I want you off my property. You're nothing but a troublemaker. Don't know what you did, but it's a shame you weren't arrested."

"Did you even ask Keaton what that was about?" Annie asked, calmer now, as she could see that this was nothing more than a misunderstanding.

"No. Wouldn't do any good. He wouldn't tell me if I had. All I know is he thinks the sun rises and sets on you. Can't understand it myself. Far as I can see, you're not that great. Keaton doesn't see that, though. He'd take a bullet for you."

Annie knew Keaton was attracted to her but not to that extent. For a moment, she held on to the happy feeling, knowing that reality would come crashing back. When next she spoke, she softened her voice. "Keaton means the world to me, and he's everything you say he is. I would never do anything to hurt him."

"Then you better tell me what happened this morning that had him as angry as I've ever seen him."

Annie's hand tightened around her phone. "Someone threatened me. The tires on my car were slashed. That's why the sheriff was here. It wasn't anything I did to Keaton."

Her explanation was met by silence.

"Oh," Mellie said after several tense moments passed, but she didn't say anything more.

Eventually Annie found the courage to ask, "May I stay in the cottage, then?"

Mellie appeared to be debating her answer.

"I'd be willing to sweeten the pot," Annie added hopefully.

"How are you going to do that?"

"Put the tea on, I'm coming over."

"Hold on a minute," Mellie said. "I —"

Annie ended the call, grabbed the bag of paperback novels she'd collected, and walked across the yard. If she knocked, she knew Mellie would refuse to answer, so she took it upon herself to find the keys. She'd watched Keaton do this several times. She lifted the cushion on the porch swing, retrieved the keys, and let herself into the house.

Mellie stood in the kitchen, frozen in place as though a spell had been cast over her. With all the boxes and other paraphernalia stacked about, there was little room to move. The entire area was like a maze, with pathways leading around tight corners. A few boxes had no tops and Annie saw newspapers with headlines dating back to the Obama inauguration, plus thirty-year-old copies of *National Geographic*. Heaven only knew what was buried in the others.

Although she'd seen glimpses of her landlord gazing out the window, Annie was surprised at how attractive she was. She wore her dark blond hair shoulder length. It was straight and parted down the middle. Her eyes were a snappy blue. She wore faded jeans, cowboy boots, and a long-sleeve plaid shirt as fashionably as a model. What surprised Annie the most was her size. Mellie was petite, probably around five-two or -three, but with the command and resoluteness of Mellie's voice, you would have thought she was seven feet tall.

"What's that?" Mellie asked, glaring at the bag in Annie's hand.

With effort, Annie kept from smiling. Mellie was curious, and that was a good sign. "A few of my favorite historical romances."

Mellie's gaze went to the bag and Annie saw the interest on her face. Wonderful. Annie's love of romances — the uplifting, powerful kind — had gone a long way toward getting her through many a sleepless night. And now it was the common ground that would allow her to connect to Mellie.

"Is the tea brewing?" Annie asked, seeking out the kitchen table, which was stacked high with more newspapers and magazines. Annie saw that Mellie had carved out a tiny space for herself, but every other inch was covered with boxes and useless stuff. On the countertop, she appeared to have every small appliance imaginable, some still in their boxes. In a single glance, Annie saw a rice cooker, a deep-fat fryer, and a pressure cooker she'd recently seen advertised on television. It appeared Mellie maintained a connection with the outside world through online shopping.

Mellie stared at her. "Don't have time for tea. I didn't invite you, so you should leave."

Taking the dismissal in stride, Annie shrugged, prepared to do as asked. She turned and started toward the door.

"Leave the books, though."

Annie met her stare. "Before I do, I want the assurance you won't cancel my lease."

Mellie pinched her lips together and reverted her eyes back to the grocery bag full of books. "Any Regency novels in that collection?" she asked.

"Several. Regencies are some of my favorites." Ready to walk away with the books, she turned the doorknob.

"Okay, fine," Mellie relented. "I'll abide by the lease. You have one year and then I want you gone."

"Fair enough," Annie agreed. In the intervening months, she'd find a way to be Mellie's friend whether she wanted one or not. She set the bag of books on top of one of the boxes and was about to return to the cottage when Mellie added another stipulation.

"With the understanding . . . ?" She paused for what could only be effect.

"Yes?"

"If you do anything, and I do mean *anything*, to hurt, embarrass, humiliate, disconcert, demean, or un-settle Keaton, your lease will automatically be terminated. Do we understand each other?"

It wasn't Annie's intention to do any of those things. "Understood."

"Good. Now don't let the door hit you in the butt on your way out."

Annie struggled to hold back a smile.

Monday morning didn't start out much better than Sunday had. When Annie arrived at Bean There, Britt refused to make eye contact with her.

Immediately concerned, she asked, "Britt, is everything all right?" From the teen's reaction, she feared the worst. She didn't see any visible signs of abuse, but that didn't mean the girl's stepfather hadn't hit her someplace where it wouldn't be easily detected.

"No, everything isn't all right at home," Britt returned in a fierce whisper. "And you're the one responsible."

"I'm sorry."

"It's a little too late for that, don't you think?"

"What happened?" Annie was afraid Carl's anger with Annie had been taken out on his family instead.

Britt's head shot up and her eyes clashed with Annie. "What *happened?*" Britt repeated, whispering furiously. "*You* happened. Why did you butt into something that was none of your business? My stepfather has been on a rampage ever since your visit. My mom has enough to deal with already without you making matters worse."

"Britt . . ." Annie pleaded, but the teenager had already cut her off.

"You make it sound easy. You don't know . . . You have no idea. Please, just stay away from me and my family." She whirled from the counter, turning her back to Annie.

Jimmy looked stricken and sneaked a worried glance at Britt. The two traded positions, and Jimmy took Annie's order. Upset and flustered, Annie needed to repeat it twice. She was shaken, and clearly he was, too.

Seeing that Britt wanted nothing more to do with her, Annie swallowed hard and told him, "Please let Britt know I'm sorry. I was only trying to help."

"I will," he said, and then lowered his voice. "Is it her stepdad?"

Annie nodded.

He briefly closed his eyes, fully aware of what was happening at home but powerless to stop it.

When Annie arrived at the clinic, Candi sent her a warning glance. "Dr. Bainbridge is here."

"On a Monday?" He normally worked on Tuesdays, Wednesdays, and Thursdays, but never on a Monday.

"He'd like to see you in his office."

Annie leaned toward her friend. "Do you know what it's about?"

Candi glanced over her shoulder to make sure no one was listening. She lowered her voice to a whisper. "Any reason you met with the sheriff this weekend?"

"I reported a crime. Why?"

Candi exhaled. "Dr. Bainbridge and the sheriff are good friends. I saw the two of them talking in the parking lot when I arrived. I didn't intentionally mean to eavesdrop, but I heard your name mentioned with Carl Hoffert's."

Annie's shoulders sagged. She had to assume Dr. Bainbridge had learned she visited the Hofferts'. She might as well accept that she was about to find herself without a job. It seemed she'd bungled her opportunity to build a new life in Oceanside. Mellie had been ready to throw her out of the cottage, and now this.

After giving her heart a moment to settle itself, she knocked gently on Dr. Bainbridge's door. "You asked to see me?" she said, trying to act like she had no clue what this was about. Pretending to be oblivious was probably not the best way to start off the conversation.

"Come in, Annie," he said from behind his desk. He gestured toward the chair for her to take a seat.

Clearing her throat, she lowered herself onto the chair and sat on her hands like a penitent child.

"What's this I hear about you visiting the Hoffert household?"

"Yes, well . . ." She found it difficult to speak because her mouth had gone dry. "Logan missed his follow-up appointment and I was concerned. Also, Mrs. Hoffert cleans houses and I went to find out if she could take on another client."

He mulled over her answer. "It was more than that, though, wasn't it?"

She weighed her options, unwilling to lie but equally unwilling to dig herself into a hole.

"I read the CPS report," he said, before she could formulate an answer. "The underlying reason for your visit was to check out the home life yourself."

"Ah . . ."

"Annie, do you have any idea of the danger you put yourself in?"

She lowered her head. "The social worker was a friend of Mr. Hoffert's . . . I think he got a pass because the other man knew him from years ago."

"So you decided to take matters into your own hands?"

She nodded, but felt the need to explain. "I didn't intend for him to know it was me who'd called in the suspected abuse. It slipped out when he insisted the boy was a sissy and his mother had overreacted and —"

"It doesn't matter how it came out," the physician said, cutting her off. "What concerns me is that you put yourself at tremendous risk. What you did was foolish, in the extreme sense of the word."

Annie stared down at her feet. "I know." And then, because she couldn't stand the suspense, she blurted out, "Are you going to fire me?"

Dr. Bainbridge took far too long to answer for Annie's comfort. "To be honest, that was my first inclination. The thing is, Annie, you're good with the patients and have gained the trust of this community in only a short amount of time. I'm only going to write you up for this, but, fair warning, if you do anything like this again, I won't have a choice but to let you go."

Annie had learned her lesson. "I understand."

She'd already felt the consequences of her lack of good judgment. The slashed tires. Mellie threatening to evict her. Plus, she'd managed to alienate Britt. Seeing how upset the teenager was, Annie didn't know if she could repair the damage. Keaton had been furious, too. Not at her, thankfully, but at Carl Hoffert. If she hadn't stopped Keaton, there was no telling what he might have done. If all that wasn't enough, she was basically holding on to her position at the clinic by the thin strand of a spiderweb.

This wasn't the way she'd intended to start her Monday.

Candi sent her a sympathetic look when Annie left Dr. Bainbridge's office. "You okay?" she asked, her face showing her worries.

Annie expelled a long sigh. "I think so. Thankfully, I still have my job."

Candi looked nearly as relieved as Annie. "Thank goodness. I didn't know what to think when I saw Dr. Bainbridge talking to the sheriff this morning."

"I've learned my lesson," Annie assured her, and she had. She knew better and was determined she wouldn't do anything to put her position in jeopardy again.

For the remainder of the week Annie did everything by the book. She didn't see Britt working at Bean There and wondered if she'd quit her job. High school graduation was a little over a month away and that might be the reason. Or, maybe, the teen had traded shifts to avoid having to deal with her. That depressed her.

To find Britt at the clinic on Friday afternoon as a patient came as a total shock. Candi told her that Britt had asked to speak privately to Annie. Surprised and wondering what this could mean, Annie entered the exam room where the teen waited.

Britt looked up, her face pale and her eyes sad and red, rimmed with tears.

"Britt," Annie said, comforting her with an arm around her shoulders. "You asked to see me?"

Britt nodded and kept her head lowered. She seemed to square her shoulders and find the courage to sit up. "I'm pregnant."

Annie sat next to the teen and took hold of her hand, giving it a gentle squeeze, hoping to comfort her. "Are you okay?"

Britt shrugged. "I can't tell Mom. She's got enough on her plate as it is."

"Oh Britt, of all people, your mother will understand."

The teenager didn't confirm or deny it. "Mom has enough worries without dealing with mine."

"Are you positive you're pregnant?" Seeing the amount of stress in the home, it wouldn't be unusual for Britt to skip a month of her menstrual cycle.

"As positive as I can get. I bought one of those tests at the drugstore, and it confirmed what I already knew in my heart."

"Did you tell the father?" Annie asked. She hated the idea of Britt keeping this secret all to herself when she would need the emotional support of those closest to her.

Avoiding eye contact, Britt shook her head no.

"Do you plan to let him know?"

Again, she shook her head and then emphasized her refusal. "No, and I'm not going to, either." She covered her face with both hands and broke into heart-wrenching tears.

Annie hugged Britt again, her own heart heavy, while she debated how best to help the teenager in the months ahead.

CHAPTER
EIGHTEEN

Unable to sleep that night, Annie gently petted Ringo, who was curled up in a tight ball, sleeping beside her. Her thoughts were full of Britt's visit to the clinic. Further conversation revealed that the teenager was terrified of letting her mother and stepfather know about her situation. Although Annie had encouraged Britt to confide in her mother, the girl insisted she couldn't. Not yet. By necessity, she would in time, but for whatever reason, she wanted to wait.

Since Teresa had become pregnant with Britt while a teenager herself, Annie hoped that the girl would be willing to confide in her mother. It was entirely understandable that she wouldn't want her stepfather to know.

Britt had refused to name the father. If Annie were to guess, she would say it was Jimmy, but that was speculation on her part. She'd noticed the way he looked at Britt and saw the love in his eyes. Clearly, he idolized her. A couple times she'd seen the two of them together in town, holding hands.

A keening howl cut into the night, slicing through the silence, jarring Annie. It sounded like a werewolf from a horror story. Climbing out of bed, she went to the kitchen and peered out the window over the sink. A large shadow silhouetted by the moonlight moved across the yard toward Mellie's.

Standing on her tiptoes to get a better look, she recognized Keaton.

It was well past midnight; she couldn't imagine what he'd be doing at Mellie's this late, until she noticed he carried what looked to be an injured animal in his arms. As he approached, the door opened, indicating that her landlord had anticipated his arrival. This was too strange. Annie had never seen Mellie open the door for any reason.

Wanting to know what was going on, Annie grabbed her jeans and sweatshirt and slipped into a pair of Converse, determined to see if she could help. Her immediate concern was that the injured dog was Lennon. Although she had no experience treating animals, she did have a medical background and might be able to assist in some way.

Racing across the yard, she found the door unlocked and let, herself in. Hearing voices down the hall, she called for Keaton, believing Mellie wouldn't be nearly as welcoming.

Keaton rounded the corner and met her.

"Is it Lennon?" she asked, her voice tight with worry.

"No."

Her relief was instantaneous.

"I was worried," Annie said. "I saw you carrying a dog."

His hands clenched her upper arms, his eyes delving into hers, looking at her like she was precious beyond measure. "I found him on the side of the road. He'd been hit by a car."

"Can I help?"

"It doesn't look good." His voice was tinged with sadness. "Mellie's with him now."

"She knows what to do?"

He nodded. "She's good in situations like this."

This apparently was a regular occurrence, which left her wondering about his involvement in animal rescue. He had brought her Ringo. It seemed Keaton's heart was as big as the rest of him. "You do this sort of thing often?" she asked.

He shrugged. "Often enough."

"You and Mellie?"

"I find hurt and neglected animals."

"And bring them to Mellie?"

"Mellie and Preston. He's at the animal shelter, but with limited funding, Preston can only do so much. Mellie has a gift with these animals. I can't really explain how she does it; she has this knack of soothing them, gaining their trust. First time I saw it, I couldn't believe my eyes."

"Keaton." Annie gasped. She cupped her hands against the sides of his face. It meant so much to her when he spoke in full sentences, as she knew it meant he trusted her. "I love hearing your voice."

His eyes narrowed, as if nothing had changed. "I always talk to you."

She wanted to ask him to continue talking for the simple pleasure of hearing his voice. This was a

186

wonderful display of his feelings for her, an indication that he was making himself vulnerable to her.

His eyes brightened with his smile. "I've been known to talk nonstop."

"Well, not to me. Not until this evening." She wanted to kiss him so he'd know how pleased she was.

Before she could, Mellie appeared in the doorway, her look decidedly unfriendly.

"He speaks to those he trusts. I'm not confident you deserve that trust. Prove me wrong and you know what it means."

Annie was about to assure her landlord, for yet another time, when the woman continued, clearly unhappy to see Annie in her home again. "Who said you could come into the house?"

"I came to see if I could help," she explained.

"It's too late. The dog died."

Annie's heart sank, and she noticed Keaton's shoulders slouch forward and his head drop.

"Oh no," she whispered. "I'm sorry."

Mellie wove her way through the maze that was her kitchen, washed her hands, and then filled the teapot with water before setting it on the burner.

Annie reached for Keaton's hand and gave it a squeeze, letting him know she shared his disappointment.

"Keaton can't save them all," Mellie muttered, "although God knows he tries."

Here was a completely different facet of this man Annie knew so little about. He looped his arm around her shoulders and brought her close to his side as

187

though seeking her warmth. Standing side by side with him, she again became aware of how tall and strong he was.

Seeing the affection between the two of them, Mellie shook her head and muttered, "Might as well stay now that you're here."

An invitation from Mellie! That was noteworthy. "I must be growing on you," she said, sharing a smile with Keaton.

"Not really," Mellie snapped.

"You like me," Annie insisted. "You just don't want to admit it."

"I like you about as much as I like going to the dentist."

"You go to the dentist?"

"No. Haven't been in years." She took three cups out of the sink, washed them, and set them on what little space was available on the kitchen counter.

Keaton left her side to reach for a pair of medical rubber gloves from a box on the table. It was buried amid piles of useless papers and would have gone unnoticed if he hadn't called her attention to it.

With her back to Annie, Mellie continued chatting. "If Keaton's talking to you, then I figure I'll give you a chance. Not that you deserve it."

"I did share my favorite books with you," Annie reminded her.

Mellie made a huffing noise to discount the gesture. She made it sound like those novels were little more than a nuisance to her.

188

While they were talking, Keaton left the kitchen and disappeared down the hall. Annie heard another door open and close.

"He went to bury the dog," Mellie explained before Annie could ask. "Does something to him every time he finds an animal too late to help. He brought in an abused dog a while back and I swear he had tears in his eyes."

"Did that dog make it?"

"He lived. Thankfully, Keaton reached him in time. Poor thing was skin and bones; he'd nearly been starved to death. He was in rough shape physically and psychologically. Kept him for weeks, gaining his trust. Didn't think he'd adjust. Preston helped. Found him a good home. Have to say, I miss having him around."

Annie had heard Preston's name mentioned several times but had never met the man. From conversations with Keaton, she understood his friend managed the local animal shelter.

"I can come by to visit if you're interested in having company on occasion." Annie was only half serious but hoped Mellie would take her up on the offer.

Mellie snorted. "I'd rather have an IRS audit."

Oh well, Annie had tried. The teakettle whistled, and Mellie poured the boiling water into a ceramic pot. "Didn't know you were such a jokester."

"Hey, I was serious."

"So was I. Was that teapot your grandmother's?" Annie asked.

Turning around so that her back was to her, Mellie nodded. "Grams loved her tea. She brewed a pot every afternoon; she and Gramps would sit on the porch together on the swing that he built. Funny thing was they didn't talk much — just sat and drank tea. Asked Gramps about it once and he told me that after fifty-five years of marriage, they'd discussed about everything that needed to be said."

Annie swallowed against the growing thickness in her throat. Her parents never would have the opportunity to grow old together. Yet another reminder that the tragedy had robbed her parents and Mike and his family of a future together.

Annie remembered a phone call she'd had with her sister-in-law only a few weeks before that Thanksgiving. Kelly mentioned that she and Mike were hoping to add to their family. For all anyone knew, Kelly might have been pregnant.

Tears welled in her eyes, and rather than embarrass herself, Annie blinked and glanced toward the door, ready to make an excuse to leave.

"Hey," Mellie said, "what's going on?" While the words were gruff, her voice wasn't.

"Sorry . . . I lost both my parents."

"Both? At the same time?"

Annie nodded. And swallowed against the hard knot in her throat.

"That's rough."

"Yeah, it is. I'd like to think they would have enjoyed time in their retirement years on the porch the way your grandparents did." Embarrassed now, Annie quickly added, "I need to get back . . . Sorry to rush off." She knew she sounded abrupt and panicky. Not wanting to explain anything more or give details, Annie hurried away.

She smeared the moisture across her cheeks, sniffling as she practically raced back to the cottage. Once inside, she fell with her back against the door. She took in deep, uneven breaths, hoping to quell her thoughts.

These bouts of tears came at the oddest times. A comment, a memory, just something little and seemingly meaningless and Annie would be tossed back emotionally to the first few weeks following the accident. When that happened, it was difficult to breathe. It was all she could do to hold herself together.

When she felt collected enough to move, she straightened, reached for a tissue, and blew her nose, her hands trembling. She couldn't begin to imagine what Mellie must be thinking. Later, when she was ready, she'd apologize and explain further. It wouldn't be soon, though. Annie avoided any discussion of the disaster; no one in this community was even aware of it, or how it continued to impact her life.

A knock sounded against her door. It could only be Keaton.

Opening it, she silently invited him inside and walked straight into his arms. He held her tightly against him, his thick arms wrapped completely around her, making her feel small and protected.

"Mellie said you lost your parents?"

Annie nodded, not wanting to talk about the tragedy. "Can you just hold me for a few minutes. No questions?"

His grip tightened slightly. "Of course."

"Thank you."

"If Mellie pressured you for details . . ."

"She didn't. Be quiet." Realizing how crazy it was to tell Keaton to keep silent, she started to laugh. The humor started low in her belly and worked its way up into her chest and finally escaped on a high-pitched sob that came out sounding like a braying donkey.

"Annie." Keaton sounded genuinely concerned now.

"Sorry, I'm fine. Really."

He led her to the sofa and sat them both down. "You don't sound like it."

"It's just funny," she said, still trying to control the urge to giggle.

It seemed impossible that he didn't see the irony of what she'd said. "Don't you see how ridiculous that was? Me asking *you* to be quiet?"

She could tell he was amused because he smiled, his mouth at the crown of her head. "Gotcha."

He did have her, in more ways than he realized.

"I'm sorry about the dog."

"Me too. I don't know what people think," he said, his voice raw with anger. "Because this is a beach town, tourists bring dogs and cats they no longer want and leave them here to fend for themselves. I can't even guess what these people think will happen to these animals."

Annie was horrified. "What? People do that?"

"More than anyone realizes. I do what I can. Preston helps. Mellie, too. People call and report seeing strays wandering around town. Preston doesn't have the time or the staff to go looking, so I do what I can. We try to find them before it's too late, but it takes time and effort."

"How do you locate them?" she asked, her heart hurting for those poor abandoned animals.

"Preston gets a report and lets me know the last place they were spotted. I set out food and then stay and wait, hoping to attract the animal so I can bring him into the shelter."

There was so much more to this man than she had ever realized. "Can I go with you sometime?"

He leaned away from her and she assumed he was looking to evaluate her sincerity. "I'd like that."

"I would, too." Any time spent with Keaton was good. She wanted to learn more about him, why he chose to speak so rarely, and what had led him to be a fearless advocate for animals.

His hold on her gradually loosened.

A chill came over her outside his arms, and she immediately felt the loss of his warmth and gentleness. His touch surprised her every time; he was unexpectedly tender for a man his size.

"You okay now?" he asked.

She nodded. "Did you rescue Lennon?" she wanted to know, hating the thought that anyone would heartlessly abandon a defenseless dog at the beach. She'd come to care about Keaton's lumbering companion.

"It was a few years back now. Found him in the nick of time."

"No," she cried, unable to bear the thought of Lennon being cast aside like unwanted garbage.

"It happens, Annie. And the horrors these animals suffer would break your heart."

"Let me go with you the next time."

"You have the stomach for this?"

"I don't know. I guess we'll find out."

"Okay, then. How about tomorrow night?"

"It's a date."

This wasn't exactly a night on the town, and yet she'd never looked forward to going out with any other man more than she did with Seth Keaton.

CHAPTER
NINETEEN

The next two nights Annie went out with Keaton on search-and-rescue missions. On the second night, by chance they found a feral mother cat who'd delivered her babies in a deserted drainage pipe. It took some effort for Keaton to cage her and to deliver the mother and litter to Preston at the animal shelter.

This was Annie's first time meeting Preston. He was a thin, wiry man with thick eyebrows and the kindest eyes she could ever remember seeing in a man.

"Annie," he said, greeting her cheerfully. "Heard about you."

She looked to Keaton and wondered under what context he had mentioned her.

"Not from him," Preston said, shaking his head. "Keaton's pretty tight-lipped about the people in his life, especially you. Guess he's nervous I'd try to steal you away," he teased, and then laughed. "Actually, it was Mellie who mentioned you."

"Mellie did?" Annie looked to Keaton and grinned proudly. "Told you I was growing on her."

Preston's thick brows bent upward. "She wants everyone to think she has a hard heart, but Keaton and I know better."

"I'm beginning to see her soft spots myself."

Preston gave Annie a tour of the shelter and she saw how hard he and his staff worked to locate good homes for the animals. She had Ringo, thanks to Keaton, and toyed with the idea of adopting one of the feral cat's litter once it was weaned. She'd wait and see if homes were found for them first.

It was late when they left the shelter. Annie leaned her head against Keaton's shoulder as he drove his pickup to the cottage, straining against the seatbelt.

"You're quiet this evening. Tired?" he asked.

"Not any more than usual. Just thinking about some things."

"Like?"

She couldn't discuss her work, and had continued to mull over Britt and the pregnancy. Since seeing the teenager at the clinic, Annie hadn't had a chance to talk to Britt, other than a few snippets of conversation in the mornings. Annie had noticed how pale she looked, and Annie feared she was barely holding it together. It wasn't only Britt, either. Annie had given a lot of thought to Teresa, too, and how best she could help her. She was a good person. Earlier in the week Annie received a note addressed to her at the clinic from Teresa, apologizing for Carl's behavior and thanking her for the job offer but that she would need to refuse.

Annie had other worries, too. Dr. Bainbridge was at retirement age and eager to slow down and travel with his wife. Recently he'd confided in her his concerns for the clinic and what would happen if he retired completely.

"What's on your mind?" Keaton asked. He seemed to enjoy having her lean against him and reached for her hand, giving it a gentle squeeze before entwining their fingers to encourage her confidence.

An idea had been brewing in her mind about Britt and Teresa, an idea in which Mellie would play a key role. Keaton would be a good sounding board, so she decided to discuss it with him.

"Who does Mellie let into the house?"

If Keaton found the question odd, he didn't mention it. "Me, Preston, and now you."

"You can't count me," she murmured. "I sort of let myself in." She smiled, thinking of how disgruntled Mellie became when Annie came inside uninvited.

"Yes, but you notice she didn't kick you out. If she wanted you out, it would have happened."

"Don't kid yourself; she was tempted," Annie said. Holding her breath for a moment, she plunged ahead. "I was shocked when I saw the condition of the kitchen."

"How so?"

"Is she a hoarder? I mean, all the junk and stuff she has piled all over the countertops and table."

Keaton's arm continued to hold her close to him, and she laid her head against his shoulder, treasuring these peaceful moments with him.

"If you think the kitchen is bad, you should see the rest of the house."

"Really?"

"She has more junk lying around than anyone I know."

Annie released a sigh. "The thought of clearing it all out probably overwhelms her."

"Don't know that she wants it gone."

"What if she did?" Annie wondered, watching him for any nonverbal clues to what he was thinking. "I could ask her."

Keaton snorted. "You going to volunteer to help her with it?"

Annie laughed. "No, but I know someone who could."

Keaton frowned. "Who?"

She broke away, and turned and looked at him square in the face. "Teresa."

"Who's Teresa?"

"Teresa Hoffert, Carl's wife. She cleans houses and she'd be perfect."

Annie had met a woman in Teresa's situation while working at the clinic in California. She had spoken frankly with the woman and asked what made her stay with a man who hurt her and her children, when there were shelters that would help her. What she'd learned surprised her. Not all women's shelters take adolescent males after a certain age, so this woman had no place to go where she could be safe. She made the difficult choice to stay with her husband. The problem had weighed heavily on Annie's mind. Many shelters in Washington had similar rules. Annie had reported the abuse, but the woman refused to press charges. She never saw or heard from her again, although from time to time she'd come to Annie's mind.

Teresa reminded her of the woman from California. If she could convince Mellie to let Teresa work for her, then Annie would have the opportunity to talk to Teresa and perhaps encourage her to get away from Carl. Although it was speculation on her part, Annie had the feeling that Mellie had been in a similar situation and had found the courage to break away.

"So, what do you think?" she asked eagerly.

Keaton didn't look convinced. "If Mellie would agree, and that's a big if."

That, of course, was the bigger question. "Yes, but if Mellie knew she was helping someone, she just might."

Keaton still had his doubts.

"I wanted her to clean for me, but as you might have guessed, Carl would never allow that. Teresa needs someone who will help her see that there's a way out of this abusive relationship. She feels trapped. If she works for Mellie, then I'd have the chance to spend time with her."

Keaton's frown deepened. "I don't think that's a good idea."

"Why not?" Personally, Annie thought it was brilliant.

Keaton's shoulder instantly tensed. "You'd be putting yourself at risk."

"Keaton, Teresa is —"

"Is married to an abuser," he finished for her. "He already slashed your tires. If he finds out you're talking to his wife, there's no telling what he'll do. Please, Annie, reconsider this. I appreciate your concern for this other woman, but you don't need to get involved. It's not your problem."

"Life is a risk, Keaton. I know what you're saying, but I want to help. It's like your rescue efforts with animals. This is my own attempt to help someone. You can understand that, can't you?"

He parked the truck outside the cottage, briefly closed his eyes, and nodded.

Annie grew more excited about the possibility of Mellie hiring Teresa. "I think the two women would be good for each other. Mellie needs her house cleaned and Teresa needs —"

"Mellie has issues, Annie," Keaton reminded her.

"We all have issues. I understand that the reasons that lead to her hoarding are complicated. It speaks of other issues Mellie has. I know she needs to address those if she's ever going to move on in her life. But Mellie needs a starting point, and if I can be a friend enough to get her to recognize it, then it's a win-win for everyone."

Keaton grew silent. He remained unconvinced. "I don't trust Carl. I don't want him getting anywhere near you."

"He won't," she told him, feeling more confident by the moment. "If Teresa works for Mellie, then I can also develop a relationship with her, and maybe help her."

"Annie . . ."

"Keaton, please trust me in this. I appreciate that you're concerned, but I have a good feeling that this could work to the benefit of both Mellie and Teresa. The potential is there if I can set everything in place."

"Mellie won't easily give up whatever she has in those boxes."

"Probably not," Annie agreed. It went without saying that Mellie letting someone else into her home would be a major obstacle, but Annie wasn't about to abandon the idea because it was difficult. Her one hope was that Mellie would be willing when she understood Teresa's circumstances.

"I'm glad you came with me," he said.

"I'm glad I came, too." She'd learned more about him in the two nights they'd been out than in all the time she'd known Keaton, and the more she discovered, the closer she felt to him. "Thank you for hearing me out. You know Mellie better than anyone. There's no guarantee any of this will work, but I feel the need to try."

Keaton didn't seem to have anything to add, yet she felt there was something on his mind. "You wanted to say something?" she asked.

He pressed his hand against the side of her face, his eyes delving into hers. "I wanted you to know I'm sorry to hear about your parents. I can only imagine how hard that must be for you and your brother to lose them both at the same time. Anytime you want to talk about it, I'm here."

Her brother. She didn't remember ever mentioning Mike, but she must have. She missed him dreadfully. Swallowing down the pain, she bit into her lower lip. "Thank you."

If she told anyone the full story of what had happened, it would be Keaton. But not tonight. To

201

bring that grief into their evening together would ruin the good feelings she had about being with him.

"You've never mentioned any brothers or sisters," she said, in an effort to turn the subject away from herself.

"There's just me. Mom died shortly after I was born."

"I'm sorry."

"Me too, My father is a brute."

His face tightened when he mentioned his father, and that look alone spoke more than a lengthy tirade. Keaton didn't need to explain to Annie that his father had physically abused him. The way he'd reacted when he'd learned she'd been threatened by Carl told her that nearly everything she'd suspected about his childhood was true.

"Is your father the reason you don't talk much to others?"

He nodded.

Her heart ached for him. Annie felt the need to show him how deeply she cared. Words were difficult and unnecessary; she understood, and she said it by framing his face between her hands. His eyes held hers as she leaned forward and pressed her lips to his.

Awkward as it was with him behind the steering wheel, Keaton's arms circled her, his mouth devouring hers. Keaton's kisses were unlike any others she'd experienced. He was her prince, although he hadn't come wrapped up in the traditional handsome package. To the rest of the world he was ungainly, and antisocial. Annie had been gifted with the ability to see him as others rarely had, and probably never had the chance to. His heart was good; he was kind and generous, talented and loveable.

Keaton broke off the kisses and buried his face in her neck, kissing her there, loving her with a gentleness that belied his strength and size.

"Go inside, Annie."

Her head was still trapped in a fog of desire. "What?" she asked.

"It would be best if you got out of the truck."

It took a moment for his words to make sense.

"If you don't get out of this truck in the next sixty seconds, I swear I'm not going to be able to resist making love to you."

Annie smiled. "Those are the sweetest words you've ever said to me, Seth Keaton."

"Annie, please, I am only so strong when it comes to you."

"Okay, okay." She opened the truck door and climbed out, blowing him a kiss as she hurried toward the cottage.

CHAPTER
TWENTY

Keaton took his lunch break from his most recent painting job. He worked as an independent contractor and had more work than he could handle. After he ate his sandwich, he drove over to the animal shelter. Earlier in the day, he'd asked Preston to drop groceries off to his father. As much as possible, Keaton avoided contact with his caustic parent. Still, he was concerned, as his father wasn't in the best of health. Keaton had long suspected the old man had cancer, although Seth Senior wouldn't admit it. Not to him, anyway.

The animal shelter was a cacophony of barking from the rescue dogs. The noise comforted him in ways he couldn't explain. Because he was often at the shelter, he recognized many of the volunteers who came to walk and feed the strays. Keaton found Preston in his office. His friend hated paperwork and put it off as long as he could. Apparently, the need had caught up with him, as it was rare to see Preston sitting.

His friend looked up when Keaton leaned against the doorjamb.

"How's he looking?" Keaton asked. Keaton didn't need to explain who he was asking about.

Preston's eyes revealed the answer. "Not good."

Keaton expected as much. "Don't suppose he's been to see Dr. Bainbridge?"

Preston leaned back in the chair. "Wouldn't tell me if he had."

Again, this didn't come as a shock. His old man was as stubborn as they came. Not much he could do about it.

Preston had done him a favor by checking on his father, and Keaton thought he would return it. "Mellie asked me to pick up a few things for her at the store. Don't suppose you'd like to make the delivery?" Knowing his friend had been in love with Mellie for years, this would be a good opportunity for Preston to spend time with her alone.

Preston's look resembled a man who had unexpectedly confronted a grizzly bear in the woods. "I . . . I don't think so."

"You're going to have to let go of the past one of these days," Keaton said, shaking his head. It was a shame Preston hadn't. The two of them would be good together. Soon after Mellie had returned, Preston had asked her out and had been harshly rejected. That was all it took to keep him from trying again.

"I will . . . *one of these days*," Preston said, repeating Keaton's words back at him. "You've been on me about Mellie ever since Annie showed up."

Keaton couldn't deny it.

"You stuck on her?" Preston asked.

"Pretty much." It wasn't like Keaton could hide it, knowing that Preston would see through the lie.

"Thought so," Preston replied. "She's what you need."

Keaton agreed and grinned, feeling a little foolish yet elated that she was in his life. He never expected his infatuation with her to develop into anything more than a few sketches of a girl he'd once met on the beach. He'd never been in love before, and the emotion made him leery. He couldn't help wondering if her attraction to him would last. He feared he was a novelty to Annie, and that when the time came, she would go back to her life in Seattle and leave him behind. The sooner he accepted it, the better it would be when it came time to let her go.

"You might want to check on your dad," Preston suggested, breaking into his thoughts. "He barely raised a fuss when I stopped by. That's not like him. Most always he tells me to take the groceries back because he doesn't need or want anything from you. He didn't do that this time."

Keaton could think of other ways to ruin a week besides visiting his father. But knowing that Preston wouldn't mention his father's failing health without cause, he decided to stop by when he'd finished work for the day.

Keaton didn't expect the visit to go well, and his dad didn't disappoint him. He arrived at about six, and after one hard knock on the door, Keaton let himself into the house. He found his father sitting in his recliner in front of the television.

206

The old man had once been as tall and big as Keaton. Over the years he'd lost two or three inches and was quite a bit lighter. His clothes hung on him from the recent weight loss. His eyes narrowed as he lowered the recliner and stood, confronting Keaton.

"What are you doing here?" the old man demanded loudly. His voice had lost its strength, and he wobbled slightly.

"Came to check on you."

"Don't want you here."

Keaton was accustomed to the lack of welcome, so it didn't faze him. "You need anything?"

"Yes. I need you to get out." Seth sank back into his recliner, nearly falling into the chair — he was that weak.

Keaton walked over and sat so he could get a better look at his father. His pallor was yellow, telling him the old man's liver wasn't functioning properly. "When was the last time you saw Dr. Bainbridge?"

"None of your business."

"He doesn't make house calls, you know."

"Leave me alone. I'll be dead soon enough."

Keaton ignored the comments. "If you need me to take you to an appointment, let me know."

"Wouldn't ask anything of you if I was dying, which I am, so go."

Knowing there was nothing more he could do, Keaton returned to his truck, where Lennon waited for him. He sat in the driver's seat for several minutes before he pulled away. This was the house where he'd been raised, where he'd lived most of his life, but it had never been a home. For whatever reason, his father had resented him from the day he was born. There'd been no love in that house, no caring.

Each visit left him feeling like a lead blanket had been placed over his head, dragging him down into the dark depths of depression. When this happened, he turned to his art. Over the years, he'd filled dozens of sketchbooks. About five years ago he'd started painting on canvases, many of which were stored in a back bedroom.

Thursday night, Keaton took Annie to the Concert in the Park. The city council provided entertainment each Thursday night for the community. These events were popular with the locals. Keaton had attended a few now and again, preferring to remain in the background. When he brought Annie, it was different. She was becoming known in the community and was making friends. The bleachers were full, so she spread a blanket on the crowded lawn. Annie refused to listen to his protest as she unpacked their dinner. Keaton had never felt comfortable in large groups. What surprised her was how many of the townsfolk greeted him by name. Lennon stretched out at his side and Annie was thoughtful enough to have packed turkey and thick tomato sandwiches for the two of them.

The entertainment that evening was a group of young musicians who played music from the Beatles. Annie sat in front of him between his outstretched legs, leaning her back against the broad expanse of his chest, bobbing her head to the musical beat. Lennon pressed his chin against her thigh, content.

Keaton had never experienced this sense of belonging before. For most of his life, he'd felt like an outcast. He'd always been the one on the outside of life, looking in, pretending not to care. Being with Annie was a good feeling. Having her this close, snuggled up against him, enjoying the sounds of the sixties, was about as close to heaven as he ever expected to get. He reached out and petted Lennon's head, his heart full.

After the concert, Annie and Keaton lingered in the park.

"What was it that Ed from the pharmacy said earlier?" she asked as she gathered the remains of their picnic basket. "You know, about when that scene would be finished?"

Keaton hesitated. He'd never mentioned the murals to Annie. Several people knew that Keaton was the artist who'd painted the murals in town. He didn't sign his name to the artwork. No need. He wasn't looking for the recognition. He painted for the sheer joy of it, of creating something beautiful the community could be proud of.

She paused and looked at him expectantly.

"Best show you," he said, rather than explain.

Walking hand-in-hand, they headed toward Center Street and turned one block off the main drive until they faced the corner around from the bank building. He stopped and stood directly in front of her.

"What are we doing here?" she asked, frowning.

He grinned, slightly embarrassed. "I paint."

"Yes, I know you're a painter," Annie commented, sounding confused. "It's how you make your living."

"Yes," he agreed. "But I paint more than just walls and houses."

Moving around the corner, they stood in front of the half-finished mural on the back side of the bank. Keaton waited for her reaction. Annie stared at the artwork and then looked at him.

Slowly her mouth sagged open. "Are you telling me you painted this?" Her voice rose half an octave with the question.

He nodded, enjoying her surprise.

"The other murals in town? You did those?"

He nodded a second time.

Gesturing toward the wall, she looked dumbfounded. "This is all *your* work?"

"It is."

Her hand flew to her heart. "Keaton, they're . . . they're wonderful."

Her praise embarrassed him, and he could feel his mouth forming an involuntary smile. "Thanks."

"Wait," she said, her arm flying out and pointing at him. "The mural by the real estate office. The woman with the single braid who's by the ocean. That's me, isn't it?"

Keaton hadn't forgotten, even though he'd painted it years earlier. "Yes."

"But that was already painted before I moved here. I asked about it and was told it's been there four or five years."

"Yes."

She stared at him, not knowing what to say.

"I met you on the beach when you were fourteen or so," he explained.

Her forehead wrinkled. "So that was how you knew I had a brother. Keaton, I feel dreadful, I don't remember meeting you."

"I know."

"Tell me about it. When did we meet? Where?"

He shook his head. "It's not important."

"It is to me," she argued. "You must have taken my picture to get my features so perfect. When I first saw the mural, it looked so much like me I was shocked."

He was uncomfortable explaining what he'd done. "I sketched you that summer."

This news seemed to fluster her. "I wish I could remember meeting you."

He grinned. "It was just the one time, and only briefly. Don't worry. I remembered you."

Using both hands, she pushed the hair away from her face. "You recognized me when I came into the real estate office after thirteen years?"

"Before. Earlier, on the beach with Lennon, before you moved here."

"After all those years?"

He nodded, watching her closely. She couldn't seem to take her eyes off the scene. Like several of his others, it was a scene from the beach with the waves heaving toward the sand. Seashells littered the beach and kites were flying overhead against the backdrop of a bright summer day, with lazy clouds dotting the horizon.

"Keaton, this is . . . amazing." She couldn't seem to find the words to adequately express herself. Keaton watched as she opened and closed her mouth several times and then shook her head. "You're so talented."

"Thank you."

She stared up at him, seeing him through fresh eyes. "Wow. I don't know what to say."

"You don't need to say anything." He enjoyed surprising her, and because he found her adorable, he leaned down and kissed her. When they broke apart, Annie looked at him, ready to melt into a puddle at his feet. He saw the look of wonder in her eyes, and it demanded all the restraint he could muster not to spend what remained of the evening making love to her.

"You are far and away the most amazing person I've ever met," Annie whispered.

Keaton basked in her praise. He so rarely received approval that he didn't know how to react to it. Once again, he struggled with the need to pull her back into his arms and kiss her senseless.

With what could be described only as sheer force of will, he moved away from her and led her back to where he'd parked his truck.

"You make me look beautiful," she said as they strolled along, the wind buffeting them. The sun was going down, casting a warm glow reflecting off the water.

"That's how I see you."

She looked up, and he noticed she had tears in her eyes. "Thank you, Keaton."

212

Little did she understand that he should be the one thanking her. For the first time in his life, he felt accepted and loved.

CHAPTER
TWENTY-ONE

Mellie called Saturday morning just as Annie was watering her garden. She'd planted lettuce and already had cuttings enough to share.

"I finished those books you brought over," Mellie announced.

"Already?" The woman had apparently spent every spare moment reading through the thirty paperback novels.

"I don't suppose you have a few more," her friend asked, ignoring Annie's comment. "But only if you're looking for someone to take them off your hands," she added, acting like she was doing Annie a favor.

"Sure," she said, mentally going through her bookshelf. She'd already given the majority of what she had to Mellie. However, this would be a great time to approach her about hiring Teresa as her housekeeper.

Annie turned her back to the house on the off-chance Mellie was watching her out the window. She didn't want the other woman to see her struggling to hold back a smile.

"I was getting ready to cut you some fresh lettuce from the garden. Would you like some of that, too?" Annie asked, remembering that her mother let the lettuce set in saltwater, to clean it of any bugs. She'd do that, too, before passing it on to Mellie.

"You can bring that to me with those books."

"Of course. Glad to do it."

"What time are you coming?" Mellie wanted to know.

My, my, she was eager. "What time are you receiving guests?"

"Ha, ha. Very funny. Just bring me those books and some of that lettuce."

"Deal. Besides, I have something I want to ask you."

"About?" Mellie demanded.

"I'll let you know later."

"Tell me now. I'm not very patient."

Annie grinned. "Really. I hadn't noticed."

"Don't keep me waiting."

It was hard not to laugh out loud. "I'll be over in a few and then you'll know all."

Mellie continued to grumble as Annie disconnected.

Their relationship was developing nicely. On the nights that Annie had been out with Keaton, they'd stopped off to check in with Mellie at the end of their searches. Annie could tell that Mellie was becoming more accustomed to having her around. At one point, Mellie had gone so far as to tell Annie that she was good for Keaton.

With a sense of purpose, Annie washed the lettuce and gathered it in a plastic bag along with a few novels she believed Mellie would enjoy, and headed across the yard. To be polite, she knocked once, and then let herself in the door off the kitchen, unlocking the various devices.

"Mellie," she called out, although she suspected the woman was keenly aware Annie was already in the house. The cat sat on the windowsill, soaking up the sunshine. Trying to be helpful, she set the crisp lettuce inside the refrigerator. When she turned around, she found Mellie standing in the doorway that led to the hall, watching.

"What are you doing snooping in my refrigerator?" she demanded.

"Just putting the lettuce away," Annie returned, holding up her hands as if Mellie had a gun pointed at her.

"I'm not feeding you, if that's what you think."

"I wouldn't dream of imposing."

"Did you bring the books?"

"I did." She pointed at the stack on the kitchen table. It was little wonder that Mellie had missed seeing them, with all the other junk that was accumulated there. "Some great stories, too."

"You have something on your mind." Mellie remained on the other side of the room, like she was afraid of what Annie had to say.

Annie ignored the question. "So, you enjoyed the others?"

Mellie shrugged, unwilling to admit it. "They were okay. Noticed a couple mysteries, too. Not bad. Kept me entertained." Stepping forward, she walked over to the table and placed her hands against the back of one of the kitchen chairs and frowned.

216

"You going to tell me what's on your mind or are you going to beat around the bush all day?"

Annie made a point of looking around the kitchen. "Have you ever thought about hiring a housekeeper?" she asked.

"No." Her response was flat and sharp.

"Organizing everything here must feel overwhelming."

"Never said I wanted anything organized. I don't like strangers in my house, and that includes you."

Annie reached for the chair directly across from Mellie, her fingers curving over the back of it. She had to approach this carefully. "I met Teresa Hoffert. Do you know her?"

"No, and I don't care to."

Annie bit into her lower lip. "She's the sole support for her family and cleans houses for a living."

"I'm not running a charity out of here. Hire her yourself if you want to do her a favor." Mellie didn't appear the least bit moved.

"I can't. I made her husband angry and he forbade her to work for me."

"Her husband?" Mellie frowned. "This have anything to do with your slashed tires?"

"Yeah. I'm pretty sure it was him."

Mellie's eyes sparked with anger.

Annie exhaled. This next part was tricky. "He's abusing her. I don't have positive proof, but I've seen the evidence."

Crossing her arms, Mellie grew thoughtful. "She ever reported him to the sheriff?"

"No." Her hands tightened around the back of the chair until her fingers were white. "I doubt she will. Okay, the truth is, I thought if Teresa started working for you as a housekeeper, that I'd have the chance to talk to her about her options. She doesn't need to stay in this marriage, but Carl has her emotionally beaten down to the point where she's terrified to do anything to defy him."

Mellie said nothing, but Annie could see that she was considering what Annie had said.

"It's a win-win for you both," Annie said quickly, before Mellie could refuse. "You'd get the help you need, and what she earns with you would help Teresa support her family."

"How are you planning to talk to her?"

"I'll find an excuse to be outside while she's at the house. We can both subtly talk to her, help her build up confidence."

Annie waited, but Mellie didn't appear to have anything to say.

"Will you consider it?" she asked, her heart racing.

"Maybe. But don't count on it."

Annie couldn't ask for anything more than that. She reached for a slip of paper and set it down on top of one of the boxes. "This is Teresa's phone number, in case you decide to hire her."

Having had her say, Annie rubbed her palms together and was ready to leave.

"You should know, Keaton mentioned Teresa yesterday."

218

"He did?" He hadn't said one word since their conversation a week earlier.

"Never had him recommend anyone before. Not like him. Seems you put him up to it."

Annie grinned. "I might have mentioned it to him."

"Time for you to leave."

"Okay. I appreciate you hearing me out." All she could do now was pray the arrangement between the two worked the way she hoped.

After spending time in her garden, Annie showered, changed clothes, and decided to take a walk along the beach. She enjoyed these walks, but she had an ulterior motive. She wanted to see Keaton, so she sent him a text.

Meet me at the beach.

Give me twenty.

Perfect.

Annie walked barefoot along the shore, and she saw Lennon racing toward her before Keaton came into view. Lennon raced past her, chasing a flock of seagulls that flew off.

Walking straight to Keaton, Annie hugged him close.

"What's that for?" he asked, his arms circling her shoulders as he smiled down on her.

"Mellie said you recommended Teresa."

He reached for her hand and they slowly started walking down the sandy shoreline.

"I might have said something. Nothing much. I figured with Mellie, the less said, the better."

"Thank you."

"It was . . ."

The rest of what he intended to say was lost when three teenage boys raced toward them on motor scooters, their wheels spitting up sand and scattering seagulls. The noise cut off any chance of conversation.

As they approached, the teenagers reduced their speed. Annie noticed that Keaton held her protectively by his side, placing his arm around her. She didn't recognize any of the youths, although they were older, probably close to Britt's age.

"Hey," the blond-haired one shouted out, and waved as they roared past, kicking up sand in their wake.

Seeing that they were friendly, Annie waved back.

"Hey," Keaton called back and chuckled.

It took her a moment to realize the boys knew Keaton. "You know these boys?" she asked.

Keaton nodded and didn't explain further. She narrowed her eyes at him, waiting. He grinned. "They're part of the school wrestling team. I help the coach out from time to time."

"You wrestle?"

"I did years ago. No longer."

"But you coach."

"Some," he said again, without elaborating.

There was more to this man than Annie ever suspected. He wasn't one to brag about himself, and he went out of his way to downplay his skills.

"You are a man of many talents, Seth Keaton," she said, and her heart melted a little as she leaned in to him, playfully bouncing her shoulder against his side.

They continued walking with Lennon racing ahead. Annie enjoyed tossing a stick for him to fetch. She noticed Keaton watching her and smiling. She didn't remember ever seeing him smile that much, and it did her heart good.

She was busy with Lennon when she noticed that Keaton had stopped. When she straightened, she saw that Carl Hoffert stood no more than a few feet away. Carl looked past Keaton and focused his gaze on her. Unafraid, Annie straightened and squared her shoulders.

Keaton stood like a wall between them. Only a fool would threaten her with Keaton by her side.

"Hello, Carl," she said.

Britt's stepfather pointed his finger at her. "Keep him away from me."

She looked at Keaton, whose eyes had narrowed menacingly.

"I think Keaton is the least of your worries, Carl."

"Just keep him away from me. Understand?"

"Is that all you want to say?" she asked.

"Yes," Carl said, backing away and nearly stumbling in the process. "Tell him to stay the hell away from me."

Annie looked from one man to the other. Apparently, far more was going on than she knew.

Far, far more.

CHAPTER
TWENTY-TWO

Keaton knew Annie was upset after the confrontation on the beach with Carl Hoffert. No way was Keaton going to let Carl walk away scot-free after he'd slashed Annie's tires. He was determined that nothing even close to that would happen again. There was only one way for Carl to get the message, which meant Keaton openly confronting him, as he'd done. Then and only then would Carl understand Annie and Carl's wife and family were off-limits.

Of course, Keaton could have sat back and waited for the sheriff to act, but Sheriff Terrance, being a good man, was bound by law. The sheriff figured Carl was responsible for the damage to Annie's car. Carl had as much as admitted it with his earlier threat. Unfortunately, without proof, no legal action could be taken.

Getting the desired results had been a matter of simply paying Carl a visit, which Keaton had done a few days earlier. His confrontation with Carl had been classic. Keaton had waited until Britt and Logan had left for school and Teresa had gone to work. Carl was home alone.

Keaton let himself into the house without knocking or ringing the doorbell. He wasn't surprised to find Carl had started drinking when it was barely nine-thirty in the morning. With an open bottle of whiskey, Carl had sat at the kitchen table with a shot glass in his hand. For as big as Keaton was, he hadn't made a sound. He'd surprised Carl and held him by the scruff of his neck, lifting him out of the chair. Carl's feet dangled above the linoleum floor.

Being a man of few words, he'd looked Carl in the eye, their faces so close their noses nearly touched. Carl stared at him in wide-eyed horror and seemed unable to find his voice.

"Don't go near Annie again," Keaton said.

Carl had nodded.

But Keaton wasn't finished. "You hurt Logan and I will do to you double what you do to him." This wasn't an idle threat.

Carl started to kick his feet and argue before Keaton increased the strength of his hold, tightening the grip on his neck. That shut him up in quick order.

"If you lay a finger on Teresa, Britt, or Annie, the same, but far worse, will happen to you." Much worse. Keaton wasn't a violent man, except when it came to a man who abused women, children, or animals.

Carl's eyes looked like they were about to bug out of his head.

"You understand me?"

Carl tried to nod but was unable to until Keaton loosened his grip.

223

When he set the man back on his feet, Carl's hands immediately went to his throat, and he made a coughing sound.

Keaton turned to leave but caught a reflection in the window. Carl had reached for the bottle of whiskey to use it as a weapon. With a single shove, Keaton wrestled the bottle out of his hand and knocked the other man to the floor. He emptied the contents down the sink. From Carl's position on the cracked linoleum, he cried out in protest.

Before he left, Keaton stood over him again, glaring down on the weakling.

To be certain Carl wasn't tempted to try anything else against Annie or his family, Keaton occasionally followed the man, letting his presence be threat enough. He wanted to let Carl know he was being closely watched and if he dared to even think about retaliation toward Annie there would be a price to pay.

What Keaton hadn't anticipated was Carl coming to Annie, looking for protection. The coward had no trouble hitting his wife and then running to another woman for help. Keaton had no intention of letting him anywhere close to Annie.

A few shell-shocked moments followed the confrontation. Annie remained strangely quiet. Sneaking looks at her while waiting for her to say something, anything, Keaton grew edgy, worried what she must be thinking.

Annie seemed to need time to mull over her feelings. He didn't blame her. She'd never seen this side of him, and she didn't know what he was capable of.

He noticed that she no longer held on to his hand and she'd stopped playing fetch with Lennon. By now Keaton knew her well enough that he could almost read her mind. Her body language told him she wasn't happy with what he'd done, and at the same time, she was grateful Carl feared the consequences.

When she spoke, it was in the form of a question. "Are you going to tell me what you did?"

"No."

"Why not?"

"I'd rather not involve you."

"Keaton, I'm already involved."

If Carl decided to press assault charges against him, the less Annie knew, the better. It was highly unlikely Carl would contact the law, though.

"I wish you hadn't threatened Carl."

He nodded, growing silent. He missed her touch, had grown addicted to it. Nothing terrified him more than losing her because she was afraid he was a violent man. Yet, given the option, he wouldn't change a thing. Carl needed to know there would be consequences if he ever tried to get close to Annie again.

She looked prepared to say more when her phone buzzed. She glanced at it with an irritated look, but once she read the name her features relaxed.

"Trevor . . . hi."

Trevor. Who is Trevor? Keaton wondered.

Holding the phone to her ear, Annie walked away from Keaton. If she wanted to keep him from listening to the conversation, that didn't help. He could still hear, albeit only one side of it. He caught the gist of the call right away. Trevor appeared to be someone she knew from when she'd lived in California.

An old boyfriend?

"You're coming to Seattle?" Annie repeated. She frowned and didn't look overly pleased with the information. "When?"

Keaton wasn't a jealous man, but then he'd never cared about a woman as strongly as he did about Annie. His mind started spinning with doubts. Unfamiliar with these feelings, he did his best to hide them. Annie was new ground for him, caring for someone the way he did, and the uncertainty twisted his gut.

Annie ended the conversation after only a few minutes. She looked over at him.

"That was a friend of mine from California."

"Trevor."

"Yes, Trevor."

She didn't offer any other information, so he mentioned what he'd heard. "He's coming to visit?"

Looking uncomfortable, Annie nodded. "He's been talking to my cousin, Gabby. She's worried about me. I made the mistake of telling her about what Carl did to my tires. She wants me to take my next free weekend and come back to Seattle."

His stomach clenched. His biggest fear when it came to Annie was that she'd grow bored with life in Oceanside and would eventually move back to either Seattle or Los Angeles. He knew from previous conversations that Annie and her cousin were close. At some point, he would need to let her go. But at least he had this year, and he was determined to treasure each day.

"So Trevor is coming to Seattle?" he said, hoping to sound casual and unconcerned. "I suppose you'll want to get away for a weekend while Trevor's in town."

"Probably not. Dr. Bainbridge needs me on standby for the weekends I don't work."

This must be a recent development. "Standby?"

"It's complicated . . . He's working more hours than he wants already." She didn't elaborate, and Keaton didn't press for an explanation.

They walked along the beach for several moments, the silence stretching between them. The tightness in his chest didn't ease. He felt Annie stealing looks at him, which he chose to ignore.

"You've gone quiet," Annie commented.

"I've been silent for a good portion of my life," he reminded her, keeping his eyes trained on the ocean waves as they slid against the smooth, glistening shore, leaving a foam trail in their wake. Being close to the water soothed him. He couldn't get the thought of Annie moving away out of his mind. His gut clenched just thinking about it.

"You don't have a problem talking to me, though. What are you thinking, Keaton? You look like you're carrying the weight of the world. Is it Trevor?"

"No," he said, shaking his head. He forced himself to smile and gave her hand a gentle squeeze. "All is well. No worries."

He doubted she believed him, but she didn't press the issue, and Keaton was grateful. When the time came, he'd have to steel himself and let her go, and be grateful she had been in his life, no matter how limited the time.

They continued walking, farther than usual. The tide was going out, and Annie bent down to retrieve a starfish.

"Have you ever been in love?" he asked, wanting to know.

She took her time answering, tossing the starfish back into the water. "I thought I was."

"When?"

"In college."

Maybe he shouldn't pry, but he was curious. Annie had shared very little of her life with him, which left him wondering, even if it didn't matter. But love. This was important, and he hoped she would fill in the details. "What happened?" he asked.

She shrugged, acting like it wasn't a big deal. "He broke up with me."

Keaton snickered. "He broke up with you? The man must have been nuts."

Annie leaned in to him the way she did when he said or did something she especially liked. Keaton treasured those little shoulder bumps of hers. Actually, he treasured everything about Annie.

"It hurt at the time. I was devastated, but in retrospect it was for the best. We weren't right for each other."

"Did he give you a reason?"

"None that made sense. We'd grown apart, I suppose, although I didn't realize it at the time. If I had, I might have noticed he'd fallen for someone else. What hurt most was seeing him with another girl just a few days after he broke it off."

Pain leaked into her voice. She'd downplayed how difficult this time had been for her. Reading between the lines, Keaton recognized this had been a pivotal moment for Annie. This college relationship had changed her.

"What about you?" she asked, in what he believed was an attempt to steer the conversation away from her.

"In love?"

"Yes, silly. Have you ever been in love?"

"Don't know."

She laughed. "You don't know?"

"Don't know," he reaffirmed. "There was a girl in high school once that I liked."

"What was her name?"

"Doesn't matter."

"Does too," she countered, smiling. She apparently was enjoying this. "I want to know her name."

"Shelly."

"Shelly," she repeated. "Does Shelly still live in Oceanside?"

"No. She moved after high school and went away to college. I haven't seen her since."

"Okay, tell me about you and Shelly."

This made him uncomfortable, but because Annie asked, he would tell her. "I thought she was pretty. She was kind to me, when others weren't." The less said about the teasing and name-calling, the better.

"Did the two of you date?"

"No." He'd barely said more than a few words to her the entire time they were in school. Those early teen years had been painful ones for Keaton. His one outlet had been wrestling, and he'd been good. Good enough to earn the right to compete at state. Then he'd got in trouble by defending Preston, and lost the opportunity to play sports.

"Did you ask her out on a date?" Annie wanted to know next.

"No."

"Never?" she asked, shocked. She shook her head in disbelief.

"Never," he repeated, although he'd wanted to ask her in the worst way until he overheard someone mentioning how Shelly had a soft heart. After hearing that, Keaton figured she was being kind because that was her nature. In their senior year, she dated one of the popular guys and he realized she was out of his league.

"In other words, you loved Shelly from afar?"

"I guess."

"She's the only one?"

Keaton locked eyes with Annie and held his breath for a moment before he confessed. "Until you."

"Me? Oh Keaton," she cried, her face full of emotion, "I don't know what I've done to deserve you."

He was the lucky one. Turning to her, he captured her face between his hands and lowered his mouth to hers. Even now, he found it hard to believe that someone as perfect and as beautiful as Annie Marlow would ever be interested in him. It'd taken a single phone call to Annie from a California friend to remind him that he shouldn't let his heart get too attached to her.

CHAPTER
TWENTY-THREE

With her grocery cart at hand, Annie headed to the checkout section and stood in line, waiting her turn. She glanced at the headlines of a bunch of magazines in front of the cash register and rolled her eyes at the latest rumors of divorces and infidelities. While living in California she had occasionally caught glimpses of celebrities. It'd become a game with her friends to talk about celebrity sightings. Once, Stephanie had dragged Annie to a location site for a television series, wasting an entire afternoon, hoping for a chance to see the actors. It'd been fun and a little crazy. That was the silly way she'd spent her time before the tragedy. It all seemed frivolous and a waste now.

As she set her items on the conveyer belt, she looked at the cashier and discovered that the woman looked vaguely familiar. Then she remembered: It was Becca, the desperate young wife who had come to the clinic, convinced she was pregnant.

From the way her eyes widened, Becca recognized Annie, too.

Not wanting Becca to be self-conscious or embarrassed, Annie started a friendly conversation. "I see the blueberries are on sale." She set two boxes on the conveyer belt.

"Yes, they're a popular item," Becca said as she slid the box of blueberries over the barcode reader. She kept her eyes down as she scanned. "I'm glad to see you again."

"You too," Annie returned.

"I saw you in the store shopping before but didn't have a chance to thank you for being so kind and patient with me that day."

"There's no need," Annie said, as she slid her debit card through the machine. "I understood your frustration."

"You were wonderful and calm, when I was nearly hysterical." She bit into her lower lip. "I want to be a mother so badly, but it doesn't seem to be in the cards for me and Lucas."

The pain in her voice touched Annie's heart. With everything in her, Annie wanted to help, but there was nothing more she could do.

"My husband and I decided to apply with an adoption agency. We were told it might take a few years."

Becca did her best to sound positive, but Annie could feel the other woman's heartache as clearly as she had that morning in the clinic.

"That's wonderful. I hope you don't need to wait long."

"Me too. We'll be good parents," she continued, as she bagged Annie's purchases.

Annie collected her groceries and set them in the cart. "If there's anything I can do, please let me know."

Becca nodded. "I will. Thank you again for being kind and for understanding."

Annie felt the strongest urge to hug Becca but didn't want to make her feel uncomfortable. She lingered for a moment, unsure what more she could say, before pushing her cart out the door and to the parking lot.

Once she was home, Annie couldn't get Becca out of her mind. She put away her groceries and took the extra box of blueberries and washed them. She'd bought them for Mellie, thinking her landlord might enjoy fresh blueberries. Without giving Mellie warning, Annie carried the bowl over to the big house.

Over the last week Annie had spent quite a bit of time with Mellie. Despite her dour mood, Mellie didn't seem to mind her infrequent visits. With each visit, Annie found an excuse to bring up Teresa's name, although she doubted that her friend appreciated her less-than-subtle hints.

Annie knocked and then let herself in the house. "Mellie," she called out.

"In here."

"In here" turned out to be what had once been the living room. It was hard to tell what it was, with the mess collected all about the room. Annie found her landlord sitting in a recliner with her feet up and a book in her hands.

"Come right in," she muttered sarcastically. "Feel free to make yourself at home."

Annie looked around her. "I would if I could find a place to sit."

"Ever think that might be the reason I keep those boxes on the chairs? I don't welcome company, not that you've taken the hint. And don't you use this as an excuse to bring up that housekeeper again."

Seeing that Mellie had made her point, Annie said, "I brought you some blueberries. They were on sale. I set them in the kitchen."

Mellie's look soured, trying to act like those berries were a major inconvenience.

"Your grandmother grew blueberries," Annie reminded her.

"You think I don't know that?"

"I didn't think you remembered."

"Of course I remember. Now Keaton's out there, digging through those brambles, cutting away years of thorny vines on a search to find those bushes again. He's so head over heels for you, he'd do just about anything you asked."

Annie couldn't hold back a smile. Together, Annie and Keaton had worked tirelessly clearing the area. Annie had the scratches and cuts on her arms to prove it. Keaton, too, even though he wore gardening gloves and long sleeves. It was a hellish task, but they'd been rewarded to find the bushes. With a little TLC, the bushes might have a chance to bear fruit again the following year.

"I suppose he did most of that work." Disapproval dripped from her words like melting wax.

"I helped." Annie had spent nearly every available minute outside in her garden and trimming away those pesky vines. Keaton, however, had done most of the work.

Mellie studied her. "Don't suppose you know it's his birthday this week."

"Keaton's?" Annie asked. He wasn't one to mention something like that. It surprised her that he would let Mellie know. "He told you?"

"No. Saw it on his driver's license. Not telling you how I happened to look inside his wallet, either. That's none of your business."

Telling Mellie that it wasn't her business wasn't something Annie felt she should mention. The only way Annie could think that Mellie had pulled it off was if Keaton had left his wallet behind and she had snuck a peek.

"Let's surprise him," Annie suggested, an idea quickly taking shape. "I'll get him a cake and balloons."

At first Annie thought Mellie would put up a fuss and object. "He likes ice cream. Vanilla."

"Of course, ice cream. I'll take care of all that, too. You can make up an excuse to get him to the house, and we'll surprise him."

From Mellie's surly look, Annie was afraid she was going to refuse to get involved. "You'd do that for him?" she demanded.

"Totally." Throwing him a surprise birthday party was minor compared to everything he'd done for her.

"Sit down," Mellie ordered, waving her arm in the general area. "You make me nervous standing over me like that. Move that stack of magazines off the ottoman."

It took Annie a minute to find the ottoman among all the accumulated boxes and things Mellie had stacked about the room.

"Why do you keep all these old magazines?" she asked, lifting away one box after another.

"They belonged to my grandmother."

"She's not going to read them again," Annie pointed out with a huff. The magazines were downright heavy.

"I know that. Cleared out all her stuff a long time ago, just haven't had time to do away with it."

"If you had help . . ."

"I told you not to mention that housekeeper again."

"All right, all right."

Shifting another box to the floor, Annie heaved a sigh. If the kitchen was crowded, the living room was twice as bad. The only clear space was the overstuffed chair where Mellie sat. A protective wall of boxes surrounded her. She felt like she was sitting in a grotto. Annie guessed that was the way Mellie liked it.

Once she found the ottoman, Annie sat down, ignoring the dust that was stirring the air. This was the first time Mellie had invited her to stay and chat.

Mellie set the book down on her lap, spine open. "I didn't like you much when you first moved here," she said.

"I sort of guessed as much," Annie replied, doing her best to hold back a smile.

Mellie snickered. "Don't be sarcastic. I'm trying to tell you something important. Like I was saying, I wasn't thrilled with you living in the cottage. Didn't like the idea of anyone being there. Keaton changed my mind, which wasn't easy. Against my better judgment, I gave in. In the short time you've been here, I've noticed some things."

"Oh?" Annie hoped it was for the good.

"Never saw Keaton smile until he met you. Don't think he had much reason. I remembered him from school. Always tried to remain in the background, which was nuts, seeing how big he is. He never said much. He hated being called on in class. His face would get as red as raspberries. The kids teased him unmercifully. He used to get into fights, lose his temper, but all that changed after the incident with Preston."

"What incident?"

"Not my story to tell. You can ask him about it."

"Okay." Annie listened intently, happy to know more about his earlier years. He hadn't said much, so she was left to speculate.

"Now you want to make something of his birthday. I don't suppose anyone ever has."

That was what Annie suspected.

"I have several reasons why I didn't want you around," she continued. "As you might have noticed, I don't like many people, and the minute I saw you, I knew you were going to be an irritation."

"Am I?"

"Oh yes. You started in on me right away, wanting to do this and that. Making demands and asking me questions I didn't want to answer."

Annie had to admit that Mellie was right. Only a week had gone by before Annie had asked Mellie if she could put in the garden.

"You're a constant nuisance."

Annie sat silently with her hands pressed between her thighs while she waited for Mellie to finish.

"If that wasn't bad enough, to insult me further, you keep suggesting I could use a housekeeper." She made a grumbling sound.

"The least you could do is meet Teresa."

"Ha, ha. I already have."

"You have?

"Yes, and she starts Monday."

In her excitement, Annie nearly leapt off the ottoman. It demanded self-control to remain seated.

"On a trial basis," Mellie added. "I told her I'd start her with three hours a week. I remember her from school, too. She was a senior when I was a freshman. She's much thinner now."

"Teresa's great."

"So you keep telling me. I made sure she understood she's to keep her hands off my grandparents' things. I'll deal with all that when I'm ready. There's a little dust here and there she can deal with and a few other household tasks I don't enjoy."

"I know she'll do a good job."

"She'd better. Far as I'm concerned, she needs to prove herself to me." Her frown deepened.

"Teresa will be respectful."

Mellie gave an unladylike snort. "Time will tell."

Annie found it impossible to hold back her excitement. "I'm so pleased, Mellie. It means a lot that you're willing to give her a shot. I'll have a chance to talk to her, to encourage her."

"Does that mean you're going to make yourself even more of a pest than you already are?" she asked.

Annie couldn't deny it. "Probably."

Mellie rolled her eyes and looked toward the ceiling. "I was afraid of that."

Pressing her hand over her heart, Annie pretended to be deeply hurt. "You wound me."

"Ha. Your hide is as thick as leather. Same as Keaton's."

The remark made Annie think about the party they were planning for Keaton. "Should we invite Preston?"

Mellie let the question hang in the air. "I suppose it wouldn't hurt."

"Do you want me to ask him, or would you rather touch base with him?"

"I'll do it."

Mellie's willingness surprised her, and Annie wondered if it was possible that she had feelings for Keaton's friend. One way to find out was to ask. "Does he have a wife? It would be rude to exclude her."

"No. He never married."

Well, that, too, was interesting.

They settled on a Sunday afternoon for Keaton's party. Annie was grateful for the opportunity to make his birthday special.

"You gonna buy the cake?" Mellie asked. "Or bake it yourself?"

"I'll bake it; no guarantees how it will turn out, though." She'd do what she could and hope for the best.

Mellie nodded approvingly and then shook her head and grumbled under her breath.

"What?" Annie asked, not knowing what she'd said to set the woman off.

Mellie set her book aside. "That's the problem."

"What is?"

"You."

Annie didn't have a clue what she'd done.

"You," Mellie said. "Bringing me blueberries, supplying me with books, showing kindness to Keaton. Not what I expected. Not sure I like it, either."

"Come on, Mellie, admit it. I'm growing on you."

She shook her head, though denial was already on her lips when she broke into a rusty, almost painful smile.

"Okay, fair enough. You're growing on me."

CHAPTER
TWENTY-FOUR

Something was up with Mellie. Keaton heard it in her voice when she called to ask him to stop by the house. In all the years he'd known her, she'd never once actually *invited* him to her home, other than when she needed something. This wasn't the first change he'd noticed in Mellie since Annie's arrival.

In fact, he'd begun to think Annie might be the force behind Mellie's transformation. She'd listened to Annie and had hired the housekeeper, which astonished him. He found it shocking that Mellie would agree to let anyone touch her stuff. Whether Mellie knew it or not, she was a hoarder. Her house was filled to the rafters with what her grandparents had accumulated over the years.

Another effect of Annie being in Mellie's life was finding Mellie reading on her iPad. Mellie chatted about a list of authors that Annie had recommended, and it seemed she'd found a few new titles on her own. Keaton never thought he'd see the day that Mellie would welcome Annie into her house, but he saw more and more of the two of them together.

As he headed over to Mellie's he wondered if Annie would be there as well, seeing that she wasn't home.

When he reached the porch, Lennon let out a lone bark, as though to announce their arrival. Unlatching the door, he walked into the kitchen to discover Mellie, Annie, and Preston standing in front of the kitchen table.

That was odd. Something was off. Really off.

In unison, all three yelled, "Surprise!" Then they parted to reveal a cake with lit candles.

Keaton stared at it, completely puzzled.

"Happy birthday, Keaton," Annie exclaimed, wearing a huge grin that took up half her face.

Keaton looked from Annie to Mellie, and then to Preston. "Is today my birthday?"

"According to your driver's license, it is," Mellie told him.

He was about to ask when she'd had a chance to look at his driver's license but thought better of it.

"Aren't you going to blow out the candles?" Preston asked.

"Make a wish," Mellie added.

Caught off guard, Keaton remained too shocked to answer. To the best of his knowledge, he'd never had a birthday cake. Nor had he ever blown out candles. He didn't have a clue about making a wish. A wish for what?

"How old are you?" Annie asked. "I guessed you must be around thirty-five."

"Thirty-three," he said, suddenly feeling anxious and uneasy. His heart beat hard and fast.

"Annie baked the cake," Preston said, motioning toward it.

"I tried my best," she added. "I've never made a layer cake before. It's a little lopsided, but I didn't think you'd mind."

All Keaton could do was stare at the cake with the candles melting and wax running down the sides.

"It's chocolate. You like chocolate, don't you?"

"Who doesn't like chocolate?" Mellie asked.

"Chocolate is okay," he said, and his tongue went dry, making conversation difficult. Every bit of liquid had completely evaporated in his mouth. He couldn't seem to take his eyes off that birthday cake.

"I had Annie get vanilla ice cream, too," Mellie added. "I remembered that you like vanilla."

Lennon barked.

Everyone was watching him. They expected him to say something. Do something. His heart felt close to exploding. This was too much.

Suddenly, Keaton had the overwhelming need to escape. He had to get out of the house. He didn't mean to offend anyone, but he had to leave. Offering a reason or an excuse would have been impossible, and so he did the only thing he could think to do. Turning away, he walked out of the house, down the stairs, struggling to breathe the entire way.

As he left, he heard the shocked gasps of the three most important people in his life. At the bottom of the steps, his knees threatened to buckle. His head was spinning, and he paused, too dizzy to continue. Leaning forward, he pressed his hands over his thighs and dragged oxygen into his lungs for fear he was about to lose consciousness. When his vision cleared, he started walking, not knowing where he was going or why. As soon as he gained his momentum he speed-walked, needing to put as much distance as possible between him and everyone else.

He heard the screen door slam and Annie shout out his name. It sounded like she was calling to him from the bottom of a deep crevasse.

"Keaton," she cried. "Wait up."

Because he could never refuse her, he stopped. If she asked him why he'd walked away, he wouldn't have an answer for her. Fleeing this way must have offended those he valued most, and yet nothing could have kept him inside that kitchen.

Annie rushed to him, and he noticed she was breathless. He hadn't realized he'd managed to put that much distance between him and the birthday cake. Unable to look at her for fear of what he would see in her eyes, he turned his head and looked to the sky. If she was angry, it would devastate him. She had baked him a cake.

A birthday cake.

With candles.

And wishes.

"Keaton," she said softly. "It's okay." Her arms circled him, and she pressed the side of her face against his chest, holding him as he trembled.

As best he could, he resisted her, keeping his arms dangling at his sides. She was impossible to ignore, and his willpower was weak when it came to Annie. He needed her. Her gentleness. Her softness. Her love. Giving in, he wrapped her in his embrace and clung to her, unable to identify the rush of emotion that cascaded through him like a riptide. By holding her close, he seemed to be able to infuse order into his mind, to make sense of what was happening. Slowly, with Annie in his arms, his mind cleared and he could think.

Her small cry of pain made him realize he was crushing her. He immediately loosened his hold.

"I'm sorry," he whispered brokenly.

"It's all right. We shouldn't have surprised you like that. It was too much for you."

Was it? From the time he was a toddler, keeping control of his emotions had been ingrained in him by his brute of a father. He couldn't remember the last time he'd cried. Tears were a sign of weakness, and he wasn't a weak man. And yet there was moisture on his face. It burned his cheeks as he held on to Annie, unable to explain the hard tightness in his chest.

"Would you like some cake?" she asked.

Nodding was all he could manage.

Annie took hold of his hand, raised his fist to her lips, and kissed his knuckles.

Together, holding hands, they walked back to the big house. When they entered the kitchen, they found Mellie and Preston sitting at the table, eating chocolate birthday cake and vanilla ice cream.

At the table.

"You cleared off the table," Keaton said. When he'd first walked in, right away he'd noticed something was different, but he'd been distracted by his three friends and the cake.

"Not me," Mellie clarified. "Teresa managed it."

The housekeeper.

Mellie had allowed the housekeeper to clear off the kitchen table? That was no small miracle. He didn't dare ask where Teresa had put everything, because, frankly, he didn't want to know.

Annie dished him up a slice of cake and a huge scoop of ice cream and set it down on the table for him.

"I blew out the candles for you," Preston said, grinning at Mellie.

"Damn near started a fire in my kitchen," she muttered.

"Did not," Preston countered.

Annie scooted her chair closer to Keaton and smiled at the two of them.

Keaton took a bite of the cake; it was the best he'd ever tasted. "Never had my own birthday cake before," he announced. He scooped up a huge bite and smiled at Annie, who closely watched him.

"I'm sorry it slid to one side."

Keaton couldn't take his eyes off her. "It's a beautiful cake."

Annie blushed with his praise. He was talking about the cake and about her.

"Do you want to open your gifts now?" she asked, seemingly embarrassed by the way he focused his attention on her. "You can wait, if you'd rather."

"Gifts?" he repeated. It was one shock after another. No one gave him gifts. "I don't need anything."

"Doesn't matter if you do or not," Mellie told him. "We got you gifts."

He never liked being the center of attention, and he didn't want everyone watching while he unwrapped packages. "I'd rather do it later."

"That's fine," Annie assured him.

"I'll take them home with me." He couldn't imagine what people would buy him. This was uncharted territory; he was uncomfortable with anyone giving him gifts.

"We wanted to make your day special," Annie said.

"Thank you," he whispered.

He stayed a while longer and ate a second huge piece of cake. Mellie insisted he take the rest of it home. She secured it in plastic wrap and gave it to him. Keaton took the cake along with his gifts. He thanked each of them, and then, with Lennon trailing behind him, he left Mellie's.

It'd been almost two weeks since he'd last seen his father. Generally, he'd avoided the man responsible for his birth. It had never been a healthy relationship. Keaton could have won a gold medal at the Olympics and it wouldn't have altered his father's opinion of him. He'd accepted that long before he was a teenager. His father had never loved him.

Unfortunately, Keaton had no memories of his mother. He had to believe she'd loved him. His father refused to let him mention her name or ask about her. Once, when he was around five or six, he'd found a box with photos of his parents. They were smiling and walking hand in hand. His father had looked happy. Keaton could never remember his father smiling.

One photo caught his attention. His mom was pregnant with him; Keaton was only a small bump in her belly. Her hand was on her stomach as she smiled into the camera, joy radiating from her. Keaton lost track of how long he'd stared at that photograph.

Somehow, some way, the look in his mother's eyes transmitted love, her love for her unborn child. For her husband. For life. Looking at it had instilled in him feelings of being wanted and having been deeply loved. Keaton knew his father blamed him for his mother's death. He knew she died of cancer, but nothing more. If she had family, he never knew them. He instinctively knew talking about her brought his father pain he was looking to avoid.

For reasons Keaton couldn't explain, after his surprise birthday party he drove to his father's house. His father lived just outside of town. He'd always been a loner. While Keaton lived at home, his father had worked as a lumberjack, felling trees. The years of hard labor had taken a toll on his health. His back was bad, and he was no longer able to walk for any distance or stand for long periods of time.

His father rarely came into town; when he did, he ran his errands quickly, then returned home. Those visits had become infrequent of late, and Keaton only heard about them from others. In all the years since Keaton had moved out, his father had never once been to see him. That had never troubled him. To Keaton, that was more of a blessing than a slight.

He parked in front of the run-down house. The roof needed replacing and the outside needed to be painted.

Moss grew along the rain gutters. Keaton would have taken care of the upkeep himself, but his father wouldn't hear of it.

Years earlier, his father had kept two dogs, which he'd trained to attack outsiders; it had infuriated Seth that neither one had ever tried to bite Keaton. Intuitively, they seemed to recognize that Keaton was a friend and not an intruder.

Without knocking, he walked into the house and saw that his father stood in the kitchen with a shotgun aimed at Keaton. "What do you want?" he demanded in a voice that rattled from years of tobacco use.

Keaton set the leftover cake on the table.

His old man's gaze drifted to the cake. "You looking to poison me, boy?"

Keaton shook his head and looked around the house for signs of trouble. His father would never ask him for anything. The old man looked worse than usual. Though standing upright, he leaned against the side of the doorway, as if it demanded too much effort to remain standing on his own. His shotgun was directed right at the center of Keaton's chest. This wasn't the first time he'd looked down the barrel of a firearm.

"You're not welcome here."

Keaton didn't need the reminder but nodded so his father would know that he understood.

Seth Keaton Sr. hadn't remembered that it was his son's birthday. It would be foolish to think he had. Stepping over to the kitchen, Keaton opened the silverware drawer and pulled out a fork. Keaton set it next to the cake, turned around, and walked away.

250

"I don't need no cake," his father shouted after him.

Most likely his father would toss it in the garbage rather than eat it. If anyone were to ask what prompted him to give the cake to his father, he wouldn't have an answer. It might be his way of letting Seth know other people cared about him. Others loved him. He didn't need anything from the old man.

It had been a day of oddities. A day of emotions and surprises.

Not until much later that night did Keaton open the gifts from his friends.

Mellie had bought him a book. A mystery.

Preston had bought him a new pair of gardening gloves, since the ones he'd used to rip out the blackberry vines were ruined.

He opened Annie's gift last. He stared at it for several minutes, unable to look away. It was a long chain with a silver medallion on the end, inscribed with his name and the date, along with an inscription:

You carry my heart with you.

He wondered if she had any idea that she carried his heart as well.

CHAPTER
TWENTY-FIVE

Britt was waiting when Annie finished work at the clinic. The teenager leaned against the side of the building and straightened when she saw Annie come out. Annie had worried about her ever since she'd learned the girl was pregnant. As best she could figure, Britt no longer worked at Bean There. If she did, she wasn't part of the morning shift any longer.

"Hello, Britt."

"Hi." The girl kept her head lowered. "Do you have a minute to talk?"

"Of course." Annie slipped her arm around the girl's thin shoulders. "How are you feeling?"

"Okay, I guess." Britt swallowed, glanced up at Annie, and continued. "I don't know if you heard — my stepfather left town. Mom reported that he was responsible for Logan's broken arm to Sheriff Terrance."

"She did?" Annie was overjoyed. She knew it had taken courage for Teresa to take that step.

"He emptied the bank account and disappeared," Britt elaborated. "Mom paid a visit to Sheriff Terrance's office, and then the man from the state who

252

was here earlier returned to talk to Mom, but by that time, Carl had packed up and left town."

"Do you know where he is?"

"No. Mom told me an arrest warrant was issued for him. Logan doesn't know that, though. Mom didn't want to tell him his father is a loser."

"Does your mom need financial assistance?" Annie could steer Teresa to resources that would help until she was able to get on her feet.

"Mom's proud. She said we'd be fine. She suspected Carl would do something like this and had squirreled away some money." Britt grinned, pleased her mother had thwarted her stepfather. "I bet Carl was surprised when he went to the bank and saw how little was on deposit. I have my own account, and he didn't have access to that."

It served Carl right, but Annie didn't say so.

"What about you, Britt? How are *you*?" Annie wouldn't mention the pregnancy unless Britt brought it up first.

"After I saw you and we talked, I told Jimmy about the baby."

It was just as Annie had suspected, Jimmy was the father.

"How did that go?" she asked, keeping her arm around Britt.

Britt released a long, slow sigh. "Not so good. He wants us to get married. I told him no, and now he's upset and won't talk to me."

"Do you love Jimmy?"

Britt sniffled and nodded vigorously. "I do. More than anything, which is why I won't marry him. He has a scholarship to the University of Washington that he would have to give up if we were married. I refuse to let him do that."

Annie had to admire Britt. It couldn't have been easy to turn Jimmy down.

"If Jimmy stays in Oceanside because of me and the baby, it will ruin any chance he has of becoming a dentist. It's all he talked about when we first started dating. His grandfather was a dentist, and that's his dream too. I refuse to take that dream away from him because I'm pregnant."

"I think that's wise, Britt."

"Maybe, but it isn't easy, and it hurts that Jimmy won't even talk to me now."

"What does your mom think?" Annie asked.

The teenager's gaze went back to the sidewalk. "I haven't told her yet."

"Oh Britt, you need to let her know." Because Annie knew Teresa, she was confident the teen's mother would support and encourage her daughter, as Teresa had been in similar circumstances herself as a teenager. Teresa would understand.

"When I first learned I was pregnant, I knew there were other options, but I can't get rid of this baby."

"Have you thought about adoption?"

She shook her head. "I don't know that I could give up my baby, either. But then I think about my mother . . ." she said, and hesitated. "Mom had me when she was eighteen. It was a summer romance, and

254

the college boy was someone she met on the beach. She wrote to tell him she was pregnant, and he insisted the baby wasn't his. After that, Mom had no contact with him. I don't even know the name of my father. He was nothing more than a sperm donor.

"Mom could have left Oceanside and gone on to school. Because of me, she never had the chance to finish her education. Then she met Carl. At first he was good to us and a hard worker. Everything changed after he was laid off from the mill and he started drinking heavily."

The entire economy of this part of Washington state had changed with the decline of the lumber industry. Annie remembered her parents talking about it.

"Mom did everything she could to make him happy. All he wanted, though, was to drink."

"I'm sorry."

"I know. It's only been in the last couple years that he's started getting physical, hitting us. I was angry when I learned you'd called the state on him, because I was afraid it would only make things worse."

"I should never have gone to your home," Annie added. That had been a major mistake on her part. Her intentions had been good, but that didn't excuse the risk she'd taken.

"I'm glad you reported him," Britt insisted. "Mom is a different person now that Carl has left."

"He could come back." Annie was afraid that once Britt's stepfather ran out of money, he would return to Oceanside and terrorize Teresa, demanding more.

"He won't." Britt seemed convinced of that. "Not with an arrest warrant filed against him. Mom said he has a brother in Alaska. That's where she thinks he went. I'm just glad he's gone."

"How's Logan handling all this?"

"He'll be better off. He'll understand it all when he gets older." Britt shrugged, as they continued walking toward the beach.

Annie had removed Logan's cast a week earlier, and he'd seemed quiet and withdrawn. On the bright side, his broken arm had healed nicely, and he was glad to be free of the cast.

"How can I help you, Britt?" she asked, wanting to do whatever she could for the teenager.

The girl's steps slowed. "Would you talk to Jimmy for me?"

Annie didn't feel that was her place, or that anything she said to the young man would help. "I don't know that I should. The two of you need to sort this out yourselves. It's more important that you tell your mother and get her advice."

Britt covered her face with both hands. "But it's hard. She's going to be disappointed in me."

"Your mother, of all people, will understand. Give her the benefit of the doubt."

Britt grew silent. "I know I should. You're probably right about her understanding. My mother wanted better for me."

Annie gently hugged the girl. "This pregnancy isn't the end of the world, Britt. If you want to consider adoption, I know of an agency that can help you find a couple who would welcome this baby into their lives. Your child would be a blessing to them. It's something to consider."

"I'll think about it."

"The choice is yours and Jimmy's. All I'm telling you is that there are loving families who would love your baby beyond measure."

Britt had tears in her eyes as she spoke. "I'm so glad you moved to Oceanside."

"I am, too." Annie had come here because it was her happy place, and it had become so much more in the months since she'd found the cottage. It had turned into her healing place, also.

After her short walk along the beach, Annie arrived home. Seeing her, Ringo woke from his nap and stretched his legs out, letting his claws sink into the rug. He'd grown since Keaton had brought him to her, and she'd come to love her special gift.

Picking the kitten up, Annie gave him attention before feeding him and headed outside to water her garden. The lettuce continued to thrive, and the other plants were starting to bud. She was looking forward to fresh tomatoes and cucumbers.

The door off Mellie's kitchen was open, and the screen door as well, which was odd. Annie had never seen either door open, other than the time Keaton delivered an injured animal. She saw Teresa scoot a heavy box onto the porch. Annie watched, transfixed, as the first box was followed by a second and then a third.

She couldn't imagine that Mellie had approved of this. Teresa was a brave woman to cross her employer.

Just as she suspected, a few minutes later Annie heard her landlord howl.

"What are you doing to me?" she screeched.

Teresa continued, undaunted. "Getting rid of this junk." Another box was set onto the porch.

"Bring everything back in the house right this minute," Mellie bellowed furiously.

Teresa stood with her hands on her hips just outside the kitchen door. "Tell me what you need with twenty-year-old newspapers?"

"Not your business."

"I'm making it my business. I can't clean if you keep ridiculously old newspapers and magazines all over the kitchen. Enough is enough."

"Fine. You're fired. Leave now."

"If that's what you want, then pay me what you owe me, and I'll be on my way."

Teresa wasn't giving in. Annie admired her for holding fast to what was good for Mellie.

Mellie stomped her foot. "Bring back those boxes first."

"If you want them, then come get them yourself."

Mellie paced back and forth before the open door like a soldier on parade. "You're the one who put everything on the porch. Now bring everything back."

"I no longer work for you."

"Okay, I'll rehire you. Bring those boxes back inside."

Teresa crossed her arms and stood just outside the door, tapping her foot. "I quit."

"You can't quit." Outraged, Mellie stopped pacing.

"I just did."

Annie was tempted to intervene but decided against it. Setting the watering container down, she sent a text to Keaton.

Looks like war has erupted between Mellie and Teresa.

No way. What's happening?

Teresa cleared out the kitchen. Boxes are stacked on the porch.

Mellie furious?

Yup. Fired Teresa then rehired her. Teresa just quit.

Wish I was there to see this.

She could feel his amusement matched her own.

It's worth the price of admission.

Annie put her phone in her pocket as the two women continued the battle of words. Teresa refused to budge. No way was she letting Mellie keep those ridiculous piles of old magazines and newspapers. Annie silently applauded her tenacity. It couldn't have been easy with Mellie shouting demands at her from inside the house. Teresa made it clear: If she couldn't properly clean the kitchen, then she was quitting.

Trying to be invisible, Annie continued watering her plants, giving all the garden plants a cool, refreshihg drink until she heard Mellie screech across the yard.

"Annie, help!"

She pretended not to hear, and cheerfully continued to water her plants.

"Annie, do something!" Mellie tried again.

"She's not helping you," the housekeeper insisted. "Annie agrees with how silly it is to keep this garbage."

"It is *not* silly, and everything inside those boxes is *not* garbage. They belonged to my grandfather."

Teresa remained unmoved. She stood on the porch, arms crossed, with her foot tapping impatiently. "Other than magazines and newspapers you should have tossed years ago, tell me what's in these boxes," she asked calmly, testing Mellie.

"I don't remember," the other woman cried. "Bring them back inside this instant or I'm calling Sheriff Terrance."

Teresa swept her arm toward Mellie. "By all means, call the authorities."

"You're taking my things away from me. That's stealing. Unless you do as I say, you're going to end up in jail."

"I am not stealing. It's all right here on your porch."

Mellie was clearly at her wits' end.

"I'm not unreasonable," Teresa said. "I'll tell you what I'll do. If you can tell me one item in those boxes that is of sentimental value, then I'll return the entire bunch."

Mellie jumped on the offer as if it were a lifeline. "Those old magazines. My grandfather saved all those. They're *National Geographic* . . . I think," she said desperately.

"And what, exactly, do you intend to do with these priceless issues?"

Mellie looked flustered and angry. "I . . . I don't know."

"My guess is the library would love to have them. Don't you think your grandfather would have wanted to see them read and enjoyed rather than rotting away in the kitchen?"

Mellie remained stubbornly silent.

"That's what I thought." Teresa had heard all she needed to hear. "I'll pull out the *National Geographic* magazines, but everything else is going to the dump."

"The dump. No way!" the woman cried, as if Teresa had threatened to dispose of priceless family heirlooms.

"Mellie," Teresa said in a calming tone. "If whatever it is you have stored in these boxes is that important to you, then come and get them yourself."

"I can't . . . You know that."

"Then that's all I need to know."

"I fired you," Mellie reminded her.

"But you changed your mind, remember?" Teresa stated calmly.

"You quit."

"I have since changed my mind."

Annie leaned over and turned off the faucet. When she suggested Teresa for Mellie's housekeeper, this was exactly what she'd hoped would happen. Being around Mellie helped Teresa, and Teresa helped Mellie. They were good for each other. This arrangement couldn't have worked out better. Even more encouraging was the fact that Carl Hoffert was out of the picture.

CHAPTER
TWENTY-SIX

Teresa solicited Keaton and Annie's help to haul away the accumulated boxes stacked on Mellie's porch. Annie knew that Mellie had already carefully gone through the remainder of the boxes before they left the house, where she had found many *Reader's Digest* books from the 1970s, which were then donated to the library. Teresa had already dropped those boxes off. Keaton parked his pickup as close to the big house as he could get, and the three of them hauled the other boxes onto his truck bed.

Annie was grateful for time with Keaton. She'd barely seen him since Sunday, and when she did, she instinctively knew he was troubled. Whatever it was, though, he kept it to himself. It'd started right after his birthday party. He'd gone back to answering her in short sentences, which was indicative of his worries.

Mellie stood framed on the other side of the doorjamb, fuming, as the three hauled boxes from the porch to Keaton's truck.

"Traitors, that's what you are," she cried out. "The lot of you. Some friends you turned out to be."

"Don't you like all the room you have in your kitchen?" Teresa asked, not the least bit perturbed by her employer's censure.

"No," Mellie insisted. "I liked everything exactly the way it was before you showed up."

"You're too stubborn," Keaton insisted, breaking off his words. Looking inside the open doorway, he seemed shocked. "The table has four chairs."

Mellie ignored the comment.

The difference in the kitchen was night and day. Annie was amazed when she'd looked inside the first time. Teresa had taken away the boxes and cleared off the countertops. Annie had no idea where she'd stored the multitude of appliances Mellie had collected over the years. The floor sparkled, along with the polished faucet and the stainless-steel sink. The room resembled the way it had looked when Annie had visited the elder Munsons as a preteen and teenager.

"Don't you dare think you're going to do this in the rest of the house," Mellie spat at Teresa. "You're not touching anything else. I want that understood right now."

"Depends on what you want me to clean," Teresa returned, huffing with the effort to lift the boxes.

"I only want you to clean the kitchen," Mellie informed her. "Nothing else from here on out."

"Thought you said something about changing your sheets and cleaning your toilets," Teresa reminded her.

"I'll do that myself."

"No need for me to clean, then," the housekeeper argued.

Both Keaton and Annie stopped to glare at Mellie. The other woman scowled back. "Why are you two looking at me like that?" she demanded, hands on her hips.

Keaton and Annie ignored the question, seeing that the answer was obvious. They carted the last of the boxes and set them in the truck bed. Once loaded, they would deliver them to the dump. After a quick inspection, they didn't find anything of value — certainly nothing worth saving.

After thanking Annie and Keaton for their help, Teresa made her excuses and headed home to her children.

Arms folded and looking glum, Mellie remained standing in the doorway. "I've had about all I can take for one day," she muttered and slammed the door. As soon as Teresa was out of sight, another rusty old truck rolled into the driveway and parked next to Keaton's.

Annie saw that it was Preston.

Keaton met Preston as he stepped out of the truck. "You're late. We're finished."

Preston grinned, removed his cap, and pushed an unruly patch of hair off his forehead. "Brought you that thing you've been asking me about," he said, and glanced sheepishly toward Annie and then the house.

Before Keaton could comment, Preston looked longingly at the house. "How's Mellie?"

"Not a happy camper," Annie informed him.

"Don't suppose now would be a good time to visit?"

"Want to get your head bit off?" Keaton asked, discouraging him.

264

Preston's smile didn't waver. "Wouldn't be the first time. Being around that woman is like trying to cuddle a porcupine."

Annie had to hold back a laugh. Preston had it right. Mellie had the personality of a prickly animal. Over the last several months, though, Annie had discovered that the brusque way her landlord treated others was merely a front. Mellie hated Teresa touching her grandparents' things and had plenty to say about it. At the same time, Annie believed that a part of Mellie was glad to be rid of the junk. If the contents of those boxes were as important as she'd made out, she would have found a way to keep them.

"Preston," Annie interjected, "Mellie might actually be in the mood for the comfort of a friend. She's had a hard day."

"Wouldn't risk it if I were you," Keaton countered.

Scratching the side of his head, Preston looked from one to the other.

"Rough day is right," Keaton added.

Annie agreed. Seeing those boxes hauled away had been tough on Mellie. "She's probably feeling out of sorts and a bit lost. We've disrupted her world, and that can't be easy. I think she might welcome you — someone she can vent to — someone who she doesn't consider a traitor."

Preston centered his gaze on the door to the kitchen. "I don't know about that."

Annie heard a weak bark from inside Preston's truck. "That'd be the critter you wanted," Preston told him. He opened the passenger side of his truck and took out a puppy who appeared to be a couple months old. It was impossible to tell what breed he was. He looked part spaniel and something else that she couldn't detect or identify.

"A puppy!" Annie cried, and immediately took the dog out of Preston's hands. "He's adorable." She nuzzled her face against him and he licked her cheek. "You're getting a puppy?" she asked Keaton.

"Not for me," Keaton explained. "For Logan."

"Teresa's son?"

Keaton gave her a weak smile. Again, she felt the urge to ask him what was bothering him. It went without saying that he wouldn't explain until he was ready, and so she bit her tongue, keeping her questions to herself.

The puppy continued to lick her hand and face. Training a puppy was exactly what Logan needed to take his mind off the father who had abandoned him. There was one small glitch, though. "Teresa know about this?"

Keaton nodded.

Annie remained concerned. Puppies weren't cheap, and she knew Teresa had financial struggles. "What about his shots? Dog food isn't cheap either."

"Taken care of," Preston supplied. "Keaton's picking up all the vet bills and food. The shelter will have him neutered when he's ready."

His thoughtfulness and generosity shouldn't surprise her by now.

"Ride with me to Logan's?" Keaton invited.

266

"I'd love to." She continued to hold the puppy while Preston retrieved a few items out of the bed of his truck and transferred them over to Keaton's vehicle.

When he'd finished, Keaton helped her into the passenger side. He joined her a minute later and she noticed that Preston stayed behind. She hoped Preston was willing to give Mellie a second chance.

Keaton slid into the driver's seat and started up the truck. "You were right," he said, his hands on the steering wheel.

"Right? That's one of the most appreciated comments you can give a girl. Now tell me, what was I right about?" The puppy settled into her lap, curled up, and promptly went to sleep, his chin resting on her arm.

"About Mellie and Teresa. I can't believe Mellie let Teresa clear her entire kitchen."

"I know."

Reaching across the seat, Keaton took hold of her hand and gave it a gentle squeeze. "Miracle."

"Everything's possible, Keaton."

He released her hand and centered his focus back on the road. "No."

In a matter of seconds, his mood sobered.

"What do you mean by that?" she asked.

"Not important."

Annie couldn't let it go any longer.

"You're sad about something."

Keaton didn't deny or confirm her assessment.

"Someone has upset you."

He gave her nothing.

"Will you tell me who?"

"No."

She let the disappointment settle before she spoke again. "Okay, I can accept that."

Keaton reached for the medallion she'd given him for his birthday. His hand folded around it. As best as she could tell, he'd worn it every day since his birthday.

They both grew quiet and introspective. Keaton turned down the road that would lead them to Teresa's house. The truck slowed to a crawl. Annie wondered if Keaton realized he'd taken his foot off the gas.

"My father's ill," he said, his voice so low Annie had to strain to hear.

"I'm sorry."

She was about to ask if there was anything she could do when Keaton spoke again.

"He hates me."

Annie didn't know how that could possibly be true. "How could he?" she asked.

Keaton shrugged. "All my life. Lived with it. Left when I could."

"Do you see him often?"

"No."

She agreed that was likely for the best. "Some people are toxic, Keaton. Your father can't love you because he doesn't love himself. If that's the way he feels, then it's best to avoid him."

"I try. He's sick. He needs help."

"Will he accept it from you?"

Keaton shook his head.

"What can I do?" she asked.

Keaton pulled over to the side of the road and let the truck idle. "Don't know," he said, and then repeated it: "Don't know."

"Is your father living alone?"

Keaton's huge hands clenched the steering wheel with a grip so tight his knuckles were white. "Yes."

"Is he able to care for himself?"

He shrugged. "Doubtful." He lifted his head and inhaled sharply. "Went to the house." He reached for the medallion.

"On your birthday?" she guessed.

Keaton turned his head to look at her. "Saw then he was weak. Went back. He's worse. Much worse."

"Would you like me to visit, assess his condition?"

"Don't want . . . venom aimed at you."

Placing her hand on his forearm, Annie did her best to reassure him. "I've worked with difficult patients before, Keaton. Don't worry, I can handle your father. If he needs to be hospitalized, I'll put everything in place to see that it happens. I don't want you upset over this."

"He won't go."

"If he's as bad as you say, perhaps hospice would be for the best. He'll have the end-of-life care he needs, and the staff will make him comfortable."

"You'd do that?"

She squeezed his arm. "Keaton, of course. You should know by now that I'm willing to do anything to help you."

"Thank you."

Annie's heart swelled. She was happy to do something for Keaton. He'd never ask. That wasn't his way. Accepting anything from anyone went against his nature. He didn't expect kindness or generosity. Knowing that pained her.

After a few minutes, Keaton pulled up in front of Teresa's house. Logan was sitting on the porch steps, looking glum.

"Hello, Logan," Annie called out from the passenger window.

His eyes brightened as he recognized her. "Hi, Dr. Annie." She'd given up correcting him and asked, "Whatcha doing?"

Logan shrugged. "Nothing."

Teresa opened the screen door and stepped out onto the porch. Several repairs had been made to the house, and Annie knew that Keaton and Preston were responsible.

"Have something for you," Keaton said, climbing out of the truck.

"For me?" Logan stood and walked to the gate, his eyes wide with curiosity.

Keaton climbed down and walked around to Annie's side of the truck. He opened the door and removed the sleeping puppy from her lap and held him against his chest.

"Really?" Logan asked.

Keaton smiled. "Yup."

"Mom," Logan cried out. "Please. Can I have him?" The ten-year-old's eyes grew huge, silently pleading with his mother.

Teresa hesitated, giving the matter serious consideration. "Are you going to care for him, feed him, and train him to go outside to take care of business?"

"Yes," Logan said eagerly. "Please, Mom. You know I've wanted a dog forever . . . since I was little."

Teresa shared a smile with Keaton. "If you can handle the responsibility, then you can keep the dog."

Logan flew to his mother and hugged her around the middle. Annie noticed that both mother and son had tears in their eyes. He ran down the sidewalk to Keaton, who placed the puppy in Logan's arms.

Keaton looked over at Annie, and she was blinded by his smile. In that moment, she realized that by Keaton helping the boy get over the pain of his father's abandonment, it helped Keaton deal with the lack of love from his own father. He spoke very little of his childhood, but reading between the lines, Annie knew there had been little nurturing in Keaton's life. That he had become the wonderful, kind, and caring man that he was left her to marvel at the depth of his inner strength.

CHAPTER
TWENTY-SEVEN

Watering her garden after work each day was a favorite task that Annie enjoyed. She glanced toward the big house for a moment, and then looked over a second time. Something was different. It took her a few minutes to realize what it was.

The windows.

They sparkled, and Annie could see into the kitchen for the first time since she'd moved to the cottage. The curtains looked fresh and white. Teresa had been busy with more than clearing out the kitchen. The woman was a miracle worker. Annie wanted to advise her to go slow with Mellie, afraid that too much change all at once would send her into a tailspin.

When Annie looked down at her plants, she jerked the hose away and gasped. She'd about drowned the fledgling green beans. Water pooled around her feet as she shook her head and hastily moved down the row.

A rusty truck she recognized rolled onto the side of the street and stopped.

Preston.

Apparently oblivious to where he'd parked, he climbed out of the truck with a clenched bouquet of daisies in his hand. He then proceeded to pace all the

272

way around his truck not once but twice. He seemed caught up in his own thoughts, and he jumped about a foot off the ground when Annie called his name.

"What?" he demanded.

Annie turned off the faucet and walked toward him. "You okay?"

"Why wouldn't I be?" Preston asked back, grumbling under his breath. He removed his cap, wiping his forearm across his brow and glancing toward the house.

"I don't know," Annie returned honestly. "You're looking agitated."

He leaned back and cocked his head toward the sky. "There's no fool like an old fool. Isn't that what they say?"

"You aren't old."

"Feel it at times."

Annie noticed Preston had a fresh haircut and wore a clean shirt.

He opened the cab of his truck and was about to climb inside when she stopped him. "Did you bring those daisies for Mellie?" she asked.

His face filled with color.

"Seems a shame not to give them to her."

Preston looked at her like he was suddenly trapped in a parallel universe.

"Preston?" she tried again, and waved her hand in front of his face, while he continued to stare into space, seeming oblivious to her. "You okay?" she asked.

"Don't know," he admitted after a long moment. His expression was a mixture of doubt and longing. "I know far more about dogs and cats than I do women.

In high school, I was crazy about Mellie. All of us boys were. But she was too pretty for me. I was a shy, skinny kid with the social skills of an ape." He paused, then gave a sad smile and added, "Come to think of it, I'm the same now, just a bit older." Preston glanced wistfully toward the big house. "When she came back, I gave it a try and got shot down. A man has his pride, you know."

"I noticed your truck was here after Keaton and I took the puppy to Logan. Everyone deserves a second chance, Preston."

"Yeah, we talked for a long time. Laughed some, too." Preston continued to stare at Mellie's house.

"That sounds like a step in the right direction."

"Yeah."

Seeing that Mellie hadn't kicked Preston out after a few minutes, the way she tended to do with everyone else, spoke volumes. As many times as Annie had been to the big house, she'd never stayed more than ten or fifteen minutes, and at that point Mellie usually made it clear it was time for Annie to go. And she wasn't always subtle about it, either.

"You think I should give her the flowers?" He studied Annie seriously, as if this was a matter of life or death.

Annie would hate to misread the situation. Mellie's rejection might crush Preston. Inhaling a deep breath, she went with her gut. "Nothing ventured, nothing gained."

He looked at the house again, and then headed with determination toward the kitchen door, swinging the bouquet at his side like a soldier in drill practice.

274

Annie had faith in Preston. She was convinced his gentleness and persistence would eventually win Mellie over. All Annie could hope was that Mellie didn't bark at him the way she so often did her.

Reassured, she returned to watering her plants. She hadn't realized how much work and effort went into the maintenance of a garden. The vegetables were developing nicely, and she would have more cucumbers and jalapeños than she could possibly use. She'd share the bounty with Keaton, Mellie, and Candi. The pumpkins and Hubbard squash were doing well, too. Annie knew her mother would have been proud of her efforts.

"Ms. Marlow."

She turned around and saw the boy from Bean There. It took her a moment to recognize him outside of the coffee shop. "Jimmy."

The young man hung his head, his shoulders slumped forward. This seemed to be her week for depressed and uncertain men.

"Britt told me you know about the baby?"

"I do," Annie confessed. She wasn't breaking any confidentiality requirements by confirming this.

"I want to marry her. Britt keeps telling me no, but I know she loves me as much as I love her. Now she's talking about adoption."

"Jimmy, I can't get involved in this decision. That's for you and Britt to discuss." Setting her tools down, Annie left the garden and led Jimmy into the cottage. She gestured toward the small kitchen table. He took a seat and immediately planted his elbows on the tabletop, holding his head as though it weighed too much for him to keep it upright without support.

Ringo wandered over. Annie scooped the kitten into her arms and set him on her lap, petting him as Jimmy continued.

"You need to make Britt listen to me about this," he pleaded. "We can get married, have the baby, and I'll go to school later. She's more important to me than becoming a dentist."

Annie didn't feel right giving him advice. "You're right, Jimmy; Britt does love you. She loves you enough to think about your future, as well as her own."

"We can make it work," he insisted, wanting to convince her. "I'll get a full-time job and put college off for a year or two until we get on our feet."

"Sounds good in theory, but that's harder to make happen than you realize. Besides, didn't I hear you have a scholarship?"

His head dipped so low his forehead nearly rested against the tabletop. "I'll give that up."

"But Britt doesn't want you to do that, does she?"

He shrugged. "No," he reluctantly confessed. "She said if I turned down the scholarship, she'd break up with me."

Annie didn't know how it'd happened that she'd become the Dear Abby of Oceanside.

"Britt told me you know an agency that would help with the adoption. A reputable one that would make sure the baby went to a good home."

Annie continued to pet Ringo, who was content in her arms. "I did mention that, yes. Adoption is an option."

Jimmy adamantly shook his head. "I'm not willing to give our baby over to strangers."

"What about Britt?"

Jimmy looked utterly miserable. "She's reading up on 'open adoption' and talked to me about it. She thinks that it might be a good idea for us, but I don't know. Britt said we could still be part of the baby's life."

"Does that feel wrong to you?" she asked.

He looked up, not quite sure how to answer her. "I don't want Britt to regret giving up our baby."

"That's a consideration," she conceded. "But I believe Britt is looking at what's best for your future, for her own, and for your baby's."

Jimmy rubbed his hand over his eyes. "I know she is, and I am, too. I don't want to lose her."

Annie admired Britt and knew this decision would be difficult for one so young.

"Do your parents know?" she asked.

Jimmy nodded. "Britt and I told both our parents at the same time. They were shocked. My dad was more upset than my mom. Britt's mom started crying and then so did my mom." He inhaled sharply and scrubbed his face with both hands, trying to wipe away the memory of the confrontation.

Annie felt bad that she couldn't do more. "I wish I could be of more help, Jimmy, but this is a matter between you, Britt, and your parents."

"You won't talk to her? She likes and trusts you. I know she'll listen if you —"

"Sorry, Jimmy, I can't do that."

He seemed to accept her answer. "I didn't think you would, but I felt I should at least ask."

Seeing that there wasn't anything more to discuss, Jimmy stood. Annie led him to the door.

After brewing a cup of tea, she mulled over the situation. It had taken courage for Britt and Jimmy to tell their parents, and it pleased her that they'd done it together. From the beginning, Annie knew Teresa would be upset, seeing history repeating itself in her daughter.

Although Annie didn't want to be involved with the decision that Britt, Jimmy, and their families needed to make, she wanted to help in any way she could.

After making a salad for dinner, Annie decided to visit Teresa at her home. She'd make the excuse of seeing how Logan was doing with the puppy.

When she arrived, she saw Keaton's truck parked at the house. A smile came over her. She hadn't seen him for a few days and missed him. He had painted Teresa's house, she noticed.

"Hey," she said when she saw Keaton. He was at his truck, putting away his equipment.

Logan was running around the front yard, the puppy nipping at his heels. The sound of his laughter filled the evening.

Keaton saw her and grinned. "Hey."

Teresa stepped onto the porch and Annie said to Keaton, "I'll check in with you later."

Keaton's face warmed as he nodded. "Later."

Annie joined Teresa on the top porch step. "Thought I'd stop by to see how everything is going," she said, leaving it up to the other woman to lead the conversation.

"It's good." Teresa folded her arms around her middle. "Logan's crazy about that puppy. I found the dog sleeping with him when I went to check this morning. Been like that every night since the pup arrived."

"I noticed Mellie's kitchen windows are sparkling clean."

"Never seen dirtier windows," Teresa mentioned.

"She still upset with you?" Mellie was a safe subject for both women.

Teresa grinned. "Oh, she put up a fuss all right, but in the end she had nothing more to say. I'll give her a few days or so before I move on to one of the other rooms. She's standing guard over her stuff, afraid that I'll cart it away, right under her nose. This morning she watched me like a hawk and wouldn't let me near her bedroom or the living room."

Annie did her best not to smile, with limited success.

"I won't be back until the end of the week. That'll give her time to adjust. Much as she complained and whined, I can see she's enjoying all the space she has in the kitchen now."

"Don't give up on her."

"I won't," Teresa promised. "I can be just as stubborn as she is."

"Good."

She wanted to ask about Britt and the pregnancy, but the subject felt awkward. Annie wasn't certain Teresa was aware that she knew.

After about twenty minutes, Annie returned home to her cottage and was happy to see Preston's truck still parked outside. This was real progress for her friend. And for Preston.

Changes, they're a-comin' to the big house, she thought. All Annie could do was pray that Mellie was able to accept all the upheaval in her life.

Keaton arrived about ten minutes after she did. Annie met him at the front door of the cottage. By standing on the top step she was almost tall enough to look him in the eyes.

"You were busy this weekend." Annie had walked past the bank and saw that the mural was nearly completed.

He grinned.

"The mural is beautiful." And it was. Keaton was a talented artist. She'd learned that he'd had no formal training, and yet his work stood out like few others in her mind.

"Got a bit more to do on it," he commented, brushing off her compliment.

As they spoke, their voices grew soft and low. Annie found herself leaning toward him as he gradually eased his head forward. His breath fanned her face and she closed her eyes, wrapped up in the familiarity that was Keaton.

His lips were close to her ear. "Your friends still coming to visit Oceanside?" He whispered the question.

280

Annie's eyes shot open. How on earth could she have forgotten? Gabby would be driving Steph and Trevor to town over Memorial Day weekend. They were scheduled to fly into Seattle, meet up with Gabby, and then spend a couple nights at the ocean.

CHAPTER
TWENTY-EIGHT

Annie's head was spinning. This opportunity couldn't have come at a worse time. If her parents were alive, she'd get their advice, although she was certain what her father would say. His face would break into a huge smile and he'd say, "Go for it. You know this was what you were born to do." With her family gone, Annie reached out to Gabby. Her cousin knew her as well as Annie knew herself.

Gabby picked up on the first ring. "I know why you're calling —"

"You don't," Annie said, abruptly cutting her off. Her mind was speeding at an alarming rate as she reviewed the conversation with Dr. Bainbridge.

"This isn't about our trip to see you?"

"No." That said, Annie leaned back in her chair, petting Ringo as she spoke, giving comfort while seeking it. "It's about Dr. Bainbridge."

"Is everything okay?"

"Not really. He's getting eager to retire. His wife wants him to slow down so they can travel. He's concerned with how much longer he'll be able to continue at this pace. He went into Seattle last week and returned with a proposition for me."

"What kind of proposition?" Gabby sounded as leery as Annie had when Dr. Bainbridge first approached her.

"First off, he told me how well I've fit into the community, which I've grown to love. I've found peace here, Gabby. It was a nice compliment and it made me feel good. He explained, other than that one minor mishap with Carl Hoffert, how much he's come to respect and trust me."

"As he should. You're great at your job," Gabby reminded her. "I can remember when we were kids you were doctoring all your dolls, covering them with Band-Aids. They didn't wear diapers; they had their heads wrapped from injuries you were treating."

Annie closed her eyes, remembering those times, too. When Gabby came for play dates, Annie would insist on Gabby being her patient so she could work on her, bandaging up her arms and legs, prescribing medication, even wheeling her down the hallway on a stool.

"Okay, sorry to interrupt. Tell me what Dr. Bainbridge wanted."

Leaning back in the chair, Annie continued. "At first I hadn't known what to think. It almost sounded like he was about to lay me off."

Sensing the tension in her, Ringo scored his claws into Annie's thigh. She carefully disentangled him from the fabric of her pants.

"Then he mentioned how difficult it is to find physicians willing to serve in these small communities, and when they do, it often doesn't go well. It takes the

283

right kind of personality, and it's often hard to find a good fit."

"Where is this leading?" Gabby asked, sounding confused.

"When Dr. Bainbridge was back in Seattle, he told the head of HR how well I was doing. Apparently, the parent clinic's health organization has started a new accelerated program for physician assistants like me that will pay my medical school expenses in exchange for a commitment to serve in a small community like Oceanside."

"Annie, that's wonderful. I don't understand why you don't sound over the moon over this chance. You always wanted to be a physician."

"Yes, I know but . . ."

"But nothing. This is a fabulous opportunity. Why aren't you excited?"

"I am, only . . . It's complicated." Annie loved hearing the enthusiasm in Gabby. She felt it herself, wanted this in the worst way. The drawback, and it was a biggie, was that it would mean leaving Oceanside . . . leaving Keaton and Mellie and Teresa.

Oceanside was her home now, and these people she'd come to love were important to her. Although she wanted to come back to serve as a physician in this community, the program gave her no guarantee she would be able to return to Oceanside.

"I am excited," Annie insisted, and she was, but at the same time she was concerned, too. Uncertain. Afraid.

"You don't sound it. Okay, yes, so you'd be away for a few years, but after that you'd be back again. Right?" Gabby was doing her best to talk her into accepting this offer. She didn't need to do too much convincing. Annie wanted to accept in the worst way, but at what cost? This wasn't a decision she could make quickly. There was more to consider than the obvious.

"Not necessarily," Annie explained. "It's not a sure thing that I'd be back in Oceanside. It might not even be in Washington state."

Once more her cousin grew quiet. "Your father always wanted you to be a doctor, but more important, you did, too, until Davis broke up with you."

Annie didn't need the reminder. "I know." A few scenarios had been floating around in Annie's mind and she didn't see how any of them would work. Keaton would be miserable living in Seattle. She would hate leaving him, and while seeing him on weekends would probably pan out for a while, she knew she would have to put all her physical and emotional energy into medical school. Relationships would need to go on the back burner. If she agreed to enter medical school, it would mean giving it her all.

"You can't pass this up, Annie," Gabby said. "If you do, you'll regret it the rest of your life."

That was true. Annie was aware that she wouldn't ever get another chance like this. She loved medicine. She was good with people and loved helping those in need. Being a family doctor had once been her dream, but she'd become impatient while in college, and eager to be done.

From the beginning, Keaton had been afraid she would leave. He seemed to be mentally prepared for her to walk away, holding back his feelings for her. Their kisses would go only so far before he'd pull himself away. He had built a barrier — a wall, of sorts — that he would raise when it came to expressing his feelings for her. Annie had been determined to prove him wrong. Now she was about to prove him right, and she feared it wouldn't go well.

"It's a hard decision to make, Gabby."

"What decision? You know you want this, Annie. Do you want me to tell Trevor and Steph that now isn't a good time to visit?" Gabby asked.

Automatically, Annie shook her head. She couldn't disappoint her friends. Not when they'd already made all their travel arrangements. "No, don't do that. I think a weekend with all of you is exactly what I need before I get back to Dr. Bainbridge."

Steph, Gabby, and Trevor showed up at the clinic just as it was closing Friday night. Annie had expected them sometime that day; she didn't have the exact time. She was happy to see them, excited.

"Annie!" Stephanie threw her arms around Annie and hugged her so tightly she found it difficult to breathe. "It's been forever." Holding her phone up, she posed for a selfie with Annie and snapped the shot.

"My turn," Trevor said, easing Steph out of the way so he could hug Annie next. With his arms circling her waist, he lifted her off the ground and gave her a noisy kiss on her cheek. "Missed you, girl."

Annie laughed and glanced over his shoulder at her cousin. Gabby's face was split in half with a huge smile. When Trevor finally set her feet back on the ground, Annie held her hand out to Gabby, who quickly grabbed hold of it, squeezing her fingers.

"I wish you'd been able to get away for a couple days," Gabby said, unwilling to hide her disappointment. "There's a music festival this weekend in Seattle that we could've all attended."

"I couldn't, Gabby, I'm sorry." Because Annie had been with the clinic not even two months, she didn't feel she could ask for four days off during a holiday in the middle of tourist season. In fact, it'd been a mad rush at the clinic every day that week. Twice she'd had to work through her lunch hour to keep up with the demand.

"Well, if Muhammad won't come to the mountain, then the mountain must come to Annie," Trevor teased. Rubbing his palms together, he asked, "What's the nightlife like around here?"

Annie laughed until she realized he wasn't joking. "Trev, this isn't L.A. We have a couple bars, but nothing like the clubs in Seattle or Beverly Hills."

"Then the local bar will have to do."

"Come on, show us this cottage you're always talking about," Steph said, looping her arm through Annie's and matching their steps as they left the clinic.

Her friends drove her to the cottage. Annie was eager to show off her place. They admired her garden, but she could tell it wasn't really their thing, which was fine. Undoubtedly, it surprised them that it was hers.

To get ready for their night out, Steph immediately invaded Annie's lone bathroom to redo her hair and makeup, while Trevor looked around her cottage. Gabby petted Ringo, lavishing attention on him.

"I didn't know you liked cats," Trevor commented.

"I didn't either until Keaton gave him to me."

"You mention Keaton every time we talk," Trevor said. "Are we going to get a chance to meet him?"

"Of course. He said he'd stop by at the bar later."

"Great. I'm looking forward to meeting this guy who's captured your heart." Her friends were crazy fun and she did miss them. At the same time, she loved her life now, too.

Trevor sat down and took Ringo away from Gabby, setting the kitten in his lap and looking at him. "Gabby mentioned the medical-school thing. It must be a hard decision, but what an opportunity!"

"It is." She wished she'd told her cousin to keep the news to herself. No one else knew about it other than Gabby, and now, Trevor and Steph. Not Mellie or Candi, and certainly not Keaton.

"Personally, I think you should go for it," Trevor continued.

Steph stuck her head out the bathroom door. "Me too. It's something you've always wanted." She looked toward Trevor. "We shouldn't try to influence Annie. She needs to make up her own mind."

"You stated your opinion. Why can't I state mine?"

"Okay, we've both let her know what we think," Steph agreed, "but in the end the decision is hers."

"It's life-changing," Annie said, sighing with the weight of it. A lot of questions remained, a whole lot to consider. She was happy with her work in Oceanside, and if she did refuse the offer, she had to assume she would remain here and be just as happy. In the back of her mind, though, she had to wonder if the day would come when she'd regret turning down something that wasn't likely to come her way again.

"I've found peace and healing here," she said, thinking out loud. "Gabby is the one who suggested I find my happy place, and I have. I'm not sure returning to Seattle is the best thing for me right now."

"What if Keaton came with you?" Gabby asked.

Although she hadn't discussed any of this with him, she knew the answer. "I doubt he would consider it."

Trevor frowned, knitting his brows together. "If he loves you . . ."

"He cares about me." Keaton might never have said anything about loving her, but she suspected he did. He didn't need to spell it out with words; she knew how he felt simply by the things he did for her. No man would work that hard and relentlessly to clear a thorn-infested garden for a woman unless he had strong feelings for her.

"Then he would want you to do what's best for you," Gabby said.

Annie didn't disagree. "The problem is I don't know what's best for me yet. Please don't say anything to him," she begged, looking from one to the other. "I haven't told him yet."

289

"He doesn't know anything about this?" Steph asked, her eyes widening with surprise as she peeked out the bathroom door again.

Annie shook her head. "It would only upset him, and that's the last thing I want. I'll let him know if I decide to accept the offer. If I make the decision to stay in Oceanside, then there's no reason to even mention it."

Gabby and Trevor exchanged a look, but Annie refused to be influenced by their disapproval. She knew Keaton, and they didn't.

Gabby, naturally, had her own opinion. "I won't say anything more other than it would be wonderful to have you living back in Seattle. I've missed you something terrible."

In a gallant effort to change the subject, Trevor said, "Are you girls ready for dinner? I'm famished."

"Heavens, no," Annie cried. "I need to get out of these work clothes."

"I want to change, too," Gabby said, leaping to her feet. "I have dibs on the bathroom next. I'll get my suitcase out of the trunk and be back in a flash."

Annie knew her friends had booked motel rooms, but apparently they were intent on getting ready in her small cottage.

It was with a sense of unrest that Annie retreated to her own room to change. She needed this night out. Now, if she could only put the medical-school decision out of her mind for the time being and enjoy being with her friends. She would need to let Dr. Bainbridge know soon enough. He wanted her answer by the end of the following week.

Annie dressed in her skinny jeans and worked like crazy getting them over her hips. It'd been a while since she wore them. She didn't remember them being this tight before. Funny, she hadn't gained weight, but her daily routine of walking had changed her figure, apparently. She put on a bohemian top and piled her hair up in a loose ponytail. When she opened her bedroom door, she found Gabby and her two friends waiting for her.

Trevor gave an appreciative whistle. "Don't know how I'm so lucky to be escorting three beautiful women."

CHAPTER
TWENTY-NINE

The evening got off to a fun start. The bar had only a few people, and Annie's friends were quick to liven it up. The music was turned up, and the first round of drinks was on the table while they waited for Keaton's arrival before ordering dinner. Annie hadn't had any alcohol in months and felt the effects immediately.

"Maybe we should order appetizers," she suggested, and waved the server over.

By the time the sliders came out of the kitchen and they'd each had their share, Keaton had arrived. He'd changed out of his work clothes and wore jeans and a short-sleeve button-down shirt. Steph stared at him with her mouth hanging open. Annie too. He looked wonderful; she couldn't keep her eyes off him.

Introductions were made.

"How's the weather up there?" Trevor teased.

Annie remembered that was one of the comments Keaton disliked the most about his height, but he cordially smiled and didn't let on that he wasn't amused. Annie appreciated his willingness to fit in with her friends.

Keaton slid into the booth next to Annie and reached for her hand. She leaned her head against his shoulder, happy to have him with her.

Trevor ordered another round of drinks. Cosmopolitans for the girls and a Manhattan for him. Keaton asked for a beer. Even with the slider in her stomach, the drink quickly went to Annie's head.

"You know we want to steal Annie away from you, right?" Steph teased Keaton as he read over the menu. "Trevor and I were originally planning to kidnap her and take her back to California with us."

"Annie, does that tempt you?" Keaton's eyes bored into hers.

"Nope." She squeezed his thigh, letting him know there was no way that was happening.

"She claims she likes living here," Trevor said, and sighed, not trying to hide his disappointment.

After the second cosmopolitan, Annie's head started to swim. "I need more food."

Keaton motioned the server over and they ordered a selection of appetizers. The band had arrived and began to play. Couples started drifting onto the dance floor.

"I'm feeling woozy," Annie told Steph.

"Then you should dance. You'll feel better if you get your body moving."

"Yes, let's dance." Trevor turned to Keaton. "Do you mind if I dance with your girl?"

He nodded toward Annie. "That's her decision."

"Annie?" Trevor asked. Even before she could answer, he tugged her onto the dance floor. It'd been ages since she'd been out like this. Ages since she'd let her hair down, laughed, or drank a little. With so much on her mind, it felt good to let loose, enjoy herself, and be with her friends again. Annie liked to think she was a decent dancer, and she wanted Keaton to know she was more than a pretty face. She giggled to herself as Trevor led her to the middle of the floor. With her arms above her head, her body swayed to the beat while Trevor danced around her. Lots of people turned their eyes on them, and more than a few wolf whistles came from the gathering crowd.

When she slid back into the booth, Annie was sweating and hot, but she didn't feel nearly as drunk.

Keaton smiled when she scooted next to him.

"It feels good to let loose. I've been uptight ever since Dr. Bainbridge approached me about —" She abruptly bit off the rest of what she was about to say.

Keaton was far too observant not to notice.

"Since he approached you about what?" he asked.

The table went quiet.

"You should tell him," Trevor advised. "He has a right to know what's going on."

"Your friends know and I don't?" Keaton asked, looking around the table, reading the looks on their faces. "Annie, what's going on?"

Her shoulders sagged with misery. The last thing she had wanted to do was lay this on Keaton so soon. "I have a decision to make, that's all."

"What kind of decision?" His eyes narrowed with doubt.

"About work," she said.

Keaton glanced around the table, his look questioning her friends, who remained stoic and quiet.

Their food arrived, and Annie had never been more grateful for an interruption.

"Would you like another round?" the server asked.

"No," Annie protested. If she hadn't been drinking she would never have slipped up. She should have known she couldn't trust herself not to say the very thing she didn't want to say, especially after drinking two cosmopolitans.

"I'm done, because I'm driving. But these two will have another," Gabby said, pointing to Steph and Trevor. The three headed back out to the dance floor, leaving Annie and Keaton alone.

Keaton remained silent. Before her eyes, Annie could see him withdrawing from her.

"You're leaving Oceanside, aren't you?" he asked.

"I . . . I haven't decided yet." Annie gave Keaton a quick rundown of the offer. "It's a wonderful opportunity, and one that's not likely to ever come again." She trained her eyes on him, her heart racing while she waited for his reaction.

Keaton shrugged. "Then you should go."

His words stunned her. "Don't you want to talk about it?"

"Not especially."

His body was stiff, and his eyes stared past her, as if looking at her was now painful.

"Don't you want me to stay?"

"Not my decision."

"But . . ." Annie was too shocked to form a viable question.

He turned to her then, and his look softened. "It's okay, Annie. I always knew you would leave. I'd hoped you'd stay for a year, but I get it. I'm grateful for the time we had."

The drink order arrived, and while Annie asked for a glass of water, Keaton quickly slipped out of the booth. She thought he was headed to the men's room but saw him walk out the door instead.

Her heart dropped at the sight of him walking away. This wasn't how she wanted things to play out. That he'd been flippant about it, acting like it was of little concern to him, cut deep. She hadn't expected that from him, and it hurt.

Trevor, Steph and Gabby returned at the end of the dance. "Where'd Keaton go?" Gabby asked.

"He left," Annie told her friends.

"He left?" Steph repeated. "That was abrupt. Was he upset about . . . you know?"

Annie nodded.

Trevor reached for his drink. "I should have kept my mouth shut. I'm sorry, Annie."

"It wasn't you. I was the one who blurted it out."

Gabby placed her hand over Annie's in a comforting way. "He'll come around. It's a shock. Give him time."

"Finding out that we knew and he didn't must have been a blow to his ego," Trevor added.

Annie suspected he was right. "I'll talk to him later and explain everything."

"I'm so sorry," Gabby said sympathetically.

"Me too," Annie whispered.

They paid their bill and left soon afterward. Gabby dropped Annie off, and the three of them went on to the motel.

As soon as she was inside the cottage, Annie tried calling Keaton. She felt horrible and wanted to do what she could to make it right. He must have turned off his phone, because her call went straight to voicemail.

She sent him a text, but that, too, went unanswered. After several tries and after leaving him two voice messages, Annie decided it was best to let him come to her when he was ready. She told him as much in her last voicemail.

They needed to talk this out.

It wasn't a done deal.

If he'd only give her a chance to explain the details.

Annie tossed and turned all night and woke with a throbbing headache. Despite a massive hangover and the unsettled situation between her and Keaton, she needed to be available to her friends. They met for brunch and were full of questions about what had happened with Keaton. Annie had nothing to tell them. He hadn't returned her calls. By noon, the three were ready to return to Seattle. Annie didn't blame them for leaving early; she was too out of sorts to be a good hostess. The rain didn't help, and Seattle had a lot more to offer.

As they were heading out, Steph hugged her close. "Don't worry. Everything will work itself out."

Annie returned the hug. She had her doubts. She'd thought she'd hear from Keaton before now and there'd been nothing.

Trevor hugged her next. "Keep in touch, okay?"

"I will," she promised.

When it came to Gabby's turn, she hugged Annie closely. "I'll call later."

Annie nodded and then stood and watched them climb into the vehicle and drive away.

After seeing them off, she turned to the cottage. It was then that she saw it. Annie gasped, and her hand automatically flew to her heart.

The medallion. The gift Annie had given Keaton for his birthday.

It was curled up in the corner to the right of the door, the silver chain glinting in contrast to the old wooden porch deck.

He'd returned her gift, carefully placing the piece where he knew she would find it . . . where he'd left her small gifts a dozen times before. Gifts she treasured.

Her stomach pitched as she reached for the medal. She held it protectively, folding her fingers around it. She stared at it for a long time, and prayed this wasn't Keaton's way of telling her good-bye.

CHAPTER
THIRTY

Annie had waited all day Saturday to hear from Keaton and didn't. This made it clear he had no intention of reaching out to her, despite her voicemail messages she'd left and the texts she'd sent. Well, fine, she'd seek him out and make him listen.

The first place she thought to look was at his home. Although she knocked loud and hard, there was no answer. Lennon barked loudly from the other side of the door, which led her to believe Keaton might be there but stubbornly refusing to answer. But, his truck was missing.

"Keaton," she called out. "It's me."

If he was inside, it was apparent that he knew it was her, but wasn't ready to clear the air, which frustrated her even more. She wanted him to know she wasn't taking back the medallion. He had her heart whether he wanted it or not, so she hung it on the door handle by the chain.

On the off-chance she was mistaken and Keaton hadn't been at the house, she drove around town, looking for his truck. That proved to be a futile effort. With nothing more to be done, she returned to the cottage, then sat depressed while she decided what to

299

do next. She felt the overwhelming need to make things right with him. It ate at her, leaving her frustrated and vexed.

It was past dinnertime, but she wasn't hungry. When she saw Preston pull up and park his truck, she hurried out of the cottage and called to him, hoping he would know something.

"Hey, Preston."

He glanced over at her and raised his hand in greeting.

Right away she noticed he was grinning, which told her things must be going well between him and Mellie.

"I'm bringing Mellie some dog food," he said, walking around to the back of his truck and hefting a twenty-five-pound bag over his shoulder.

Annie didn't think Mellie was currently caring for any injured dogs and suspected Preston used the dog food as an excuse to visit. He might not realize he was being obvious, but he was. No worries. If Mellie didn't want him visiting, she'd find a way to tell him so there'd be no question and he'd know it.

"Have you been in touch with Keaton today?" she asked, anxious to find out what she could.

Preston shook his head. "Haven't seen him in a couple days. That's not unusual. He'll show up when he's ready."

Annie was worried. They usually connected at least once a day. Often by text.

She returned to the house and reached for her phone. Although she'd tried several times earlier, she

300

felt compelled to try again. Aware that he wouldn't answer his phone, she sent a text.

Please call me.

Setting her phone down on the kitchen counter, Annie stared at it, waiting for it to ding, hoping he would text right away.

He didn't.

Keaton couldn't ignore her forever. Eventually he would need to talk to her.

Annie didn't sleep well on Saturday night and spent an anxious Sunday until she remembered that Keaton had mentioned he'd be working on the mural. He generally worked on it late at night. She waited until a few minutes after ten and walked into town, keeping in the shadows until she was at the bank building where Keaton had nearly finished his current mural.

Just as he'd casually mentioned earlier, Keaton stood in front of the mural. Only he wasn't painting. Instead, he was working frantically, whitewashing the work he'd already done, obliterating the hours and hours he'd already put into the project. He was destroying the scene, one stroke at a time.

"Keaton," she cried, horrified. "What are you doing?"

He paused but ignored her.

"Keaton, please! Don't!"

He reacted by doing exactly the opposite, painting over a portion of the mural that she had openly admired.

"Stop it! Stop!" she demanded, growing angrier by the minute. She clenched her fists, outraged that he would destroy something she found incredibly beautiful.

He continued, slopping white paint in frenzied movements, unable to obliterate the scene fast enough.

"It hurts me to see you doing this. What's wrong with you? Why would you destroy all your work?"

He turned to look at her, his face a hard mask. "Go. Leave."

"Leave?" she repeated, gesturing toward him with her hands, swallowing down the hurt. "Apparently all of this is your way of saying that you can't wait to see me gone. If that's what you want, then that's exactly what I'll do."

He shrugged, as if it made no difference to him.

Turning on her heel, she all but ran away, determined to get as far from him as she could. By the time she returned to the cottage, her lungs ached with pain, anger, and frustration.

Keaton had made it clear he intended to cut her out of his life. While she recognized he was trying to protect his own heart, it didn't hurt *her* heart any less. All she could do was pray he'd realize how unfair he was being to himself and to her.

Exhausted, she sank down on the top step of her small porch and buried her face in her hands while she struggled to control her raging emotions. When her phone rang, she had a fleeting hope it was Keaton, calling to apologize.

It died a quick death when she saw Mellie's name appear on the screen.

"What's going on?" she demanded. "You hurt your leg or something?"

"It's nothing." Annie was in no mood to explain what was happening between her and Keaton.

"Yeah, right. You're sitting under the porch light like you're carrying the weight of the world. Get over here. I'll make us coffee."

Annie debated if she should go, then decided talking this out with a friend would help. The kitchen door was unlocked when she tried the handle.

Mellie was standing by her coffee machine, brewing a cup, when Annie let herself into the house.

"Sit," she ordered, pointing toward the table. When the cup finished brewing she carried it over to Annie and set it down before returning to brew her own. Once she'd finished, she joined Annie at the table. Not one to waste time, she sipped her coffee, looked Annie in the eye, and said, "Spill."

"It's Keaton," Annie managed to whisper.

"I suspected as much. Better tell me what you did." She braced her elbows on the table and leaned forward to listen.

If there was anything amusing in this scenario, it was the way Mellie had automatically blamed her. She briefly went over her conversation with Dr. Bainbridge.

"In other words, you're breaking your lease and moving away from Oceanside." She made it a statement rather than a question.

"I . . . I don't know yet. I wasn't going to say anything until I'd made my decision, but I blurted it out when my friends were visiting." She leaned against the table and brushed the hair away from her face. "Being a doctor is something I've always wanted. And my dad would want me to do this."

"Your dad. I get it. You lost your parents, and you're thinking that this would have made them happy?"

Annie swallowed hard. "It isn't just my parents that I lost, Mellie," she said, pain bleeding into her voice as she struggled to keep her voice even. "My entire family died."

A moment of stunned silence followed. "Your entire family? What the hell happened?"

"A mudslide."

"Wait a minute," Mellie said, her head jerking back. "I remember hearing about that. It was all over the news. It was on an early Thanksgiving morning well over a year ago, right?"

Annie nodded, grateful it was unnecessary to go into the details. "I should have been with them that day," she continued, doing her best to hold back tears. "Mom wanted me home, so the entire family could be together." Her voice cracked as she continued. "I lost both my parents, my brother and his wife and Bella . . . She'd just started walking. A baby. She was just a baby." She began to softly cry.

"Damn," Mellie whispered. "I'm so sorry, Annie."

"I know . . . everyone is sorry, but sorry doesn't make up for the fact that my entire family is gone. The reason I came to Oceanside in the first place is because

304

of all the good memories I had from my family vacations here."

"So that's why it was so important for you to rent the cottage."

Annie nodded her head. "Our family stayed there a week every summer for several years."

"A lot of families used the cottage. I'm sorry that I don't remember yours, Annie." Mellie was full of sympathy.

"I didn't want people to pity me. Moving here was a fresh start for me . . . a way to look toward the future, because I was drowning in the past. I had to do *something*. I was depressed and sinking deeper into despair every day. I was afraid if anyone knew what had happened, that's all anyone would want to talk about, and I couldn't . . . I just couldn't let that tragedy continue to define me."

Nodding, Mellie reached across the table and gripped hold of her hand. "I understand."

"Thank you," Annie whispered.

"Did you tell Keaton about the disaster, about losing your entire family?"

Annie shook her head. "The only thing he knows is that I lost both my parents."

Mellie reached for her mug and took another sip. "Keaton is a complicated person."

Annie snorted. "You're telling me?"

Mellie smiled. "Yeah, I guess you know that as much or better than me. He's opened up to you in ways he never has with me. He's afraid of losing you, Annie, that's all."

"He made it sound like he didn't care one way or another what I decided."

"And you believe that? Think again, Annie. He's dying inside. So what are you going to do about fixing this?"

Annie hung her head. She couldn't do a single thing if he refused to talk to her. "I don't know," she whispered miserably.

It pained her to hurt Keaton. "He refuses to talk to me, to listen. He knows practically nothing about this offer. All he said was that I should take it, and then he walked away."

Her friend mulled this over. "Give him a chance. He's like one of those injured dogs he brings to me. He's lashing out at you, but once he understands the full situation, he'll come around."

The thought of comparing Keaton to a hurt dog made Annie smile for the first time that day. "I can only hope that you're right."

"I don't want to sound like I'm an expert when it comes to relationships, because I'm not. I grew up around Keaton. Far as I can remember, Preston was his only friend. He could have made other friends, but Keaton wasn't interested."

"Probably because that would mean he had to talk."

Mellie nodded. "You're right, most likely. He was always self-conscious about how big he is, although that could have worked to his advantage if he'd let it. He never did, preferring to stay in the background. Wrestling coach finally talked him into coming out for the team, and he did great. One on one, Keaton could handle anyone, but he didn't enjoy the attention. He could have been a state champion but chose not to compete. Coach never forgave him. The school didn't either."

Annie could well picture how painfully shy Keaton must have been as a teenager.

"All the years I've known him, I've never seen him as happy as he has been with you, Annie. I might like to read romances, but I don't believe much in love and all that rot. I like the fantasy of it all, and who doesn't? But you and Keaton have given me hope that finding love is possible."

"I want the same thing."

"That seems to be something we're all looking for," Mellie said.

Annie could only agree.

CHAPTER
THIRTY-ONE

It came as no surprise to Annie that Keaton returned the medallion a second time. She wasn't willing to fight him on the issue. If he was determined to cut her out of his life without knowing the details, then there wasn't a thing she could say. He basically had made the decision for her. After carefully considering her options and giving it a lot of thought and prayer, Annie decided to pursue the opportunity. She told Mellie she would be leaving at the end of the summer, and offered to pay off her lease. Mellie refused. Annie was certain Mellie told Keaton that she would be moving come September.

When Annie told Dr. Bainbridge that she would gratefully accept the health organization's offer, he was delighted. Annie was, too, although she missed Keaton every minute of every day. Whether he wanted it or not, he still owned her heart. She bought a shorter silver chain and wore the medallion herself.

Britt McDuffee and her boyfriend, Jimmy Lane, graduated from high school in the middle of June. Annie was honored that Britt sent her an invitation and personally asked her to attend the graduation ceremony.

On Britt's big day, Annie sat next to Teresa, who dabbed at her eyes with a tissue throughout the ceremony. Logan was restless on the other side of her, swinging his feet, anxious to get home to his puppy. While they chatted before the graduation, Teresa didn't mention her daughter's pregnancy, and that was fine. Only those who were close to Britt knew about the baby. Although the teenager was more than six months along, she barely showed.

Annie didn't know what the couple had decided when it came to their future or that of their child. She had her own opinion, but Annie didn't feel it was her place to share it. She would support Britt and Jimmy with whatever choice they made.

When the school principal awarded Britt a scholarship, one chosen by the faculty, Teresa, in her joy, grabbed hold of Annie's hand, squeezing hard.

Teresa leaned toward Annie and whispered, "I never had the chance to attend college. I so wanted Britt to have the opportunity. I was willing to take on more houses, anything I could do. This scholarship is really going to help."

After the graduation exercises, Teresa invited Annie and several of Britt's friends to her home for a small party. With Carl out of the picture, she was free to live the way she wanted to. No one had heard from Carl, who apparently had left the state.

The graduation party was a big success. Teresa was a wonderful hostess. She must have cooked for days. Annie had never seen Britt happier, and she knew Teresa felt good to be able to do this for her daughter. She knew Keaton had been invited and had to assume he'd stayed away because of her. It hurt Annie that he went to such lengths to avoid her.

Keaton had scarcely been to visit Mellie, too, she noticed. If he did stop by, he apparently made certain it was at times he knew she wouldn't be at the cottage. She mentioned as much to Mellie.

"Haven't seen Keaton in two weeks," her friend complained. "He asked Preston to bring me my groceries and mail. His father is in hospice care now, so he's using that as an excuse to keep away, but you and I know the real reason."

The news about Keaton and his father upset Annie, and although she tried to hide it, Mellie knew. The other woman patted Annie's hand to comfort her. "Don't worry. Keaton won't stay away forever."

She wanted to believe that was true, but she had her doubts.

"He's a man," Mellie explained. "It simply takes them longer to come to their senses. He wants what's best for you but feels the need to protect his heart even if that means behaving like a damn fool."

"He has all summer. I don't understand why we can't enjoy the time we do have together."

Mellie grumbled under her breath, "I'm the last person you should ask about understanding men. Every relationship I've ever had has gone down in flames. Keaton doesn't want my advice. All I can suggest is that you give him time."

The rest of the summer was busy at the clinic with the crush of cases from the heavy tourist season. Annie treated everything from sunburns to the more serious case of a young man who'd had a serious surfing accident. She'd held his hand and comforted him before he was airlifted to a Seattle hospital with a serious spinal injury.

Working the hours that she did, Annie often arrived home exhausted. The blueberries and raspberries were responding well to the fertilizer and sunshine. Combined with the wild berries she found, she was able to make several batches of jam, sharing with Mellie and the clinic staff. She couldn't look at those thriving bushes and not think of Keaton and all the work he'd put into clearing the area enough for them to flourish. On a regular basis Annie stopped to look in on Keaton's father while he was in hospice care. She didn't do it out of obligation, but as a means of expressing appreciation to Keaton for all he'd done for her. It was a small thing, and while Keaton might never know, it made her feel good.

Teresa was gradually making progress in cleaning out Mellie's house. Not without a lot of complaining and whining from Mellie, of course. Thankfully, Preston was there to encourage and comfort her.

One afternoon in late July, Annie heard Mellie shouting at Teresa as the housekeeper opened the door and stepped onto the porch.

"That yarn belonged to my grandmother," Mellie cried, as if Teresa had walked away with a priceless artifact.

Refusing to listen, Teresa hauled the large bag stuffed with skeins of yarn out the kitchen door and onto the porch.

"I refuse to let you steal my grandmother's yarn," the homeowner screeched. "I was going to use that."

Teresa shouted back, "Do you knit or crochet?"

Mellie paused and childishly stamped her foot. "No, but I might someday."

"If you haven't by now, you probably won't."

"You don't know that," Mellie insisted, standing in the open doorway, swaying back and forth, almost tempted to leave the security of the house to retrieve the long-ignored yarn.

"If you feel that strongly, then come and get it," Teresa challenged.

Frowning, Mellie hesitated. She was tempted, just not enough.

"That's what I thought," Teresa said, and then added in a gentle tone, "Besides, it was in the newspaper recently that the women at the senior center are looking for yarn so they can knit hats, mittens, and scarves for the children in refugee camps overseas. Some of those women were probably friends of your grandmother's. She would have wanted them to have it."

Giving in, Mellie tossed her hands in the air. "Okay, fine, you can take the yarn."

This wasn't easy for her friend, and Annie was proud of her.

Mellie added, "Next thing I know, you'll be wanting to get rid of the family silverware."

"No worries," Teresa assured her. "The silver is safely tucked away in a drawer in the dining room."

"Well . . . thank God for that," Mellie muttered sarcastically.

"I do every single day," Teresa called back, smiling, as Mellie turned away from the screen door.

Annie couldn't be happier with her landlord's progress. When she had first moved into the cottage, Mellie wouldn't even open her door. Looking at the yard was more than she could bear. She frequently did so now. Recently, Annie saw her stand in the doorway, eagerly awaiting Preston's arrival.

With most of her evenings free these days, Annie had continued working in the yard, clearing the flowerbed, planting, and trimming back the bushes. She did volunteer work at the food bank and the hospice center, too.

Mellie and Annie saw each other often these days. Mellie was grateful — well, as grateful as she was willing to voice — for the work Annie had put into the yard. More than once, Mellie commented on the garden.

According to Preston, Mellie was excited to see the changes taking place on the property. It was almost back to the way it'd been when her grandparents were alive. Preston and Annie chatted a few times when he came to see Mellie. She wanted to ask him about Keaton, and he seemed to sense that and quickly made an exit to avoid the conversation.

All summer, Preston was a regular visitor at Mellie's house. Rarely a day went by when he didn't have one excuse or another to stop by. He often stayed late, too, she noticed. Annie was convinced it was his devotion to Mellie that had taken the sharp edge off her brusque personality.

In the first week of August, Annie learned Mellie was nursing a badly malnourished set of three puppies. She knew Keaton had most likely been the one to bring them to her. Because the mother had died, the puppies needed to be bottle-fed. When she was off work in the evenings, Annie helped Mellie with the feedings.

The third day after the puppies arrived, Annie sat on the floor, holding one in her lap, feeding him with the bottle. He was adorable, tempting her with the idea of adopting him herself. She would if she wasn't returning to Seattle and starting medical school. She spoke softly to the puppy as he greedily sucked away at the miniature bottle. The other two puppies had been fed and were napping.

Annie heard the door off the kitchen open and assumed it was Preston, until she heard a familiar voice.

Keaton.

"Need help?" he asked Mellie, referring to the puppies. He remained a man of few words.

"No thanks, Annie's been lending me a hand," she heard Mellie tell him.

She listened intently, wondering if Keaton would ask about her, anything to show she remained in his thoughts.

He didn't.

"Meant to come sooner."

Annie frowned; he sounded troubled.

"What's going on?" Mellie seemed to have sensed it, too.

"Not much."

"Keaton," Mellie chastised gently, "we've been friends too long for you to give me that. This has to do with your father, doesn't it? Don't know what your problem is. You haven't been the same since Annie —"

"Told you," he barked, "don't say her name. Ever."

Annie flinched and lowered her head, releasing a slow breath. When she looked up, to her surprise, she found Keaton standing in the doorway to the room. Her breath caught in her lungs. He looked shocked, too, as though seeing her threw him off balance.

Despite whatever was troubling him now, Keaton looked good to Annie. She was reminded of how big and muscular he was, especially when she was on the floor, looking up at him. His hair was longer than she remembered and his eyes a bit duller, like he hadn't slept in a while.

"Keaton," she managed to say, although her voice came out in more of a whisper.

He didn't return her greeting. Instead, he turned around and walked away. A few seconds later she heard the kitchen door open and close.

Clearly he was averse to even making polite conversation with her.

Mellie joined Annie a few minutes later. "Keaton's got a lot on his mind, so don't take his behavior personally," she told her, going out of her way to make excuses for Keaton. "His father only has a short time left to live."

From her time volunteering at the hospice center, Annie was aware of his father's condition. Knowing the rocky relationship Keaton had with his father, this couldn't have been easy for him. That explained the fatigue on his face.

Hospice was the best place for the older man. Annie decided to stop by the next day. She'd do what she could, for no other reason than the fact that he had fathered Keaton. There was no need for Keaton to know.

"Keaton looked tired," she said.

"He did," Mellie agreed. "Still crazy about you."

Annie shook her head. "You don't need to lie. I heard what he said. He can't bear to hear the sound of my name."

Her friend shook her head. "Think he'd give a horse's butt if he didn't care? He can't get you out of his mind, although heaven knows he's giving it his best shot. Don't be discouraged. He's angry with himself for lowering his guard and for falling in love, and then frustrated that his feelings aren't strong enough to keep you here."

Annie knew Mellie was right, although she wished he'd given her the chance to discuss her options with him and to get his feedback. Instead, he'd behaved like a wounded bear, cutting her completely out of his life.

The next afternoon, Annie stopped by the hospice center, a home that had been donated to the community. She checked in with the volunteer currently on shift.

The woman, Linda McKoen, was someone Annie knew. Linda was a gentle soul, and a retired nurse.

When Annie asked about Keaton's father, Linda shook her head and muttered, "That man's a piece of work."

After what Keaton had told her, this came as no surprise.

Being as quiet as possible, she checked on Seth and found him sleeping. Even from a prone position she could tell the older man probably used to be as tall as Keaton, though much thinner, almost skin and bones. The cancer had ravaged his body. From previous visits, she could see no resemblance between father and son except his height, and she guessed that Keaton must have taken after his mother more than his father. For several minutes, she stood and watched him sleep.

Not wanting to disturb him, Annie walked away. Besides, she didn't know what she'd say if he was awake. Even though she'd been by a few other times, they'd never spoken; he didn't know her, and Annie was certain Keaton wouldn't have mentioned her, either.

"Do you want me to let him know you stopped by?" Linda asked when Annie returned.

"No."

"You know Keaton?" Linda asked gently. "He's such a pleasant young man."

Annie could only agree. "He's a really good person."

"He is," Linda concurred. "Checks on his dad frequently. Won't go in and see him, but stops by and asks about him."

"If Seth needs anything, please let me know."

"I will."

Annie left shortly afterward and continued home. When she arrived at the cottage, she found Britt sitting on her front porch, waiting for her.

"Britt," she greeted her, seeing that the baby bump was clearly noticeable now.

"Hi," Britt said, and stood. "I wanted you to know Jimmy and I talked it over, and we've decided to consider the adoption agency you mentioned. Would you mind coming with us for our first visit?"

"Of course. I'd be more than happy to do that."

"Thank you, Annie," Britt said, and then reached out and impulsively hugged her.

While leaving Oceanside was going to be hard, Annie couldn't help but feel good that she'd been able to help others as much as they'd helped her.

CHAPTER
THIRTY-TWO

Annie was finishing up her dinner dishes when a loud clap of noise came from the yard next door, jolting her. Standing on her tiptoes, she looked out the window and noticed Preston marching down the steps of Mellie's place like he couldn't get away fast enough.

Uh-oh — looks like trouble is brewing in paradise.

Over the last few weeks she'd seen a softening in Mellie. She'd been more willing to let go of the piles of stuff that littered nearly every corner of the house. Teresa had not only cleared the kitchen and dining room but had made progress in the living room, too. With each truckload, Mellie had made less and less of a fuss.

Looking out the window again, Annie saw that when Preston reached his truck, he looked back at the house. His face was scrunched up with a mixture of anger, regret, and disappointment. For a long moment, he continued looking, before opening the door and sliding in. His shoulders sagged as he glanced one last time over his shoulder, started the engine, and drove off.

Mellie was looking out the kitchen window, watching Preston. Although it was difficult to tell from this distance, it looked like Mellie's face was red. Whether with anger or tears, Annie couldn't tell.

Annie debated going to check on her friend. It would go either of two ways: Annie would be the last person Mellie wanted to see and would demand that she get out and leave her alone; or, she would welcome Annie and cry on her shoulder.

She gave it a couple hours.

Preston didn't return.

Hoping to smooth the way, Annie baked peanut butter brownies, cut them in neat squares, and set them on a plate. It was her favorite "your man done you wrong" recipe. Armed with the goodies, she walked to Mellie's.

Knocking, she let herself into the kitchen, where she was most likely to find her friend. Mellie looked up, her eyes bright with anticipation, until she saw it was Annie. The light quickly faded.

Annie waited for more of a reaction and got none. "Thought you might need my special brownies."

Mellie scowled at the plate.

"These are my 'your man done you wrong' brownies."

"Oh," she said, ignoring the offering, which Annie set on the table. "I guess you heard Preston slam out of the house."

"I heard something. You two have a difference of opinion?"

Mellie grabbed a brownie off the plate. "Something like that."

"I won't ask about it."

"Wouldn't do you any good if you did."

Annie had already figured that would be the case. Mellie wasn't the type to share confidences or seek advice. "Misery loves company, and seeing that we're both on the outs with our men, I figured we could drown our sorrow in brownies."

"I'm more inclined to bring out the Fireball whiskey."

"Not a bad idea," Annie said, amused and only half serious.

She should have known Mellie wasn't joking. Before Annie could say anything more, Mellie dragged a stepstool to the cabinet above the refrigerator and retrieved a large bottle. Next she brought out two glasses, filled both with ice, and poured a liberal amount of whiskey in each glass before handing one to Annie.

"What should we toast to?" Mellie asked, at a loss to find a reason good enough to raise her glass.

"To sisterhood," Annie suggested.

"The sisterhood of rotten men," Mellie added, frowning.

Annie shook her head, disliking that idea. "Keaton's not rotten; he's stubborn."

"So is Preston," Mellie said and raised her glass a second time. "To the sisterhood of stubborn men."

They clicked glasses, and each took a healthy sip. The whiskey burned all the way to Annie's stomach, but it was a good burn.

Mellie set her glass down on the kitchen table and stared into the distance. "I told Preston what to expect when he first started showing up. I was perfectly clear that I wasn't interested in a relationship. I didn't want to mislead him; I didn't hide anything. He knew how I felt about anything romantic between us."

It appears that Preston's heart had been rejected not once but twice now, Annie thought to herself.

"He said he understood that," Mellie continued.

Annie wasn't going to ply her friend with questions, seeing that Mellie hadn't asked for advice. If she wanted Annie's opinion, then she'd ask for it. What Mellie needed, Annie figured, was someone willing to listen.

"I told him all I could offer him was friendship."

She stared down at the table, and Annie swore she could see tears glistening in Mellie's eyes. It was either the pain she felt from her disagreement with Preston or the result of the hard liquor. Annie couldn't tell which.

Reading between the lines, she realized Preston must have let Mellie know his feelings. She knew he had loved Mellie for a long time.

"I don't need a man in my life."

"Don't have one in mine," Annie added. Unlike her friend, she would have liked to discuss options with Keaton, to figure out ways to make their relationship work. He refused to give her the chance to do so.

Mellie held on to the glass with both hands. "It's my fault," she said, staring down into the glass. "I let him get too close. He claimed I encouraged him, and he's right, I did. He'd stop by, and we'd sit and chat. Didn't know I had that much to talk about with anyone. We'd sometimes be at it for hours. When he left, I was sorry

322

to see him go and I'd think about all the things that I wanted to tell him next time."

It was different for Annie and Keaton. Words hadn't seemed necessary. She could spend hours with him without either of them speaking a single word. It was that companionable silence she missed the most. The way he'd smile at her, like she was the most precious thing in the world, or take hold of her hand and raise it to his lips for a gentle kiss. He never asked her prying questions, never made demands. She'd needed that, needed him. Annie didn't realize how much until he was no longer there. The quiet felt completely different now, echoing loneliness and loss. Keaton had filled the empty space in her heart that she'd been convinced had been forever taken from her.

Mellie took another sip and hitched her breath. "Preston admitted he loved me."

Annie patted Mellie's shoulder, hoping that would comfort her. Her friend jerked away as a quick reminder that she didn't like to be touched.

"He said he'd had a crush on me from as far back as high school. Loved me from afar for years." She shook her head to chase away his words. "Doubt he said ten words to me all through school. You'd think he'd have let me know then."

"You'd think," Annie agreed, although she was certain it'd taken Preston all these years to work up the nerve to tell Mellie how he felt.

"What do you know?" Mellie snapped back.

"Hey, I'm agreeing with you." The whiskey had already gone to her head. It was liquor that had caused her trouble with Keaton in the first place. She knew better than to indulge in the hard stuff, no matter how it helped to ease the pain.

"He kissed me," Mellie whispered.

"Was it awful?" Annie scrunched up her face.

"No," she whispered. "It was wonderful."

"Oh no."

"Right. Not what I wanted to feel, either. We had a good thing going as friends. I never realized how much we had in common. We share a history, both of us growing up in Oceanside. Most everyone leaves, but not us. Well, I did leave for a while, but I came back. He has a soft spot for animals, the same as me."

"Right."

"He plays World of Warcraft and so do I. Haven't had a friend like Preston since I ran off with Cal." She rubbed her face and muttered, "Biggest mistake of my life, that Cal. I should have turned tail and hightailed it the minute he started spewing his charm on me. I hate how stupid and naïve I was to listen to that scumbag." She closed her eyes and shook her head. "When I think of all the garbage I put up with because of him, I want to punish myself." She shook her head again, trying to chase away the memories. "How stupid can a woman get?"

"Weren't you a teenager when you ran off with him?" She wanted to help Mellie understand she'd been young and foolish. Everyone made stupid mistakes, no matter what their age. The key was growing from the experience, becoming wiser and smarter.

Mellie refused to respond.

It was then that it hit Annie.

Bull's-eye.

Directly in the middle of her forehead.

Mellie hadn't moved forward. She hadn't forgiven herself. She lived in fear, afraid of making the same mistake. As for wanting to punish herself, she was doing exactly that. By not leaving the house, by rejecting Preston's love. This was all a form of self-punishment.

"Preston isn't Cal, Mellie," she reminded her, and realized the instant the words left her mouth that she'd said the wrong thing.

"You know Cal?" she demanded, eyes flashing with instant fire.

"Uh, no."

"Then you know nothing."

"I know nothing," Annie repeated, hoping that would appease her friend.

"He was a cheating man-whore. Every word out of his mouth was a bald-faced lie. I wanted to believe him, so I accepted everything he said as gospel truth. Grandpa read him like a book. Five minutes after I introduced the two of them, Grandpa forbade me to see Cal ever again. I should have listened. It would have saved me years of grief."

"I'm sorry," Annie whispered.

"I thank God every day that we never married."

"You weren't married?"

"Another Cal lie. He was already married. Naturally, he forgot to mention that when I ran away with him. Fact was, he had two or three other wives strewn across

325

five states. I didn't learn that for a year or two. Should have left him then. But I'm too big of an idiot to realize all he ever wanted from me was my trust fund. Thankfully, I didn't have full access to it until I was thirty."

Mellie reached for the Fireball and refilled her glass, splashing some over the edges in her eagerness to top it off.

"I don't think Preston ever married." Annie remembered Keaton telling her that.

Mellie ignored the comment. "Did you know he is able to finish the Sunday edition of the *New York Times* crossword puzzle?"

"No." She wasn't aware of the significance of that feat.

"In ink!" she added in awe. "I don't usually make it past Wednesday. They get harder each day of the week, in case you didn't know."

"I didn't."

"He's so smart. I never paid that much attention to grades when I was in school. What a waste. I might have learned something."

Thinking she needed food in her stomach to neutralize the alcohol, Annie reached for a brownie. Mellie slapped her hand. "Those are mine."

"But I baked them."

"Bake more. I'm not sharing. Preston likes —" She stopped talking abruptly as she studied the plate of brownies. After an awkward moment, she shoved it closer to Annie. "Help yourself. Preston won't be back."

"You don't know that. Weren't you the one who told me to give Keaton time? Seems like you need to take your own advice."

"I told him to leave."

This wasn't good. No wonder Preston had seemed hurt and rejected.

"Said I never wanted to see him again."

Annie wanted to groan. Poor Preston. It'd probably taken him all these weeks of visiting Mellie in her home to build up his courage to tell her how he felt. How devastating it must have been to be kicked out of the house and be told that he wasn't welcome back. Annie's heart hurt for Preston.

"You love him," Annie said softly, uncertain how Mellie would react to the truth.

"I don't," the other woman insisted, stiffening with resolve.

"You do. He's all you talk about."

"I do not. You keep asking about him."

"No, Mellie, I haven't. You're the one who brought him up, not me."

She looked like she was about to argue, then didn't. She appeared to be mentally reviewing their conversation. Her eyes widened, realizing that Annie might be right. She had been talking nonstop about Preston.

Gradually a thoughtful frown developed. "You think I love Preston?"

Annie grinned. "Yup."

"All I ever wanted was for us to be friends."

"You are friends; that's what makes this wonderful. Love based on shared experiences and friendship is what helps relationships last." Ironic, Annie thought, that she should be giving Mellie advice, when her own experiences with falling in love had been gigantic failures.

"I've never enjoyed anyone's company as much as I do Preston's," Mellie admitted.

"You can laugh with Preston and cry with him, too, Mellie. And, most important, you can be yourself. Preston is willing to love you, Mellie. Forgive me for being blunt, but you're not an easy woman to love."

Annie closed her eyes, ready for her friend to lambast her for being brutally honest.

"I know," she conceded.

If Mellie was willing to accept a few hard-to-accept truths, then Annie figured she'd drop another. "You mentioned earlier how much you regretted running off with Cal."

She nodded. "Stupidest mistake of my life."

"And you wanted to punish yourself for that."

Her friend narrowed her eyes. "I said that? I did, didn't I?"

"Yes, you did, and Mellie, my dear, dear friend, that's exactly what you're doing. You're punishing yourself by holing up inside this house. You're refusing to forgive yourself for your willingness to accept Cal's lies and for wasting all those senseless years."

Mellie's face hardened. "Thank you, Dr. Phil." She shoved the plate of brownies back at Annie. "I think it's time you left. Take these with you. I don't need your sympathy any more than I need your advice."

Scooting back her chair, Annie took her glass over to the sink. "These are people who care about you, Mellie. Preston loves you and I count you as one of my dearest friends. You can accept that love and friendship, or you can reject it. The choice is yours."

Mellie refused to look at her. After what seemed an eternity, she murmured, "Like I said, it's time for you to go."

CHAPTER
THIRTY-THREE

Keaton stopped off at the animal shelter to check on his friend Preston. He hadn't seen much of him lately, since Preston had taken over duties with Mellie. Unfortunately, it seemed Mellie and Preston's relationship had abruptly ended. He didn't know the details, and he wasn't inclined to pry into his friend's personal life. Preston had accepted that Keaton was no longer involved with Annie, and Keaton didn't feel he could do any differently when it came to his friend and Mellie. Privately, he wished it would have worked out for the two of them, seeing how much Preston cared about Mellie.

He waited until the animal shelter was closed before he went in, so they could catch up without constant interruptions. Keaton was determined not to mention Mellie, but he knew something was up and it wasn't good, which Preston confirmed when he told Keaton that he'd no longer be available to deliver the mail and groceries to her.

Keaton had his own code and let himself into the shelter. He found Preston hauling the heavy bag of dog food from stall to stall, filling the dogs' bowls. The barking was a tumultuous uproar, the dogs all eagerly awaiting their turn to be fed. They made it impossible for Preston to realize he was no longer alone. Rather than announce himself, Keaton picked up a second bag and pitched in with the row of dogs in the stalls on the opposite side of the kennel.

Preston glanced up, saw that he had help, and thanked Keaton with an abrupt nod.

"You okay?" Keaton asked, once they were directly across from each other.

"Any reason I shouldn't be?" Preston flared back.

Yup, Preston was having relationship problems. Not that Keaton was any kind of expert. He'd made peace with the fact that Annie would soon be leaving town. It was inevitable, and had been from the start, only he hadn't wanted to believe it. He'd been a fool to think she'd even consider staying, although he had expected she'd complete the contracted year. It seemed a signed contract, plus the lease on the cottage, weren't enough to keep her in Oceanside. At the first opportunity, she'd found an excuse to walk away. He'd hoped . . . He stopped, refusing to let his mind drift into a minefield of negativity. It'd been a huge mistake to involve his heart. He knew it at the time, but that hadn't kept him from falling hard for a woman who many would consider miles out of his league. Letting Annie go hurt about as bad as anything he'd endured in his life, but he was wiser now, accepting it. He wished her well, but for his own protection, he wanted nothing more to do with her.

Preston made a few grumbling noises. If he'd said anything, it had completely bypassed Keaton. Keaton had promised himself to leave matters alone, but it was clear from the sunken look about Preston that he was brokenhearted. Keaton recognized that pain all too well. He didn't know if he could help, but he decided to try.

"You on the outs with Mellie?"

"What if I am?"

Keaton set down the bag of dog food and leaned against the kennel door. This wasn't the Preston he knew of late. Since spending nearly every free moment with Mellie this summer, his friend had been like a big puppy, happy and carefree.

"Anything I can do?" Keaton asked, opening the kennel door. A terrier mix leapt into his arms.

"Nope. Not a thing."

They continued to work in silence for several minutes.

"You take Mellie her mail?" Preston asked. The words seemed to be wrenched from him like he hated asking but couldn't help himself.

"Yeah."

"She say anything?"

"Not to me." Now that he thought about it, that wasn't like Mellie. "Never knew her not to have a complaint about something."

A hint of a smile came and went from Preston.

"She was shockingly subdued when I stopped by."

Preston nodded, that coming as no surprise to him. He finished feeding the dogs. Keaton noticed that the cats and other animals had already been fed. His row had several empty stalls, so he was finished at about the same time. Preston stored the food, turned off the lights, and locked the doors.

Keaton walked with him and stopped abruptly, his steps faltering. Standing in the middle of the shelter parking lot was Annie.

It felt like he'd been sucker-punched, and for one wild moment he couldn't breathe. Generally, he was better prepared and could control his reaction when he saw her, but this time she'd caught him off guard. Right away his eyes locked on to her as if pulled by a magnetic force beyond his control.

She looked as stunned as he felt, but after a second she acknowledged him with a tight nod.

"Preston, do you have a minute?" she asked, dragging her eyes away from Keaton.

His friend stuffed his hands into his back pockets. "What's on your mind?"

"It's Mellie."

Preston's entire body tensed. "What's the problem?"

"She loves you."

He snickered loudly and shook his head in denial. "She loves me so much she kicked me out of her house. Damn near shoved me out the door."

"You frightened her."

"Me? Look at me, Annie. Am I a scary guy?"

Annie wasn't backing down. "You said you loved her."

Keaton turned to his friend. He'd known that Preston had loved Mellie since he was a skinny high school kid. It'd broken his heart when she ran off all those years ago. When she'd come back to town,

333

Keaton had urged him to make his move, only to be rejected.

Five years.

It'd taken Preston a long time to work up courage enough to let Mellie know how he felt. For a while everything seemed to be working out for him.

"Yeah, well, that was a big mistake."

"It wasn't a mistake," Annie said gently. "She's miserable —"

"Listen," Preston said, cutting Annie off mid-sentence. "I gave it my best shot and learned my lesson. No guy wants to toss his heart in the ring and then have it stomped on, and that's what Mellie did."

"I know what you're saying, but . . ."

Preston walked over to his truck and opened the door. "And no guy wants to hear that his declaration of love makes someone miserable. As far as I'm concerned it's over."

"Preston, please listen."

"No!" he shouted adamantly. "I had my say, and I'm done making a fool out of myself."

Both Keaton and Annie gasped. For as long as Keaton had known Preston, he'd never heard his friend raise his voice.

"I'm finished," Preston insisted. "I've pined after that woman for years. Well, no more. It's over, understand? I don't want anything more to do with her. Mellie made it plain she doesn't have feelings for me. Fine. I've accepted her decision and am grateful for the honesty. Didn't really think I had a shot, anyway."

334

"Can't a woman change her mind?" Annie asked, and then, looking to Keaton, added in a low hush, "Or a man?"

Preston remained unconvinced. "You can tell her for me that it's too late."

Keaton had no clue Preston could be this stubborn.

"Won't you at least talk to her?" Annie pleaded.

Preston was sticking to his resolve and refused to budge. "Heard all I want to hear from Mellie."

"Okay, I understand how you feel. But tell me, what would it take for you to give her another chance?"

"Not happening." Preston wasn't bending.

"Come on, be reasonable," Annie pleaded.

Keaton had to admire his friend. He didn't know if he'd have the strength to refuse Annie. The woman wasn't giving up easily.

Desperate now, seeing that Preston remained steadfastly stubborn, she looked to Keaton for help. He shook his head, refusing to get involved. He didn't feel it was his place to champion Mellie. She was the one who'd broken Preston's heart.

Preston removed his cap and slapped it against his thigh. Keaton had seen him do this before, whenever he grew frustrated or uncertain. He turned to face Annie. "Mellie know you're here?" Preston asked.

Annie's face turned pink. She didn't need to answer for him to know the truth. Mellie had no idea what Annie was doing.

Preston huffed and shook his head. "That's what I thought."

Trying again, Annie turned to Keaton. "Say something," she pleaded. "I could use some help here."

Keaton shook his head.

Climbing into the cab of his truck, Preston was about to drive off when he rolled down his window. Annie stepped up to the truck.

"Tell you what," Preston said. "I'll give Mellie one last chance, but she has to come to me."

"Come to you?" Annie repeated, frowning. "What do you mean?"

"Exactly what I said. She has to step out of that house and come to me."

Annie leaned forward, not sure she had heard him correctly. "You do realize she hasn't set foot outside that house in five years, don't you?"

"Yup," Preston confirmed. "If she loves me the way you say she does, then she can prove it."

"But, Preston —"

Whatever it was Annie had to say, Preston wasn't listening. He stepped on the gas and drove off, leaving Keaton standing alone with Annie in the parking lot of the animal shelter.

He was taken by surprise when Annie whirled around and confronted him. "You were no help whatsoever."

The accusation in her voice caused him to raise both hands as if she'd pointed a gun in his direction.

"You saw Mellie, you know how unhappy she is, and still you refuse to help. What kind of friend are you?"

"One who minds his own business."

"Fine. Whatever." In a huff of righteous indignation, she stomped over to where she'd parked.

Keaton knew he shouldn't try to stop her. Now that he'd seen her, though, it was way too hard to let her go.

"I heard you've stopped by the hospice center to check on Seth." He wouldn't call that man Father. He didn't deserve the title.

Her steps slowed. "Just . . . I expected he would have died by now."

The staff said much the same thing. The old man lingered, barely conscious of where he was or why.

"He's too mean to die."

"He's certainly not the most popular patient."

Knowing his father as well as Keaton did, that was understandable. "Don't go visit him out of any sense of duty to me."

Her eyes flared as she let out an angry retort. "Okay, fine. I won't. Is there something else you want to tell me?" she asked, arms akimbo, glaring at him.

"Not particularly. You're leaving. I wish you well. Surprised you hung around as long as you did."

Annie's eyes spit fire, and she pounded her foot with enough outrage for the sound to echo around him like a sonic boom. "The thing is, Keaton, I was given the opportunity of a lifetime."

"So I heard," he said, unable to hide his sarcasm. "Congratulations. You must be happy to get away from this hole-in-the-wall town."

"You know that's not true."

He heard the pain in her voice and chose to ignore it.

Annie started to walk away when she unexpectedly turned around and faced him. "Keaton, please, you need to help Mellie. I'll never ask anything of you again, I promise."

His chest ached, and he found it nearly impossible to refuse her. He thought he had become immune to her, and finding out that he wasn't came as a blow to the weeks he'd spent forcing her out of his thoughts, convincing himself it was over. He was trying his best to let her go without regrets. It angered him that she continued to have this emotional impact on him. He thought he was stronger than this.

"I understand why Mellie is the way she is," Annie continued. "She's punishing herself for abandoning her grandparents. She was their only grandchild and they pampered her. She left them for a man unworthy of her love, choosing him over her family —"

"She told you all this?" he asked, interrupting her.

"Yes, and it involved Fireball whiskey."

"That explains it," he muttered.

"Mellie stayed with Cal for all those years because she was too proud to admit that her grandparents were right. When she was finally ready, it was too late. That's why she's refused to give up anything that belonged to them. All those boxes and containers were filled with their things."

"That doesn't explain why she won't leave the house."

"But it does," she countered. "It's a form of self-punishment. She refused to forgive herself, so she remained holed up in the one place where she once had comfort and love."

"What do you want from me?" he demanded, frustrated because he felt himself giving in, when he was determined he wouldn't.

"Talk to Preston, and I'll deal with Mellie. I'll explain to her what Preston said. If she's willing to step outside the house, then that should tell him how much she loves him."

"But does she?" Keaton had his doubts. Like his friend, he'd given love a try and walked away with a wounded heart. He was also holding on to what was left of his pride, refusing to show Annie that it was killing him inside to let her go.

Annie's eyes went soft and glistened in the late-afternoon sun. "SHE. LOVES. HIM." From the way she spoke, Keaton could almost believe she wasn't talking about Mellie and Preston but her own feelings for him.

Keaton felt the pull toward her. It took all the reserve strength he could muster to ignore the powerful need to hold her. This was the longest conversation they'd had in nearly two months, and every moment that passed, he felt himself weakening. He needed to get away from her.

"What do you want me to say to Preston?" he snapped.

"I don't know. Just get him to the house late Monday afternoon after I'm done at the clinic."

Keaton shook his head. She was asking the impossible.

"Use any excuse you can. Make something up, I don't care."

"Do you honestly think you can convince Mellie to walk out that door?" He had serious doubts.

She nodded. "I'm going to give it my best shot. And if she can, that should tell Preston everything he needs to know."

The woman was dreaming, but Keaton resolved to do his part because Annie had asked it of him. In his mind, there wasn't a snowball's chance in hell that Mellie would leave that house for Preston, for love or for anything else.

CHAPTER
THIRTY-FOUR

Men were difficult.

That was an understatement if Annie had ever heard one. She'd given up trying to figure out Keaton. She still couldn't understand why he'd severed their relationship without giving her a chance to discuss their options. He'd completely shut her out of his life. Annie had been stunned and hurt, but as time wore on, she'd become annoyed. She wasn't going to plead with him to hear her out. She could be just as proud as he was.

The only encouragement she'd received to this point was his willingness to arrange for Preston to come to Mellie's house on Monday afternoon. She'd practically had to throw herself from a cliff to get him to agree to do that.

Preston seemed to be cut from the same cloth as Keaton. No wonder they had remained friends through the years. Preston was unwilling to bend when it came to Mellie. He'd said his piece, accepted her rejection, and refused to give her one more chance without her proving herself to him. And he wasn't making it easy. Annie didn't know how she was going to convince Mellie to let go of her fears to prove to Preston that she had feelings for him, too.

Part one of her plan had been a success, and that was to get Preston to see Mellie again. Now she had to convince Mellie to meet Preston halfway. Annie figured if she could stand up against Preston's stubborn pride, then she could deal with Mellie. Or so she hoped.

Using a convenient excuse, Annie stopped off at her neighbor's on Monday afternoon, once she was home from the clinic.

"Knock, knock," she said, letting herself into the house. "I brought you some fresh basil and cucumbers."

Mellie sat at the kitchen table, playing one of her video games. She looked up from the computer screen when Annie arrived. She seemed to be caught up in her own world.

"Would you like me to put them in the refrigerator for you?" she asked.

Mellie shrugged. Over the last week, she'd noticed that Mellie had grown more and more withdrawn. It was seeing these changes in her that had prompted Annie to reach out to Preston.

After setting the produce in the fridge, Annie pulled out the kitchen chair across from Mellie and planted her elbows on the table. "Guess who I saw?" she asked.

"Why should I care?"

"You might, knowing it was Preston."

Again, she shrugged. "Big deal."

"You're in love with him. You can't deny it."

"Am not."

Annie did her best not to roll her eyes. "Liar, liar, pants on fire."

Mellie's lips quirked, trying hard not to smile. Her hand curled around the mouse. "All right, since you're in such a happy mood, you might as well get it over with and tell me what Preston said. Not that I'm expecting it to be anything good."

"What would you like to know?"

Mellie's eyes went soft as she struggled to disguise her feelings. Annie recognized that façade on Mellie's face, as she'd so often needed to hide her emotions from her aunt and cousin following the tragedy. She'd become good at pretending nothing was amiss.

"Is . . . he okay?"

"If what you're really asking is if he misses you, then I can categorically tell you that he's even more miserable than you are."

Mellie's throat cleared, struggling to hold back tears. "Does he really miss me?"

"Yes, but the difference is he's hurt and angry."

Hanging her head, Mellie shut down the computer and pushed it aside. "I said some ugly things to him."

Annie hoped the damage was repairable. When confronted, Mellie could react like an angry rattlesnake. She would strike without much thought and leave a poisoned, festering wound for her victim to tend to. Early in her relationship with Mellie, Annie had been bitten a time or two herself.

"Are you sorry?" Annie asked.

Mellie nodded. "Don't think that will do me much good now."

"Did you let him know?"

"I . . . tried, but he blocked my number. When he left here he said it was for good, and apparently he meant it. I . . . I haven't seen or heard from him since, and I don't expect that I will." She raised her pain-filled eyes and looked directly at Annie. "Did . . . Did he mention me?"

"Not until I did."

"What did he say?" she asked eagerly.

It was highly unusual for Mellie to react with anything other than anger or irritation. Annie almost didn't know how to respond.

"He said a lot of things," Annie answered, wondering how best to lead up to Preston's stipulation. Annie could sense that she might be in over her head, and she was fearful that her interference could make matters even worse.

"I can take it," Mellie said, stiffening and bracing herself. "You can tell me whatever it is."

Annie didn't realize she was this readable. "I'll tell you what I told Preston," she offered. "I explained that you reacted in fear, and that you loved him, too."

Mellie cast her gaze downward. "I can imagine what he said to that. Didn't believe a word of it, did he? Well, he's the one to blame. He should never have sprung his feelings on me like that. I liked the way things were before he went and ruined it. Being with him was fun and easy, and then he had to go and talk about his feelings."

She grew quiet for a moment, as though reliving the scene. "Took him several minutes to get it out. He

344

started by telling me how he'd always admired me in our high school days, and said that it hit him hard when I left with Cal, but he never forgot me and was happy when I moved back. Happy enough to ask me to dinner, which I turned down back then. I wasn't in a good place then, and not much better now, I suppose. He went on to say how much he enjoyed spending time with me, and figured I should know how much he loved me."

"Maybe Preston should have waited a bit, given you time to take it all in," Annie suggested.

Agreeing with her wasn't what Mellie had expected from Annie. "I . . . I didn't think I'd miss him as much as I do. Never needed anyone the way I need him. Don't know that I can do anything now to mend the fences."

This was exactly the opening Annie had been waiting for, exactly what she wanted to hear from Mellie. "What if I were to tell you that you could make everything right with Preston? A way for everything to go back to the way it was before, only better?"

Mellie's head jerked upright, her eyes wide and hopeful. "Is he willing to come back to me?"

"He is."

"Then why isn't he here?"

Drawing in a deep, steadying breath, Annie told her. "He said if you loved him, then you had to be willing to go to him."

Annie watched as the color drained from Mellie's face.

"He can't be serious."

"He said that's the only way he'll believe you truly love him."

"He couldn't ask for something easy, now could he?" Mellie rubbed her hands up and down her thighs several times. "He knows better than anyone that I can't leave this house."

"But you *can* leave, Mellie," she reminded her gently.

"Easy for you to say."

"Yes, it is easy. The bigger question is: Will you do it to show him you truly love him?"

"You know I do. But I can't leave the house. Stop telling me I can, because I don't want to hear it."

"Okay, I'll rephrase it. You *won't* leave this house."

"You're right, I *won't*," she agreed, adamantly shaking her head.

"Even for Preston?"

Mellie pressed the heels of her hands against her eyes. "I want to, but I don't know that I can. Not for anyone. I tried once, and I made it all the way to the door, opened it, looked outside, and nearly passed out. I was sweating, and my chest felt like I was having a heart attack. I was hyperventilating."

"Those are classic symptoms of a panic attack."

Mellie exhaled, and her shoulders deflated. "I figured as much. Five years is a long time."

"Yes, it is. I tried my hardest to get Preston to listen to reason," Annie told her. "He wouldn't budge, Mellie. He said this was what you had to do to prove to him you cared. He wouldn't back down. Keaton was there . . ."

"Keaton," Mellie repeated. "He went with you to talk to Preston?"

"No," she explained. "He was at the shelter when I showed up."

"He talked to you?"

Annie nodded. After months of avoiding her and having nothing to say to her, seeing Keaton again had been an emotional jolt that had left her reeling.

"I asked Keaton for his help," Annie clarified.

"And he agreed?"

"He did. He's bringing Preston by this afternoon."

"Here?" Hope elevated her voice. "Today?"

"Yes, and soon." Even now, Annie didn't know how Keaton would manage it, but he'd agreed to find a way.

"What's going to happen?" Mellie asked, sitting on the edge of her chair, her eyes wide and expectant.

Annie waited, hoping her hesitation would help Mellie take in the seriousness of her response. "One of two things. Either you walk out that door and go to him or —"

"Or Preston will leave and never return," Mellie finished for her.

"That's pretty much it."

Mellie looked at her watch. "When will he arrive?"

No sooner had the words left her mouth when Annie heard a truck door closing, followed by a second door. The sound reverberated into the house.

"I think they're here now," Annie said.

Mellie reached across the table and gripped Annie's forearm in a punishing hold. Annie was certain to get bruises and gritted her teeth to hide the ache.

"I'm not ready," Mellie cried. "You should have told me earlier and I could have mentally prepared. I can't, Annie. I can't do this."

Annie breathed deeply, hoping her calm attitude would rub off on Mellie. "Then it's over for you and Preston."

"This is grossly unfair. I already told you I can't do this. It could kill me if I left the house."

"You're much too young to have a heart attack. I didn't give you much notice because I didn't want you to have time to think about it."

"In other words, you sprung it on me at the last minute on purpose."

Annie sighed and nodded. "I've had all weekend to think it over. I believed the longer you had to dwell on it, the bigger this would grow in your mind."

"I can't," she reiterated. "Not for anything . . . even . . . even Preston."

"What's the worst that can happen to you?" Annie asked. "I can promise that you won't die."

"I . . . could faint, which would be humiliating." She covered her face at the thought.

"Yes, it probably would be embarrassing. Put that up against never seeing Preston again. You can faint, or you could have the love of a good man."

Mellie's mouth tightened into a flat, tense line. "If I don't leave the house, he'll eventually change his mind . . . and we can go back to the way things were." She looked to Annie for confirmation.

"Maybe," Annie agreed, although from what he'd said Friday night that didn't seem likely. "But what if he doesn't? Do you really want to take that chance?"

Mellie looked pale enough to pass out already, and she hadn't even risen from the table. Annie really didn't

348

think her friend could make it to the door, let alone walk out to meet Preston.

The door off the kitchen opened, and Keaton walked inside. Even knowing he would be coming with Preston, Annie was unprepared for the impact of seeing him again. For one elongated moment they simply stared at each other.

He broke eye contact first.

"Preston's outside," Keaton announced.

Annie nodded. "I didn't mention any of this to Mellie until a few minutes ago," she told him.

He frowned disapprovingly.

"She's going to need a few minutes," Annie added.

Shaking his head, Keaton said, "Don't know that she has a lot of time. It was hard enough getting Preston here as it was."

Mellie looked up, paler than ever. "Preston's really here?"

"Outside. Waiting." The look he exchanged with Annie said it'd taken every bit of persuasiveness he possessed to make this happen.

Annie left her seat and placed her arm around Mellie. "Tell him to be patient."

"That won't work," Keaton mumbled. "He didn't want to come as it was, and I don't think he's going to be willing to stick around for long."

Mellie scooted back her chair. "Tell him to give me a chance," she snapped. "This isn't easy for me."

"He wants proof. Do you love him, Mellie?"

"I do."

"Then you're going to need to show him you're sincere."

"Okay, fine, then that's what I'll do. Just make sure one of you is close enough to catch me if I faint."

Keaton and Annie exchanged looks. "I'll do it," he volunteered. "You're likely to go down with her."

It was one small sign that he cared. That was enough for Annie to live on for the time being.

Mellie stood, and almost right away her knees went out from under her. She cried out, fell back in her chair, and then buried her face in her hands.

"I can't do it," she cried. "I can't."

CHAPTER
THIRTY-FIVE

"I'm sorry," Mellie whispered brokenly. "So sorry." Her eyes filled with tears and devastation.

"I'll tell Preston," Keaton said, leaving the kitchen.

"I was the one who instigated this," Annie said, following him out the door, stopping it from closing. "I should be the one to tell him."

Preston was pacing the area in front of the steps, and when he saw Keaton and Annie both leave at the same time, he stopped walking and looked at them expectantly. "Well?" he demanded. "Is she coming or not?"

Annie and Keaton exchanged glances. His look told Annie that if she wanted to be the one to relay the news, then she should do it.

With her arm wrapped around the column at the top step, Annie faced him, struggling to find the words to explain. "She loves you, Preston. She'd give anything to take back all the unkind things she said. She didn't mean any of it."

Hope left his eyes and his face went hard. "Just answer the question. Is she coming or not?"

Annie swallowed tightly and descended the stairs. "Not."

"That's what I thought." He turned and started to walk toward the truck.

Keaton stopped him. "Listen for a minute, would you? Let Annie explain what happened."

"When did you become an advocate for Annie?" Preston demanded. "You snapped my head off every time I mentioned her name, and now suddenly you want me to listen to her? Not going to do it."

"Please, Preston," Annie pleaded, holding her hands out to him, palms up. "You should know Mellie was determined to come to you, but her legs went out from under her. She was paralyzed with fear. More than anything, she wanted to do as you asked, but she can't."

"Sorry to hear that." He glared at Keaton. "I'm leaving. You coming with me or not?"

"I didn't tell Mellie what you were asking of her until just this afternoon," Annie cried, wanting to stop him. "She hasn't had a chance to build up her courage," she tried again, feeling nearly desperate.

Preston froze.

"Why do you have to be so stubborn, Preston? Why isn't it enough for Mellie to admit she loves you?" she demanded, hoping he could explain why his ego and pride demanded a pound of flesh.

"What is it with you? Love isn't enough for you? What is it you want? Blood?" Although she was shouting at Preston, she was talking to Keaton at the same time.

"I'm leaving, with or without you, Keaton," Preston reiterated, ignoring her outburst.

"Wait. Please wait." A small voice came from the house.

All three of them turned to the open door upon hearing Mellie's fragile request. Framed in the opening was Mellie, pale as a ghost, holding on to both sides in a determined effort to remain upright. She swayed once, as if she was close to collapsing.

Preston stood transfixed, not quite able to believe what he was seeing. For that matter, neither could Annie. She stared in disbelief: Mellie had done it. She had pushed herself from the table and managed to walk all the way to the open door. Now all that she needed to do was take that next step out of the house and onto the porch.

"You said I had to prove that I love you." She spoke directly to Preston, her trembling voice barely above a whisper.

Preston wasn't budging. "It's a start."

"How far do I need to go?" she asked, holding on to the doorframe with both hands.

Standing at the bottom of the stairs now, Preston looked at Mellie, encouraging her with a broad smile. "Depends on how important I am to you, Mellie," he answered, his voice softening.

"Important enough to risk a heart attack," Mellie flared back, her voice gaining strength. Color was gradually returning to her cheeks.

"You haven't left the house yet," he informed her, as if she hadn't figured that out.

"I know," she shot right back. "Is the porch good enough?"

He cocked his head, considering this a question of great importance. "The deal was you had to come to me."

"Down the stairs?" she cried. He might as well have asked her to swim across the Pacific Ocean all the way to Hawaii.

"Six steps. If you love me, Mellie, you can walk down six steps."

"If you loved me, Preston, you wouldn't ask that of me."

"Who said I loved you?" he asked.

"You did," she reminded him.

"A lot of good it did me," he countered.

"Are you two going to stand there and argue?" Annie asked, growing impatient with them both. Knowing how difficult this was for her friend, she felt it was important that Mellie see this to the end. She'd never have guessed Preston could be this unreasonable and demanding. That was the attitude she expected from Mellie, not the soft-spoken Preston.

Mellie took one tiny step out of the house. She continued to hold on to the doorframe to keep her steady.

Preston grinned, looking almost boyish. "One small step for mankind . . ."

"Don't get sarcastic with me, Preston Young." She took another step, and then another, until she had no option but to let go of the doorframe.

Annie's eyes grew wide with astonishment. After her talk with Mellie earlier, she didn't think this was remotely possible. She glanced toward Preston and noticed the tightness had left his features, replaced by a smile, his eyes bright with happiness.

"The steps," Mellie called out. "Are you seriously going to make me walk down these steps?"

"Preston," Keaton whispered, even thinking that Preston was asking too much.

"You coming to me, Mellie?" Preston asked, his sole focus on her.

Her concentration was on her feet, willing them to move. Her steps were minuscule, and progress was slow, but it was progress. "If that's what it takes to prove I love you."

"You do, don't you?"

Mellie grabbed hold of the column closest to the steps. "You have to know you're the only person in the world I would leave this house for."

Watching her friend, Annie covered her mouth with her fingertips, afraid of what might happen when Mellie started down the stairs. As it was, she looked unsteady on her feet. What if Mellie lost her balance? It seemed a good possibility that she just might.

Mellie started to lower her foot to the top step while still holding on to the porch column.

"Enough," Preston cried, racing up the stairs and grabbing hold of Mellie around the waist. "You've gone far enough." With both arms wrapped around her waist, he whirled her around and around before setting her back down on her feet. His hands cupped her face before he kissed her.

Tears welled in Annie's eyes until the couple blurred in front of her.

She turned to Keaton, who looked as amazed as she did. "We did it, Keaton; we did it." Overcome with emotion, she rushed to him and hugged him with both arms around his middle while pressing the side of her face against him. "I didn't think she'd do it."

"Love does funny things to people," he said, sounding just as happy as she was. His arms came around her and he squeezed her back. He held her tightly, each of them savoring the moment. He released her, and Annie turned to view Mellie and Preston. The joy on their faces was as visible as if it were written in the clouds.

While Annie wiped the tears from her cheeks, Keaton's arms went around her from behind. Leaning against him, she was grateful for his support, grateful that he'd agreed to help her. She'd promised she'd never ask anything of him again and she'd meant it. This could be the last time she'd see him, other than in passing, and she was taking full advantage of his lowered guard.

Preston and Mellie continued to kiss, unable to get enough of each other.

It was then that Annie felt Keaton's lips on the top of her head in the same familiar way he'd once kissed her. Twisting around, she looked up at him, her eyes holding his for several time-altering seconds. Her heart pounded hard and loud enough to echo in her ears.

Annie longed to say something but feared if she did it would break the spell. That was the last thing she wanted. This was the closest she'd been to Keaton since that night almost three months ago.

She tried to read the look in his eyes and all she saw was hesitation and remorse, as if he didn't know how he'd allowed himself to hold her, that he'd regretted letting her get close to him again.

Just as she feared, he dropped his arms and stepped back as though her touch had burned him.

Annie placed her arms around herself in a protective way. Keaton looked away rather than meet her eyes.

Out of nowhere, Lennon barked. He was in the truck and had apparently been napping earlier.

Keaton walked over to let him out. Immediately the dog raced over to Annie. She squatted and petted his ears. It'd been a long time since she'd seen Keaton's dog. Lennon couldn't get enough of her and was licking her face.

"Lennon," Keaton called, his voice firm and hard.

The dog glanced up at his master.

"Heel."

Lennon paused.

"Heel," Keaton repeated, louder this time.

Lennon reluctantly left her side and joined Keaton. His gait was slow and defiant, head down.

As Annie righted herself, she noticed that Mellie and Preston had gone back into the house.

Preston had driven his truck, which meant Keaton was stuck waiting for his friend, or he had to leave on foot and take Lennon with him. Given the option, Annie knew what his choice would be. He would do almost anything to avoid her company.

"Do you remember all the walks we once took along the beach?" she asked.

He nodded stiffly.

"We rarely spoke."

"Your point?" he asked.

"I . . . I enjoyed those walks."

He shrugged, not wanting to admit he had, too.

"Would you sit with me a bit?"

"Here?"

"On Mellie's porch."

From the looks of it, the swing hadn't been used in years. It was time someone took the opportunity. On second thought, that might not be a good idea. The swing might not hold them, seeing how big Keaton was.

"Just on the steps," she suggested.

He hesitated, as if tempted.

"No need to talk," she added. He could wait for Preston there, and she would wait with him. It seemed a reasonable request, and she hoped Keaton would agree.

Every second it took for him to decide felt like an hour to Annie, until she couldn't bear the wait any longer. She walked over to the steps, climbed to the top, and sat down.

Lennon left Keaton's side, leapt up the stairs, and joined her. Annie planted her hands in his thick fur and slowly, lovingly stroked his head, letting him know how much she'd missed him and their times on the beach. What she wouldn't give for sand beneath her feet and a piece of driftwood to throw to Lennon. His eyes told her he was thinking of the same thing.

The dog made the decision for Keaton. After another lengthy pause, Keaton joined her, sitting as far away from her as space would allow.

Annie smiled and then snuck a glance at Keaton, and was taken by surprise to find him smiling, too.

Lennon twisted and pressed his chin to her thigh.

Time passed, and Annie couldn't remember being this content in weeks. She felt completely at ease. Keeping her promise, she didn't speak, didn't ask him a single question, didn't fill in any of the details of her decision. Instead, she drank in the peacefulness of spending time with him.

Ten minutes went by before Keaton stood, his face filled with pain. His eyes locked with hers. The sadness she saw there nearly made her collapse.

"Oh Annie," he whispered. "Tell me. Where am I going to find the strength to let you go?"

CHAPTER
THIRTY-SIX

The phone call came in the middle of the night from Teresa. "Britt's in labor. She wanted me to call you."

Annie blinked the sleep out of her eyes. The hospital in Aberdeen was forty minutes away from Oceanside, and Britt had already checked in. Earlier in the summer, Annie had gone with the teenage couple to the adoption agency and introduced them to the social worker there. They trusted Annie because she was impartial, whereas both sets of parents had definite views as to what Britt and Jimmy should do. Annie appreciated that this was a difficult decision and guided them with love, compassion, and understanding. They had chosen the family for their baby, and their choice couldn't have pleased Annie more.

"I'll be there within the hour."

"Thank you." Teresa, who was normally calm and cool, sounded shaken and emotional.

"It's going to be fine," Annie assured her.

"I know. I know. It's just that it's hard for me to see my daughter in so much pain."

"Britt's strong and healthy," Annie reminded her. "Is Jimmy with her?"

"Yes. He's not handling it well. I think Britt wants you here so you can help him through this."

Annie figured as much. Once the adopting parents had been selected, Jimmy and Britt had requested that the couple be there for the birth of their baby. They wanted their parents and Annie to witness when they handed their child over to the parents who would raise their daughter. Because this was important to Jimmy and Britt, Annie arranged to take time off from the clinic.

For Teresa, Annie knew, this was history repeating itself. She was the same age as Britt when she gave birth, only Teresa didn't have the support and encouragement of Britt's father. Thankfully, Teresa's family had stepped in to help, as she was willing to do for Britt now.

Annie quickly dressed and petted Ringo. Not knowing how long she'd be away, she filled his dishes with food and water before she left. By the time she arrived at the hospital, Britt had reached the second stage of delivery. She'd insisted she wanted to have a natural childbirth. Annie had coached her and Jimmy on what to expect, but they hadn't attended the classes, although she had urged them to sign up. Time, distance, and funds made it impossible for the young couple.

"How are you doing?" Annie asked, stroking the hair away from Britt's forehead, encouraging her with a gentle smile.

"This is a lot more painful than I thought it'd be."

"I know it is," Annie said. She had no firsthand experience with childbirth, but as part of her training she'd worked in a delivery room and realized why the birthing process was called labor. It was hard work.

Jimmy was a wreck, pacing the small room at the birthing center. He looked completely exhausted, acting like he was the one giving birth and not Britt. "Can't they give her something to deal with the pain?"

"Yes, of course," Annie assured him. "All she needs to do is ask."

"Britt keeps refusing any drugs."

"I don't think they're good for the baby," Britt insisted.

"I'm more concerned about you," Jimmy said, collapsing onto the chair beside the bed. "Please, Britt, do it for me. I can't stand to see you suffer like this."

"I'll ask for them soon; I promise." She closed her eyes as a contraction took over. Moaning softly, she arched her back. As the contraction grew in intensity, she twisted her head back and forth and bit into her lower lip to escape the ripping pain.

"Remember what I told you about the breathing exercises," Annie told her softly.

The contraction eased, and Britt relaxed. Opening her eyes, she reached for Jimmy's hand. "It was easier to practice those exercises when I wasn't in labor."

Annie figured that was true enough.

"Where's my mom?"

"She's in the waiting room," Annie told her. She'd noticed Teresa slipping out almost as soon as Annie arrived. From the open door, Annie noticed Britt's mother taking a seat next to the family who would be adopting the baby girl.

Britt's eyes connected with Annie's as she asked, "Will you get Becca for me?"

"Certainly, Britt." Annie had nothing to do with the teenagers choosing a family from Oceanside. As it happened, it was Becca, the very woman Annie had met the first day she'd started work at the clinic. As soon as Britt and Jimmy had read the application, they'd been assured that their daughter would be raised by a family that loved her, and in the same small town they called home.

"And take Jimmy with you to talk to Lucas, will you, Annie?" He was in a near-panicked state, unable to hold still, pacing or leaping in and out of the chair.

"I'm not leaving you," Jimmy insisted, his eyes flashing defiance.

"Yes, you are. I love you, Jimmy, but right now you're more of a distraction than a help. I need to concentrate, and I can't do it with you playing leapfrog all over this room."

Jimmy was about to argue, but then he changed his mind. "I'll send Becca in," he told Annie. "But don't leave Britt. She needs you with her."

"Okay." Annie stayed and reached for Britt's hand after yet another powerful contraction. "It won't be long now," she whispered, hoping that would encourage her.

"Becca wants to name the baby Grace. It's perfect, isn't it?" Britt told her.

"It's a beautiful name. Becca will be a good mother."

"I think so, too," Britt said, her voice raw with emotion. "Jimmy and I liked the idea of Grace growing up in Oceanside. They want us to be part of her life, too, like an extra aunt and uncle." Her hold tightened on Annie's hand as another contraction overcame her. They were coming faster now, growing in intensity.

It wasn't long before Britt was ready for the delivery. Her mother held one hand, Becca the other, while Annie stood at Britt's head, whispering encouragement as the physician prepared to receive the baby. Jimmy and Lucas Calder were called into the room and sat close by. Both men were pale, and Annie feared if they stood they might be in danger of fainting.

Britt pushed down hard and grunted as the baby slid from her body. Soon the birthing room was filled with the loud cry of the newborn. Annie's eyes clouded with tears and she noticed that Becca was weeping, too. The baby squalled, turning pink and showing off her amazing pair of healthy lungs.

After cleaning the crying infant and wrapping her in a blanket, the nurse handed little Grace to Britt.

Gazing down on her baby, Britt kissed her forehead and then looked to Becca. With tears clouding her eyes, she handed the infant to the other woman. "Congratulations, Becca," she whispered softly. "You have a daughter, and I know you will love her and be a good mother."

"Thank you," Becca said through her own tears of joy. "Thank you, Britt. Thank you, Jimmy."

Annie looked over and saw that Lucas was weeping, too. Both Britt and Jimmy's faces were wreathed in huge smiles. Jimmy joined Britt and gripped her hand with both of his. "We did the right thing," he whispered.

Britt agreed, and Jimmy bent over and kissed her forehead. Teresa remained at her daughter's side, and her eyes, too, were filled with tears.

An hour later, Annie arrived back in Oceanside. No sooner had she stepped inside the cottage when she received a call from the hospice center.

"You asked to be notified when Seth Keaton was close to passing."

"Yes," she said, recognizing the voice as belonging to Linda, the volunteer at the hospice center.

"It will be only a matter of hours."

Annie let the news sink in. "Thank you for letting me know." Her first thought was whether Keaton had been notified, too, and she thought that he must have been. If the hospice center had contacted her, then there was every likelihood they had reached out to Keaton, too. She knew he'd stopped in regularly to check on his father. That was the kind of man he was. Even knowing his father hated him and wanted nothing to do with him, Keaton still cared. Seeing Keaton seemed to upset the old man, and she'd learned that Keaton frequently checked with the volunteer and then left without visiting his father. It was better for them both that Keaton kept his distance.

The irony didn't escape Annie.

Life and death in the same day.

Although she'd recently returned from the hospital, she headed out again and drove to the hospice center where Seth had been staying. Annie had stopped by a few times to see how he was doing. The man was defiant, difficult, disagreeable, and often crude. His pain level was managed with heavy doses of morphine. According to Linda, not once had he showed his appreciation for the care given him. When Annie was there, she'd sit at his bedside and do what she could to make him comfortable, though he seemed to resent her presence. Seth never spoke to her.

Annie debated if she should be with him now. But she knew that Keaton was likely to stay away, and the thought of Seth Keaton dying alone didn't seem right, no matter what kind of father he'd been.

At a loss on how best to handle the situation, Annie went inside. She was grateful Linda was on duty. That helped Annie make the decision. She would sit with Seth until he passed. Keaton never needed to know she was there.

When she entered his room, Seth was sleeping. Pulling up the chair, she took a seat next to him. After a few minutes, his eyes fluttered open. From a previous conversation with Linda, Annie had learned that Seth fluctuated between unconsciousness and lucidity.

Awake now, he stared at her, uncertain of who she was. This wasn't unusual for a man so close to death. He blinked and released a slow, ragged breath that rattled in his throat. "I'm dying."

"Yes. It won't be long now."

"Expect so." He faced death calmly, unafraid.

At least he wasn't demanding that she leave. "Is there anything you want to tell anyone?" As an afterthought, she added, "Any regrets?" Naturally, her hope was that his parting words would be those of love for his son.

"I only have one regret in this life," he murmured. "With everything in me, I regret ever having a son."

Horrified, Annie jumped from the chair. She stared down at this dying man, dismayed that he would say anything so unkind and cruel. "How can you say that? You clearly have no idea the kind of person Keaton is, do you? He's a good man, generous and talented and —"

"He took my Maggie from me." His voice gained strength with his conviction.

"What?"

The old man made no sense.

He closed his eyes, and for a moment Annie was afraid he'd lost consciousness. It took effort for him to open his eyes again. He twisted his head back to get a better look at her before he spoke. "Maggie loved him more than me and it killed her."

"I don't understand."

"Cancer," he whispered, growing weaker now, his voice little more than a whisper. "We learned she had cancer when she was pregnant with him. The doctor said the treatment would kill the baby . . . Maggie refused . . . She wanted the baby. He killed her . . . She wanted him . . . loved him more than me."

Tears blurred Annie eyes and her throat grew thick with emotion. "Old man, don't you understand? She was giving you a gift."

"A gift?" he spat. "Some gift. He's a freak."

Annie refused to listen to him say ugly things about Keaton, and she put herself in Maggie's shoes. She would have made the same decision. "First off, Keaton is no freak. Your wife, your Maggie, loved you *and* her baby. She gave her very life to give you a son. It was her love for *you* that led her to make that decision. She knew, in every likelihood, this would be her only opportunity to have a child. She was willing to take the chance that she could beat the cancer after the baby arrived."

"Maggie shouldn't have died."

"Do you seriously believe that she *wanted* to die? I'm certain she wanted more than anything to live, and she took a gamble that she would live." Perhaps he was delusional after all.

He didn't answer. "Keaton has my body and Maggie's looks. Every time I look at my son, I see her face. She was an artist and everything that was good. I couldn't believe she fell in love with me. Still don't know how it happened that she agreed to marry me."

"Your Maggie gave you the best part of herself," Annie insisted, imagining what it'd be like to be Maggie. "You say she was an artist. Keaton is, too, and where do you think he got that talent? From his mother. I bet you don't even know he's the one who painted those beautiful murals in town."

The question hung between them for several tense seconds.

"Keaton did those?"

Annie nodded. "He also rescues and cares for injured animals and . . . people." She placed herself in the last category. "You don't even know your son. You don't realize what a good, decent man he is. Despite your hate, despite your mistreatment, he's a kind, caring person. No one could ask for a better son than Keaton."

"Keaton is an artist?"

It shocked Annie that Seth knew so little about him, but it shouldn't have.

"Yes, he's an artist and so much more. For you to say you regret giving him life is wrong on a hundred different levels."

Staring up at her, Seth's eyes narrowed, almost in disbelief at what she was telling him.

Annie wasn't finished. "You have no idea how many lives Keaton has touched. How much good he's done in this community. I'll agree, some people think he's different because he's prone not to speak, yet he's genuinely liked and admired." Her voice grew stronger as she spoke. "Your Maggie gave you the best part of herself in Keaton, and you squandered that gift. If there's anyone to feel sorry for here, it's you."

When she finished speaking, it looked like Seth had drifted away. Death was close now. Annie could feel its approach.

"Maggie?" His hand moved, reaching out to his dead wife, the woman he'd loved and lost. "Oh . . . Maggie." His eyes opened and connected with Annie's. "My Maggie."

Annie realized he thought she was his dead wife. At this point, Seth Keaton had one foot in life and the other stepping across the line into death.

"I'm sorry," he whispered, his voice a low rattle. "So sorry."

His eyes closed, and in that instant he was gone.

Annie waited a moment, checked his pulse, and found there was none. She noted the time and sat with him for several more moments while she tried to make sense of their conversation as best she could.

Linda entered the room. "He passed?"

"Yes." She gave the hospice worker the time.

"I'll let his son know," Linda said.

That relieved Annie of the task, and she was grateful. She didn't want to be the one to tell Keaton that his father was dead. At some point in the future, if he was willing, she would explain that she'd been at Seth's side at his passing and what his last words had been.

Although she promised herself to never reveal Seth's one regret in life. Even knowing what she did about Keaton's mother, she couldn't understand how his father didn't understand or appreciate the gift that his beloved wife had given him.

CHAPTER
THIRTY-SEVEN

At his father's request, no funeral services were held. Seth Keaton Sr. was buried in the cemetery in the space next to Margaret Elizabeth Keaton. A couple days after he'd been laid to rest, Annie stopped by the grave site and brought flowers. Standing over the freshly dug earth, she remembered her last conversation with Keaton's father, bent down, and set the flowers on Maggie's grave instead. She decided that his mother was more deserving of the bouquet.

The same afternoon, Keaton unexpectedly joined Annie as she walked along the beach. The day was cloudy and windy, with threatening rainclouds. Lennon raced to her side, his tongue lolling out of the side of his mouth. Annie bent down on one knee to rub his ears. She'd missed him almost as much as she missed her times with Keaton. When she looked up, she found him looming over her. They hadn't spoken since the day Mellie had stepped onto the porch. She'd waited for him to come to her and had waited in vain.

After giving Lennon attention, Annie sat on a beached log and looked out over the tide as it slowly eased its way out. Her heart expanded when Keaton sat down next to her, with Lennon resting between them.

Seagulls circled overhead, their cries blending in with the sound of the waves. The scent of the ocean was heavy in the air.

Not surprisingly, it took him a few moments before he spoke. "I heard you were with my father when he passed."

"Yes." She didn't explain further. This was something she'd learned from him and his silent ways. Her answer was simple and precise, giving him nothing more than required.

"I appreciate it."

She shrugged off his gratitude. Elaborating the events of that day wasn't necessary, and in Seth's case, they wouldn't be helpful. His father had never loved nor appreciated his son, and Keaton knew it; he'd always known it. That was something she found astonishing about Keaton. That he could have withstood that complete lack of tenderness and become the caring person he was. Her admiration for him kept expanding in equal measure to her love for him. The last time they'd spoken, he mentioned he didn't know how he was going to let her go. She had her own pressing question. Annie didn't know how she could bear leaving him.

"I know you're moving back to Seattle soon," he said. Even mentioning it seemed to cause him pain.

"I only have a couple weeks left at the clinic."

He nodded and looked down at the sand, scooting it around with his feet, trying to find the words he wanted to say. "You'll make a good doctor."

"Thank you."

His feet had built a small pile of sand. "It's selfish of me to not want you to go."

"The truth is, the thought of leaving Oceanside fills me with dread."

"I reacted badly, Annie. I'm sorry."

Leaning sideways, Annie braced her shoulder against him. "Your blessing would mean the world to me, Keaton."

"You have it, Annie, right along with my heart."

Tears clouded her vision, and she swallowed hard before she thanked him. "That means more than you know."

"I'm going to Dad's house," Keaton said.

"Moving there?"

"No. Cleaning it out. Selling it."

"Would you like some help?" She wanted to spend as much time as she could with him before she left.

"You'd do that?"

"Of course; I'd be happy to, Keaton," she said, pressing against his shoulder with her own. "You didn't hesitate to bring your strength and tools to help me when I needed it. I carry a mean broom and sponge."

They set a time to meet, and Keaton agreed to pick her up.

On Saturday afternoon, he arrived a little before five. Annie had been over to see Mellie earlier in the day, and her friend was busy making dinner preparations for her and Preston. Mellie remained entrenched in the house, but Annie suspected Preston was working on convincing her to move beyond the porch and back into the real world. Annie believed it wouldn't be long before Mellie agreed, as much in love with Preston as she was.

On the drive to the cabin, Keaton was silent, but this wasn't his normal silence. He seemed to have something on his mind, something he wanted to say but found it difficult to find the words for. After all these months, she knew him better than she realized. He often had trouble expressing emotions. Of course, cleaning out his father's home would be traumatic enough.

Once they arrived, it came as no surprise to find the house in complete disarray. Seth had been sick for several months and housekeeping chores had long been neglected. Dust and cobwebs were everywhere. The windows were dirty, the floors sticky and smudged with dried mud.

"Where would you like me to start?" she asked, as Keaton brought in several packing boxes.

He stood in the middle of the living room and seemed overwhelmed. "Kitchen, I guess."

"Okay." She carried two of the larger boxes into that area. The contents were sparse. A few pots and pans, a skillet, a few utensils, and that was about it. All those were stacked in the sink, which made it necessary to wash nearly everything that required packing. Nothing was of much value or worth saving. It took her less than an hour to clear it out and clean what was necessary. After wiping down the counters, she mopped the floor.

Keaton had disappeared into the bedroom that had belonged to his father. She hadn't seen him since they'd arrived.

374

When she'd finished the kitchen, she found Keaton sitting on the end of the bed, his head down. Unsure what to do or say, Annie silently sat down next to him.

"I didn't love him," Keaton said. "Didn't think I'd miss him."

Because of her last conversation with Seth, Annie felt she understood Keaton better. "He was a bitter, angry man who didn't appreciate love."

"Never able to give it to me."

Annie had become painfully aware of that because of Seth's deathbed declaration.

Reaching for her hand, Keaton entwined their fingers, raised them to his lips, and kissed her knuckles. "I heard."

"What did you hear?" she asked, staring down at their joined hands.

"You. With my father, just before he died."

Annie tried to hide her surprise. "You were there . . . at the hospice center?"

He nodded. "They called me to let me know. I was determined to let him die alone, but then I couldn't do it. I went and saw that you were at his bedside."

Annie bit into her lower lip, knowing that if Keaton had been listening he would have heard his father mention his one regret. Her heart ached that he had heard those hurtful, demeaning words.

"He didn't mean it," she whispered.

"He meant every word. He blamed me for her death from the minute I was born. He never loved me. Never wanted me, especially since my birth is what cost my mother her life."

Annie had no words of comfort; nothing she could say would take away the brutal sting of Seth's dying words. "I'm sorry you heard any of that."

"I'm not. It helped me understand my father, understand why he was never able to love me."

Annie was confident she hadn't heard him right. "You mean you didn't know that your mother had decided to refuse cancer treatment because she was pregnant with you?" If his father hadn't said anything, his mother's relatives certainly would have, she assumed.

"Her name was never mentioned. If not for a few photos I found of her when I was young, I would know nothing about my mother. Once she was dead, it seemed that she was forever erased from my father's mind. I know now that just the opposite was true."

Annie didn't know that she would ever understand a man like Keaton's father.

"What I didn't know until I met you . . . what I didn't appreciate, was my father's feelings," Keaton continued.

"I don't get what you're telling me."

He looked uncomfortable. "I'd never been in love before, Annie. I never knew what it was to give another person your heart. At the very thought of losing you, the only thing I could do was withdraw. The thought of you leaving Oceanside devastated me. I had to accept that once you left you were never coming back, much in the same way my father had to accept that my mother would never return."

"But, Keaton —"

"No, please, let me finish. I didn't love my father. I never understood what I had done that was so bad that he could hate me the way he did. I realize what it was now."

Annie closely studied him as he spoke and saw the intensity on his face, knowing the words were hard to speak. "Until my mother, I don't think my father had anyone who loved him, and I was the one who took her away from him."

"But it wasn't anything you did, Keaton. Cancer is what took her away. Not you. Your mother wanted you enough to risk her own life to have you."

"I know that now. What I didn't realize was that she was everything to him. To lose her was to lose the only love my father had ever known."

His eyes were dark and intense as they met Annie's. "I've known little love in my life. For a good portion of my youth, I felt like an outsider. My size and home life didn't help. When you came back to town, Annie, that first time on the beach, it was like I'd taken a hit to my abdomen. Lennon saw you first. He knew. It was at that moment that I realized you were my destiny. Then later, there was the pain that I felt, knowing that I was eventually going to need to let you go."

Annie continued to lock eyes with him and found it impossible to speak.

"You don't understand. That day on the beach — I thought I was losing it. A girl I'd admired years earlier was back, but now she was a beautiful woman. I was convinced after all that time that you weren't real, and that I had imagined things. Then, to see you again, right before my eyes, and learn that you were looking for a house to rent. If that wasn't enough, you were interested in Mellie's cottage."

She smiled and leaned her head against his shoulder.

"Having you close, living right here in Oceanside, overwhelmed me. I didn't know what to think. God's truth, Annie, you terrified me."

"Why . . ." She didn't finish her thought. Keaton knew what she meant.

"How was I to know if this was love?" he asked. "It felt more like an obsession. You were in every thought; every day I looked for ways to spend time with you. I was convinced these feelings would fade in time, and when they didn't, I didn't know what was happening to me. It didn't take me long to understand that you owned my heart."

"And you own mine."

He exhaled. "Just when I thought it might be possible for the two of us to forge a future together, you decided to return to medical school. You planned to leave me, and I knew nothing about it. The news caught me off guard, but then to make it worse — all along, I'd been sharing my heart with you, sharing the pain of my youth, only to learn from Mellie that you'd lost your entire family. You kept that from me while I shared the deepest parts of my heart with you."

"Oh Keaton, I should have explained, should have told you. In retrospect, I would do it all so differently."

"I needed to protect myself," he said, and kissed the top of her head. "I was so desperately in love with you that I realized you had the power to utterly destroy me.

The only option I felt I had to survive was to separate myself completely from you.

"As time progressed, another deeper fear took hold of me. I was afraid that without you in my life I'd end up like my father, lost and bitter, angry at the world."

"You could never be like your father." That was beyond the scope of Annie's imagination.

His hand tightened around hers until it was almost painful. She was convinced he didn't realize how tight his grip had become.

"I love you, Annie, so much so that it feels like my heart is going to bust wide open."

Annie bit into her lower lip. "I love you, too, so much I don't know that I can leave you. Other than my aunt and Gabby, I don't have any family left. You, Mellie, Teresa, and Preston are my family now. The only home I know is right here with you, and leaving you, leaving Oceanside, seems unimaginable. I . . . I don't know that I can do it."

Keaton bowed his head. "You're my family, too, and as painful as this is to say, you should move back to Seattle and attend medical school. You need to become the doctor you were always meant to be."

"I don't know that I can make it through medical school without you, Keaton."

"But you have me," he assured her, his arm holding her closer to his side. "I'm not going anywhere. If you want me to come be with you every weekend, then that's what I'll do."

"I can't do it. I can't leave you."

"Annie, no. You're going to medical school. Please don't fight me on this. It's hard enough as it is to let you go. I'll do everything within my power to help you. Everything and anything."

"Anything?" She looked up at him, her heart in her eyes.

"Annie, of course. What do you need?"

She didn't hesitate. "You."

"You have me. Heart and soul. You've always had me." He stretched his arm out and touched the medallion she wore around her neck, letting it slide between his thick fingers. "It's fitting that you are the one to wear that, seeing that you carry my heart with you."

Her hand wrapped around his.

A half-smile formed. "I was wondering if you'd be willing to give it back to me?"

Annie grinned. "I love you, Keaton. Your heart is safe with me. It always has been. It took losing those I loved most to wake me up to the fact that life is fragile. I'm not the same person I was back then. Their deaths taught me what's most important. The answer is love. You're important, Keaton. I'm making a new life for myself, giving and receiving love. You're a huge part of this transformation because you taught me what it meant to give my heart to someone.

"You said you felt I was your destiny," Annie continued. "What you don't understand is that you're mine as well. I came to Oceanside because I'd been happy here as a teenager. What I discovered by living here is that my happy place is with *you*, wherever *you* are. I can go back to medical school. I can leave, but only if you're willing to come with me. Can you leave Oceanside? Can you do that for me?"

Taking her face in both of his hands, Keaton leaned forward and pressed his lips to hers in a searing kiss that left them both breathless, their hearts beating in unison.

His eyes delved into hers. "I can go anywhere as long as we're together, Annie. That's what is important."

"You're sure about that?" She couldn't believe that he'd agree.

"More than sure."

Life had taken Annie on this rugged path. It wasn't one she would have voluntarily chosen, but it had led her to this point, and to these friends who had become her new family. She had found home, and it was with them.

She removed the medallion from around her neck and handed it to Keaton. "I think it's time this goes back to where it belongs."

He bent forward and bowed his head as she put it around his neck. Tucking his arms around her waist, Keaton lifted her feet from the ground and hugged her against his massive chest, holding her as gently as an orchid, his eyes closed, his heart beating solidly against her own.

Annie tilted back her head and looked toward the sky, and for just an instant she was convinced she could feel her parents' presence, peeking through the clouds, smiling down on her.

CHAPTER
THIRTY-EIGHT

"You coming?" Preston called impatiently from the driver's side of his truck.

"Give me a minute," Keaton said. He was busy getting ready to make the move to Seattle with Annie and had a hundred different matters on his mind that required his attention.

"Maybe it would be best if I met you at Mellie's," Keaton called out to his friend, who was too eager to be on his way to wait with even a modicum of patience.

Keaton realized Preston had been working for the last few weeks on a surprise for his sweetheart, building her a swing for the porch. His friend had persistently encouraged Mellie to venture beyond the emotionally protective walls of the big house and had met with limited success. This latest project was a means of readying her for the next step in more ways than one.

Love had turned Keaton's life around, and it did him good to see similar changes in both Preston and Mellie. A warm happy feeling stole over him as Annie came to mind. She was never far from his thoughts. His hand automatically went to the medallion she'd given him. When she'd returned it, and personally placed it around his neck — it had been like a promise, a renewed commitment between them. Never again would he allow his fears to stand in the way of loving her. He'd had to let her go for them both to move forward, he'd learned. In the process, he'd come to realize that he'd never really lost her.

Annie knew about Mellie's surprise and had had to keep it a secret, which had been hard, seeing that they now talked many times a week. Preston was pacing, nervous and agitated. His nerves were due to more than the swing.

Keaton helped Preston unload the swing from the back of his truck and carried it up the steps leading to the porch. They set it down and then removed the old one that Mellie's grandfather had installed forty years earlier, before Mellie had been born.

No sooner had they started working when the door off the kitchen opened and Mellie called out from inside the kitchen, "What's all that racket?"

"You'll find out soon enough," Keaton told her.

"Preston?" Mellie shouted from the other side of the screen door, unwilling to move beyond it to discover the answer herself. "What are you doing now?"

"Hush, woman."

"Hush?" she repeated sarcastically. "Preston, did you seriously tell me to hush?"

"Yes, but only for a few minutes while I finish this up."

"Finish what?" she demanded.

"You'll see for yourself in a bit. Patience, my love."

Mellie wasn't having any of it. "Preston Young, you should know by now that I'm not a patient woman."

"That I do."

Annie arrived, having come separately from the clinic, where she was finishing up and saying her good-byes. In Keaton's mind, it was in the nick of time. She parked, hurried up the steps, paused long enough to kiss him, and then went on to distract Mellie.

"What are they doing?" he heard Mellie demand as Annie eased her away from the door.

"You'll see. Why don't we make a pitcher of iced tea?" Annie suggested.

Even with Keaton helping, it took the two of them about thirty minutes to get the swing installed. It would have been a hundred times easier if Preston had ordered a mass-produced swing. Instead, he'd insisted on building it himself. Mellie's grandfather had handmade the original, and any replacement, to Preston's way of thinking, had to be done by hand.

Once they had it installed, Keaton studied his friend and noticed how pale he was. "You okay?"

"No," Preston was honest enough to tell him. "I'd rather face a rabid dog."

Keaton slapped him across the back. "You know she loves you; you don't have anything to worry about."

"Nothing is a sure thing when it comes to Mellie."

His friend was right about that.

"You ready?" he asked.

Preston swallowed hard and nodded. "As ready as I'll ever be."

They approached the screen door, and within seconds Mellie stood on the other side. "You're going to make me go out on the porch, aren't you?"

Preston didn't answer with words. Instead, he opened the screen door and held out his hand. Mellie hesitated, almost ready to refuse.

"Please," Preston added.

Mellie huffed and angrily shook her head. "You know I can't say no to you when you look at me like that."

Keaton's sole purpose for coming was to help his friend install the swing. Thinking Preston wouldn't want an audience, he said, "Annie and I'll leave the two of you —"

"No," Preston protested. "Don't go. Not yet." He silently pleaded with Keaton, imploring him with a look to stay put.

Keaton relented, although he felt uneasy staying. Annie sent a questioning look that he answered with a reassuring smile.

Mellie inhaled a deep breath, and with her hand tightly gripping Preston's, she moved outside the kitchen and onto the porch. "Where are you taking me?" she asked, as he continued to lead her toward the swing.

That she hadn't noticed the new swing astonished Keaton until he realized her complete concentration was on moving her feet forward, one step at a time.

"I've been working on this for some time," Preston said.

Keaton knew his friend was referring to more than the swing.

"Working on what?" Mellie asked, standing next to the swing, still oblivious to what was different.

"This swing."

Mellie's eyes widened when she realized it wasn't the one her grandfather had built years earlier. "You built this swing?"

Pride radiated from Preston. "Got the plans, studied them a long time, made a model first. I wanted it to be perfect for you. I made a few mistakes, but nothing anyone would notice without looking close."

"Oh Preston," she said and sighed. "You did that for me?"

Looking well pleased with himself, he smiled and stuffed his fingertips into his back pockets.

Mellie sat on the wooden swing and appreciatively ran her hands over the polished wood. Keaton knew his friend had spent countless hours working on the project, hoping his effort would reveal the depth of his feelings for Mellie.

Annie carried out a tray with four glasses of iced tea.

With her eyes on Preston, Mellie patted the seat next to her. "Aren't you going to sit with me?"

"I . . ." Preston reached for the porch railing looking like he was about to pass out.

"Preston." Alarmed, Mellie leapt to her feet. "What's wrong?"

"I'm okay," he choked out. "Sit, please."

Annie set the tray down and Keaton brought her to his side and wrapped his arm around her waist.

Preston bent down on one knee. He remained deathly pale but was determined. "Guess you know I love you. Never could hide the way I feel. Never really expected you'd feel anything near love for me."

"I proved I did, if you remember," she reminded him. "Wouldn't be sitting in this swing right now if I didn't have strong feelings for you."

"Strong enough to last a lifetime?" Preston asked.

Mellie frowned and studied him before she asked, "Are you proposing to me, Preston?"

"Not down here on my knee looking for evidence of termites."

Keaton did his best not to laugh, but a snicker escaped. Annie elbowed him in the ribs to keep him from spoiling the moment.

Preston sucked in a big gulp of air before he continued speaking. "I'm not a romantic guy, Mellie. I know you read all those romance novels where men know the perfect thing to say. I read a few love poems, wanting to do this right, but I was afraid if I recited any of that nonsense you'd never take me seriously."

"It's not nonsense. But I need to know if you're serious about getting married."

"Serious enough. In case you haven't noticed, I'm something of a wreck here. Fact is, I'm about to keel over. Now let me finish, Mellie. I've been working on what I want to say for a long time."

For once she remained completely silent, her eyes bright, her lips trembling, as she waited for Preston to finish.

"I know I'm not much to look at," he continued. "I'll never be rich, but what I can offer you can't be bought with money. You have my devotion, my heart, and my love."

Mellie's eyes went wide and bright. Slowly, a lone tear wove a moist trail down her cheek.

"I'm willing to commit my life to you as your husband. I have loved you from the time we were teenagers; don't know that it's in me to love anyone else. If you decide you don't want to marry me, it would hurt, but I'd accept it."

"Would you please kindly shut up?" Mellie whispered.

Confused, Preston glanced over his shoulder at Keaton, hoping Keaton would tell him what she wanted. Keaton shrugged, letting his friend know he didn't have a clue.

"Stop rambling on and get to the point," Mellie clarified.

"The point?" Preston repeated, afraid of losing his train of thought.

"Just ask me," she advised. "Before you make a bigger mess of this than you have already."

"Okay." He swallowed again, his Adam's apple moving up and down in his throat. "Mellie Johnson, will you marry me?"

"No," she blurted out. Her response was sharp and fast.

Preston hung his head and slumped down onto the porch.

"Oh stop," Mellie snapped. "Of course I'll marry you, Preston. I'd be a damn fool to refuse someone who's loved me longer than I've loved myself. Truth is, I consider myself lucky, knowing you love me. You bring me an engagement ring?"

Preston nearly turned his pocket inside out, searching for the ring. He opened the case, removed the diamond and slipped it on Mellie's finger. Holding her face between his hands, he leaned forward and kissed her.

Watching the pair, Keaton grinned, happy for them.

Seeing that his buddy didn't need any further assistance, he gestured to Annie that it was time for them to go. They walked out to the truck, where Lennon waited patiently, asleep in the front seat with both windows rolled down. He lifted his head when he saw Annie and Keaton and then promptly went back to sleep.

"That went about as well as can be expected from Mellie," Keaton said as they walked across the yard together.

"It was sweet," Annie agreed. "He loves her enough to want to spend the rest of his life at her side."

"He does." Keaton was probably the only one who knew how hard it'd been for Preston to propose. "I remember a time when Preston would get tongue-tied with the mere mention of Mellie's name."

"Mellie is his destiny," she said pointedly.

"In a roundabout way, I guess you could say that you are mine," Keaton said, getting ready to climb into the truck. It was an off-handed comment, and he was surprised when Annie stood frozen at his side.

"What?" he asked.

"Are you going to marry me?" Annie posed the question, hands on her hips.

Keaton frowned and rubbed his hand down the side of his face. "Is that what you want?"

"Keaton," she cried, "what do you think?"

"Ah," he muttered, feeling completely out of his element. He glanced at Annie and dropped his hands, afraid he was going to disappoint her. "I didn't know there was going to be a test. I don't do well with tests."

"Do you love me?"

He nodded.

"Check." She made a checking motion with her hand on an invisible chalkboard.

"Do you want to spend the rest of your life with me?"

Again, he nodded.

"Check." She made the same motion again. "What about children at some point in our future?"

"Children? You mean as in babies?" This question wasn't as easy to answer as the others had been. He didn't have a single doubt when it came to his feelings for Annie. "I've never been around babies. I'm at a loss with how well I'd do with them."

"Do you or do you not want children?" she prodded.

"Do you?" he asked, turning to her for the answer.

"Yes. Several."

"Several," he repeated, feeling the color drain from his face. Suddenly, he felt lightheaded. The vision of crying babies filled his mind. Diapers. Dirty diapers. Baby bottles. Burping. Tiny creatures who depended on him for their very survival. "Define *several*."

"Three, minimum."

"Three," he repeated slowly, those same visions circling around inside his head. "How about one . . . maybe two, seeing how it goes with the first one."

Annie frowned, seriously taking his suggestion into consideration. "Can we make that decision later?"

"I suppose." He opened the driver's-side door to his truck when the realization hit him. "When do you want to do this?"

"Do what?"

Funny. Annie should know, seeing that she was the one who brought it up in the first place. "Get married."

"I'm starting medical school in a week," she snapped. "I can't think about that now."

"Then why did you bring it up? Was it because Preston proposed to Mellie and you're feeling left out?"

Annie hesitated and then grinned. "Maybe. I want to marry you, Keaton, more than I want to be a doctor, more than anything. And when the time is right, I am confident we're going to have the most incredible children in the universe."

He didn't miss the reference to more than one child.

"How about tomorrow?" he asked, thinking he didn't want to wait a minute longer than necessary. "We'll get the license right away . . . don't know if there's a waiting period but if there is, we'll make it as soon as that is over. The pastor of the little Seaside Church by the park could perform the ceremony, unless, of course, you want something big and fancy. I don't. Never did like being the center of attention, but for you, I'd do it."

Annie stood with her mouth hanging open, gawking at him.

"What?" he asked.

"Words are falling out of your mouth again. I'm still getting used to it."

Words. His woman was getting hung up on words. Keaton swore he would never understand women, but that was fine, because he didn't really need to understand them to love Annie.

"Are we getting married or not?" he asked.

"Married."

"Good. You ready to go now?"

Annie nodded.

Keaton grinned. "Check." He made a checkmark in the air, walked around, lifted her off her feet, and kissed her so she'd know beyond a shadow of a doubt how much he loved her.

Epilogue

Three years later
Thanksgiving

Annie put the finishing touches on the Thanksgiving table in Mellie and Preston's dining room. The house was cleared out now and the table was set with the fine china from the cabinet that had once been completely obscured by mountains of boxes filled with accumulated junk.

An orange, yellow, and brown floral arrangement graced the center of the table. It was picture perfect.

Keaton came to stand behind her, his hands on her shoulders. "You okay?"

Of all the holidays, Thanksgiving was the hardest for Annie, bringing to the surface memories of that dreadful event.

"I'm good." Annie's studies continued, and it wouldn't be long before she joined a staff, hopefully right here in Oceanside, where it had all started for her and Keaton.

Somewhat to her surprise, Keaton had adjusted well to life in Seattle. He continued working as a painter with a big contractor in town and studied art on the side. His paintings had gained the notice of a prominent artist who had become a mentor to her husband. Keaton truly was gifted.

"Everything going okay in the kitchen?" Annie asked her husband.

"Teresa and Mellie have everything under control." Annie had tried to help, but the two women had swooshed her away to set the table. That was for the best, as Mellie and Teresa were disagreeing on the best starch to thicken the turkey gravy. Annie didn't want to get caught in the middle.

Her husband's lips grazed the side of her neck and Annie closed her eyes, enjoying the small display of love and affection. Keaton had proved to be an attentive lover.

"Dinner is ready," Preston said, as he carried out the platter filled with sliced turkey.

Teresa trailed behind with a huge bowl of mashed potatoes. Britt and Logan followed with a variety of other dishes. Stuffing and green beans. Jimmy brought in a bowl of gravy. It was like an assembly line.

Soon they were all seated and a prayer was said, one of gratitude and thankfulness. Home from college, Britt and Jimmy sat next to each other. They had been to see Grace earlier that morning and were full of talk about how big she was getting. The day before, Annie had run into Becca and Lucas in town with the toddler. They were a beautiful family, and their love and pride in their daughter was evident to all.

Teresa and Logan sat across from each other. Teresa had managed to get an uncontested divorce from Carl. An arrest warrant remained out in his name. No one had heard from him since he'd disappeared. Logan was growing and had shot up about an inch since the beginning of the school year. Teresa was a hard worker. In addition to her housekeeping clients, she'd started night classes to become a legal assistant. Annie suspected Mellie was helping her financially, but she hadn't asked.

Mellie and Preston sat next to each other, surrounded by their friends, but they might as well have been alone, as they only had eyes for each other. The two remained deeply in love. Mellie's baby bump was evident now that she was six months along. Annie saw the changes love had made in each of their lives. Mellie's rough edges had softened, and Preston sat up taller and with pride. Annie's gaze drifted to her husband. Annie looked forward to finishing her training so that they could start their own family. It wouldn't be much longer now.

After the prayer was said, Keaton released her hand. As she looked around the table, Annie thought about her parents, about Mike, Kelly, and baby Bella, about the family she'd lost in that horrific accident. Their deaths had helped her to define her life, to give it a framework. It had led her to Oceanside and to the chance to become what she was always meant to be. Everything in her life had shifted on that fateful Thanksgiving Day. Only now, years later, was she beginning to understand that the relationships with those she had lost weren't over. Yes, it was different, but her family remained with her, a part of her. In many ways, she believed it was her family who had led her to

Oceanside — to Keaton, Mellie, Preston, and to the others.

They were her new family. While they might not have a blood connection, they were as close to her as if they had always been a part of her life.

Her new life. The one she had built for herself.

Keaton passed her the mashed potatoes. Annie set a scoop on her plate and passed the bowl on to Teresa.

Mellie sat with her hand pressed against her abdomen. Preston noticed. "Is our little princess kicking?" he asked.

Nodding, Mellie grinned and stretched out her hand to her husband. Preston gripped it and kissed her fingers.

As Annie looked around the table, her heart swelled with love.

A fresh start.

A future.

Her family.

Other titles published by Ulverscroft:

IF NOT FOR YOU

Debbie Macomber

If not for her loving but controlling parents, Beth might never have taken charge of her life. If not for her friend Nichole, Beth would never have met Sam Carney — a tattooed mechanic who is her conservative parents' worst nightmare. And if not for Sam — who witnessed a terrible accident and rushed to her aid — Beth might never have survived and fallen in love. Yet there are skeletons in Sam's closet that prevent him from ever trusting a woman again. Will he be able to overcome his past and fight for love?

SILVER LININGS

Debbie Macomber

Since opening the Rose Harbor Inn, Jo Marie Rose and handyman Mark Taylor are becoming more than just friends, yet he still won't reveal anything about his past. Then he tells her he's moving out of town. As Jo Marie tries to convince Mark to stay, she welcomes two visitors who are seeking answers of their own: Coco and Katie, who have returned to Cedar Cove for their high school reunion. Coco wants to confront the boy who broke her heart, while Katie wants to reconnect with her old boyfriend, the one who got away. As Katie hopes for a second chance, Coco starts to believe that people can change — and that the future might hold exciting possibilities for them both.

TWELVE DAYS OF CHRISTMAS

Debbie Macomber

Julia is infuriated by her grumpy neighbour, Cain, who can't even be pleasant when they bump into each other. So on the suggestion of her best friend, Cammie, Julia concocts a plan. She starts a blog in order to clinch her perfect job, and now she has a subject. Over the next twelve days, she is going to kill Cain with kindness — and Christmas cheer — and document it for all to read about. But as the experiment goes on, Julia realises she underestimated the effect it would have on Cain, and on their relationship, as things take an unexpected turn . . .

MY ABSOLUTE DARLING

Gabriel Tallent

At fourteen, Turtle Alveston knows the use of every gun on her wall; that chaos is coming, and only the strong will survive it; that her daddy, Martin, loves her more than anything else in this world. But chinks begin to appear in Turtle's armor as she learns that other people live differently from them. She meets Jacob, a high school boy who tells jokes, lives in a big clean house, and looks at Turtle as if she is the sunrise. And for the first time, the larger world begins to come into focus. Turtle begins to imagine escape, using the very survival skills that Martin devoted himself to teaching her. But changing her life will not be without risk — especially when Martin is driven into a downward spiral of fear and cruelty . . .

ALICE'S ADVENTURES IN WONDERLAND
AND THROUGH THE LOOKING-GLASS

ALICE'S ADVENTURES IN WONDERLAND

AND

THROUGH THE LOOKING-GLASS

By Lewis Carroll

With the original engravings by
JOHN TENNIEL
of which 8 have been redrawn in colour by
DIANA STANLEY

LONDON: J. M. DENT & SONS LTD
NEW YORK: E. P. DUTTON & CO. INC.

CHARLES LUTWIDGE DODGSON, *who wrote verse and fiction under the pen-name of* LEWIS CARROLL, *was born at Daresbury, Cheshire, where his father, the Rev. Charles Dodgson (afterwards Archdeacon of Richmond), was Perpetual Curate, on 27th January 1832.*

He was educated at Richmond School (Yorkshire) and Rugby, before proceeding to Christ Church, Oxford, in 1851, where he became Student and Mathematical Lecturer in 1855. He relinquished his lectureship in 1881, but retained the studentship for life. He was ordained Deacon in 1861 but did not proceed to full orders and seldom preached He died in his sisters' house at Guildford on 14th January 1898.

He made friends with a large number of children, mainly little girls, the most famous of whom were Alice Liddell and her sisters Lorina and Edith, to whom he told the story of 'Alice's Adventures Underground' on 4th July 1862 during a picnic on the Thames at Godstow just outside Oxford. This grew into Alice's Adventures in Wonderland *(1865), followed by* Through the Looking-Glass, and What Alice Found There, *published in 1871. These two books rank as the supreme example of imaginative and humorous fiction for children in English—perhaps in any language.*

Dodgson followed these with The Hunting of the Snark *(1876), a worthy pendant, being the only example of a long 'nonsense' poem that is completely successful. His last book for children,* Sylvie and Bruno *(two parts, 1889 and 1893), was unsatisfactory as a whole, though containing flashes of his original genius. He also wrote simple books on Logic and several mathematical puzzles for children (as 'Lewis Carroll') and a number of advanced mathematical works under his own name. He is also remembered as the best photographer of children of the Victorian period and one of the principal figures in the early history of photography in this country.*

ALL in the golden afternoon
　　Full leisurely we glide;
For both our oars, with little skill,
　　By little arms are plied,
While little hands make vain pretence
　　Our wanderings to guide.

Ah, cruel Three! In such an hour
　　Beneath such dreamy weather,
To beg a tale of breath too weak
　　To stir the tiniest feather!
Yet what can one poor voice avail
　　Against three tongues together?

Imperious Prima flashes forth
　　Her edict 'to begin it'—
In gentler tone Secunda hopes
　　'There will be nonsense in it!'
While Tertia interrupts the tale
　　Not *more* than once a minute.

Anon, to sudden silence won,
　　In fancy they pursue
The dream-child moving through a land
　　Of wonders wild and new,
In friendly chat with bird or beast—
　　And half believe it true.

And ever, as the story drained
　　The wells of fancy dry,
And faintly strove that weary one
　　To put the subject by,
'The rest next time—' 'It *is* next time!'
　　The happy voices cry.

Thus grew the tale of Wonderland:
  Thus slowly, one by one,
Its quaint events were hammered out—
  And now the tale is done,
And home we steer, a merry crew,
  Beneath the setting sun.

Alice! a childish story take,
  And with a gentle hand
Lay it where Childhood's dreams are twined
  In Memory's mystic band,
Like pilgrim's wither'd wreath of flowers
  Pluck'd in a far-off land.

AUTHOR'S NOTE

INQUIRIES have been so often addressed to me, as to whether any answer to the Hatter's Riddle (see p. 58) can be imagined, that I may as well put on record here what seems to me to be a fairly appropriate answer, viz. 'Because it can produce a few notes, though they are *very* flat; and it is never put with the wrong end in front!' This, however, is merely an afterthought: the Riddle, as originally invented, had no answer at all.

Christmas, 1896.

CONTENTS

ALICE'S ADVENTURES IN WONDERLAND

THROUGH THE LOOKING-GLASS

ILLUSTRATIONS

IN COLOUR

x

CHAPTER I

DOWN THE RABBIT-HOLE

ALICE was beginning to get very tired of sitting by her sister on the bank, and of having nothing to do: once or twice she had peeped into the book her sister was reading, but it had no pictures or conversations in it, 'and what is the use of a book,' thought Alice, 'without pictures or conversation?'

So she was considering in her own mind (as well as she could, for the hot day made her feel very sleepy and stupid) whether the pleasure of making a daisy-chain would be worth the trouble of getting up and picking the daisies, when suddenly a White Rabbit with pink eyes ran close by her.

There was nothing so *very* remarkable in that; nor did Alice think it so *very* much out of the way to hear the Rabbit say to itself, 'Oh dear! Oh dear! I shall be too late!' (when she thought it over afterwards, it occurred to her that she ought to have wondered at this, but at the time it all seemed quite natural); but when the Rabbit actually *took a watch out of its waistcoat-pocket*, and looked at it, and then hurried on, Alice started to her feet, for it flashed across her mind that she had never before seen a rabbit with either a waistcoat-pocket, or a watch to take out of it, and burning with curiosity, she ran across the field after it, and fortunately was just in time to see it pop down a large rabbit-hole under the hedge.

In another moment down went Alice after it, never once considering how in the world she was to get out again.

The rabbit-hole went straight on like a tunnel for some way, and then dipped suddenly down, so suddenly that Alice had not a moment to think about stopping herself before she found herself falling down a very deep well.

Either the well was very deep, or she fell very slowly, for she had plenty of time as she went down to look about her, and to wonder what was going to happen next. First, she tried to look down and make out what she was coming to, but it was too dark to see anything; then she looked at the sides of the well, and noticed that they were filled with cupboards and book-shelves: here and there she saw maps and pictures hung upon pegs. She took down a jar from one of the shelves as she passed; it was labelled 'ORANGE MARMALADE,' but to her great disappointment it was empty: she did not like to drop the jar for fear of killing somebody, so managed to put it into one of the cupboards as she fell past it.

'Well!' thought Alice to herself. 'After such a fall as this, I shall think nothing of tumbling down stairs! How brave they'll all think me at home! Why, I wouldn't say anything about it, even if I fell off the top of the house!' (Which was very likely true.)

Down, down, down. Would the fall *never* come to an end? 'I wonder how many miles I've fallen by this time?' she said aloud. 'I must be getting somewhere near the centre of the earth. Let me see: that would be four thousand miles down, I think—' (for, you see, Alice had learnt several things of this sort in her lessons in the schoolroom, and though this was not a *very* good opportunity for showing off her knowledge, as there was no one to listen to her, still it was good practice to say it over) '—yes, that's about the right distance—but then I wonder what Latitude or Longitude I've got to?' (Alice had no idea what Latitude was, or Longitude either, but thought they were nice grand words to say.)

Presently she began again. 'I wonder if I shall fall right *through* the earth! How funny it'll seem to come out among the people that walk with their heads downwards! The Antipathies, I think—' (she was rather glad there *was* no one listening, this time, as it didn't sound at all the right word) '—but I shall have to ask them what the name of the country is, you know. Please, Ma'am, is this New Zealand or Australia?' (and she tried to curtsy as she spoke—fancy *curtsying* as you're falling through the air! Do you think you could manage it?) 'And what an ignorant little girl she'll think me! No, it'll never do to ask: perhaps I shall see it written up somewhere.'

Down, down, down. There was nothing else to do, so Alice soon began talking again. 'Dinah'll miss me very much to-night, I should think!' (Dinah was the cat.) 'I hope they'll remember her saucer of milk at

tea-time.   Dinah, my dear, I wish you were down here
with me!   There are no mice in the air, I'm afraid, but
you might catch a bat, and that's very like a mouse, you
know.   But do cats eat bats, I wonder?'   And here
Alice began to get rather sleepy, and went on saying to
herself, in a dreamy sort of way, 'Do cats eat bats?   Do
cats eat bats?' and sometimes, 'Do bats eat cats?' for,
you see, as she couldn't answer either question, it didn't
much matter which way she put it.   She felt that she
was dozing off, and had just begun to dream that she
was walking hand in hand with Dinah, and saying to her
very earnestly, 'Now, Dinah, tell me the truth: did you
ever eat a bat?' when suddenly, thump! thump! down
she came upon a heap of dry leaves, and the fall was
over.

Alice was not a bit hurt, and she jumped up on to her
feet in a moment: she looked up, but it was all dark overhead; before her was another long passage, and the White
Rabbit was still in sight, hurrying down it.   There was
not a moment to be lost: away went Alice like the wind,
and was just in time to hear it say, as it turned a corner,
'Oh my ears and whiskers, how late it's getting!'   She
was close behind it when she turned the corner, but the
Rabbit was no longer to be seen: she found herself in a
long, low hall, which was lit up by a row of lamps hanging
from the roof.

There were doors all round the hall, but they were all
locked; and when Alice had been all the way down one
side and up the other, trying every door, she walked sadly
down the middle, wondering how she was ever to get
out again.

Suddenly she came upon a little three-legged table, all
made of solid glass; there was nothing on it except a tiny
golden key, and Alice's first thought was that it might
belong to one of the doors of the hall; but, alas! either

the locks were too large, or the key was too small, but at any rate it would not open any of them. However, the second time round, she came upon a low curtain she had not noticed before, and behind it was a little door about fifteen inches high: she tried the little golden key in the lock, and to her great delight it fitted!

Alice opened the door and found that it led into a small passage, not much larger than a rat-hole: she knelt down and looked along the passage into the love-liest garden you ever saw. How she longed to get out of that dark hall, and wander about among those beds of bright flowers and those cool fountains, but she could not even get her head through the doorway; 'and even if my head would go through,' thought poor Alice, 'it would be of very little use without my shoulders. Oh, how I wish I could shut up like a telescope! I think I could, if I only knew how to begin.' For, you see, so many out-of-the-way things had happened lately, that Alice had begun to think that very few things indeed were really impossible.

There seemed to be no use in waiting by the little door, so she went back to the table, half hoping she might find another key on it, or at any rate a book of rules for shutting people up like telescopes: this time she found a little bottle on it ('which certainly was not here before,' said Alice), and round its neck a paper label, with the words 'DRINK ME' beautifully printed on it in large letters.

It was all very well to say 'Drink me,' but the wise little Alice was not going to do *that* in a hurry. 'No, I'll look first,' she said, 'and see whether it's marked "*poison*" or not'; for she had read several nice little histories about children who had got burnt, and eaten up by wild beasts, and many other unpleasant things, all because they *would* not remember the simple rules their friends had taught them: such as, that a red-hot poker will burn you if you hold it too long; and that, if you cut your finger *very* deeply with a knife, it usually bleeds; and she had never forgotten that, if you drink much from a bottle marked 'poison,' it is almost certain to disagree with you, sooner or later.

However, this bottle was *not* marked 'poison,' so Alice ventured to taste it, and finding it very nice (it had, in fact, a sort of mixed flavour of cherry-tart, custard, pine-apple, roast turkey, toffee, and hot buttered toast), she very soon finished it off.

'What a curious feeling!' said Alice. 'I must be shutting up like a telescope.'

And so it was indeed: she was now only ten inches high, and her face brightened up at the thought that she was now the right size for going through the little door into that lovely garden. First, however, she waited for a few minutes to see if she was going to shrink any further: she felt a little nervous about this; 'for it might end, you know,' said Alice, 'in my going out altogether, like a candle. I wonder what I should be like then?' And she tried to fancy what the flame of a candle is like after it is blown out, for she could not remember ever having seen such a thing.

After a while, finding that nothing more happened, she decided on going into the garden at once; but, alas for poor Alice! when she got to the door, she found she had forgotten the little golden key, and when she went back to the table for it, she found she could not possibly reach it: she could see it quite plainly through the glass, and she tried her best to climb up one of the table-legs, but it was too slippery; and when she had tired herself out with trying, the poor little thing sat down and cried.

'Come, there's no use in crying like that!' said Alice to herself, rather sharply. 'I advise you to leave off this minute!' She generally gave herself very good advice (though she very seldom followed it), and sometimes she scolded herself so severely as to bring tears into her eyes; and once she remembered trying to box her own ears for having cheated herself in a game of croquet she was playing against herself, for this curious child was very fond of pretending to be two people. 'But it's no use now,' thought poor Alice, 'to pretend to be two people! Why, there's hardly enough of me left to make *one* respectable person!'

Soon her eye fell on a little glass box that was lying under the table: she opened it, and found in it a very small cake, on which the words 'EAT ME' were beautifully marked in currants. 'Well, I'll eat it,' said Alice, 'and if it makes me larger, I can reach the key; and if it makes me smaller, I can creep under the door; so either way I'll get into the garden, and I don't care which happens!'

She ate a little bit, and said anxiously to herself, 'Which way? Which way?' holding her hand on the top of her head to feel which way it was growing, and she was quite surprised to find that she remained the same size: to be sure, this generally happens when one eats cake, but Alice had got so much into the way of expecting nothing but out-of-the-way things to happen, that it seemed quite dull and stupid for life to go on in the common way.

So she set to work, and very soon finished off the cake.

*   *   *   *

*   *   *   *

*   *   *   *   *

CHAPTER II

THE POOL OF TEARS

'CURIOUSER and curiouser!' cried Alice (she was so much surprised, that for the moment she quite forgot how to speak good English); 'now I'm opening out like the largest telescope that ever was! Good-bye, feet!' (for when she looked down at her feet, they seemed to be almost out of sight, they were getting so far off). 'Oh, my poor little feet, I wonder who will put on your shoes and stockings for you now, dears? I'm sure I shan't be able! I shall be a great deal too far off to trouble myself about you: you must manage the best way you can—but I must be kind to them,' thought Alice, 'or perhaps they won't walk the way I want to go! Let me see: I'll give them a new pair of boots every Christmas.'

And she went on planning to herself how she would manage it. 'They must go by the carrier,' she thought;

'and how funny it'll seem, sending presents to one's own feet! And how odd the directions will look!

> *Alice's Right Foot, Esq.*
>> *Hearthrug,*
>>> *near the Fender,*
>>>> (*with Alice's love*).

Oh dear, what nonsense I'm talking!'

Just then her head struck against the roof of the hall: in fact she was now more than nine feet high, and she at once took up the little golden key and hurried off to the garden door.

Poor Alice! It was as much as she could do, lying down on one side, to look through into the garden with one eye; but to get through was more hopeless than ever: she sat down and began to cry again.

'You ought to be ashamed of yourself,' said Alice, 'a great girl like you' (she might well say this), 'to go on crying in this way! Stop this moment, I tell you!' But she went on all the same, shedding gallons of tears, until there was a large pool all round her, about four inches deep and reaching half down the hall.

After a time she heard a little pattering of feet in the distance, and she hastily dried her eyes to see what was coming. It was the White Rabbit returning, splendidly dressed, with a pair of white kid gloves in one hand and a large fan in the other: he came trotting along in a great hurry, muttering to himself as he came, 'Oh! the Duchess, the Duchess! Oh! won't she be savage if I've kept her waiting!' Alice felt so desperate that she was ready to ask help of anyone, so, when the Rabbit came near her, she began, in a low, timid voice, 'If you please, sir——' The Rabbit started violently, dropped the white kid gloves and the fan, and scurried away into the darkness as hard as he could go.

Alice took up the fan and gloves, and, as the hall was very hot, she kept fanning herself all the time she went on talking: 'Dear, dear! How queer everything is to-day! And yesterday things went on just as usual. I wonder

if I've been changed in the night? Let me think: was I the same when I got up this morning? I almost think I can remember feeling a little different. But if I'm not the same, the next question is, Who in the world am I? Ah, *that*'s the great puzzle!' And she began thinking over all the children she knew that were of the same age as herself, to see if she could have been changed for any of them.

'I'm sure I'm not Ada,' she said, 'for her hair goes in such long ringlets, and mine doesn't go in ringlets at all; and I'm sure I can't be Mabel, for I know all sorts of things, and she, oh! she knows such a very little! Besides, *she*'s she, and *I*'m I, and—oh dear, how puzzling it all is! I'll try if I know all the things I used to know. Let me see: four times five is twelve, and four times six is thirteen, and four times seven is—oh dear! I shall never get to twenty at that rate! However, the Multiplication Table doesn't signify: let's try Geography. London is the capital of Paris, and Paris is the capital of Rome, and Rome—no, *that*'s all wrong, I'm certain! I must have been changed for Mabel! I'll try and say "*How doth the little*—"' and she crossed her hands on her lap as if she were saying lessons, and began to repeat it, but her voice sounded hoarse and strange, and the words did not come the same as they used to do:

> *How doth the little crocodile*
> *Improve his shining tail,*
> *And pour the waters of the Nile*
> *On every golden scale!*
>
> *How cheerfully he seems to grin,*
> *How neatly spread his claws,*
> *And welcomes little fishes in*
> *With gently smiling jaws!*'

'I'm sure those are not the right words,' said poor Alice, and her eyes filled with tears again as she went on, 'I must be Mabel after all, and I shall have to go and live in that poky little house, and have next to no toys to play with, and oh! ever so many lessons to learn! No, I've made up my mind about it; if I'm Mabel, I'll stay down here! It'll be no use their putting their heads down and saying "Come up again, dear!" I shall only look up and say "Who am I then? Tell me that first, and

then, if I like being that person, I'll come up: if not, I'll
stay down here till I'm somebody else"—but, oh dear!'
cried Alice, with a sudden burst of tears, 'I do wish they
would put their heads down! I am so *very* tired of
being all alone here!'

As she said this she looked down at her hands, and
was surprised to see that she had put on one of the
Rabbit's little white kid gloves while she was talking.
'How *can* I have done that?' she thought. 'I must be
growing small again.' She got up and went to the table
to measure herself by it, and found that, as nearly as she
could guess, she was now about two feet high, and was
going on shrinking rapidly: she soon found out that the
cause of this was the fan she was holding, and she dropped
it hastily, just in time to avoid shrinking away altogether.

'That *was* a narrow escape!' said Alice, a good deal
frightened at the sudden change, but very glad to find herself still in existence; 'and now for the garden!' and she ran
with all speed back to the little door: but, alas! the little
door was shut again, and the little golden key was lying on
the glass table as before, 'and things are worse than ever,'
thought the poor child, 'for I never was so small as this
before, never! And I declare it's too bad, that it is!'

As she said these words her foot slipped, and in another
moment, splash! she was up to her chin in salt water.
Her first idea was that she had somehow fallen into the
sea, 'and in that case I can go back by railway,' she said
to herself. (Alice had been to the seaside once in her
life, and had come to the general conclusion, that where-
ever you go to on the English coast you find a number of
bathing machines in the sea, some children digging in
the sand with wooden spades, then a row of lodging
houses, and behind them a railway station.) However,
she soon made out that she was in the pool of tears which
she had wept when she was nine feet high.

'I wish I hadn't cried so much!' said Alice, as she swam about, trying to find her way out. 'I shall be punished for it now, I suppose, by being drowned in my own tears! That *will* be a queer thing, to be sure! However, everything is queer to-day.'

Just then she heard something splashing about in the pool a little way off, and she swam nearer to make out what it was: at first she thought it must be a walrus or hippopotamus, but then she remembered how small she was now, and she soon made out that it was only a mouse that had slipped in like herself.

'Would it be of any use, now,' thought Alice, 'to speak to this mouse? Everything is so out-of-the-way down here, that I should think very likely it can talk: at any rate, there's no harm in trying.' So she began: 'O Mouse, do you know the way out of this pool? I am very tired of swimming about here, O Mouse!' (Alice thought this must be the right way of speaking to a mouse: she had never done such a thing before, but she remembered having seen in her brother's Latin Grammar, 'A mouse—of a mouse—to a mouse—a mouse—O mouse!') The Mouse looked at her rather inquisitively, and seemed to her to wink with one of its little eyes, but it said nothing.

'Perhaps it doesn't understand English,' thought Alice;
'I dare say it's a French mouse, come over with William
the Conqueror.' (For, with all her knowledge of history,
Alice had no very clear notion how long ago anything
had happened.) So she began again: 'Où est ma chatte?'

which was the first sentence in her French lesson-book.
The Mouse gave a sudden leap out of the water, and
seemed to quiver all over with fright. 'Oh, I beg your
pardon!' cried Alice hastily, afraid that she had hurt the
poor animal's feelings. 'I quite forgot you didn't like cats.'

'Not like cats!' cried the Mouse, in a shrill, passionate
voice. 'Would *you* like cats if you were me?'

'Well, perhaps not,' said Alice in a soothing tone: 'don't
be angry about it. And yet I wish I could show you our
cat Dinah: I think you'd take a fancy to cats if you
could only see her. She is such a dear quiet thing,' Alice
went on, half to herself, as she swam lazily about in the
pool, 'and she sits purring so nicely by the fire, licking
her paws and washing her face—and she is such a nice
soft thing to nurse—and she's such a capital one for
catching mice——Oh, I beg your pardon!' cried Alice

again, for this time the Mouse was bristling all over, and she felt certain it must be really offended. 'We won't talk about her any more if you'd rather not.'

'We, indeed!' cried the Mouse, who was trembling down to the end of his tail. 'As if *I* would talk on such a subject! Our family always *hated* cats: nasty, low, vulgar things! Don't let me hear the name again!'

'I won't indeed!' said Alice, in a great hurry to change the subject of conversation. 'Are you—are you fond—of—of dogs?' The Mouse did not answer, so Alice went on eagerly: 'There is such a nice little dog near our house I should like to show you! A little bright-eyed terrier, you know, with oh, such long curly brown hair! And it'll fetch things when you throw them, and it'll sit up and beg for its dinner, and all sorts of things—I can't remember half of them—and it belongs to a farmer, you know, and he says it's so useful, it's worth a hundred pounds! He says it kills all the rats and—oh dear!' cried Alice in a sorrowful tone, 'I'm afraid I've offended it again!' For the Mouse was swimming away from her as hard as it could go, and making quite a commotion in the pool as it went.

So she called softly after it, 'Mouse dear! Do come back again, and we won't talk about cats or dogs either, if you don't like them!' When the Mouse heard this, it turned round and swam slowly back to her: its face was quite pale (with passion, Alice thought), and it said in a low trembling voice, 'Let us get to the shore, and then I'll tell you my history, and you'll understand why it is I hate cats and dogs.'

It was high time to go, for the pool was getting quite crowded with the birds and animals that had fallen into it: there were a Duck and a Dodo, a Lory and an Eaglet, and several other curious creatures. Alice led the way, and the whole party swam to the shore.

CHAPTER III

A CAUCUS-RACE AND A LONG TALE

THEY were indeed a queer-looking party that assembled on the bank—the birds with draggled feathers, the animals with their fur clinging close to them, and all dripping wet, cross, and uncomfortable.

The first question of course was, how to get dry again: they had a consultation about this, and after a few minutes it seemed quite natural to Alice to find herself talking familiarly with them, as if she had known them all her life. Indeed, she had quite a long argument with the Lory, who at last turned sulky, and would only say 'I am older than you, and must know better'; and this Alice would not allow without knowing how old it was, and, as the Lory positively refused to tell its age, there was no more to be said.

At last the Mouse, who seemed to be a person of authority among them, called out 'Sit down, all of you, and listen to me! *I*'ll soon make you dry enough!' They all sat down at once, in a large ring, with the Mouse in the middle. Alice kept her eyes anxiously fixed on it, for she felt sure she would catch a bad cold if she did not get dry very soon.

'Ahem!' said the Mouse with an important air. 'Are you all ready? This is the driest thing I know. Silence all round, if you please! "William the Conqueror, whose cause was favoured by the pope, was soon submitted to by the English, who wanted leaders, and had been of late much accustomed to usurpation and conquest. Edwin and Morcar, the earls of Mercia and Northumbria—''

'Ugh!' said the Lory, with a shiver.

'I beg your pardon!' said the Mouse, frowning, but very politely. 'Did you speak?'

'Not I!' said the Lory hastily.

'I thought you did,' said the Mouse. '—I proceed. "Edwin and Morcar, the earls of Mercia and Northumbria, declared for him: and even Stigand, the patriotic archbishop of Canterbury, found it advisable—''

'Found *what*?' said the Duck.

'Found *it*,' the Mouse replied rather crossly: 'of course you know what "it" means.'

'I know what "it" means well enough, when *I* find a thing,' said the Duck: 'it's generally a frog or a worm. The question is, what did the archbishop find?'

The Mouse did not notice this question, but hurriedly went on, '"—found it advisable to go with Edgar Atheling to meet William and offer him the crown. William's conduct at first was moderate. But the insolence of his Normans—" How are you getting on now, my dear?' it continued, turning to Alice as it spoke.

'As wet as ever,' said Alice in a melancholy tone: 'it doesn't seem to dry me at all.'

'In that case,' said the Dodo solemnly, rising to its feet, 'I move that the meeting adjourn, for the immediate adoption of more energetic remedies——'

'Speak English!' said the Eaglet. 'I don't know the meaning of half those long words, and, what's more, I don't believe you do either!' And the Eaglet bent down its head to hide a smile: some of the other birds tittered audibly.

'What I was going to say,' said the Dodo in an offended

tone, 'was, that the best thing to get us dry would be a Caucus-race.'

'What *is* a Caucus-race?' said Alice; not that she much wanted to know, but the Dodo had paused as if it thought that *somebody* ought to speak, and no one else seemed inclined to say anything.

'Why,' said the Dodo, 'the best way to explain it is to do it.' (And, as you might like to try the thing yourself some winter day, I will tell you how the Dodo managed it.)

First it marked out a racecourse, in a sort of circle ('the exact shape doesn't matter,' it said), and then all the party were placed along the course, here and there. There was no 'One, two, three, and away,' but they began running when they liked, and left off when they liked, so that it was not easy to know when the race was over. However, when they had been running half an hour or so, and were quite dry again, the Dodo suddenly called out 'The race is over!' and they all crowded round it, panting, and asking 'But who has won?'

This question the Dodo could not answer without a great deal of thought, and it sat for a long time with one finger pressed upon its forehead (the position in which you usually see Shakespeare, in the pictures of him), while the rest waited in silence. At last the Dodo said '*Everybody* has won, and all must have prizes.'

'But who is to give the prizes?' quite a chorus of voices asked.

'Why, *she*, of course,' said the Dodo, pointing to Alice with one finger; and the whole party at once crowded round her, calling out in a confused way, 'Prizes! Prizes!'

Alice had no idea what to do, and in despair she put her hand in her pocket, and pulled out a box of comfits (luckily the salt water had not got into it), and handed them round as prizes. There were exactly one a-piece all round.

'But she must have a prize herself, you know,' said the Mouse.

'Of course,' the Dodo replied very gravely. 'What else have you got in your pocket?' he went on, turning to Alice.

'Only a thimble,' said Alice sadly.

'Hand it over here,' said the Dodo.

Then they all crowded round her once more, while the Dodo solemnly presented the thimble, saying 'We beg your acceptance of this elegant thimble'; and, when it had finished this short speech, they all cheered.

Alice thought the whole thing very absurd, but they all looked so grave that she did not dare to laugh; and, as she could not think of anything to say, she simply bowed, and took the thimble, looking as solemn as she could.

The next thing was to eat the comfits: this caused some noise and confusion, as the large birds complained that they could not taste theirs, and the small ones choked and had to be patted on the back. However, it was over at last, and they sat down again in a ring, and begged the Mouse to tell them something more.

'You promised to tell me your history, you know,' said Alice, 'and why it is you hate—C and D,' she added in a whisper, half afraid that it would be offended again.

'Mine is a long and a sad tale!' said the Mouse, turning to Alice and sighing.

'It *is* a long tail, certainly,' said Alice, looking down with wonder at the Mouse's tail; 'but why do you call it

sad?' And she kept on puzzling about it while the
Mouse was speaking, so that her idea of the tale was
something like this:—'Fury said to a

mouse, That
he met in the
house, "Let
us both go
to law: *I*
will prose-
cute *you*.—
Come, I 'll
take no de-
nial: We
must have
the trial;
For really
this morn-
ing I 've
nothing
to do."
Said the
mouse to
the cur,
"Such a
trial, dear
sir, With
no jury
or judge,
would
be wast-
ing our
breath."
"I 'll be
judge,
I 'll be
jury,"
said
cun-
ning
old
Fury;
"I 'll
try
the
whole
cause,
and
con-
demn
you to
death."'

'You are not attending!' said the Mouse to Alice severely. 'What are you thinking of?'

'I beg your pardon,' said Alice very humbly: 'you had got to the fifth bend, I think?'

'I had *not*!' cried the Mouse, angrily.

'A knot!' said Alice, always ready to make herself useful, and looking anxiously about her. 'Oh, do let me help to undo it!'

'I shall do nothing of the sort,' said the Mouse, getting up and walking away. 'You insult me by talking such nonsense!'

'I didn't mean it!' pleaded poor Alice. 'But you're so easily offended, you know!'

The Mouse only growled in reply.

'Please come back and finish your story!' Alice called after it. And the others all joined in chorus, 'Yes, please do!' but the Mouse only shook its head impatiently and walked a little quicker.

'What a pity it wouldn't stay!' sighed the Lory, as soon as it was quite out of sight; and an old Crab took the opportunity of saying to her daughter 'Ah, my dear! Let this be a lesson to you never to lose *your* temper!' 'Hold your tongue, Ma!' said the young Crab, a little snappishly. 'You're enough to try the patience of an oyster!'

'I wish I had our Dinah here, I know I do!' said Alice aloud, addressing nobody in particular. 'She'd soon fetch it back!'

'And who is Dinah, if I might venture to ask the question?' said the Lory.

Alice replied eagerly, for she was always ready to talk about her pet: 'Dinah's our cat. And she's such a capital one for catching mice you can't think! And oh, I wish you could see her after the birds! Why, she'll eat a little bird as soon as look at it!'

This speech caused a remarkable sensation among the

party. Some of the birds hurried off at once: one old
Magpie began wrapping itself up very carefully, remarking, 'I really must be getting home; the night air doesn't
suit my throat!' and a Canary called out in a trembling
voice to its children 'Come away, my dears! It's high
time you were all in bed!' On various pretexts they all
moved off, and Alice was soon left alone.

'I wish I hadn't mentioned Dinah!' she said to herself
in a melancholy tone. 'Nobody seems to like her, down
here, and I'm sure she's the best cat in the world! Oh,
my dear Dinah! I wonder if I shall ever see you any
more!' And here poor Alice began to cry again, for she
felt very lonely and low-spirited. In a little while, however, she again heard a little pattering of footsteps in the
distance, and she looked up eagerly, half hoping that the
Mouse had changed his mind, and was coming back to
finish his story.

CHAPTER IV

THE RABBIT SENDS IN A LITTLE BILL

IT was the White Rabbit, trotting slowly back again, and looking anxiously about as it went, as if it had lost something; and she heard it muttering to itself, 'The Duchess! The Duchess! Oh my dear paws! Oh my fur and whiskers! She'll get me executed, as sure as ferrets are ferrets! Where *can* I have dropped them, I wonder?' Alice guessed in a moment that it was looking for the fan and the pair of white kid gloves, and she very good-naturedly began hunting about for them, but they were nowhere to be seen—everything seemed to have changed since her swim in the pool, and the great hall, with the glass table and the little door, had vanished completely.

Very soon the Rabbit noticed Alice, as she went hunting about, and called out to her in an angry tone, 'Why, Mary Ann, what *are* you doing out here? Run home this moment, and fetch me a pair of gloves and a fan! Quick, now!' And Alice was so much frightened that she ran off at once in the direction it pointed to, without trying to explain the mistake it had made.

'He took me for his housemaid,' she said to herself as she ran. 'How surprised he'll be when he finds out who I am! But I'd better take him his fan and gloves —that is, if I can find them.' As she said this, she came upon a neat little house, on the door of which was a bright brass plate with the name 'W. RABBIT' engraved upon it. She went in without knocking, and hurried upstairs, in great fear lest she should meet the

real Mary Ann, and be turned out of the house before
she had found the fan and gloves.

'How queer it seems,' Alice said to herself, 'to be
going messages for a rabbit!   I suppose Dinah'll be
sending me on messages next!'   And she began fancying
the sort of thing that would happen: '"Miss Alice!
Come here directly, and get ready for your walk!"
"Coming in a minute, nurse!   But I've got to watch
this mouse-hole till Dinah comes back, and see that the
mouse doesn't get out."   Only I don't think,' Alice
went on, 'that they'd let Dinah stop in the house if it
began ordering people about like that!'

By this time she had found her way into a tidy little
room with a table in the window, and on it (as she had
hoped) a fan and two or three pairs of tiny white kid
gloves: she took up the fan and a pair of the gloves, and
was just going to leave the room, when her eye fell upon
a little bottle that stood near the looking-glass.   There
was no label this time with the words ' DRINK ME,'
but nevertheless she uncorked it and put it to her lips.
'I know *something* interesting is sure to happen,' she said
to herself, 'whenever I eat or drink anything; so I'll just
see what this bottle does.   I do hope it'll make me grow
large again, for really I'm quite tired of being such a tiny
little thing!'

It did so indeed, and much sooner than she had
expected: before she had drunk half the bottle, she found
her head pressing against the ceiling, and had to stoop
to save her neck from being broken.   She hastily put
down the bottle, saying to herself 'That's quite enough
—I hope I shan't grow any more—As it is, I can't
get out at the door—I do wish I hadn't drunk quite so
much!'

Alas! it was too late to wish that!   She went on growing, and growing, and very soon had to kneel down on the

floor: in another minute there was not even room for this,
and she tried the effect of lying down with one elbow
against the door, and the other arm curled round her
head.   Still she went on growing, and, as a last resource,
she put one arm out of the window, and one foot up the
chimney, and said to herself 'Now I can do no more,
whatever happens.   What *will* become of me?'

Luckily for Alice, the little magic bottle had now had
its full effect, and she grew no larger: still it was very
uncomfortable, and, as there seemed to be no sort of
chance of her ever getting out of the room again, no
wonder she felt unhappy.

'It was much pleasanter at home,' thought poor Alice,
'when one wasn't always growing larger and smaller, and
being ordered about by mice and rabbits.   I almost wish
I hadn't gone down that rabbit-hole—and yet—and yet
—it's rather curious, you know, this sort of life! I do
wonder what *can* have happened to me!   When I used
to read fairy-tales, I fancied that kind of thing never

happened, and now here I am in the middle of one! There ought to be a book written about me, that there ought! And when I grow up, I'll write one—but I'm grown up now,' she added in a sorrowful tone; 'at least there's no room to grow up any more *here*.'

'But then,' thought Alice, 'shall I *never* get any older than I am now? That'll be a comfort, one way—never to be an old woman—but then—always to have lessons to learn! Oh, I shouldn't like *that*!'

'Oh, you foolish Alice!' she answered herself. 'How can you learn lessons in here? Why, there's hardly room for *you*, and no room at all for any lesson-books!'

And so she went on, taking first one side and then the other, and making quite a conversation of it altogether; but after a few minutes she heard a voice outside, and stopped to listen.

'Mary Ann! Mary Ann!' said the voice. 'Fetch me my gloves this moment!' Then came a little pattering of feet on the stairs. Alice knew it was the Rabbit coming to look for her, and she trembled till she shook the house, quite forgetting that she was now about a thousand times as large as the Rabbit, and had no reason to be afraid of it.

Presently the Rabbit came up to the door, and tried to open it; but, as the door opened inwards, and Alice's elbow was pressed hard against it, that attempt proved a failure. Alice heard it say to itself 'Then I'll go round and get in at the window.'

'*That* you won't!' thought Alice, and, after waiting till she fancied she heard the Rabbit just under the window, she suddenly spread out her hand, and made a snatch in the air. She did not get hold of anything, but she heard a little shriek and a fall, and a crash of broken glass, from which she concluded that it was just possible it had fallen into a cucumber-frame, or something of the sort.

Next came an angry voice—the Rabbit's—'Pat! Pat! Where are you?' And then a voice she had never heard before, 'Sure then I'm here! Digging for apples, yer honour!'

'Digging for apples, indeed!' said the Rabbit angrily. 'Here! Come and help me out of *this*!' (Sounds of more broken glass.)

'Now tell me, Pat, what's that in the window?'

'Sure, it's an arm, yer honour!' (He pronounced it 'arrum.')

'An arm, you goose! Who ever saw one that size? Why, it fills the whole window!'

'Sure, it does, yer honour: but it's an arm for all that.'

'Well, it's got no business there, at any rate: go and take it away!'

There was a long silence after this, and Alice could only hear whispers now and then; such as, 'Sure, I don't like it, yer honour, at all, at all!' 'Do as I tell you, you coward!' and at last she spread out her hand again, and made another snatch in the air. This time there were *two* little shrieks, and more sounds of broken glass. 'What a number of cucumber-frames there must be!' thought Alice. 'I wonder what they'll do next! As for pulling me out of the window, I only wish they *could*! I'm sure *I* don't want to stay in here any longer!'

She waited for some time without hearing anything

more: at last came a rumbling of little cart-wheels, and the sound of a good many voices all talking together: she

made out the words: 'Where's the other ladder?—Why I hadn't to bring but one; Bill's got the other—Bill! Fetch it here, lad!—Here, put 'em up at this corner—No, tie 'em together first—they don't reach half high enough yet—Oh! they'll do well enough; don't be particular — Here, Bill! catch hold of this rope—Will the roof bear!—Mind that loose slate—Oh, it's coming down! Heads below!' (a loud crash)—'Now, who did that? —It was Bill, I fancy—Who's to go down the chimney?— Nay, *I* shan't! *You* do it!— *That* I won't, then!—Bill's to go down—Here, Bill! the master says you've to go down the chimney!'

'Oh! So Bill's got to come down the chimney, has he?' said Alice to herself. 'Why, they seem to put everything upon Bill! I wouldn't be in Bill's place for a good deal: this fire-place is narrow, to be sure; but I *think* I can kick a little!'

She drew her foot as far down the chimney as she could, and waited till she heard a little animal (she couldn't guess of what sort it was) scratching and scrambling about

in the chimney close above her: then, saying to herself
'This is Bill,' she gave one sharp kick, and waited to see
what would happen next.

The first thing she heard was a general chorus of
'There goes Bill!' then the Rabbit's voice alone—'Catch
him, you by the hedge!' then silence and then another
confusion of voices—'Hold up his head—Brandy now—
Don't choke him—How was it, old fellow? What
happened to you? Tell us all about it!'

At last came a little feeble, squeaking voice ('That's
Bill,' thought Alice), 'Well, I hardly know—No more,
thank ye; I'm better now—but I'm a deal too flustered
to tell you—all I know is, something comes at me like a
Jack-in-the-box, and up I goes like a sky-rocket!'

'So you did, old fellow!' said the others.

'We must burn the house down!' said the Rabbit's
voice. And Alice called out as loud as she could, 'If
you do, I'll set Dinah at you!'

There was a dead silence instantly, and Alice thought
to herself 'I wonder what they *will* do next! If they
had any sense, they'd take the roof off.' After a minute
or two, they began moving about again, and Alice heard
the Rabbit say 'A barrowful will do, to begin with.'

'A barrowful of *what*?' thought Alice. But she had
not long to doubt, for the next moment a shower of little
pebbles came rattling in at the window, and some of them
hit her in the face. 'I'll put a stop to this,' she said to
herself, and shouted out 'You'd better not do that
again!' which produced another dead silence.

Alice noticed with some surprise that the pebbles
were all turning into little cakes as they lay on the floor,
and a bright idea came into her head. 'If I eat one of
these cakes,' she thought, 'it's sure to make *some* change
in my size; and, as it can't possibly make me larger, it
must make me smaller, I suppose.'

So she swallowed one of the cakes, and was delighted to find that she began shrinking directly. As soon as she was small enough to get through the door, she ran out of the house, and found quite a crowd of little animals and birds waiting outside. The poor little Lizard, Bill, was in the middle, being held up by two guinea-pigs, who were giving it something out of a bottle. They all made a rush at Alice the moment she appeared; but she ran off as hard as she could, and soon found herself safe in a thick wood.

'The first thing I've got to do,' said Alice to herself, as she wandered about in the wood, 'is to grow to my right size again; and the second thing is to find my way into that lovely garden. I think that will be the best plan.'

It sounded an excellent plan, no doubt, and very neatly and simply arranged; the only difficulty was, that she had not the smallest idea how to set about it; and, while she was peering about anxiously among the trees, a little sharp bark just over her head made her look up in a great hurry.

An enormous puppy was looking down at her with large round eyes, and feebly stretching out one paw, trying to touch her. 'Poor little thing!' said Alice, in a coaxing tone, and she tried hard to whistle to it; but she was terribly frightened all the time at the thought that it might be hungry, in which case it would be very likely to eat her up in spite of all her coaxing.

Hardly knowing what she did, she picked up a little bit of stick, and held it out to the puppy; whereupon the puppy jumped into the air off all its feet at once, with a yelp of delight, and rushed at the stick, and made believe to worry it; then Alice dodged behind a great thistle, to keep herself from being run over; and, the moment she appeared on the other side, the puppy made another rush at the stick, and tumbled head over heels in its hurry to get hold of it; then Alice, thinking it was very like having a game of play with a cart-horse, and expecting every

moment to be trampled under its feet, ran round the thistle again; then the puppy began a series of short charges at the stick, running a very little way forwards each time and a long way back, and barking hoarsely all the while, till at last it sat down a good way off, panting, with its tongue hanging out of its mouth, and its great eyes half shut.

This seemed to Alice a good opportunity for making her escape; so she set off at once, and ran till she was quite tired and out of breath, and till the puppy's bark sounded quite faint in the distance.

'And yet what a dear little puppy it was!' said Alice, as she leant against a buttercup to rest herself, and fanned herself with one of the leaves. 'I should have liked teaching it tricks very much, if—if I'd only been the right size to do it! Oh dear! I'd nearly forgotten that I've got to grow up again! Let me see—how *is* it to be managed? I suppose I ought to eat or drink something or other; but the great question is, what?'

The great question certainly was, what? Alice looked all round her at the flowers and the blades of grass, but she could not see anything that looked like the right thing to eat or drink under the circumstances. There was a large mushroom growing near her, about the same height as herself; and, when she had looked under it, and on both sides of it, and behind it, it occurred to her that she might as well look and see what was on the top of it.

She stretched herself up on tiptoe, and peeped over the edge of the mushroom, and her eyes immediately met those of a large blue caterpillar, that was sitting on the top with its arms folded, quietly smoking a long hookah, and taking not the smallest notice of her or of anything else.

CHAPTER V

ADVICE FROM A CATERPILLAR

THE Caterpillar and Alice looked at each other for some time in silence: at last the Caterpillar took the hookah out of its mouth, and addressed her in a languid, sleepy voice.

'Who are *you*?' said the Caterpillar.

This was not an encouraging opening for a conversation. Alice replied, rather shyly, 'I—I hardly know, sir, just at present—at least I know who I *was* when I got up this morning, but I think I must have been changed several times since then.'

'What do you mean by that?' said the Caterpillar sternly. 'Explain yourself!'

'I can't explain *myself*, I'm afraid, sir,' said Alice, 'because I'm not myself, you see.'

'I don't see,' said the Caterpillar.

'I'm afraid I can't put it more clearly,' Alice replied very politely, 'for I can't understand it myself to begin with; and being so many different sizes in a day is very confusing.'

'It isn't,' said the Caterpillar.

'Well, perhaps you haven't found it so yet,' said Alice; 'but when you have to turn into a chrysalis—you will some day, you know—and then after that into a butterfly, I should think you'll feel it a little queer, won't you?'

'Not a bit,' said the Caterpillar.

'Well, perhaps your feelings may be different,' said Alice; 'all I know is, it would feel very queer to *me*.'

'You!' said the Caterpillar contemptuously. 'Who are *you*?'

Which brought them back again to the beginning of the conversation. Alice felt a little irritated at the Caterpillar's making such *very* short remarks, and she drew herself up and said, very gravely, 'I think you ought to tell me who *you* are, first.'

'Why?' said the Caterpillar.

Here was another puzzling question; and as Alice could not think of any good reason, and as the Caterpillar seemed to be in a *very* unpleasant state of mind, she turned away.

'Come back!' the Caterpillar called after her. 'I've something important to say!'

This sounded promising, certainly: Alice turned and came back again.

'Keep your temper,' said the Caterpillar.

'Is that all?' said Alice, swallowing down her anger as well as she could.

'No,' said the Caterpillar.

Alice thought she might as well wait, as she had nothing else to do, and perhaps after all it might tell her something worth hearing. For some minutes it puffed away without speaking, but at last it unfolded its arms, took the hookah out of its mouth again, and said, 'So you think you're changed, do you?'

'I'm afraid I am, sir,' said Alice; 'I can't remember things as I used—and I don't keep the same size for ten minutes together!'

'Can't remember *what* things?' said the Caterpillar.

'Well, I've tried to say "*How doth the little busy bee,*" but it all came different!' Alice replied in a very melancholy voice.

'Repeat "*You are old, Father William,*"' said the Caterpillar.

Alice folded her hands, and began:

'*You are old, Father William,*' *the young man
    said,*
  '*And your hair has become very white;*
And yet you incessantly stand on your head—
  Do you think, at your age, it is right?'

'*In my youth,*' *Father William replied to his son,*
  '*I feared it might injure the brain;*
But, now that I'm perfectly sure I have none,
  Why, I do it again and again.'

'*You are old,*' *said the youth,* '*as I mentioned*
before,
And have grown most uncommonly fat;
Yet you turned a back-somersault in at the door—
Pray, what is the reason of that?'

'*In my youth,*' *said the sage, as he shook his grey*
locks,
'*I kept all my limbs very supple*
By the use of this ointment—one shilling the box—
Allow me to sell you a couple?'

'You are old,' said the youth, 'and your jaws are
    too weak
  For anything tougher than suet;
Yet you finished the goose, with the bones and the
    beak—
  Pray how did you manage to do it?'

'In my youth,' said his father, 'I took to the law,
  And argued each case with my wife;
And the muscular strength, which it gave to my
    jaw,
  Has lasted the rest of my life.'

'You are old,' said the youth, 'one would hardly
    suppose
  That your eye was as steady as ever;
Yet you balanced an eel on the end of your nose—
  What made you so awfully clever?'

'I have answered three questions, and that is
    enough,'
  Said his father; 'don't give yourself airs!
Do you think I can listen all day to such stuff?
  Be off, or I'll kick you downstairs!'

'That is not said right,' said the Caterpillar.

'Not *quite* right, I'm afraid,' said Alice, timidly; 'some of the words have got altered.'

'It is wrong from beginning to end,' said the Caterpillar decidedly, and there was silence for some minutes.

The Caterpillar was the first to speak.

'What size do you want to be?' it asked.

'Oh, I'm not particular as to size,' Alice hastily replied; 'only one doesn't like changing so often, you know.'

'I *don't* know,' said the Caterpillar.

Alice said nothing; she had never been so much contradicted in all her life before, and she felt that she was losing her temper.

'Are you content now?' said the Caterpillar.

'Well, I should like to be a *little* larger, sir, if you wouldn't mind,' said Alice: 'three inches is such a wretched height to be.'

'It is a very good height indeed!' said the Caterpillar angrily, rearing itself upright as it spoke (it was exactly three inches high).

'But I'm not used to it!' pleaded poor Alice in a piteous tone. And she thought to herself, 'I wish the creatures wouldn't be so easily offended!'

'You'll get used to it in time,' said the Caterpillar; and it put the hookah into its mouth and began smoking again.

This time Alice waited patiently until it chose to speak again. In a minute or two the Caterpillar took the hookah out of its mouth and yawned once or twice, and shook itself. Then it got down off the mushroom, and crawled away into the grass, merely remarking as it went, 'One side will make you grow taller, and the other side will make you grow shorter.'

'One side of *what*? The other side of *what*?' thought Alice to herself.

'Of the mushroom,' said the Caterpillar, just as if she had asked it aloud; and in another moment it was out of sight.

Alice remained looking thoughtfully at the mushroom for a minute, trying to make out which were the two sides of it; and as it was perfectly round, she found this a very difficult question. However, at last she stretched her arms round it as far as they would go, and broke off a bit of the edge with each hand.

'And now which is which?' she said to herself, and nibbled a little of the right-hand bit to try the effect: the next moment she felt a violent blow underneath her chin: it had struck her foot!

She was a good deal frightened by this very sudden change, but she felt that there was no time to be lost, as she was shrinking rapidly; so she set to work at once to eat some of the other bit. Her chin was pressed so closely against her foot, that there was hardly room to open her mouth; but she did it at last, and managed to swallow a morsel of the left-hand bit.

*   *   *   *   *

   *   *   *   *

*   *   *   *   *

'Come, my head's free at last!' said Alice in a tone of delight, which changed into alarm in another moment, when she found that her shoulders were nowhere to be found: all she could see, when she looked down, was an immense length of neck, which seemed to rise like a stalk out of a sea of green leaves that lay far below her.

'What *can* all that green stuff be?' said Alice. 'And where *have* my shoulders got to? And oh, my poor hands, how is it I can't see you?' She was moving them about as she spoke, but no result seemed to follow, except a little shaking among the distant green leaves.

As there seemed to be no chance of getting her hands up to her head, she tried to get her head down to them, and was delighted to find that her neck would bend about easily in any direction, like a serpent. She had just succeeded in curving it down into a graceful zigzag, and was going to dive in among the leaves, which she found to be nothing but the tops of the trees under which she had been wandering, when a sharp hiss made her draw back in a hurry: a large pigeon had flown into her face, and was beating her violently with its wings.

'Serpent!' screamed the Pigeon.

'I'm *not* a serpent!' said Alice indignantly. 'Let me alone!'

'Serpent, I say again!' repeated the Pigeon, but in a more subdued tone, and added with a kind of sob, 'I've tried every way, and nothing seems to suit them!'

'I haven't the least idea what you're talking about,' said Alice.

'I've tried the roots of trees, and I've tried banks, and I've tried hedges,' the Pigeon went on, without attending to her; 'but those serpents! There's no pleasing them!'

Alice was more and more puzzled, but she thought there was no use in saying anything more till the Pigeon had finished.

'As if it wasn't trouble enough hatching the eggs,' said the Pigeon; 'but I must be on the look-out for serpents night and day! Why, I haven't had a wink of sleep these three weeks!'

'I'm very sorry you've been annoyed,' said Alice, who was beginning to see its meaning.

'And just as I'd taken the highest tree in the wood,' continued the Pigeon, raising its voice to a shriek, 'and just as I was thinking I should be free of them at last, they must needs come wriggling down from the sky! Ugh, Serpent!'

'But I'm *not* a serpent,' I tell you!' said Alice. 'I'm a—I'm a——'

'Well! *What* are you?' said the Pigeon. 'I can see you're trying to invent something!'

'I—I'm a little girl,' said Alice, rather doubtfully, as she remembered the number of changes she had gone through, that day.

'A likely story indeed!' said the Pigeon in a tone of the deepest contempt. 'I've seen a good many little girls in my time, but never *one* with such a neck as that! No, no! You're a serpent; and there's no use denying it. I suppose you'll be telling me next that you never tasted an egg!'

'I *have* tasted eggs, certainly,' said Alice, who was a very truthful child; 'but little girls eat eggs quite as much as serpents do, you know.'

'I don't believe it,' said the Pigeon: 'but if they do, why then they're a kind of serpent, that's all I can say.'

This was such a new idea to Alice, that she was quite silent for a minute or two, which gave the Pigeon the opportunity of adding 'You're looking for eggs, I know *that* well enough; and what does it matter to me whether you're a little girl or a serpent?'

'It matters a good deal to *me*,' said Alice hastily; 'but I'm not looking for eggs, as it happens; and if I was, I shouldn't want *yours*: I don't like them raw.'

'Well, be off, then!' said the Pigeon in a sulky tone, as it settled down again into its nest. Alice crouched down among the trees as well as she could, for her neck kept getting entangled among the branches, and every now and then she had to stop and untwist it. After a while she remembered that she still held the pieces of mushroom in her hands, and she set to work very carefully, nibbling first at one and then at the other, and growing sometimes taller and sometimes shorter, until

she had succeeded in bringing herself down to her usual
height.

It was so long since she had been anything near the
right size, that it felt quite strange at first; but she got
used to it in a few minutes, and began talking to herself,
as usual. 'Come, there's half my plan done now! How
puzzling all these changes are! I'm never sure what
I'm going to be, from one minute to another! However,
I've got back to my right size: the next thing is, to get
into that beautiful garden—how *is* that to be done, I
wonder?' As she said this, she came suddenly upon an
open place, with a little house in it about four feet high.
'Whoever lives there,' thought Alice, 'it'll never do to
come upon them *this* size: why, I should frighten them
out of their wits!' So she began nibbling at the right-
hand bit again, and did not venture to go near the house
till she had brought herself down to nine inches high.

CHAPTER VI

PIG AND PEPPER

FOR a minute or two she stood looking at the house,
and wondering what to do next, when suddenly a footman
in livery came running out of the wood—(she considered
him to be a footman because he was in livery: otherwise,
judging by his face only, she would have called him a fish)
—and rapped loudly at the door with his knuckles. It
was opened by another footman in livery, with a round
face, and large eyes like a frog; and both footmen, Alice
noticed, had powdered hair that curled all over their
heads. She felt very curious to know what it was all
about, and crept a little way out of the wood to listen.

See page 47

'*For the Duchess.   An invitation from the Queen to play croquet*'

The Fish-Footman began by producing from under
his arm a great letter, nearly as large as himself, and this
he handed over to the other, saying, in a solemn tone,
'For the Duchess. An invitation from the Queen to
play croquet.' The Frog-Footman repeated, in the same
solemn tone, only changing the order of the words a little,
'From the Queen. An invitation for the Duchess to
play croquet.'

Then they both bowed low, and their curls got entangled together.

Alice laughed so much at this, that she had to run back
into the wood for fear of their hearing her; and, when she
next peeped out, the Fish-Footman was gone, and the
other was sitting on the ground near the door, staring
stupidly up into the sky.

Alice went timidly up to the door, and knocked.

'There's no sort of use in knocking,' said the Footman,
'and that for two reasons. First, because I'm on the
same side of the door as you are; secondly, because they're
making such a noise inside, no one could possibly hear
you.' And certainly there was a most extraordinary
noise going on within—a constant howling and sneezing,
and every now and then a great crash, as if a dish or
kettle had been broken to pieces.

'Please, then,' said Alice, 'how am I to get in?'

'There might be some sense in your knocking,' the
Footman went on without attending to her, 'if we had
the door between us. For instance, if you were *inside*,
you might knock, and I could let you out, you know.'
He was looking up into the sky all the time he was speaking, and this Alice thought decidedly uncivil. 'But
perhaps he can't help it,' she said to herself; 'his eyes
are so *very* nearly at the top of his head. But at any rate
he might answer questions.—How am I to get in?' she
repeated, aloud.

'I shall sit here,' the Footman remarked, 'till to-morrow——'

At this moment the door of the house opened, and a large plate came skimming out, straight at the Footman's head: it just grazed his nose, and broke to pieces against one of the trees behind him.

'——or next day, maybe,' the Footman continued in the same tone, exactly as if nothing had happened.

'How am I to get in?' asked Alice again, in a louder tone.

'*Are* you to get in at all?' said the Footman. 'That's the first question, you know.'

It was, no doubt: only Alice did not like to be told so. 'It's really dreadful,' she muttered to herself, 'the way all the creatures argue. It's enough to drive one crazy!'

The Footman seemed to think this a good opportunity for repeating his remark, with variations. 'I shall sit here,' he said, 'on and off, for days and days.'

'But what am *I* to do?' said Alice.

'Anything you like,' said the Footman, and began whistling.

'Oh, there's no use in talking to him,' said Alice desperately: 'he's perfectly idiotic!' And she opened the door and went in.

The door led right into a large kitchen, which was full of smoke from one end to the other: the Duchess was sitting on a three-legged stool in the middle, nursing a baby; the cook was leaning over the fire, stirring a large cauldron which seemed to be full of soup.

'There's certainly too much pepper in that soup!' Alice said to herself, as well as she could for sneezing.

There was certainly too much of it in the air. Even the Duchess sneezed occasionally; and the baby was sneezing and howling alternately without a moment's pause. The only things in the kitchen that did not sneeze, were the cook, and a large cat which was sitting on the hearth and grinning from ear to ear.

'Please would you tell me,' said Alice a little timidly, for she was not quite sure whether it was good manners for her to speak first, 'why your cat grins like that?'

'It's a Cheshire cat,' said the Duchess, 'and that's why. Pig!'

She said the last word with such sudden violence that Alice quite jumped; but she saw in another moment that it was addressed to the baby, and not to her, so she took courage, and went on again:

'I didn't know that Cheshire cats always grinned; in fact, I didn't know that cats *could* grin.'

'They all can,' said the Duchess; 'and most of 'em do.'

'I don't know of any that do,' Alice said very politely, feeling quite pleased to have got into a conversation.

'You don't know much,' said the Duchess; 'and that's a fact.'

Alice did not at all like the tone of this remark, and thought it would be as well to introduce some other subject of conversation. While she was trying to fix on one, the cook took the cauldron of soup off the fire, and at once set to work throwing everything within her reach at the Duchess and the baby—the fire-irons came first; then followed a shower of saucepans, plates, and dishes. The Duchess took no notice of them even when they hit her; and the baby was howling so much already, that it was quite impossible to say whether the blows hurt it or not.

'Oh, *please* mind what you're doing!' cried Alice, jumping up and down in an agony of terror. 'Oh, there goes his *precious* nose'; as an unusually large saucepan flew close by it, and very nearly carried it off.

'If everybody minded their own business,' the Duchess said in a hoarse growl, 'the world would go round a deal faster than it does.'

'Which would *not* be an advantage,' said Alice, who felt very glad to get an opportunity of showing off a little of her knowledge. 'Just think what work it would make with the day and night! You see, the earth takes twenty-four hours to turn round on its axis——'

'Talking of axes,' said the Duchess, 'chop off her head!'

Alice glanced rather anxiously at the cook, to see if she meant to take the hint; but the cook was busily engaged in stirring the soup, and did not seem to be listening, so she ventured to go on again: 'Twenty-four hours, I *think*; or is it twelve? I——'

'Oh, don't bother *me*,' said the Duchess; 'I never could abide figures!' And with that she began nursing her child again, singing a sort of lullaby to it as she did so, and giving it a violent shake at the end of every line:

'Speak roughly to your little boy,
    And beat him when he sneezes:
He only does it to annoy,
    Because he knows it teases.'

CHORUS

(In which the cook and the baby joined):
'Wow! wow! wow!'

While the Duchess sang the second verse of the song, she kept tossing the baby violently up and down, and the poor little thing howled so, that Alice could hardly hear the words:

'I speak severely to my boy,
    I beat him when he sneezes;
For he can thoroughly enjoy
    The pepper when he pleases!'

CHORUS

'Wow! wow! wow!'

'Here! you may nurse it a bit, if you like!' the Duchess said to Alice, flinging the baby to her as she spoke. 'I must go and get ready to play croquet with the Queen,' and she hurried out of the room. The cook threw a frying-pan after her as she went out, but it just missed her.

Alice caught the baby with some difficulty, as it was a queer-shaped little creature, and held out its arms and legs in all directions, 'just like a star-fish,' thought Alice. The poor little thing was snorting like a steam-engine when she caught it, and kept doubling itself up and straightening itself out again, so that altogether, for the first minute or two, it was as much as she could do to hold it.

As soon as she had made out the proper way of nursing it (which was to twist it up into a sort of knot, and then keep tight hold of its right ear and left foot, so as to prevent its undoing itself), she carried it out into the open air. 'If I don't take this child away with me,' thought Alice, 'they're sure to kill it in a day or two: wouldn't it be murder to leave it behind?' She

said the last words out loud, and the little thing grunted in reply (it had left off sneezing by this time). 'Don't grunt,' said Alice; 'that's not at all a proper way of expressing yourself.'

The baby grunted again, and Alice looked very anxiously into its face to see what was the matter with it. There could be no doubt that it had a *very* turn-up nose, much more like a snout than a real nose; also its eyes were getting extremely small for a baby: altogether Alice did not like the look of the thing at all. 'But perhaps it was only sobbing,' she thought, and looked into its eyes again, to see if there were any tears.

No, there were no tears. 'If you're going to turn into a pig, my dear,' said Alice, seriously, 'I'll have nothing more to do with you. Mind now!' The poor little thing sobbed again (or grunted, it was impossible to say which), and they went on for some while in silence.

Alice was just beginning to think to herself, 'Now, what am I to do with this creature when I get it home?' when it grunted again, so violently, that she looked down into its face in some alarm. This time there could be *no* mistake about it: it was neither more nor less than a pig, and she felt that it would be quite absurd for her to carry it any further.

So she set the little creature down, and felt quite relieved to see it trot away quietly into the wood. 'If it had grown up,' she said to herself, 'it would have made a dreadfully ugly child: but it makes rather a handsome pig, I think.' And she began thinking over other children she knew, who might do very well as pigs, and was just saying to herself, 'if one only knew the right way to change them——' when she was a little startled by seeing the Cheshire Cat sitting on a bough of a tree a few yards off.

The Cat only grinned when it saw Alice. It looked good-natured, she thought: still it had *very* long claws and a great many teeth, so she felt that it ought to be treated with respect.

'Cheshire Puss,' she began, rather timidly, as she did not at all know whether it would like the name: however, it only grinned a little wider. 'Come, it's pleased so far,' thought Alice, and she went on. 'Would you tell me, please, which way I ought to go from here?'

'That depends a good deal on where you want to get to,' said the Cat.

'I don't much care where——' said Alice.

'Then it doesn't matter which way you go,' said the Cat.

'——so long as I get *somewhere*,' Alice added as an explanation.

'Oh, you're sure to do that,' said the Cat, 'if you only walk long enough.'

Alice felt that this could not be denied, so she tried another question. 'What sort of people live about here?'

'In *that* direction,' the Cat said, waving its right paw round, 'lives a Hatter: and in *that* direction,' waving the other paw, 'lives a March Hare. Visit either you like: they're both mad.'

'But I don't want to go among mad people,' Alice remarked.

'Oh, you can't help that,' said the Cat: 'we're all mad here. I'm mad. You're mad.'

'How do you know I'm mad?' said Alice.

'You must be,' said the Cat, 'or you wouldn't have come here.'

Alice didn't think that proved it at all: however, she went on. 'And how do you know that you're mad?'

'To begin with,' said the Cat, 'a dog's not mad. You grant that?'

'I suppose so,' said Alice.

'Well, then,' the Cat went on, 'you see a dog growls when it's angry, and wags its tail when it's pleased.

Now *I* growl when I'm pleased, and wag my tail when I'm angry. Therefore I'm mad.'

'*I* call it purring, not growling,' said Alice.

'Call it what you like,' said the Cat. 'Do you play croquet with the Queen to-day?'

'I should like it very much,' said Alice, 'but I haven't been invited yet.'

'You'll see me there,' said the Cat, and vanished.

Alice was not much surprised at this, she was getting so used to queer things happening. While she was looking at the place where it had been, it suddenly appeared again.

'By the bye, what became of the baby?' said the Cat. 'I'd nearly forgotten to ask.'

'It turned into a pig,' Alice quietly said, just as if it had come back in a natural way.

'I thought it would,' said the Cat, and vanished again.

Alice waited a little, half expecting to see it again, but it did not appear, and after a minute or two she walked on in the direction in which the March Hare was said to live. 'I've seen hatters before,' she said to herself; 'the March Hare will be much the most interesting, and perhaps, as this is May, it won't be raving mad—at least not so mad as it was in March.'   As she said this, she looked up, and there was the Cat again, sitting on a branch of a tree.

'Did you say pig, or fig?' said the Cat.

'I said pig,' replied Alice; 'and I wish you wouldn't keep appearing and vanishing so suddenly: you make one quite giddy.'

'All right,' said the Cat; and this time it vanished quite slowly, beginning with the end of the tail, and ending with the grin, which remained some time after the rest of it had gone.

'Well! I've often seen a cat without a grin,' thought Alice; 'but a grin without a cat!   It's the most curious thing I ever saw in all my life!'

She had not gone much further before she came in sight of the house of the March Hare: she thought it must be the right house, because the chimneys were shaped like ears and the roof was thatched with fur.   It was so large a house, that she did not like to go nearer till she had nibbled some more of the left-hand bit of mushroom, and raised herself to about two feet high: even then she walked up towards it rather timidly, saying to herself 'Suppose it should be raving mad after all!   I almost wish I'd gone to see the Hatter instead!'

CHAPTER VII

A MAD TEA-PARTY

THERE was a table set out under a tree in front of the
house, and the March Hare and the Hatter were having
tea at it: a Dormouse was sitting between them, fast
asleep, and the other two were resting their elbows on it,
and talking over its head. 'Very uncomfortable for the
Dormouse,' thought Alice; 'only, as it's asleep, I suppose
it doesn't mind.'

The table was a large one, but the three were all
crowded together at one corner of it. 'No room! No
room!' they cried out when they saw Alice coming.
'There's *plenty* of room!' said Alice indignantly, and she
sat down in a large arm-chair at one end of the table.

'Have some wine,' the March Hare said in an encouraging tone.

Alice looked all round the table, but there was nothing
on it but tea. 'I don't see any wine,' she remarked.

'There isn't any,' said the March Hare.

'Then it wasn't very civil of you to offer it,' said Alice
angrily.

'It wasn't very civil of you to sit down without being
invited,' said the March Hare.

'I didn't know it was *your* table,' said Alice; 'it's laid
for a great many more than three.'

'Your hair wants cutting,' said the Hatter. He had
been looking at Alice for some time with great curiosity,
and this was his first speech.

'You shouldn't make personal remarks,' Alice said with
some severity; 'it's very rude.'

The Hatter opened his eyes very wide on hearing this; but all he *said* was 'Why is a raven like a writing-desk?'

'Come, we shall have some fun now!' thought Alice. 'I'm glad they've begun asking riddles—I believe I can guess that,' she added aloud.

'Do you mean that you think you can find out the answer to it?' said the March Hare.

'Exactly so,' said Alice.

'Then you should say what you mean,' the March Hare went on.

'I do,' Alice hastily replied: 'at least—at least I mean what I say—that's the same thing, you know.'

'Not the same thing a bit!' said the Hatter. 'You might just as well say that "I see what I eat" is the same thing as "I eat what I see"!'

'You might just as well say,' added the March Hare, 'that "I like what I get" is the same thing as "I get what I like"!'

'You might just as well say,' added the Dormouse, who seemed to be talking in his sleep, 'that "I breathe when I sleep" is the same thing as "I sleep when I breathe"!'

'It *is* the same thing with you,' said the Hatter, and here the conversation dropped, and the party sat silent for a minute, while Alice thought over all she could remember about ravens and writing-desks, which wasn't much.

The Hatter was the first to break the silence. 'What day of the month is it?' he said, turning to Alice: he had taken his watch out of his pocket, and was looking at it uneasily, shaking it every now and then, and holding it to his ear.

Alice considered a little, and then said 'The fourth.'

'Two days wrong!' sighed the Hatter. 'I told you butter wouldn't suit the works!' he added, looking angrily at the March Hare.

'Your hair wants cutting,' said the Hatter

See page 57

'It was the *best* butter,' the March Hare meekly replied.

'Yes, but some crumbs must have got in as well,' the Hatter grumbled: 'you shouldn't have put it in with the bread-knife.'

The March Hare took the watch and looked at it gloomily: then he dipped it into his cup of tea, and looked at it again: but he could think of nothing better to say than his first remark, 'It was the *best* butter, you know.'

Alice had been looking over his shoulder with some curiosity. 'What a funny watch!' she remarked. 'It tells the day of the month, and doesn't tell what o'clock it is!'

'Why should it?' muttered the Hatter. 'Does *your* watch tell you what year it is?'

'Of course not,' Alice replied very readily: 'but that's because it stays the same year for such a long time together.'

'Which is just the case with *mine*,' said the Hatter.

Alice felt dreadfully puzzled. The Hatter's remark seemed to have no meaning in it, and yet it was certainly English. 'I don't quite understand,' she said, as politely as she could.

'The Dormouse is asleep again,' said the Hatter, and he poured a little hot tea upon its nose.

The Dormouse shook its head impatiently, and said, without opening its eyes, 'Of course, of course; just what I was going to remark myself.'

'Have you guessed the riddle yet?' the Hatter said, turning to Alice again.

'No, I give it up,' Alice replied: 'what's the answer?'

'I haven't the slightest idea,' said the Hatter.

'Nor I,' said the March Hare.

Alice sighed wearily. 'I think you might do something better with the time,' she said, 'than waste it asking riddles with no answers.'

'If you knew Time as well as I do,' said the Hatter, 'you wouldn't talk about wasting *it*. It's *him*.'

'I don't know what you mean,' said Alice.

'Of course you don't!' the Hatter said, tossing his head contemptuously. 'I dare say you never even spoke to Time!'

'Perhaps not,' Alice cautiously replied: 'but I know I have to beat time when I learn music.'

'Ah! that accounts for it,' said the Hatter. 'He won't stand beating. Now, if you only kept on good terms with him, he'd do almost anything you liked with the clock. For instance, suppose it were nine o'clock in the morning, just time to begin lessons: you'd only have to whisper a hint to Time, and round goes the clock in a twinkling! Half-past one, time for dinner!'

('I only wish it was,' the March Hare said to itself in a whisper.)

'That would be grand, certainly,' said Alice thoughtfully: 'but then—I shouldn't be hungry for it, you know.'

'Not at first, perhaps,' said the Hatter: 'but you could keep it to half-past one as long as you liked.'

'Is that the way *you* manage?' Alice asked.

The Hatter shook his head mournfully. 'Not I!' he replied. 'We quarrelled last March——just before *he* went mad, you know——' (pointing with his teaspoon at the March Hare) '——it was at the great concert given by the Queen of Hearts, and I had to sing

> "*Twinkle, twinkle, little bat!*
> *How I wonder what you're at!*"

You know the song, perhaps?'

'I've heard something like it,' said Alice.

'It goes on, you know,' the Hatter continued, 'in this way:

> "*Up above the world you fly,*
> *Like a tea-tray in the sky.*
>   *Twinkle, twinkle—*"'

Here the Dormouse shook itself, and began singing in its sleep '*Twinkle, twinkle, twinkle, twinkle*——' and went on so long that they had to pinch it to make it stop.

'Well, I'd hardly finished the first verse,' said the Hatter, 'when the Queen jumped up and bawled out "He's murdering the time! Off with his head!"'

'How dreadfully savage!' exclaimed Alice.

'And ever since that,' the Hatter went on in a mournful tone, 'he won't do a thing I ask! It's always six o'clock now.'

A bright idea came into Alice's head. 'Is that the reason so many tea-things are put out here?'she asked.

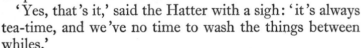

'Yes, that's it,' said the Hatter with a sigh: 'it's always tea-time, and we've no time to wash the things between whiles.'

'Then you keep moving round, I suppose?' said Alice.

'Exactly so,' said the Hatter: 'as the things get used up.'

'But what happens when you come to the beginning again?' Alice ventured to ask.

'Suppose we change the subject,' the March Hare interrupted, yawning. 'I'm getting tired of this. I vote the young lady tells us a story.'

'I'm afraid I don't know one,' said Alice, rather alarmed at the proposal.

'Then the Dormouse shall!' they both cried. 'Wake up, Dormouse!' And they pinched it on both sides at once.

The Dormouse slowly opened his eyes. 'I wasn't asleep,' he said in a hoarse, feeble voice: 'I heard every word you fellows were saying.'

'Tell us a story!' said the March Hare.

'Yes, please do!' pleaded Alice.

'And be quick about it,' added the Hatter, 'or you'll be asleep again before it's done.'

'Once upon a time there were three little sisters,' the Dormouse began in a great hurry; 'and their names were Elsie, Lacie, and Tillie; and they lived at the bottom of a well——'

'What did they live on?' said Alice, who always took a great interest in questions of eating and drinking.

'They lived on treacle,' said the Dormouse, after thinking a minute or two.

'They couldn't have done that, you know,' Alice gently remarked; 'they'd have been ill.'

'So they were,' said the Dormouse; '*very* ill.'

Alice tried to fancy to herself what such an extraordinary way of living would be like, but it puzzled her too much, so she went on: 'But why did they live at the bottom of a well?'

'Take some more tea,' the March Hare said to Alice, very earnestly.

'I've had nothing yet,' Alice replied in an offended tone, 'so I can't take more.'

'You mean you can't take *less*,' said the Hatter: 'it's very easy to take *more* than nothing.'

'Nobody asked *your* opinion,' said Alice.

'Who's making personal remarks now?' the Hatter asked triumphantly.

Alice did not quite know what to say to this: so she helped herself to some tea and bread and butter, and then turned to the Dormouse, and repeated her question. 'Why did they live at the bottom of a well?'

The Dormouse again took a minute or two to think about it, and then said 'It was a treacle-well.'

'There's no such thing!' Alice was beginning very

angrily, but the Hatter and the March Hare went 'Sh!
sh!' and the Dormouse sulkily remarked 'If you can't be
civil, you'd better finish the story for yourself.'

'No, please go on!' Alice said. 'I won't interrupt
again. I dare say there may be *one*.'

'One, indeed!' said the Dormouse indignantly. However, he consented to go on. 'And so these three little
sisters—they were learning to draw, you know——'

'What did they draw?' said Alice, quite forgetting her
promise.

'Treacle,' said the Dormouse, without considering at
all this time.

'I want a clean cup,' interrupted the Hatter: 'let's all
move one place on.'

He moved on as he spoke, and the Dormouse followed
him: the March Hare moved into the Dormouse's place,
and Alice rather unwillingly took the place of the March
Hare. The Hatter was the only one who got any advantage
from the change: and Alice was a good deal worse off, as
the March Hare had just upset the milk-jug into his plate.

Alice did not wish to offend the Dormouse again, so
she began very cautiously: 'But I don't understand.
Where did they draw the treacle from?'

'You can draw water out of a water-well,' said the
Hatter; 'so I should think you could draw treacle out of a
treacle-well—eh, stupid?'

'But they were *in* the well,' Alice said to the Dormouse,
not choosing to notice this last remark.

'Of course they were,' said the Dormouse; '——well in.'

This answer so confused poor Alice, that she let the
Dormouse go on for some time without interrupting it.

'They were learning to draw,' the Dormouse went on,
yawning and rubbing its eyes, for it was getting very
sleepy; 'and they drew all manner of things—everything
that begins with an M——'

'Why with an M?' said Alice.

'Why not?' said the March Hare.

Alice was silent.

The Dormouse had closed its eyes by this time, and was going off into a doze; but, on being pinched by the Hatter, it woke up again with a little shriek, and went on:

'——that begins with an M, such as mouse-traps, and the moon, and memory, and muchness—you know you say things are "much of a muchness"—did you ever see such a thing as a drawing of a muchness?'

'Really, now you ask me,' said Alice, very much confused, 'I don't think——'

'Then you shouldn't talk,' said the Hatter.

This piece of rudeness was more than Alice could bear: she got up in great disgust, and walked off; the Dormouse fell asleep instantly, and neither of the others took the least notice of her going, though she looked back once or twice, half hoping that they would call after her: the last time she saw them, they were trying to put the Dormouse into the teapot.

'At any rate I'll never go *there* again!' said Alice as she picked her way through the wood. 'It's the stupidest tea-party I ever was at in all my life!'

Just as she said this, she noticed that one of the trees had a door leading right into it. 'That's very curious!' she thought. 'But everything's curious to-day. I think I may as well go in at once.' And in she went.

Once more she found herself in the long hall, and close to the little glass table. 'Now, I'll manage better this time,' she said to herself, and began by taking the little golden key, and unlocking the door that led into the garden. Then she set to work nibbling at the mushroom (she had kept a piece of it in her pocket) till she was about a foot high: then she walked down the little passage: and *then*—she found herself at last in the beautiful garden, among the bright flower-beds and the cool fountains.

CHAPTER VIII

THE QUEEN'S CROQUET-GROUND

A LARGE rose-tree stood near the entrance of the garden: the roses growing on it were white, but there were three gardeners at it, busily painting them red. Alice thought this a very curious thing, and she went nearer to watch them, and just as she came up to them she heard one of them say 'Look out now, Five! Don't go splashing paint over me like that!'

'I couldn't help it,' said Five, in a sulky tone. 'Seven jogged my elbow.'

On which Seven looked up and said 'That's right, Five! Always lay the blame on others!'

'*You*'d better not talk!' said Five. 'I heard the Queen say only yesterday you deserved to be beheaded!'

'What for?' said the one who had first spoken.

'That's none of *your* business, Two!' said Seven.

'Yes, it *is* his business!' said Five. 'And I'll tell him—it was for bringing the cook tulip-roots instead of onions.'

Seven flung down his brush, and had just begun 'Well, of all the unjust things——' when his eye chanced to fall upon Alice, as she stood watching them, and he checked himself suddenly: the others looked round also, and all of them bowed low.

'Would you tell me,' said Alice, a little timidly, 'why you are painting those roses?'

Five and Seven said nothing, but looked at Two. Two began in a low voice, 'Why, the fact is, you see, Miss, this here ought to have been a *red* rose-tree, and we put a white one in by mistake; and if the Queen was to find it out, we should all have our heads cut off, you know. So you see, Miss, we're doing our best, afore she comes, to——' At this moment, Five, who had been anxiously looking across the garden, called out 'The Queen! The Queen!' and the three gardeners instantly threw themselves flat upon their faces. There was a sound of many footsteps, and Alice looked round, eager to see the Queen.

See page 75

The Duchess tucked her arm affectionately into Alice's

First came ten soldiers carrying clubs; these were all shaped like the three gardeners, oblong and flat, with their hands and feet at the corners; next the ten courtiers; these were ornamented all over with diamonds, and walked two and two, as the soldiers did.   After these came the royal children; there were ten of them, and the little dears came jumping merrily along hand in hand, in couples: they were all ornamented with hearts.   Next came the guests, mostly Kings and Queens, and among them Alice recognized the White Rabbit: it was talking in a hurried, nervous manner, smiling at everything that was said, and went by without noticing her.   Then followed the Knave of Hearts, carrying the King's crown on a crimson velvet cushion; and, last of all this grand procession, came THE KING AND QUEEN OF HEARTS.

Alice was rather doubtful whether she ought not to lie down on her face like the three gardeners, but she could not remember ever having heard of such a rule at processions; 'and besides, what would be the use of a procession,' thought she, 'if people had all to lie down upon their faces, so that they couldn't see it?'   So she stood still where she was, and waited.

When the procession came opposite to Alice, they all stopped and looked at her, and the Queen said severely, 'Who is this?'   She said it to the Knave of Hearts, who only bowed and smiled in reply.

'Idiot!' said the Queen, tossing her head impatiently; and, turning to Alice, she went on, 'What's your name, child?'

'My name is Alice, so please your Majesty,' said Alice very politely; but she added, to herself, 'Why, they're only a pack of cards, after all.   I needn't be afraid of them!'

'And who are *these*?' said the Queen, pointing to the three gardeners who were lying round the rose-tree; for, you see, as they were lying on their faces, and the pattern on their backs was the same as the rest of the pack, she could not tell whether they were gardeners, or soldiers, or courtiers, or three of her own children.

'How should *I* know?' said Alice, surprised at her own courage. 'It's no business of *mine*.'

The Queen turned crimson with fury, and, after glaring at her for a moment like a wild beast, screamed 'Off with her head! Off——'

'Nonsense!' said Alice, very loudly and decidedly, and the Queen was silent.

The King laid his hand upon her arm, and timidly said 'Consider, my dear: she is only a child!'

The Queen turned angrily away from him, and said to the Knave 'Turn them over!'

The Knave did so, very carefully, with one foot.

'Get up!' said the Queen, in a shrill, loud voice, and the three gardeners instantly jumped up, and began bowing to the King, the Queen, the royal children, and everybody else.

'Leave off that!' screamed the Queen. 'You make me giddy.' And then, turning to the rose-tree, she went on, 'What *have* you been doing here?'

'May it please your Majesty,' said Two, in a very humble tone, going down on one knee as he spoke, 'we were trying——'

'*I* see!' said the Queen, who had meanwhile been examining the roses. 'Off with their heads!' and the procession moved on, three of the soldiers remaining behind to execute the unfortunate gardeners, who ran to Alice for protection.

'You shan't be beheaded!' said Alice, and she put them into a large flower-pot that stood near. The three soldiers wandered about for a minute or two, looking for them, and then quietly marched off after the others.

'Are their heads off?' shouted the Queen.

'Their heads are gone, if it please your Majesty!' the soldiers shouted in reply.

'That's right!' shouted the Queen. 'Can you play croquet?'

The soldiers were silent, and looked at Alice, as the question was evidently meant for her.

'Yes!' shouted Alice.

'Come on, then!' roared the Queen, and Alice joined the procession, wondering very much what would happen next.

'It's—it's a very fine day!' said a timid voice at her side. She was walking by the White Rabbit, who was peeping anxiously into her face.

'Very,' said Alice: '—where's the Duchess?'

'Hush! Hush!' said the Rabbit in a low hurried tone. He looked anxiously over his shoulder as he spoke, and then raised himself upon tiptoe, put his mouth close to her ear, and whispered 'She's under sentence of execution.'

'What for?' said Alice.

'Did you say "What a pity!"?' the Rabbit asked.

'No, I didn't,' said Alice: 'I don't think it's at all a pity. I said "What for?"'

'She boxed the Queen's ears—' the Rabbit began. Alice gave a little scream of laughter. 'Oh, hush!' the Rabbit whispered in a frightened tone. 'The Queen will hear you! You see she came rather late, and the Queen said—'

'Get to your places!' shouted the Queen in a voice of thunder, and people began running about in all directions, tumbling up against each other; however, they got settled down in a minute or two, and the game began. Alice thought she had never seen such a curious croquet-ground in all her life; it was all ridges and furrows; the balls were live hedgehogs, the mallets live flamingoes, and the soldiers had to double themselves up and to stand upon their hands and feet, to make the arches.

The chief difficulty Alice found at first was in managing her flamingo: she succeeded in getting its body tucked away, comfortably enough, under her arm, with its legs hanging down, but generally, just as she had got its neck nicely straightened out, and was going to give the hedge-hog a blow with its head, it *would* twist itself round and look up in her face, with such a puzzled expression that she could not help bursting out laughing: and when she had got its head down, and was going to begin again, it was very provoking to find that the hedgehog had unrolled itself, and was in the act of crawling away: besides all this, there was generally a ridge or a furrow in the way wherever she wanted to send the hedgehog to, and, as the doubled-up soldiers were always getting up and walking off to other parts of the ground, Alice soon came to the conclusion that it was a very difficult game indeed.

The players all played at once without waiting for turns, quarrelling all the while, and fighting for the hedgehogs; and in a very short time the Queen was in a furious passion, and went stamping about, and shouting 'Off with his head!' or 'Off with her head!' about once in a minute.

Alice began to feel very uneasy: to be sure she had not as yet had any dispute with the Queen, but she knew that it might happen any minute, 'and then,' thought she, 'what would become of me? They're dreadfully fond of beheading people here; the great wonder is that there's anyone left alive!'

She was looking about for some way of escape, and wondering whether she could get away without being seen, when she noticed a curious appearance in the air: it puzzled her very much at first, but, after watching it a minute or two, she made it out to be a grin, and she said to herself 'It's the Cheshire Cat: now I shall have some-body to talk to.'

'How are you getting on?' said the Cat, as soon as there was mouth enough for it to speak with.

Alice waited till the eyes appeared, and then nodded. 'It's no use speaking to it,' she thought, 'till its ears have come, or at least one of them.' In another minute the whole head appeared, and then Alice put down her flamingo, and began an account of the game, feeling very glad she had someone to listen to her. The Cat seemed to think that there was enough of it now in sight, and no more of it appeared.

'I don't think they play at all fairly,' Alice began, in rather a complaining tone, 'and they all quarrel so dreadfully one can't hear oneself speak—and they don't seem to have any rules in particular; at least, if there are, nobody attends to them—and you've no idea how confusing it is all the things being alive; for instance, there's the arch I've got to go through next walking about at the other end of the ground—and I should have croqueted the Queen's hedgehog just now, only it ran away when it saw mine coming!'

'How do you like the Queen?' said the Cat in a low voice.

'Not at all,' said Alice: 'she's so extremely—' Just then she noticed that the Queen was close behind her listening: so she went on, '—likely to win, that it's hardly worth while finishing the game.'

The Queen smiled and passed on.

'Who *are* you talking to?' said the King, coming up to Alice, and looking at the Cat's head with great curiosity.

'It's a friend of mine—a Cheshire Cat,' said Alice: 'allow me to introduce it.'

'I don't like the look of it at all,' said the King: 'however, it may kiss my hand if it likes.'

'I'd rather not,' the Cat remarked.

'Don't be impertinent,' said the King, 'and don't look at me like that!' He got behind Alice as he spoke.

'A cat may look at a king,' said Alice. 'I've read that in some book, but I don't remember where.'

'Well, it must be removed,' said the King very decidedly, and he called to the Queen, who was passing at the moment, 'My dear! I wish you would have this cat removed!'

The Queen had only one way of settling all difficulties, great or small. 'Off with his head!' she said, without even looking round.

'I'll fetch the executioner myself,' said the King eagerly, and he hurried off.

Alice thought she might as well go back and see how the game was going on, as she heard the Queen's voice in the distance, screaming with passion. She had already heard her sentence three of the players to be executed for having missed their turns, and she did not like the look of things at all, as the game was in such confusion that she never knew whether it was her turn or not. So she went in search of her hedgehog.

The hedgehog was engaged in a fight with another hedgehog, which seemed to Alice an excellent opportunity for croqueting one of them with the other: the only difficulty was, that her flamingo was gone across to the other side of the garden, where Alice could see it trying in a helpless sort of way to fly up into one of the trees.

By the time she had caught the flamingo and brought it back, the fight was over, and both the hedgehogs were out of sight: 'but it doesn't matter much,' thought Alice, 'as all the arches are gone from this side of the ground.' So she tucked it under her arm, that it might not escape again, and went back for a little more conversation with her friend.

When she got back to the Cheshire Cat, she was surprised to find quite a large crowd collected round it:

there was a dispute going on between the executioner, the King, and the Queen, who were all talking at once, while all the rest were quite silent, and looked very uncomfortable.

The moment Alice appeared, she was appealed to by all three to settle the question, and they repeated their arguments to her, though, as they all spoke at once, she found it very hard indeed to make out exactly what they said.

The executioner's argument was, that you couldn't cut off a head unless there was a body to cut it off from: that he had never had to do such a thing before, and he wasn't going to begin at *his* time of life.

The King's argument was, that anything that had a head could be beheaded, and that you weren't to talk nonsense.

The Queen's argument was, that if something wasn't done about it in less than no time, she'd have everybody executed, all round. (It was this last remark that had made the whole party look so grave and anxious.)

Alice could think of nothing else to say but 'It belongs to the Duchess: you'd better ask *her* about it.'

'She's in prison,' the Queen said to the executioner: 'fetch her here.' And the executioner went off like an arrow.

The Cat's head began fading away the moment he was gone, and, by the time he had come back with the Duchess, it had entirely disappeared; so the King and the executioner ran wildly up and down looking for it, while the rest of the party went back to the game.

CHAPTER IX

THE MOCK TURTLE'S STORY

'YOU can't think how glad I am to see you again, you dear old thing!' said the Duchess, as she tucked her arm affectionately into Alice's, and they walked off together.

Alice was very glad to find her in such a pleasant temper, and thought to herself that perhaps it was only the pepper that had made her so savage when they met in the kitchen.

'When *I*'m a Duchess,' she said to herself (not in a very hopeful tone though), 'I won't have any pepper in my kitchen *at all*. Soup does very well without—

Maybe it's always pepper that makes people hot-tempered,' she went on, very much pleased at having found out a new kind of rule, 'and vinegar that makes them sour—and camomile that makes them bitter—and —and barley-sugar and such things that make children sweet-tempered. I only wish people knew *that*: then they wouldn't be so stingy about it, you know——'

She had quite forgotten the Duchess by this time, and was a little startled when she heard her voice close to her ear. 'You're thinking about something, my dear, and that makes you forget to talk. I can't tell you just now what the moral of that is, but I shall remember it in a bit.'

'Perhaps it hasn't one,' Alice ventured to remark.

'Tut, tut, child!' said the Duchess. 'Everything's got a moral, if only you can find it.' And she squeezed herself up closer to Alice's side as she spoke.

Alice did not much like her keeping so close to her: first, because the Duchess was *very* ugly; and secondly, because she was exactly the right height to rest her chin upon Alice's shoulder, and it was an uncomfortably sharp chin. However, she did not like to be rude, so she bore it as well as she could. 'The game seems to be going on rather better now,' she said.

''Tis so,' said the Duchess: 'and the moral of it is— "Oh, 'tis love, 'tis love, that makes the world go round!"'

'Somebody said,' whispered Alice, 'that it's done by everybody minding their own business!'

'Ah, well! It means much the same thing,' said the Duchess, digging her sharp little chin into Alice's shoulder as she added, 'and the moral of *that* is—"Take care of the sense, and the sounds will take care of themselves."'

'How fond she is of finding morals in things!' Alice thought to herself.

'I dare say you're wondering why I don't put my arm round your waist,' the Duchess said after a pause: 'the reason is, that I'm doubtful about the temper of your flamingo. Shall I try the experiment?'

'He might bite,' Alice cautiously replied, not feeling at all anxious to have the experiment tried.

'Very true,' said the Duchess: 'flamingoes and mustard both bite. And the moral of that is—"Birds of a feather flock together."'

'Only mustard isn't a bird,' Alice remarked.

'Right as usual,' said the Duchess: 'what a clear way you have of putting things!'

'It's a mineral, I *think*,' said Alice.

'Of course it is,' said the Duchess, who seemed ready to agree to everything that Alice said; 'there's a large mustard-mine near here. And the moral of that is—"The more there is of mine, the less there is of yours."'

'Oh, I know!' exclaimed Alice, who had not attended to this last remark. 'It's a vegetable. It doesn't look like one, but it is.'

'I quite agree with you,' said the Duchess; 'and the moral of that is—"Be what you would seem to be"— or if you'd like it put more simply—"Never imagine yourself not to be otherwise than what it might appear to others that what you were or might have been was not otherwise than what you had been would have appeared to them to be otherwise."'

'I think I should understand that better,' Alice said very politely, 'if I had it written down: but I'm afraid I can't quite follow it as you say it.'

'That's nothing to what I could say if I chose,' the Duchess replied, in a pleased tone.

'Pray don't trouble yourself to say it any longer than that,' said Alice.

'Oh, don't talk about trouble!' said the Duchess. 'I make you a present of everything I've said as yet.'

'A cheap sort of present!' thought Alice. 'I'm glad

they don't give birthday presents like that!' But she did not venture to say it out loud.

'Thinking again?' the Duchess asked with another dig of her sharp little chin.

'I've a right to think,' said Alice sharply, for she was beginning to feel a little worried.

'Just about as much right,' said the Duchess, 'as pigs have to fly; and the m——'

But here, to Alice's great surprise, the Duchess's voice died away, even in the middle of her favourite word "moral," and the arm that was linked into hers began to tremble. Alice looked up, and there stood the Queen in front of them, with her arms folded, frowning like a thunderstorm.

'A fine day, your Majesty!' the Duchess began in a low, weak voice.

'Now, I give you fair warning,' shouted the Queen, stamping on the ground as she spoke; 'either you or your head must be off, and that in about half no time! Take your choice!'

The Duchess took her choice, and was gone in a moment.

'Let's go on with the game,' the Queen said to Alice; and Alice was too much frightened to say a word, but slowly followed her back to the croquet-ground.

The other guests had taken advantage of the Queen's absence, and were resting in the shade: however, the moment they saw her, they hurried back to the game, the Queen merely remarking that a moment's delay would cost them their lives.

All the time they were playing the Queen never left off quarrelling with the other players, and shouting 'Off with his head!' or 'Off with her head!' Those whom she sentenced were taken into custody by the soldiers, who of course had to leave off being arches to do this, so that by the end of half an hour or so there were no arches left, and all the players, except the King, the Queen, and Alice, were in custody and under sentence of execution.

Then the Queen left off, quite out of breath, and said to Alice, 'Have you seen the Mock Turtle yet?'

'No,' said Alice. 'I don't even know what a Mock Turtle is.'

'It's the thing Mock Turtle Soup is made from,' said the Queen.

'I never saw one, or heard of one,' said Alice.

'Come on, then,' said the Queen, 'and he shall tell you his history.'

As they walked off together, Alice heard the King say in a low voice, to the company generally, 'You are all pardoned,' 'Come, *that*'s a good thing!' she said to herself, for she had felt quite unhappy at the number of executions the Queen had ordered.

They very soon came upon a Gryphon, lying fast asleep in the sun. (If you don't know what a Gryphon is, look at the picture.) 'Up, lazy thing!' said the Queen, 'and take this young lady to see the Mock Turtle, and to hear his history. I must go back and see after some executions I have ordered,' and she walked off, leaving Alice alone with the Gryphon. Alice did not quite like the look of the creature, but on the whole she thought it would be quite as safe to stay with it as to go after that savage Queen: so she waited.

The Gryphon sat up and rubbed its eyes: then it watched the Queen till she was out of sight: then it chuckled. 'What fun!' said the Gryphon, half to itself, half to Alice.

'What *is* the fun?' said Alice.

'Why, *she*,' said the Gryphon. 'It's all her fancy, that: they never executes nobody, you know. Come on!'

'Everybody says "come on!" here,' thought Alice, as she went slowly after it: 'I never was so ordered about in all my life, never!'

They had not gone far before they saw the Mock Turtle in the distance, sitting sad and lonely on a little ledge of rock, and, as they came nearer, Alice could hear him sighing as if his heart would break. She pitied him deeply. 'What is his sorrow?' she asked the Gryphon, and the Gryphon answered, very nearly in the same words as before, 'It's all his fancy, that: he hasn't got no sorrow, you know. Come on!'

So they went up to the Mock Turtle, who looked at them with large eyes full of tears, but said nothing.

'This here young lady,' said the Gryphon, 'she wants for to know your history, she do.'

'I'll tell it her,' said the Mock Turtle, in a deep, hollow tone: 'sit down, both of you, and don't speak a word till I've finished.'

So they sat down, and nobody spoke for some minutes. Alice thought to herself, 'I don't see how he can *ever* finish, if he doesn't begin.' But she waited patiently.

'Once,' said the Mock Turtle at last, with a deep sigh, 'I was a real Turtle.'

These words were followed by a very long silence, broken only by an occasional exclamation of 'Hjckrrh!'

from the Gryphon, and the constant heavy sobbing of the Mock Turtle. Alice was very nearly getting up and saying 'Thank you, sir, for your interesting story,' but she could not help thinking there *must* be more to come, so she sat still and said nothing.

'When we were little,' the Mock Turtle went on at last, more calmly, though still sobbing a little now and then, 'we went to school in the sea.   The master was an old Turtle—we used to call him Tortoise——'

'Why did you call him Tortoise, if he wasn't one?' Alice asked.

'We called him Tortoise because he taught us,' said the Mock Turtle angrily: 'really you are very dull!'

'You ought to be ashamed of yourself for asking such a simple question,' added the Gryphon; and then they both sat silent and looked at poor Alice, who felt ready to sink into the earth.   At last the Gryphon said to the Mock Turtle, 'Drive on, old fellow!   Don't be all day about it!' and he went on in these words:

'Yes, we went to school in the sea, though you mayn't believe it——'

'I never said I didn't!' interrupted Alice.

'You did,' said the Mock Turtle.

'Hold your tongue!' added the Gryphon, before Alice could speak again.   The Mock Turtle went on:

'We had the best of educations—in fact, we went to school every day——'

'*I*'ve been to a day-school, too,' said Alice; 'you needn't be so proud as all that.'

'With extras?' asked the Mock Turtle a little anxiously.

'Yes,' said Alice, 'we learned French and music.'

'And washing?' said the Mock Turtle.

'Certainly not!' said Alice indignantly.

'Ah! then yours wasn't a really good school,' said the Mock Turtle in a tone of great relief.   'Now at *ours* they had at the end of the bill, "French, music, and *washing*—extra."'

'You couldn't have wanted it much,' said Alice; 'living at the bottom of the sea.'

'I couldn't afford to learn it,' said the Mock Turtle with a sigh.   'I only took the regular course.'

'What was that?' inquired Alice.

'Reeling and Writhing, of course, to begin with,' the Mock Turtle replied; 'and then the different branches of Arithmetic—Ambition, Distraction, Uglification, and Derision.'

'I never heard of "Uglification,"' Alice ventured to say. 'What is it?'

The Gryphon lifted up both its paws in surprise. 'What! Never heard of uglifying!' it exclaimed. 'You know what to beautify is, I suppose?'

'Yes,' said Alice doubtfully: 'it means—to—make—anything—prettier.'

'Well, then,' the Gryphon went on, 'if you don't know what to uglify is, you *must* be a simpleton.'

Alice did not feel encouraged to ask any more questions about it, so she turned to the Mock Turtle, and said 'What else had you to learn?'

'Well, there was Mystery,' the Mock Turtle replied, counting off the subjects on his flappers, '—Mystery, ancient and modern, with Seaography: then Drawling—the Drawling-master was an old conger-eel, that used to come once a week: *he* taught us Drawling, Stretching, and Fainting in Coils.'

'What was *that* like?' said Alice.

'Well, I can't show it you myself,' the Mock Turtle said: 'I'm too stiff. And the Gryphon never learnt it.'

'Hadn't time,' said the Gryphon: 'I went to the Classical master, though. He was an old crab, *he* was.'

'I never went to him,' the Mock Turtle said with a sigh: 'he taught Laughing and Grief, they used to say.'

'So he did, so he did,' said the Gryphon, sighing in his turn; and both creatures hid their faces in their paws.

'And how many hours a day did you do lessons?' said Alice, in a hurry to change the subject.

'Ten hours the first day,' said the Mock Turtle: 'nine the next, and so on.'

'What a curious plan!' exclaimed Alice.

'That's the reason they're called lessons,' the Gryphon remarked: 'because they lessen from day to day.'

This was quite a new idea to Alice, and she thought it over a little before she made her next remark. 'Then the eleventh day must have been a holiday?'

'Of course it was,' said the Mock Turtle.

'And how did you manage on the twelfth?' Alice went on eagerly.

'That's enough about lessons,' the Gryphon interrupted in a very decided tone: 'tell her something about the games now.'

CHAPTER X

THE LOBSTER QUADRILLE

THE Mock Turtle sighed deeply, and drew the back of one flapper across his eyes. He looked at Alice, and tried to speak, but, for a minute or two, sobs choked his voice. 'Same as if he had a bone in his throat,' said the Gryphon: and it set to work shaking him and punching him in the back. At last the Mock Turtle recovered his voice, and, with tears running down his cheeks, went on again:

'You may not have lived much under the sea—' ('I haven't,' said Alice) 'and perhaps you were never even introduced to a lobster—' (Alice began to say 'I once tasted——' but checked herself hastily, and said 'No, never') '—so you can have no idea what a delightful thing a Lobster Quadrille is!'

'No, indeed,' said Alice. 'What sort of a dance is it?'

'Why,' said the Gryphon, 'you first form into a line along the seashore——'

'Two lines!' cried the Mock Turtle. 'Seals, turtles, and so on; then, when you've cleared the jelly-fish out of the way——'

'*That* generally takes some time,' interrupted the Gryphon.

'——you advance twice——'

'Each with a lobster as a partner!' cried the Gryphon.

'Of course,' the Mock Turtle said: 'advance twice, set to partners——'

'——change lobsters, and retire in same order,' continued the Gryphon.

'Then, you know,' the Mock Turtle went on, 'you throw the——'

'The lobsters!' shouted the Gryphon, with a bound into the air.

'——as far out to sea as you can——'

'Swim after them!' screamed the Gryphon.

'Turn a somersault in the sea!' cried the Mock Turtle, capering wildly about.

'Change lobsters again!' yelled the Gryphon.

'Back to land again, and—that's all the first figure,' said the Mock Turtle, suddenly dropping his voice; and the two creatures, who had been jumping about like mad things, sat down again very sadly and quietly, and looked at Alice.

'It must be a very pretty dance,' said Alice, timidly.

'Would you like to see a little of it?' said the Mock Turtle.

'Very much indeed,' said Alice.

'Let's try the first figure!' said the Mock Turtle to the Gryphon. 'We can do without lobsters, you know. Which shall sing?'

'Oh, *you* sing,' said the Gryphon. 'I've forgotten the words.'

So they began solemnly dancing round and round Alice, every now and then treading on her toes when they passed too close, and waving their forepaws to mark the time, while the Mock Turtle sang this, very slowly and sadly:

'"Will you walk a little faster?" said a whiting to a snail.
"There's a porpoise close behind me, and he's treading on my tail.
See how eagerly the lobsters and the turtles all advance!
They are waiting on the shingle—will you come and join the dance?
  Will you, won't you, will you, won't you, will you join the dance?
  Will you, won't you, will you, won't you, won't you join the dance?

"You can really have no notion how delightful it will be,
When they take us up and throw us, with the lobsters out to sea!"
But the snail replied "Too far, too far!" and gave a look askance—
Said he thanked the whiting kindly, but he would not join the dance.
  Would not, could not, would not, could not, would not join the dance.
  Would not, could not, would not, could not, could not join the dance.

"What matters it how far we go?" his scaly friend replied.
"There is another shore, you know, upon the other side.
The further off from England the nearer is to France—
Then turn not pale, beloved snail, but come and join the dance.
  Will you, won't you, will you, won't you, will you join the dance?
  Will you, won't you, will you, won't you, won't you join the dance?"'

'Thank you, it's a very interesting dance to watch,' said Alice, feeling very glad that it was over at last: 'and I do so like that curious song about the whiting!'

'Oh, as to the whiting,' said the Mock Turtle, 'they —you've seen them, of course?'

'Yes,' said Alice, 'I've often seen them at dinn——' she checked herself hastily.

'I don't know where Dinn may be,' said the Mock Turtle, 'but if you've seen them so often, of course you know what they're like.'

'I believe so,' Alice replied thoughtfully. 'They have their tails in their mouths—and they're all over crumbs.'

'You're wrong about the crumbs,' said the Mock
Turtle: 'crumbs would all wash off in the sea. But they
have their tails in their mouths; and the reason is—'
here the Mock Turtle yawned and shut his eyes. 'Tell
her about the reason and all that,' he said to the Gryphon.

'The reason is,' said the Gryphon, 'that they *would* go
with the lobsters to the dance. So they got thrown out
to sea. So they had to fall a long way. So they got
their tails fast in their mouths. So they couldn't get
them out again. That's all.'

'Thank you,' said Alice, 'it's very interesting. I
never knew so much about a whiting before.'

'I can tell you more than that, if you like,' said the
Gryphon. 'Do you know why it's called a whiting?'

'I never thought about it,' said Alice. 'Why?'

'*It does the boots and shoes,*' the Gryphon replied very solemnly.

Alice was thoroughly puzzled. 'Does the boots and shoes!' she repeated in a wondering tone.

'Why, what are *your* shoes done with?' said the Gryphon. 'I mean, what makes them so shiny?'

Alice looked down at them, and considered a little before she gave her answer. 'They're done with blacking, I believe.'

'Boots and shoes under the sea,' the Gryphon went on in a deep voice, 'are done with whiting. Now you know.'

'And what are they made of?' Alice asked in a tone of great curiosity.

'Soles and eels, of course,' the Gryphon replied rather impatiently: 'any shrimp could have told you that.'

'If I'd been the whiting,' said Alice, whose thoughts were still running on the song, 'I'd have said to the porpoise, "Keep back, please: we don't want *you* with us!"'

'They were obliged to have him with them,' the Mock Turtle said: 'no wise fish would go anywhere without a porpoise.'

'Wouldn't it really?' said Alice in a tone of great surprise.

'Of course not,' said the Mock Turtle: 'why, if a fish came to *me*, and told me he was going a journey, I should say "With what porpoise?"'

'Don't you mean "purpose"?' said Alice.

'I mean what I say,' the Mock Turtle replied in an offended tone. And the Gryphon added 'Come, let's hear some of *your* adventures.'

'I could tell you my adventures—beginning from this morning,' said Alice a little timidly: 'but it's no use going back to yesterday, because I was a different person then.'

'Explain all that,' said the Mock Turtle.

'No, no! The adventures first,' said the Gryphon in an impatient tone: 'explanations take such a dreadful time.'

So Alice began telling them her adventures from the time when she first saw the White Rabbit. She was a little nervous about it just at first, the two creatures got so close to her, one on each side, and opened their eyes and mouths so *very* wide, but she gained courage as she went on. Her listeners were perfectly quiet till she got to the part about her repeating '*You are old, Father William,*' to the Caterpillar, and the words all coming different, and then the Mock Turtle drew a long breath, and said 'That's very curious.'

'It's all about as curious as it can be,' said the Gryphon.

'It all came different!' the Mock Turtle repeated thoughtfully. 'I should like to hear her repeat something now. Tell her to begin.' He looked at the Gryphon as if he thought it had some kind of authority over Alice.

'Stand up and repeat "*'Tis the voice of the sluggard,*"' said the Gryphon.

'How the creatures order one about, and make one repeat lessons!' thought Alice. 'I might as well be at school at once.' However, she got up, and began to repeat it, but her head was so full of the Lobster Quadrille, that she hardly knew what she was saying, and the words came very queer indeed:

'*'Tis the voice of the Lobster; I heard him declare,*
"*You have baked me too brown, I must sugar my hair.*"
As a duck with its eyelids, so he with his nose
Trims his belt and his buttons, and turns out his toes.
When the sands are all dry, he is gay as a lark,
And will talk in contemptuous tones of the Shark:
But, when the tide rises and sharks are around,
His voice has a timid and tremulous sound.'

'That's different from what *I* used to say when I was a child,' said the Gryphon.

'Well, I never heard it before,' said the Mock Turtle; 'but it sounds uncommon nonsense.'

Alice said nothing; she had sat down with her face in her hands, wondering if anything would *ever* happen in a natural way again.

'I should like to have it explained,' said the Mock Turtle.

'She can't explain it,' hastily said the Gryphon. 'Go on to the next verse.'

'But about his toes?' the Mock Turtle persisted. 'How *could* he turn them out with his nose, you know?'

'It's the first position in dancing,' Alice said; but was

dreadfully puzzled by it all, and longed to change the subject.

'Go on with the next verse,' the Gryphon repeated: 'it begins with the words "*I passed by his garden.*"'

Alice did not dare to disobey, though she felt sure it would all come wrong, and she went on in a trembling voice:

> '*I passed by his garden, and marked, with one eye,*
> *How the Owl and the Panther were sharing a pie:*
> *The Panther took pie-crust, and gravy, and meat,*
> *While the Owl had the dish as its share of the treat.*
> *When the pie was all finished, the Owl, as a boon,*
> *Was kindly permitted to pocket the spoon:*
> *While the Panther received knife and fork with a*
>   *growl,*
> *And concluded the banquet——*'

'What *is* the use of repeating all that stuff,' the Mock Turtle interrupted, 'if you don't explain it as you go on? It's by far the most confusing thing *I* ever heard!'

'Yes, I think you'd better leave off,' said the Gryphon: and Alice was only too glad to do so.

'Shall we try another figure of the Lobster Quadrille?' the Gryphon went on. 'Or would you like the Mock Turtle to sing you a song?'

'Oh, a song, please, if the Mock Turtle would be so kind,' Alice replied, so eagerly that the Gryphon said, in a rather offended tone. 'Hm! No accounting for tastes! Sing her "*Turtle Soup,*" will you, old fellow?'

The Mock Turtle sighed deeply, and began, in a voice sometimes choked with sobs, to sing this:

> '*Beautiful Soup, so rich and green,*
> *Waiting in a hot tureen!*
> *Who for such dainties would not stoop?*
> *Soup of the evening, beautiful Soup!*

> *Soup of the evening, beautiful Soup!*
> *Beau—ootiful Soo—oop!*
> *Beau—ootiful Soo—oop!*
> *Soo—oop of the e—e—evening,*
> *Beautiful, beautiful Soup!*
>
> *Beautiful Soup! Who cares for fish,*
> *Game, or any other dish?*
> *Who would not give all else for two p*
> *ennyworth only of beautiful Soup?*
> *Pennyworth only of beautiful Soup?*
> *Beau—ootiful Soo—oop!*
> *Beau—ootiful Soo—oop!*
> *Soo—oop of the e—e—evring,*
> *Beautiful, beauti—FUL—SOUP!'*

'Chorus again!' cried the Gryphon, and the Mock Turtle had just begun to repeat it, when a cry of 'The trial's beginning!' was heard in the distance.

'Come on!' cried the Gryphon, and, taking Alice by the hand, it hurried off, without waiting for the end of the song.

'What trial is it?' Alice panted as she ran; but the Gryphon only answered 'Come on!' and ran the faster, while more and more faintly came, carried on the breeze that followed them, the melancholy words:

> *'Soo—oop of the e—e—evening,*
> *Beautiful, beautiful Soup!'*

CHAPTER XI

WHO STOLE THE TARTS ?

THE King and Queen of Hearts were seated on their throne when they arrived, with a great crowd assembled about them—all sorts of little birds and beasts, as well as the whole pack of cards: the Knave was standing before them, in chains, with a soldier on each side to guard him; and near the King was the White Rabbit, with a trumpet in one hand, and a scroll of parchment in the other. In the very middle of the court was a table, with a large dish of tarts upon it: they looked so good, that it made Alice quite hungry to look at them—'I wish they'd get the trial done,' she thought, 'and hand round the refreshments!' But there seemed to be no chance of this, so she began looking about her, to pass away the time.

Alice had never been in a court of justice before, but she had read about them in books, and she was quite pleased to find that she knew the name of nearly everything there. 'That's the judge,' she said to herself, 'because of his great wig.'

The judge, by the way, was the King; and as he wore his crown over the wig (look at the frontispiece if you want to see how he did it), he did not look at all comfortable, and it was certainly not becoming.

'And that's the jury-box,' thought Alice, 'and those twelve creatures' (she was obliged to say 'creatures,' you see, because some of them were animals, and some were birds), 'I suppose they are the jurors.' She said this last word two or three times over to herself, being rather proud of it: for she thought, and rightly too, that very few little girls of her age knew the meaning of it at all. However, 'jurymen' would have done just as well.

The twelve jurors were all writing very busily on slates. 'What are they all doing?' Alice whispered to the Gryphon. 'They can't have anything to put down yet, before the trial's begun.'

'They're putting down their names,' the Gryphon whispered in reply, 'for fear they should forget them before the end of the trial.'

'Stupid things!' Alice began in a loud, indignant voice, but she stopped hastily, for the White Rabbit cried out 'Silence in the court!' and the King put on his spectacles and looked anxiously round, to see who was talking.

Alice could see, as well as if she were looking over their shoulders, that all the jurors were writing down 'stupid things!' on their slates, and she could even make out that one of them didn't know how to spell 'stupid,' and that he had to ask his neighbour to tell him. 'A nice muddle their slates will be in before the trial's over!' thought Alice.

One of the jurors had a pencil that squeaked. This, of course, Alice could *not* stand, and she went round the court and got behind him, and very soon found an opportunity of taking it away. She did it so quickly that the poor little juror (it was Bill, the Lizard) could not make out at all what had become of it; so, after hunting all about for it, he was obliged to write with one finger for the rest of the day; and this was of very little use, as it left no mark on the slate.

'Herald, read the accusation!' said the King.

On this the White Rabbit blew three blasts on the trumpet, and then unrolled the parchment scroll, and read as follows:

> *'The Queen of Hearts, she made some tarts,*
> *All on a summer day:*
> *The Knave of Hearts, he stole those tarts,*
> *And took them quite away!'*

'Consider your verdict,' the King said to the jury.

'Not yet, not yet!' the Rabbit hastily interrupted. 'There's a great deal to come before that!'

'Call the first witness,' said the King; and the White Rabbit blew three blasts on the trumpet, and called out 'First witness!'

The first witness was the Hatter. He came in with a teacup in one hand and a piece of bread and butter in the other. 'I beg pardon, your Majesty,' he began, 'for bringing these in: but I hadn't quite finished my tea when I was sent for.'

'You ought to have finished,' said the King. 'When did you begin?'

The Hatter looked at the March Hare, who had followed him into the court, arm-in-arm with the Dormouse. 'Fourteenth of March, I *think* it was,' he said.

'Fifteenth,' said the March Hare.

'Sixteenth,' added the Dormouse.

'Write that down,' the King said to the jury, and the jury eagerly wrote down all three dates on their slates, and then added them up, and reduced the answer to shillings and pence.

'Take off your hat,' the King said to the Hatter.

'It isn't mine,' said the Hatter.

'*Stolen!*' the King exclaimed, turning to the jury, who instantly made a memorandum of the fact.

'I keep them to sell,' the Hatter added as an explanation: 'I've none of my own.   I'm a hatter.'

Here the Queen put on her spectacles, and began staring hard at the Hatter, who turned pale and fidgeted.

'Give your evidence,' said the King; 'and don't be nervous, or I'll have you executed on the spot.'

This did not seem to encourage the witness at all: he kept shifting from one foot to the other, looking uneasily at the Queen, and in his confusion he bit a large piece out of his teacup instead of the bread and butter.

Just at this moment Alice felt a very curious sensation, which puzzled her a good deal until she made out what it was: she was beginning to grow larger again, and she thought at first she would get up and leave the court; but on second thoughts she decided to remain where she was as long as there was room for her.

'I wish you wouldn't squeeze so,' said the Dormouse, who was sitting next to her.   'I can hardly breathe.'

'I can't help it,' said Alice very meekly: 'I'm growing.'

'You've no right to grow *here*,' said the Dormouse.

'Don't talk nonsense,' said Alice more boldly: 'you know you're growing too.'

'Yes, but *I* grow at a reasonable pace,' said the Dormouse: 'not in that ridiculous fashion.'   And he got up very sulkily and crossed over to the other side of the court.

All this time the Queen had never left off staring at the

Hatter, and, just as the Dormouse crossed the court, she said to one of the officers of the court, 'Bring me the list of the singers in the last concert!' on which the wretched Hatter trembled so, that he shook both his shoes off.

'Give your evidence,' the King repeated angrily, 'or I'll have you executed, whether you're nervous or not.'

'I'm a poor man, your Majesty,' the Hatter began, in a trembling voice, '—and I hadn't begun my tea—not above a week or so—and what with the bread and butter getting so thin—and the twinkling of the tea——'

'The twinkling of the *what*?' said the King.

'It *began* with the tea,' the Hatter replied.

'Of course twinkling begins with a T!' said the King sharply. 'Do you take me for a dunce? Go on!'

'I'm a poor man,' the Hatter went on, 'and most things twinkled after that—only the March Hare said——'

'I didn't!' the March Hare interrupted in a great hurry.

'You did!' said the Hatter.

'I deny it!' said the March Hare.

'He denies it,' said the King: 'leave out that part.'

'Well, at any rate, the Dormouse said——' the Hatter went on, looking anxiously round to see if he would deny it too: but the Dormouse denied nothing, being fast asleep.

'After that,' continued the Hatter, 'I cut some more bread and butter——'

'But what did the Dormouse say?' one of the jury asked.

'That I can't remember,' said the Hatter.

'You *must* remember,' remarked the King, 'or I'll have you executed.'

The miserable Hatter dropped his teacup and bread and butter, and went down on one knee. 'I'm a poor man, your Majesty,' he began.

'You're a *very* poor *speaker*,' said the King.

Here one of the guinea-pigs cheered, and was immediately suppressed by the officers of the court. (As that is rather a hard word, I will just explain to you how it was done. They had a large canvas bag which tied up at the mouth with strings: into this they slipped the guinea-pig, head first, and then sat upon it.)

'I'm glad I've seen that done,' thought Alice. 'I've so often read in the newspapers, at the end of trials, "There was some attempt at applause, which was immediately suppressed by the officers of the court," and I never understood what it meant till now.'

'If that's all you know about it, you may stand down,' continued the King.

'I can't go no lower,' said the Hatter: 'I'm on the floor, as it is.'

'Then you may *sit* down,' the King replied.

Here the other guinea-pig cheered, and was suppressed.

'Come, that finishes the guinea-pigs!' thought Alice. 'Now we shall get on better.'

'I'd rather finish my tea,' said the Hatter, with an anxious look at the Queen, who was reading the list of singers.

'You may go,' said the King; and the Hatter hurriedly left the court, without even waiting to put his shoes on.

'—and just take his head off outside,' the Queen added to one of the officers; but the Hatter was out of sight before the officer could get to the door.

'Call the next witness!' said the King.

The next witness was the Duchess's cook. She carried the pepperbox in her hand, and Alice guessed who it was, even before she got into the court, by the way the people near the door began sneezing all at once.

'Give your evidence,' said the King.

'Shan't,' said the cook.

The King looked anxiously at the White Rabbit, who said in a low voice, 'Your Majesty must cross-examine *this* witness.'

'Well, if I must, I must,' the King said with a melancholy air, and, after folding his arms and frowning at the cook till his eyes were nearly out of sight, he said in a deep voice, 'What are tarts made of?'

'Pepper, mostly,' said the cook.

'Treacle,' said a sleepy voice behind her.

'Collar that Dormouse,' the Queen shrieked out. 'Behead that Dormouse! Turn that Dormouse out of court! Suppress him! Pinch him! Off with his whiskers!'

For some minutes the whole court was in confusion, getting the Dormouse turned out, and, by the time they had settled down again, the cook had disappeared.

'Never mind!' said the King, with an air of great relief. 'Call the next witness.' And, he added in an undertone to the Queen, 'Really, my dear, *you* must cross-examine the next witness. It quite makes my forehead ache!'

Alice watched the White Rabbit as he fumbled over the list, feeling very curious to see what the next witness would be like, '—for they haven't got much evidence *yet*,' she said to herself. Imagine her surprise, when the White Rabbit read out, at the top of his shrill little voice, the name 'Alice!'

CHAPTER XII

ALICE'S EVIDENCE

'HERE!' cried Alice, quite forgetting in the flurry of the moment how large she had grown in the last few minutes, and she jumped up in such a hurry that she tipped over the jury-box with the edge of her skirt, upsetting all the jurymen on to the heads of the crowd below, and there they lay sprawling about, reminding her very much of a globe of goldfish she had accidentally upset the week before.

'Oh, I *beg* your pardon!' she exclaimed in a tone of great dismay, and began picking them up again as quickly as she could, for the accident of the goldfish kept running in her head, and she had a vague sort of idea that they must be collected at once and put back into the jury-box, or they would die.

'The trial cannot proceed,' said the King in a very grave voice, 'until all the jurymen are back in their proper places—*all*,' he repeated with great emphasis, looking hard at Alice as he said so.

Alice looked at the jury-box, and saw that, in her haste, she had the Lizard in head downwards, and the poor little thing was waving its tail about in a melancholy way, being quite unable to move. She soon got it out again, and put it right; 'not that it signifies much,' she said to herself; 'I should think it would be *quite* as much use in the trial one way up as the other.'

As soon as the jury had a little recovered from the shock of being upset, and their slates and pencils had been found and handed back to them, they set to work very diligently to write out a history of the accident, all except the Lizard, who seemed too much overcome to do anything but sit with its mouth open, gazing up into the roof of the court.

'What do you know about this business?' the King said to Alice.

'Nothing,' said Alice.

'Nothing *whatever*?' persisted the King.

'Nothing whatever,' said Alice.

'That's very important,' the King said, turning to the jury. They were just beginning to write this down on their slates, when the White Rabbit interrupted:

'*Un*important, your Majesty means, of course,' he said in a very respectful tone, but frowning and making faces at him as he spoke.

'*Un*important, of course, I meant,' the King hastily said, and went on to himself in an undertone, 'important—unimportant—unimportant—important——' as if he were trying which word sounded best.

Some of the jury wrote it down 'important,' and some 'unimportant.' Alice could see this, as she was near enough to look over their slates; 'but it doesn't matter a bit,' she thought to herself.

At this moment the King, who had been for some time busily writing in his note-book, called out 'Silence!' and read out from his book, 'Rule Forty-two. *All persons more than a mile high to leave the court.*'

Everybody looked at Alice.

'*I*'m not a mile high,' said Alice.

'You are,' said the King.

'Nearly two miles high,' added the Queen.

'Well, I shan't go, at any rate,' said Alice: 'besides, that's not a regular rule: you invented it just now.'

'It's the oldest rule in the book,' said the King.

'Then it ought to be Number One,' said Alice.

The King turned pale, and shut his note-book hastily. 'Consider your verdict,' he said to the jury, in a low trembling voice.

'There's more evidence to come yet, please your Majesty,' said the White Rabbit, jumping up in a great hurry: 'this paper has just been picked up.'

'What's in it?' said the Queen.

'I haven't opened it yet,' said the White Rabbit, 'but it seems to be a letter, written by the prisoner to—to somebody.'

'It must have been that,' said the King, 'unless it was written to nobody, which isn't usual, you know '

'Who is it directed to?' said one of the jurymen.

'It isn't directed at all,' said the White Rabbit; 'in fact, there's nothing written on the *outside*.' He unfolded the paper as he spoke, and added 'It isn't a letter, after all: it's a set of verses.'

'Are they in the prisoner's handwriting?' asked another of the jurymen.

'No, they're not,' said the White Rabbit, 'and that's the queerest thing about it.' (The jury all looked puzzled.)

'He must have imitated somebody else's hand,' said the King. (The jury all brightened up again.)

'Please your Majesty,' said the Knave, 'I didn't write it, and they can't prove I did: there's no name signed at the end.'

'If you didn't sign it,' said the King, 'that only makes the matter worse. You *must* have meant some mischief, or else you'd have signed your name like an honest man.'

There was a general clapping of hands at this: it was the first really clever thing the King had said that day.

'That *proves* his guilt,' said the Queen.

'It proves nothing of the sort!' said Alice. 'Why, you don't even know what they're about!'

'Read them,' said the King.

The White Rabbit put on his spectacles. 'Where shall I begin, please your Majesty?' he asked.

'Begin at the beginning,' the King said gravely, 'and go on till you come to the end: then stop.'

These were the verses the White Rabbit read:

> '*They told me you had been to her,*
> *And mentioned me to him:*
> *She gave me a good character,*
> *But said I could not swim.*

He sent them word I had not gone,
  (We know it to be true):
If she should push the matter on,
  What would become of you?

I gave her one, they gave him two,
  You gave us three or more;
They all returned from him to you,
  Though they were mine before.

If I or she should chance to be
  Involved in this affair,
He trusts to you to set them free,
  Exactly as we were.

My notion was that you had been
  (Before she had this fit)
An obstacle that came between
  Him, and ourselves, and it.

Don't let him know she liked them best,
  For this must ever be
A secret, kept from all the rest,
  Between yourself and me.'

'That's the most important piece of evidence we've heard yet,' said the King, rubbing his hands; 'so now let the jury——'

'If any one of them can explain it,' said Alice (she had grown so large in the last few minutes that she wasn't a bit afraid of interrupting him), 'I'll give him sixpence. *I* don't believe there's an atom of meaning in it.'

The jury all wrote down on their slates, '*She* doesn't believe there's an atom of meaning in it,' but none of them attempted to explain the paper.

'If there's no meaning in it,' said the King, 'that saves a world of trouble, you know, as we needn't try to find any. And yet I don't know,' he went on, spreading out the verses on his knee, and looking at them with one eye; 'I seem to see some meaning in them, after all. "——*said I could not swim*—" you can't swim, can you?' he added, turning to the Knave.

The Knave shook his head sadly. 'Do I look like it?' he said. (Which he certainly did *not*, being made entirely of cardboard.)

'All right, so far,' said the King, and he went on muttering over the verses to himself: '"*We know it to be true*—" that's the jury, of course—"*I gave her one, they gave him two*—" why, that must be what he did with the tarts, you know——'

'But it goes on "*they all returned from him to you*,"' said Alice.

'Why, there they are!' said the King triumphantly, pointing to the tarts on the table. 'Nothing can be clearer than *that*. Then again—"*before she had this fit*—" you never had fits, my dear, I think?' he said to the Queen.

'Never!' said the Queen furiously, throwing an ink-stand at the Lizard as she spoke. (The unfortunate little Bill had left off writing on his slate with one finger, as he found it made no mark, but he now hastily began again, using the ink, that was trickling down his face, as long as it lasted.)

'Then the words don't *fit* you,' said the King, looking round the court with a smile. There was a dead silence.

'It's a pun!' the King added in an offended tone, and everybody laughed.

'Let the jury consider their verdict,' the King said, for about the twentieth time that day.

'No, no!' said the Queen. 'Sentence first—verdict afterwards.'

'Stuff and nonsense!' said Alice loudly. 'The idea of having the sentence first!'

'Hold your tongue!' said the Queen, turning purple.

'I won't!' said Alice.

'Off with her head!' the Queen shouted at the top of her voice. Nobody moved.

'Who cares for you?' said Alice (she had grown to her full size by this time). 'You're nothing but a pack of cards!'

At this the whole pack rose up into the air, and came flying down upon her: she gave a little scream, half of fright and half of anger, and tried to beat them off, and found herself lying on the bank, with her head in the lap of her sister, who was gently brushing away some dead leaves that had fluttered down from the trees upon her face.

'Wake up, Alice dear!' said her sister. 'Why, what a long sleep you've had!'

'Oh, I've had such a curious dream!' said Alice, and she told her sister, as well as she could remember them, all these strange Adventures of hers that you have just been reading about; and when she had finished, her sister kissed her, and said 'It *was* a curious dream, dear, certainly: but now run in to your tea; it's getting late.' So Alice got up and ran off, thinking while she ran, as well she might, what a wonderful dream it had been.

But her sister sat still just as she left her, leaning her head on her hand, watching the setting sun, and thinking of little Alice and all her wonderful Adventures, till she too began dreaming after a fashion, and this was her dream:

First, she dreamed of little Alice herself, and once again the tiny hands were clasped upon her knee, and the bright eager eyes were looking up into hers—she could hear the very tones of her voice, and see that queer little toss of her head to keep back the wandering hair that *would* always get into her eyes—and still as she listened, or seemed to listen, the whole place around her became alive with the strange creatures of her little sister's dream.

The long grass rustled at her feet as the White Rabbit hurried by—the frightened Mouse splashed his way through the neighbouring pool—she could hear the rattle of the teacups as the March Hare and his friends shared their never-ending meal, and the shrill voice of the Queen ordering off her unfortunate guests to execution—once more the pig-baby was sneezing on the Duchess's knee, while plates and dishes crashed around it—once more the shriek of the Gryphon, the squeaking of the Lizard's slate-pencil, and the choking of the suppressed guinea-pigs, filled the air, mixed up with the distant sobs of the miserable Mock Turtle.

So she sat on with closed eyes, and half believed herself in Wonderland, though she knew she had but to open them again, and all would change to dull reality—the grass would be only rustling in the wind, and the pool rippling to the waving of the reeds—the rattling teacups would change to the tinkling sheep-bells, and the Queen's shrill cries to the voice of the shepherd boy—and the sneeze of the baby, the shriek of the Gryphon, and all the other queer noises, would change (she knew) to the confused clamour of the busy farmyard—while the lowing of the cattle in the distance would take the place of the Mock Turtle's heavy sobs.

Lastly, she pictured to herself how this same little sister of hers would, in the after-time, be herself a grown woman; and how she would keep, through all her riper years, the simple and loving heart of her childhood: and how she would gather about her other little children, and make *their* eyes bright and eager with many a strange tale, perhaps even with the dream of Wonderland of long ago: and how she would feel with all their simple sorrows, and find a pleasure in all their simple joys, remembering her own child-life, and the happy summer days.

THROUGH THE LOOKING-GLASS

AND WHAT ALICE FOUND THERE

DRAMATIS PERSONAE

(As arranged before commencement of game)

WHITE				RED	
PIECES			PAWNS	PAWNS	PIECES
Tweedledee	.	.	. Daisy	Daisy .	. Humpty Dumpty
Unicorn	.	.	. Haigha	Messenger .	. Carpenter
Sheep	.	.	. Oyster	Oyster .	. Walrus
W. Queen	.	.	. 'Lily'	Tiger-lily .	. R. Queen
W. King	.	.	. Fawn	Rose . .	. R. King
Aged man	.	.	. Oyster	Oyster .	. Crow
W. Knight	.	.	. Hatta	Frog . .	. R. Knight
Tweedledum	.	.	. Daisy	Daisy .	. Lion

WHITE.

White Pawn (Alice) to play, and win in eleven moves

CHILD of the pure unclouded brow
  And dreaming eyes of wonder!
Though time be fleet, and I and thou
  Are half a life asunder,
Thy loving smile will surely hail
The love-gift of a fairy-tale.

I have not seen thy sunny face,
  Nor heard thy silver laughter;
No thought of me shall find a place
  In thy young life's hereafter—
Enough that now thou wilt not fail
To listen to my fairy-tale.

A tale begun in other days,
  When summer suns were glowing—
A simple chime, that served to time
  The rhythm of our rowing—
Whose echoes live in memory yet,
Though envious years would say 'forget.'

Come, hearken then, ere voice of dread,
  With bitter tidings laden,
Shall summon to unwelcome bed
  A melancholy maiden!
We are but older children, dear,
Who fret to find our bedtime near.

Without, the frost, the blinding snow,
  The storm-wind's moody madness—
Within, the firelight's ruddy glow
  And childhood's nest of gladness.
The magic words shall hold thee fast:
Thou shalt not heed the raving blast.

And though the shadow of a sigh
  May tremble through the story,
For 'happy summer days' gone by,
  And vanish'd summer glory—
It shall not touch with breath of bale
The pleasance of our fairy-tale.

PREFACE

As the chess problem, given on a previous page, has puzzled some of my readers, it may be well to explain that it is correctly worked out, so far as the *moves* are concerned. The *alternation* of Red and White is perhaps not so strictly observed as it might be, and the 'castling' of the three Queens is merely a way of saying that they entered the palace: but the 'check' of the White King at move 6, the capture of the Red Knight at move 7, and the final 'checkmate' of the Red King, will be found, by anyone who will take the trouble to set the pieces and play the moves as directed, to be strictly in accordance with the laws of the game.

Christmas, 1887.

CHAPTER I

LOOKING-GLASS HOUSE

ONE thing was certain, that the *white* kitten had had nothing to do with it: it was the black kitten's fault entirely. For the white kitten had been having its face washed by the old cat for the last quarter of an hour (and bearing it pretty well, considering); so you see that it *couldn't* have had any hand in the mischief.

The way Dinah washed her children's faces was this: first she held the poor thing down by its ear with one paw, and then with the other paw she rubbed its face all over, the wrong way, beginning at the nose: and just now, as I said, she was hard at work on the white kitten, which was lying quite still and trying to purr—no doubt feeling that it was all meant for its good.

But the black kitten had been finished with earlier in the afternoon, and so, while Alice was sitting curled up in a corner of the great arm-chair, half talking to herself and half asleep, the kitten had been having a grand game of romps with the ball of worsted Alice had been trying to wind up, and had been rolling it up and down till it had all come undone again; and there it was, spread over the hearth-rug, all knots and tangles, with the kitten running after its own tail in the middle.

'Oh, you wicked wicked little thing!' cried Alice, catching up the kitten, and giving it a little kiss to make it understand that it was in disgrace. 'Really, Dinah ought to have taught you better manners! You *ought*, Dinah, you know you ought!' she added, looking reproachfully at the old cat, and speaking in as cross a voice as she could manage—and then she scrambled back into the arm-chair, taking the kitten and worsted with her, and began winding up the ball again. But she didn't get on very fast, as she was talking all the time, sometimes to the kitten, and sometimes to herself. Kitty sat very demurely on her knee, pretending to watch the progress of the winding, and now and then putting out one paw and gently touching the ball, as if it would be glad to help if it might.

'Do you know what to-morrow is, Kitty?' Alice began. 'You'd have guessed if you'd been up in the window with me——only Dinah was making you tidy, so you couldn't. I was watching the boys getting in sticks for the bonfire ——and it wants plenty of sticks, Kitty! Only it got so cold, and it snowed so, they had to leave off. Never mind, Kitty, we'll go and see the bonfire to-morrow.' Here Alice wound two or three turns of the worsted round the kitten's neck, just to see how it would look: this led to a scramble, in which the ball rolled down upon the floor, and yards and yards of it got unwound again.

'Do you know, I was so angry, Kitty,' Alice went on, as soon as they were comfortably settled again, 'when I saw all the mischief you had been doing, I was very nearly opening the window, and putting you out into the snow! And you'd have deserved it, you little mischievous

darling! What have you got to say for yourself? Now
don't interrupt me!' she went on, holding up one finger.
I am going to tell you all your faults. Number one: you
squeaked twice while Dinah was washing your face this

morning. Now you can't deny it, Kitty, for I heard
you! What's that you say?' (pretending that the kitten
was speaking). 'Her paw went into your eye? Well,
that's *your* fault, for keeping your eyes open—if you'd
shut them tight up, it wouldn't have happened. Now
don't make any more excuses, but listen! Number two:
you pulled Snowdrop away by the tail just as I had put
down the saucer of milk before her! What, you were

thirsty, were you? How do you know she wasn't thirsty too? Now for number three: you unwound every bit of the worsted while I wasn't looking!

'That's three faults, Kitty, and you've not been punished for any of them yet. You know I'm saving up all your punishments for Wednesday week—Suppose they had saved up all *my* punishments!' she went on, talking more to herself than the kitten. 'What *would* they do at the end of a year? I should be sent off to prison, I suppose, when the day came. Or—let me see —suppose each punishment was to be going without a dinner: then, when the miserable day came, I should have to go without fifty dinners at once! Well, I shouldn't mind *that* much! I'd far rather go without them than eat them!

'Do you hear the snow against the window-panes, Kitty? How nice and soft it sounds! Just as if some-one was kissing the window all over outside. I wonder if the snow *loves* the trees and fields, that it kisses them so gently? And then it covers them up snug, you know, with a white quilt; and perhaps it says "Go to sleep, darlings, till the summer comes again." And when they wake up in the summer, Kitty, they dress themselves all in green, and dance about——whenever the wind blows——oh, that's very pretty!' cried Alice, dropping the ball of worsted to clap her hands. 'And I do so *wish* it was true! I'm sure the woods look sleepy in the autumn, when the leaves are getting brown.

'Kitty, can you play chess? Now, don't smile, my dear, I'm asking it seriously. Because, when we were playing just now, you watched just as if you understood it: and when I said "Check!" you purred! Well, it *was* a nice check, Kitty, and really I might have won, if it hadn't been for that nasty Knight, that came wriggling down among my pieces. Kitty, dear, let's pretend——'
And here I wish I could tell you half the things Alice

used to say, beginning with her favourite phrase 'Let's
pretend.' She had had quite a long argument with her
sister only the day before—all because Alice had begun
with 'Let's pretend we're kings and queens'; and her
sister, who liked being very exact, had argued that they
couldn't, because there were only two of them, and Alice
had been reduced at last to say 'Well, *you* can be one of
them then, and *I*'ll be all the rest.' And once she had
really frightened her old nurse by shouting suddenly in
her ear, 'Nurse! Do let's pretend that I'm a hungry
hyena, and you're a bone!'

But this is taking us away from Alice's speech to the
kitten. 'Let's pretend that you're the Red Queen,
Kitty! Do you know, I think, if you sat up and folded
your arms, you'd look exactly like her. Now do try,
there's a dear!' And Alice got the Red Queen off the
table, and set it up before the kitten as a model for it to
imitate: however, the thing didn't succeed, principally,
Alice said, because the kitten wouldn't fold its arms
properly. So, to punish it, she held it up to the Looking-
glass, that it might see how sulky it was '—and if you're
not good directly,' she added, 'I'll put you through into
Looking-glass House. How would you like *that*?

'Now, if you'll only attend, Kitty, and not talk so
much, I'll tell you all my ideas about Looking-glass
House. First, there's the room you can see through the
glass—that's just the same as our drawing-room, only
the things go the other way. I can see all of it when I
get upon a chair—all but the bit just behind the fire-place.
Oh! I do so wish I could see *that* bit! I want so much
to know whether they've a fire in the winter: you never
can tell, you know, unless our fire smokes, and then smoke
comes up in that room too—but that may be only pretence, just to make it look as if they had a fire. Well
then, the books are something like our books, only the

words go the wrong way; I know that, because I've held up one of our books to the glass, and then they hold up one in the other room.

'How would you like to live in Looking-glass House, Kitty? I wonder if they'd give you milk, there? Perhaps Looking-glass milk isn't good to drink—But oh, Kitty! now we come to the passage. You can just see a little *peep* of the passage in Looking-glass House, if you leave the door of our drawing-room wide open: and it's very like our passage as far as you can see, only you know it may be quite different on beyond. Oh, Kitty! how nice it would be if we could only get through into Looking-glass House! I'm sure it's got, oh! such beautiful things in it! Let's pretend there's a way of getting through into it somehow, Kitty. Let's pretend the glass has got soft like gauze, so that we can get through. Why, it's turning into a sort of mist now, I declare! It'll be easy enough to get through——' She was up on the chimney-piece while she said this, though she hardly knew how she had got there. And certainly the glass *was* beginning to melt away, just like a bright silvery mist.

In another moment Alice was through the glass, and had jumped lightly down into the Looking-glass room. The very first thing she did was to look whether there was a fire in the fireplace, and she was quite pleased to find that there was a real one, and blazing away as brightly as the one she had left behind. 'So I shall be as warm here as I was in the old room,' thought Alice: 'warmer, in fact, because there'll be no one here to scold me away from the fire. Oh, what fun it'll be, when they see me through the glass in here, and can't get at me!'

Then she began looking about, and noticed that what could be seen from the old room was quite common and uninteresting, but that all the rest was as different as possible. For instance, the pictures on the wall next the fire seemed to be all alive, and the very clock on the chimney-piece (you know you can only see the back of it in the Looking-glass) had got the face of a little old man, and grinned at her.

'They don't keep this room so tidy as the other,' Alice thought to herself, as she noticed several of the chessmen down in the hearth among the cinders: but in another moment, with a little 'Oh!' of surprise, she was down on her hands and knees watching them. The chessmen were walking about, two and two!

'Here are the Red King and the Red Queen,' Alice

said (in a whisper, for fear of frightening them), 'and there
are the White King and the White Queen sitting on the
edge of the shovel—and here are two Castles walking arm
in arm—I don't think they can hear me,' she went on, as

she put her head closer down, 'and I'm nearly sure they
can't see me. I feel as if I were invisible——'

Here something began squeaking on the table, and
made Alice turn her head just in time to see one of the
White Pawns roll over and begin kicking: she watched
it with great curiosity to see what would happen next.

'It is the voice of my child!' the White Queen cried

out, as she rushed past the King, so violently that she knocked him over among the cinders. 'My precious Lily! My imperial kitten!' and she began scrambling wildly up the side of the fender.

'Imperial fiddlestick!' said the King, rubbing his nose, which had been hurt by the fall. He had a right to be a

little annoyed, for he was covered with ashes from head to foot.

Alice was very anxious to be of use, and, as the poor little Lily was nearly screaming herself into a fit, she hastily picked up the Queen and set her upon the table by the side of her noisy little daughter.

The Queen gasped, and sat down: the rapid journey through the air had quite taken away her breath, and for a minute or two she could do nothing but hug the little Lily in silence. As soon as she had recovered her breath a little, she called out to the White King, who was sitting sulkily among the ashes, 'Mind the volcano!'

'What volcano?' said the King, looking up anxiously into the fire, as if he thought that was the most likely place to find one.

'Blew——me——up,' panted the Queen, who was still a little out of breath. 'Mind you come up——the regular way——don't get blown up!'

Alice watched the White King as he slowly struggled up from bar to bar, till at last she said, 'Why, you'll be hours and hours getting to the table, at that rate. I'd far better help you, hadn't I?' But the King took no notice of the question: it was quite clear that he could neither hear her nor see her.

So Alice picked him up very gently, and lifted him across more slowly than she had lifted the Queen, that she mightn't take his breath away: but, before she put him on the table, she thought she might as well dust him a little, he was so covered with ashes.

She said afterwards that she had never seen in all her life such a face as the King made, when he found himself

held in the air by an invisible hand, and being dusted: he
was far too much astonished to cry out, but his eyes and
his mouth went on getting larger and larger, and rounder
and rounder, till her hand shook so with laughing that
she nearly let him drop upon the floor.

'Oh! *please* don't make such faces, my dear!' she cried
out, quite forgetting that the King couldn't hear her.
'You make me laugh so that I can hardly hold you!
And don't keep your mouth so wide open! All the ashes
will get into it—there, now I think you're tidy enough!'
she added, as she smoothed his hair, and set him down
very carefully upon the table near the Queen.

The King immediately fell flat on his back, and lay
perfectly still: and Alice was a little alarmed at what she
had done, and went round the room to see if she could
find any water to throw over him. However, she could
find nothing but a bottle of ink, and when she got back
with it she found he had recovered, and he and the Queen
were talking together in a frightened whisper—so low,
that Alice could hardly hear what they said.

The King was saying 'I assure you, my dear, I turned
cold to the very ends of my whiskers!'

To which the Queen replied 'You haven't got any
whiskers.'

'The horror of that moment,' the King went on, 'I
shall never, *never* forget!'

'You will, though,' the Queen said, 'if you don't make
a memorandum of it.'

Alice looked on with great interest as the King took
an enormous memorandum-book out of his pocket, and
began writing. A sudden thought struck her, and she
took hold of the end of the pencil, which came some way
over his shoulder, and began writing for him.

The poor King looked puzzled and unhappy, and
struggled with the pencil for some time without saying

anything; but Alice was too strong for him, and at last he panted out, 'My dear! I really *must* get a thinner pencil. I can't manage this one a bit; it writes all manner of things that I don't intend——'

'What manner of things?' said the Queen, looking

over the book (in which Alice had put '*The White Knight is sliding down the poker. He balances very badly*'). 'That's not a memorandum of *your* feelings!'

There was a book lying near Alice on the table, and while she sat watching the White King (for she was still a little anxious about him, and had the ink all ready to throw over him, in case he fainted again), she turned over the leaves, to find some part that she could read, '—for it's all in some language I don't know,' she said to herself.

It was like this.

JABBERWOCKY

'Twas brillig, and the slithy toves
Did gyre and gimble in the wabe;
All mimsy were the borogoves,
And the mome raths outgrabe.

She puzzled over this for some time, but at last a bright thought struck her. 'Why, it's a Looking-glass book, of course! And if I hold it up to a glass, the words will all go the right way again.'

This was the poem that Alice read.

JABBERWOCKY

'Twas brillig, and the slithy toves
　　Did gyre and gimble in the wabe;
All mimsy were the borogoves,
　　And the mome raths outgrabe.

'Beware the Jabberwock, my son!
　　The jaws that bite, the claws that catch!
Beware the Jubjub bird, and shun
　　The frumious Bandersnatch!'

He took his vorpal sword in hand:
　　Long time the manxome foe he sought—
So rested he by the Tumtum tree,
　　And stood awhile in thought.

And as in uffish thought he stood,
　　The Jabberwock, with eyes of flame,
Came whiffling through the tulgey wood,
　　And burbled as it came!

One, two! One, two! And through and through
　　The vorpal blade went snicker-snack!
He left it dead, and with its head
　　He went galumphing back.

'And hast thou slain the Jabberwock?
　　Come to my arms, my beamish boy!
O frabjous day! Callooh! Callay!'
　　He chortled in his joy.

'Twas brillig, and the slithy toves
　　Did gyre and gimble in the wabe;
All mimsy were the borogoves,
　　And the mome raths outgrabe.

'It seems very pretty,' she said when she had finished it, 'but it's *rather* hard to understand!' (You see she didn't like to confess even to herself, that she couldn't make it out at all.) 'Somehow it seems to fill my head with ideas—only I don't exactly know what they are!

However, *somebody* killed *something*: that's clear, at any rate——

'But oh!' thought Alice, suddenly jumping up, 'if I don't make haste I shall have to go back through the Looking-glass, before I've seen what the rest of the house is like! Let's have a look at the garden first!' She was out of the room in a moment, and ran downstairs —or, at least, it wasn't exactly running, but a new invention for getting downstairs quickly and easily, as Alice said to herself. She just kept the tips of her fingers on the handrail, and floated gently down without even touching the stairs with her feet; then she floated on through the hall, and would have gone straight out at the door in the same way, if she hadn't caught hold of the door-post. She was getting a little giddy with so much floating in the air, and was rather glad to find herself walking again in the natural way.

CHAPTER II

THE GARDEN OF LIVE FLOWERS

'I SHOULD see the garden far better,' said Alice to herself, 'if I could get to the top of that hill: and here's a path that leads straight to it—at least, no, it doesn't do that——' (after going a few yards along the path, and turning several sharp corners), 'but I suppose it will at last. But how curiously it twists! It's more like a corkscrew than a path! Well, *this* turn goes to the hill, I suppose—no, it doesn't! This goes straight back to the house! Well then, I'll try it the other way.'

And so she did: wandering up and down, and trying

turn after turn, but always coming back to the house, do what she would. Indeed, once, when she turned a corner rather more quickly than usual, she ran against it before she could stop herself.

'It's no use talking about it,' Alice said, looking up at the house and pretending it was arguing with her. 'I'm *not* going in again yet. I know I should have to get through the Looking-glass again—back into the old room—and there'd be an end of all my adventures!'

So, resolutely turning her back upon the house, she set out once more down the path, determined to keep straight on till she got to the hill. For a few minutes all went on well, and she was just saying, 'I really *shall* do it this time——' when the path gave a sudden twist and shook itself (as she described it afterwards), and the next moment she found herself actually walking in at the door.

'Oh, it's too bad!' she cried. 'I never saw such a house for getting in the way! Never!'

However, there was the hill full in sight, so there was nothing to be done but start again. This time she came upon a large flower-bed, with a border of daisies, and a willow-tree growing in the middle.

'O Tiger-lily,' said Alice, addressing herself to one that was waving gracefully about in the wind, 'I *wish* you could talk!'

'We *can* talk,' said the Tiger-lily: 'when there's anybody worth talking to.'

Alice was so astonished that she couldn't speak for a minute: it quite seemed to take her breath away. At length, as the Tiger-lily only went on waving about, she spoke again, in a timid voice—almost in a whisper. 'And can *all* the flowers talk?'

'As well as *you* can,' said the Tiger-lily. 'And a great deal louder.'

'It isn't manners for us to begin, you know,' said the

Rose, 'and I really was wondering when you'd speak! Said I to myself, "Her face has got *some* sense in it, though it's not a clever one!"   Still, you're the right colour, and that goes a long way.'

'I don't care about the colour,' the Tiger-lily remarked.   'If only her petals curled up a little more, she'd be all right.'

Alice didn't like being criticized, so she began asking questions: 'Aren't you sometimes frightened at being planted out here, with nobody to take care of you?'

'There's the tree in the middle,' said the Rose. 'What else is it good for?'

'But what could it do, if any danger came?' Alice asked.

'It could bark,' said the Rose.

'It says "Bough-wough!"' cried a Daisy: 'that's why its branches are called boughs!'

'Didn't you know *that*?' cried another Daisy, and here they all began shouting together, till the air seemed quite full of little shrill voices. 'Silence, every one of you!' cried the Tiger-lily, waving itself passionately from side to side, and trembling with excitement. 'They know I can't get at them!' it panted, bending its quivering head towards Alice, 'or they wouldn't dare do it!'

'Never mind!' Alice said in a soothing tone, and stooping down to the daisies, who were just beginning again, she whispered 'If you don't hold your tongues, I'll pick you!'

There was silence in a moment, and several of the pink daisies turned white.

'That's right!' said the Tiger-lily. 'The daisies are worst of all. When one speaks, they all begin together, and it's enough to make one wither to hear the way they go on!'

'How is it you can all talk so nicely?' Alice said, hoping to get it into a better temper by a compliment. 'I've been in many gardens before, but none of the flowers could talk.'

'Put your hand down, and feel the ground,' said the Tiger-lily. 'Then you'll know why.'

Alice did so. 'It's very hard,' she said, 'but I don't see what that has to do with it.'

'In most gardens,' the Tiger-lily said, 'they make the beds too soft—so that the flowers are always asleep.'

This sounded a very good reason, and Alice was quite pleased to know it. 'I never thought of that before!' she said.

'It's *my* opinion you never think *at all*,' the Rose said in a rather severe tone.

'I never saw anybody that looked stupider,' a Violet

said, so suddenly, that Alice quite jumped; for it hadn't spoken before.

'Hold *your* tongue!' cried the Tiger-lily. 'As if *you* ever saw anybody! You keep your head under the leaves, and snore away there till you know no more what's going on in the world, than if you were a bud!'

'Are there any more people in the garden besides me?' Alice said, not choosing to notice the Rose's last remark.

'There's one other flower in the garden that can move about like you,' said the Rose. 'I wonder how you do it——' ('You're always wondering,' said the Tiger-lily), 'but she's more bushy than you are.'

'Is she like me?' Alice asked eagerly, for the thought crossed her mind, 'There's another little girl in the garden somewhere!'

'Well, she has the same awkward shape as you,' the Rose said: 'but she's redder—and her petals are shorter, I think.'

'Her petals are done up close, almost like a dahlia,' the Tiger-lily interrupted: 'not tumbled about anyhow, like yours.'

'But that's not *your* fault,' the Rose added kindly: 'you're beginning to fade, you know—and then one can't help one's petals getting a little untidy.'

Alice didn't like this idea at all: so, to change the subject, she asked 'Does she ever come out here?'

'I dare say you'll see her soon,' said the Rose. 'She's one of the thorny kind.'

'Where does she wear the thorns?' Alice asked with some curiosity.

'Why, all round her head, of course,' the Rose replied. 'I was wondering *you* hadn't got some too. I thought it was the regular rule.'

'She's coming!' cried the Larkspur. 'I hear her footsteps, thump, thump, along the gravel-walk!'

Alice looked round eagerly, and found that it was the Red Queen. 'She's grown a good deal!' was her first remark. She had indeed: when Alice first found her in the ashes, she had been only three inches high—and here she was, half a head taller than Alice herself!

'It's the fresh air that does it,' said the Rose: 'wonderfully fine air it is, out here.'

'I think I'll go and meet her,' said Alice, for, though the flowers were very interesting, she felt that it would be far grander to have a talk with a real Queen.

'You can't possibly do that,' said the Rose: '*I* should advise you to walk the other way.'

This sounded nonsense to Alice so she said nothing, but set off at once towards the Red Queen. To her surprise, she lost sight of her in a moment, and found herself walking in at the front door again.

A little provoked, she drew back and, after looking everywhere for the Queen (whom she spied out at last, a long way off), she thought she would try the plan, this time, of walking in the opposite direction.

It succeeded beautifully. She had not been walking a minute before she found herself face to face with the Red Queen, and full in sight of the hill she had been so long aiming at.

'Where do you come from?' said the Red Queen. 'And where are you going? Look up, speak nicely, and don't twiddle your fingers all the time.'

Alice attended to all these directions, and explained, as well as she could, that she had lost her way.

'I don't know what you mean by *your* way,' said the Queen: 'all the ways about here belong to *me*—but why did you come out here at all?' she added in a kinder tone. 'Curtsy while you're thinking what to say. It saves time.'

Alice wondered a little at this, but she was too much

in awe of the Queen to disbelieve it. 'I'll try it when I go home,' she thought to herself, 'the next time I'm a little late for dinner.'

'It's time for you to answer now,' the Queen said, looking at her watch: 'open your mouth a *little* wider when you speak, and always say "your Majesty."'

'I only wanted to see what the garden was like, your Majesty——'

'That's right,' said the Queen, patting her on the head, which Alice didn't like at all: 'though, when you say "garden," *I*'ve seen gardens, compared with which this would be a wilderness.'

Alice didn't dare to argue the point, but went on: '——and I thought I'd try and find my way to the top of that hill——'

'When you say "hill,"' the Queen interrupted, '*I* could show you hills, in comparison with which you'd call that a valley.'

'No, I shouldn't,' said Alice, surprised into contradicting her at last: 'a hill *can't* be a valley, you know. That would be nonsense——'

The Red Queen shook her head. 'You may call it

"nonsense" if you like,' she said, 'but *I*'ve heard nonsense, compared with which that would be as sensible as a dictionary!'

Alice curtsied again, as she was afraid from the Queen's tone that she was a *little* offended: and they walked on in silence till they got to the top of the little hill.

For some minutes Alice stood without speaking, looking out in all directions over the country—and a most curious country it was. There were a number of little brooks running across from side to side, and the ground between was divided up into squares by a number of hedges, that reached from brook to brook.

'I declare it's marked out just like a large chess-board!' Alice said at last. 'There ought to be some men moving about somewhere—and so there are!' she added in a tone of delight, and her heart began to beat quick with excitement as she went on. 'It's a great game of chess that's being played—all over the world—if this *is* the world at all, you know. Oh, what fun it is! How I *wish* I was one of them! I wouldn't mind being a Pawn, if only I might join—though of course I should *like* to be a Queen, best.'

She glanced rather shyly at the real Queen as she said this, but her companion only smiled pleasantly, and said 'That's easily managed. You can be the White Queen's Pawn, if you like, as Lily's too young to play; and you're in the Second Square to begin with: when you get into the Eighth Square you'll be a Queen——' Just at this moment, somehow or other, they began to run.

Alice never could quite make out, in thinking it over afterwards, how it was that they began: all she remembers is, that they were running hand in hand, and the Queen went so fast that it was all she could do to keep up with her: and still the Queen kept crying 'Faster!' but Alice felt she *could not* go faster, though she had no breath to say so.

The most curious part of the thing was, that the trees

and the other things round them never changed their places at all: however fast they went, they never seemed to pass anything. 'I wonder if all the things move along with us?' thought poor puzzled Alice. And the Queen seemed to guess her thoughts, for she cried 'Faster! Don't try to talk!'

Not that Alice had any idea of doing *that*. She felt as if she would never be able to talk again, she was getting so out of breath: and still the Queen cried 'Faster! Faster!' and dragged her along. 'Are we nearly there?' Alice managed to pant out at last.

'Nearly there!' the Queen repeated. 'Why, we passed it ten minutes ago! Faster!' And they ran on for a time in silence, with the wind whistling in Alice's ears, and almost blowing her hair off her head, she fancied.

'Now! Now!' cried the Queen. 'Faster! Faster!' And they went so fast that at last they seemed to skim through the air, hardly touching the ground with their feet, till suddenly, just as Alice was getting quite exhausted, they stopped, and she found herself sitting on the ground, breathless and giddy.

The Queen propped her against a tree, and said kindly, 'You may rest a little now.'

Alice looked round her in great surprise. 'Why, I do believe we've been under this tree all the time! Everything's just as it was!'

'Of course it is,' said the Queen: 'what would you have it?'

'Well, in *our* country,' said Alice, still panting a little, 'you'd generally get to somewhere else—if you ran very fast for a long time, as we've been doing.'

'A slow sort of country!' said the Queen. 'Now, *here*, you see, it takes all the running *you* can do, to keep in the same place. If you want to get somewhere else, you must run at least twice as fast as that!'

'I'd rather not try, please!' said Alice. 'I'm quite content to stay here—only I *am* so hot and thirsty!'

'I know what *you*'d like!' the Queen said good-naturedly, taking a little box out of her pocket. 'Have a biscuit?'

Alice thought it would not be civil to say 'No,' though it wasn't at all what she wanted. So she took it, and ate it as well as she could: and it was *very* dry; and she thought she had never been so nearly choked in all her life.

'While you're refreshing yourself,' said the Queen, 'I'll just take the measurements.' And she took a ribbon out of her pocket, marked in inches, and began measuring out the ground, and sticking little pegs in here and there.

'At the end of two yards,' she said, putting in a peg to mark the distance, 'I shall give you your directions—have another biscuit?'

'No, thank you,' said Alice: 'one's *quite* enough!'

'Thirst quenched, I hope?' said the Queen.

Alice did not know what to say to this, but luckily the Queen did not wait for an answer, but went on. 'At the end of *three* yards I shall repeat them—for fear of your forgetting them. At the end of *four*, I shall say good-bye. And at the end of *five*, I shall go!'

She had got all the pegs put in by this time, and Alice looked on with great interest as she returned to the tree, and then began slowly walking down the row.

At the two-yard peg she faced round, and said 'A pawn goes two squares in its first move. So you'll go *very* quickly through the Third Square—by railway, I should think—and you'll find yourself in the Fourth Square in no time. Well, *that* square belongs to Tweedle-dum and Tweedledee—the Fifth is mostly water—the Sixth belongs to Humpty Dumpty—But you make no remark?'

'I—I didn't know I had to make one—just then,' Alice faltered out.

'You *should* have said,' the Queen went on in a tone of grave reproof, '"It's extremely kind of you to tell me all this"—however, we'll suppose it said—the Seventh Square is all forest—however, one of the Knights will show you the way—and in the Eighth Square we shall be Queens together, and it's all feasting and fun!' Alice got up and curtsied, and sat down again.

At the next peg the Queen turned again, and said 'Speak in French when you can't think of the English for a thing—turn out your toes as you walk—and remember who you are!' She did not wait for Alice to curtsy this time, but walked on quickly to the next peg, where she turned to say 'good-bye,' and then hurried on to the last.

How it happened, Alice never knew, but exactly as she came to the last peg, she was gone. Whether she vanished into the air, or ran quickly into the wood ('and she *can* run very fast!' thought Alice), there was no way of guessing, but she was gone, and Alice began to remember that she was a Pawn, and that it would soon be time to move.

CHAPTER III

LOOKING-GLASS INSECTS

OF course the first thing to do was to make a grand survey of the country she was going to travel through. 'It's something very like learning geography,' thought Alice, as she stood on tiptoe in hopes of being able to see a little further. 'Principal rivers—there *are* none.

Principal mountains—I'm on the only one, but I don't think it's got any name. Principal towns—why what *are* those creatures, making honey down there? They can't be bees—nobody ever saw bees a mile off, you know——' and for some minutes she stood silent, watching one of them that was bustling about among the flowers, poking its proboscis into them, 'just as if it was a regular bee,' thought Alice.

However, this was anything but a regular bee: in fact, it was an elephant—as Alice soon found out, though the idea quite took her breath away at first. 'And what enormous flowers they must be!' was her next idea. 'Something like cottages with the roofs taken off, and stalks put to them—and what quantities of honey they must make! I think I'll go down and—no, I won't go *just* yet,' she went on, checking herself just as she was beginning to run down the hill, and trying to find some excuse for turning shy so suddenly. 'It'll never do to go down among them without a good long branch to brush them away—and what fun it'll be when they ask me how I liked my walk. I shall say—"Oh, I liked it well enough——" (here came the favourite little toss of the head), "only it was so dusty and hot, and the elephants did tease so!"

'I think I'll go down the other way,' she said after a pause: 'and perhaps I may visit the elephants later on. Besides, I do so want to get into the Third Square!'

So with this excuse she ran down the hill and jumped over the first of the six little brooks.

'Tickets, please!' said the Guard, putting his head in at the window. In a moment everybody was holding out a ticket: they were about the same size as the people, and quite seemed to fill the carriage.

'Now then! Show your ticket, child!' the Guard went on, looking angrily at Alice. And a great many voices all said together ('like the chorus of a song,' thought Alice), 'Don't keep him waiting, child! Why, his time is worth a thousand pounds a minute!'

'I'm afraid I haven't got one,' Alice said in a frightened tone: 'there wasn't a ticket-office where I came from.' And again the chorus of voices went on. 'There wasn't room for one where she came from. The land there is worth a thousand pounds an inch!'

'Don't make excuses,' said the Guard: 'you should have bought one from the engine-driver.' And once more the chorus of voices went on with 'The man that drives the engine. Why, the smoke alone is worth a thousand pounds a puff!'

Alice thought to herself, 'Then there's no use in speaking.' The voices didn't join in this time, as she hadn't spoken, but, to her great surprise, they all *thought* in chorus (I hope you understand what *thinking in chorus* means—for I must confess that *I* don't), 'Better say nothing at all. Language is worth a thousand pounds a word!'

'I shall dream about a thousand pounds to-night, I know I shall!' thought Alice.

All this time the Guard was looking at her, first through a telescope, then through a microscope, and then through an opera-glass. At last he said 'You're travelling the wrong way,' and shut up the window and went away.

'So young a child,' said the gentleman sitting opposite to her (he was dressed in white paper), 'ought to know which way she's going, even if she doesn't know her own name!'

A Goat, that was sitting next to the gentleman in white,

shut his eyes and said in a loud voice, 'She ought to know her way to the ticket-office, even if she doesn't know her alphabet!'

There was a Beetle sitting next the Goat (it was a very queer set of passengers altogether), and, as the rule seemed to be that they should all speak in turn, *he* went on with 'She'll have to go back from here as luggage!'

Alice couldn't see who was sitting beyond the Beetle, but a hoarse voice spoke next. 'Change engines——' it said, and there it choked and was obliged to leave off.

'It sounds like a horse,' Alice thought to herself. And an extremely small voice, close to her ear, said 'You might make a joke on that—something about "horse" and "hoarse," you know.'

Then a very gentle voice in the distance said 'She must be labelled "Lass, with care," you know——'

And after that other voices went on ('What a number of people there are in the carriage!' thought Alice), saying 'She must go by post, as she's got a head on her——'

'She must be sent as a message by the telegraph——'
'She must draw the train herself the rest of the way——,'
and so on.

But the gentleman dressed in white paper leaned
forwards and whispered in her ear, 'Never mind what
they all say, my dear, but take a return ticket every time
the train stops.'

'Indeed I shan't!' Alice said rather impatiently. 'I
don't belong to this railway journey at all—I was in a
wood just now—and I wish I could get back there!'

'You might make a joke on *that*,' said the little voice close to
her ear: 'something about "you *would* if you could," you know.'

'Don't tease so,' said Alice, looking about in vain to
see where the voice came from; 'if you're so anxious to
have a joke made, why don't you make one yourself?'

The little voice sighed deeply: it was *very* unhappy,
evidently, and Alice would have said something pitying
to comfort it, 'if it would only sigh like other people!'
she thought. But this was such a wonderfully small sigh,
that she wouldn't have heard it at all, if it hadn't come
quite close to her ear. The consequence of this was that
it tickled her ear very much, and quite took off her
thoughts from the unhappiness of the poor little creature.

'I know you are a friend,' the little voice went on; 'a dear friend,
and an old friend. And you won't hurt me, though I *am* an insect.'

'What kind of insect?' Alice inquired a little anxiously.
What she really wanted to know was, whether it could
sting or not, but she thought this wouldn't be quite a
civil question to ask.

'What, then you don't——' the little voice began, when it was
drowned by a shrill scream from the engine, and everybody
jumped up in alarm, Alice among the rest.

The Horse, who had put his head out of the window,
quietly drew it in and said 'It's only a brook we have to
jump over.' Everybody seemed satisfied with this,

though Alice felt a little nervous at the idea of trains
jumping at all. 'However, it'll take us into the Fourth
Square, that's some comfort!' she said to herself. In
another moment she felt the carriage rise straight up into
the air, and in her fright she caught at the thing nearest
to her hand, which happened to be the Goat's beard.

   *   *   *   *   *

      *   *   *   *

   *   *   *   *   *

But the beard seemed to melt away as she touched it,
and she found herself sitting quietly under a tree—while
the Gnat (for that was the insect she had been talking to)
was balancing itself on a twig just over her head, and
fanning her with its wings.

It certainly was a *very* large Gnat: 'about the size of a
chicken,' Alice thought. Still, she couldn't feel nervous
with it, after they had been talking together so long.

'—then you don't like all insects?' the Gnat went on,
as quietly as if nothing had happened.

'I like them when they can talk,' Alice said. 'None
of them ever talk, where *I* come from.'

'What sort of insects do you rejoice in, where *you* come
from?' the Gnat inquired.

'I don't *rejoice* in insects at all,' Alice explained,
'because I'm rather afraid of them—at least the large
kinds. But I can tell you the names of some of them.'

'Of course they answer to their names?' the Gnat
remarked carelessly.

'I never knew them do it.'

'What's the use of their having names,' the Gnat said,
'if they won't answer to them?'

'No use to *them*,' said Alice; 'but it's useful to the
people that name them, I suppose. If not, why do
things have names at all?'

'I can't say,' said the Gnat. 'In the wood down there, they've got no names—however, go on with your list of insects.'

'Well there's the Horse-fly,' Alice began, counting off the names on her fingers.

'All right,' said the Gnat: 'half-way up that bush, you'll see a Rocking-horse-fly, if you look. It's made entirely of wood, and gets about by swinging itself from branch to branch.'

'What does it live on?' Alice asked, with great curiosity.

'Sap and sawdust,' said the Gnat. 'Go on with the list.'

Alice looked at the Rocking-horse-fly with great interest, and made up her mind that it must have been just repainted, it looked so bright and sticky; and then she went on.

'And there's the Dragon-fly.'

'Look on the branch above your head,' said the Gnat, 'and there you'll find a Snap-dragon-fly. Its body is made of plum-pudding, its wings of holly-leaves, and its head is a raisin burning in brandy.'

'And what does it live on?' Alice asked, as before.

'Frumenty and mince-pie,' the Gnat replied; 'and it makes its nest in a Christmas-box.'

'And then there's the Butterfly,' Alice went on, after she had taken a good look at the insect with its head on fire, and had thought to herself, 'I wonder if that's the

reason insects are so fond of flying into candles—because they want to turn into Snap-dragon-flies!'

'Crawling at your feet,' said the Gnat (Alice drew her feet back in some alarm), 'you may observe a Bread-and-butter-fly. Its wings are thin slices of bread and butter, its body is a crust, and its head is a lump of sugar.'

'And what does *it* live on?'

'Weak tea with cream in it.'

A new difficulty came into Alice's head. 'Supposing it couldn't find any?' she suggested.

'Then it would die, of course.'

'But that must happen very often,' Alice remarked thoughtfully.

'It always happens,' said the Gnat.

After this, Alice was silent for a minute or two, pondering. The Gnat amused itself meanwhile by humming round and round her head: at last it settled again and remarked, 'I suppose you don't want to lose your name?'

'No, indeed,' Alice said, a little anxiously.

'And yet I don't know,' the Gnat went on in a careless tone: 'only think how convenient it would be if you could manage to go home without it! For instance, if the governess wanted to call you to your lessons, she would call out "Come here—," and there she would have to leave off, because there wouldn't be any name for her to call, and of course you wouldn't have to go, you know.'

'That would never do, I'm sure,' said Alice: 'the governess would never think of excusing me lessons for that. If she couldn't remember my name, she'd call me "Miss!" as the servants do.'

'Well, if she said "Miss," and didn't say anything more,' the Gnat remarked, 'of course you'd miss your lessons. That's a joke. I wish *you* had made it.'

'Why do you wish *I* had made it?' Alice asked. 'It's a very bad one.'

But the Gnat only sighed deeply, while two large tears came rolling down its cheeks.

'You shouldn't make jokes,' Alice said, 'if it makes you so unhappy.'

Then came another of those melancholy little sighs, and this time the poor Gnat really seemed to have sighed itself away, for, when Alice looked up, there was nothing whatever to be seen on the twig, and, as she was getting quite chilly with sitting still so long, she got up and walked on.

She very soon came to an open field, with a wood on the other side of it: it looked much darker than the last wood, and Alice felt a *little* timid about going into it. However, on second thoughts, she made up her mind to go on: 'for I certainly won't go *back*,' she thought to herself, and this was the only way to the Eighth Square.

'This must be the wood,' she said thoughtfully to herself, 'where things have no names. I wonder what'll become of *my* name when I go in! I shouldn't like to lose it at all—because they'd have to give me another, and it would be almost certain to be an ugly one. But then the fun would be, trying to find the creature that had got my old name! That's just like the advertisements, you know, when people lose dogs—"*answers to the name of 'Dash': had on a brass collar*"—just fancy calling everything you met "Alice," till one of them answered! Only they wouldn't answer at all, if they were wise.'

She was rambling on in this way when she reached the wood: it looked very cool and shady. 'Well, at any rate it's a great comfort,' she said as she stepped under the trees, 'after being so hot, to get into the—into the—into *what*?' she went on, rather surprised at not being able to think of the word. 'I mean to get under the—under the—under *this*, you know!' putting her hand on the trunk of the tree. 'What *does* it call itself? I do believe it's got no name—why, to be sure it hasn't!'

She stood silent for a minute, thinking: then she suddenly began again. 'Then it really *has* happened, after all! And now, who am I? I *will* remember, if I can! I'm determined to do it!' But being determined didn't help her much, and all she could say, after a great deal of puzzling, was, 'L, I *know* it begins with L!'

Just then a Fawn came wandering by: it looked at Alice with its large gentle eyes, but didn't seem at all frightened. 'Here then! Here then!' Alice said, as she held out her hand and tried to stroke it; but it only started back a little, and then stood looking at her again.

'What do you call yourself?' the Fawn said at last. Such a soft sweet voice it had!

'I wish I knew!' thought poor Alice. She answered, rather sadly, 'Nothing, just now.'

'Think again,' it said: 'that won't do.'

Alice thought, but nothing came of it. 'Please, would you tell me what *you* call yourself?' she said timidly. 'I think that might help a little.'

'I'll tell you, if you'll come a little further on,' the Fawn said. 'I can't remember here.'

So they walked on together through the wood, Alice with her arms clasped lovingly round the soft neck of the Fawn, till they came out into another open field, and here the Fawn gave a sudden bound into the air, and shook itself free from Alice's arms. 'I'm a Fawn!' it cried out in a voice of delight. 'And, dear me, you're a human child!' A sudden look of alarm came into its beautiful brown eyes, and in another moment it had darted away at full speed.

Alice stood looking after it, almost ready to cry with vexation at having lost her dear little fellow traveller so suddenly. 'However, I know my name now,' she said: 'that's *some* comfort. Alice—Alice—I won't forget it again. And now, which of these fingerposts ought I to follow, I wonder?'

It was not a difficult question to answer, as there was only one road, and the fingerposts both pointed along it. 'I'll settle it,' Alice said to herself, 'when the road divides and they point different ways.'

But this did not seem likely to happen. She went on and on, a long way, but wherever the road divided there were sure to be two fingerposts pointing the same way, one marked 'TO TWEEDLEDUM'S HOUSE,' and the other 'TO THE HOUSE OF TWEEDLE-DEE.'

'I do believe,' said Alice at last, 'that they live in the same house! I wonder I never thought of that before— But I can't stay there long. I'll just call and say "How d'ye do?" and ask them the way out of the wood. If I could only get to the Eighth Square before it gets dark!' So she wandered on, talking to herself as she went, till, on turning a sharp corner, she came upon two fat little men, so suddenly that she could not help starting back, but in another moment she recovered herself, feeling sure that they must be——

CHAPTER IV

TWEEDLEDUM AND TWEEDLEDEE

THEY were standing under a tree, each with an arm round the other's neck, and Alice knew which was which in a moment, because one of them had 'DUM' embroidered on his collar, and the other 'DEE.'   'I suppose they've each got "TWEEDLE" round at the back of the collar,' she said to herself.

They stood so still that she quite forgot they were alive, and she was just looking round to see if the word 'TWEEDLE' was written at the back of each collar, when she was startled by a voice coming from the one marked 'DUM.'

'If you think we're wax-works,' he said, 'you ought to pay, you know. Wax-works weren't made to be looked at for nothing.   Nohow!'

'Contrariwise,' added the one marked 'DEE,' 'if you think we're alive, you ought to speak.'

'I'm sure I'm very sorry,' was all Alice could say; for the words of the old song kept ringing through her head like the ticking of a clock, and she could hardly help saying them out loud:

> *'Tweedledum and Tweedledee*
> *Agreed to have a battle;*
> *For Tweedledum said Tweedledee*
> *Had spoiled his nice new rattle.*
>
> *Just then flew down a monstrous crow,*
> *As black as a tar-barrel;*
> *Which frightened both the heroes so,*
> *They quite forgot their quarrel.'*

I know what you're thinking about,' said Tweedledum: 'but it isn't so, nohow.'

'Contrariwise,' continued Tweedledee, 'if it was so, it might be; and if it were so, it would be: but as it isn't, it ain't. That's logic.'

'I was thinking,' Alice said very politely, 'which is the best way out of this wood: it's getting so dark. Would you tell me, please?'

But the fat little men only looked at each other and grinned.

They looked so exactly like a couple of great schoolboys, that Alice couldn't help pointing her finger at Tweedledum, and saying 'First Boy!'

'Nohow!' Tweedledum cried out briskly, and instantly shut his mouth up again with a snap.

'Next Boy!' said Alice, passing on to Tweedledee, though she felt quite certain he would only shout out 'Contrariwise!' and so he did.

'You've begun wrong!' cried Tweedledum. 'The

first thing in a visit is to say "How d'ye do?" and shake hands!' And here the two brothers gave each other a hug, and then they held out the two hands that were free, to shake hands with her.

Alice did not like shaking hands with either of them first, for fear of hurting the other one's feelings; so, as the best way out of the difficulty, she took hold of both hands at once: the next moment they were dancing round in a ring. This seemed quite natural (she remembered afterwards), and she was not even surprised to hear music playing: it seemed to come from the tree under which they were dancing, and it was done (as well as she could make it out) by the branches rubbing one across the other, like fiddles and fiddlesticks.

'But it certainly *was* funny' (Alice said afterwards, when she was telling her sister the history of all this) 'to find myself singing "*Here we go round the mulberry bush.*" I don't know when I began it, but somehow I felt as if I'd been singing it a long, long time!'

The other two dancers were fat, and very soon out of breath. 'Four times round is enough for one dance,' Tweedledum panted out, and they left off dancing as suddenly as they had begun: the music stopped at the same moment.

Then they let go of Alice's hands, and stood looking at her for a minute: there was a rather awkward pause, as Alice didn't know how to begin a conversation with people she had just been dancing with. 'It would never do to say "How d'ye do?" *now*,' she said to herself: 'we seem to have got beyond that, somehow!'

'I hope you're not much tired?' she said at last.

'Nohow. And thank you *very* much for asking,' said Tweedledum.

'So *much* obliged!' added Tweedledee. 'You like poetry?'

'Ye-es, pretty well—*some* poetry,' Alice said doubtfully. 'Would you tell me which road leads out of the wood?'

'What shall I repeat to her?' said Tweedledee, looking round at Tweedledum with great solemn eyes, and not noticing Alice's question.

'"*The Walrus and the Carpenter*" is the longest,' Tweedledum replied, giving his brother an affectionate hug.

Tweedledee began instantly:

> '*The sun was shining—*'

Here Alice ventured to interrupt. 'If it's *very* long,' she said, as politely as she could, 'would you tell me first which road——'

Tweedledee smiled gently, and began again:

> '*The sun was shining on the sea,*
> *Shining with all his might:*
> *He did his very best to make*
> *The billows smooth and bright—*
> *And this was odd, because it was*
> *The middle of the night.*
>
> *The moon was shining sulkily,*
> *Because she thought the sun*
> *Had got no business to be there*
> *After the day was done—*
> *"It's very rude of him," she said,*
> *"To come and spoil the fun!"*
>
> *The sea was wet as wet could be,*
> *The sands were dry as dry.*
> *You could not see a cloud, because*
> *No cloud was in the sky:*
> *No birds were flying overhead—*
> *There were no birds to fly.*

The Walrus and the Carpenter
Were walking close at hand;
They wept like anything to see
Such quantities of sand:
"If this were only cleared away,"
They said, "it would be grand!"

"If seven maids with seven mops
Swept it for half a year,
Do you suppose," the Walrus said,
"That they could get it clear?"
"I doubt it," said the Carpenter,
And shed a bitter tear.

"O Oysters, come and walk with us!"
The Walrus did beseech.
"A pleasant walk, a pleasant talk,
Along the briny beach:
We cannot do with more than four,
To give a hand to each."

The eldest Oyster looked at him,
But never a word he said:
The eldest Oyster winked his eye,
And shook his heavy head—
Meaning to say he did not choose
To leave the oyster-bed.

But four young Oysters hurried up,
All eager for the treat:
Their coats were brushed, their faces washed,
Their shoes were clean and neat—
And this was odd, because, you know,
They hadn't any feet.

Four other Oysters followed them,
And yet another four;
And thick and fast they came at last,
And more, and more, and more—
All hopping through the frothy waves,
And scrambling to the shore.

The Walrus and the Carpenter
Walked on a mile or so,
And then they rested on a rock
Conveniently low:
And all the little Oysters stood
And waited in a row.

"The time has come," the Walrus said,
"To talk of many things:
Of shoes—and ships—and sealing-wax—
Of cabbages—and kings—
And why the sea is boiling hot—
And whether pigs have wings."

> "*But wait a bit,*" *the Oysters cried,*
>   "*Before we have our chat;*
> *For some of us are out of breath,*
>   *And all of us are fat!*"
> "*No hurry!*" *said the Carpenter.*
>   *They thanked him much for that.*
>
> "*A loaf of bread,*" *the Walrus said,*
>   "*Is what we chiefly need:*
> *Pepper and vinegar besides*
>   *Are very good indeed—*
> *Now if you're ready, Oysters dear,*
>   *We can begin to feed.*"
>
> "*But not on us!*" *the Oysters cried,*
>   *Turning a little blue.*
> "*After such kindness, that would be*
>   *A dismal thing to do!*"
> "*The night is fine,*" *the Walrus said.*
>   "*Do you admire the view?*
>
> "*It was so kind of you to come!*
>   *And you are very nice!*"
> *The Carpenter said nothing but*

"*Cut us another slice:*
I wish you were not quite so deaf—
I've had to ask you twice!"

"*It seems a shame,*" *the Walrus said,*
  "*To play them such a trick,*
After we've brought them out so far,
  And made them trot so quick!"
The Carpenter said nothing but
  "*The butter's spread too thick!*"

"*I weep for you,*" *the Walrus said:*
  "*I deeply sympathize.*"
With sobs and tears he sorted out
  Those of the largest size
Holding his pocket-handkerchief
  Before his streaming eyes.

"*O Oysters,*" *said the Carpenter,*
  "*You've had a pleasant run!*
Shall we be trotting home again?"
  But answer came there none—
And this was scarcely odd, because
  They'd eaten every one.'

'I like the Walrus best,' said Alice: 'because you see he was a *little* sorry for the poor oysters.'

'He ate more than the Carpenter, though,' said Tweedledee. 'You see he held his handkerchief in front, so that the Carpenter couldn't count how many he took: contrariwise.'

'That was mean!' Alice said indignantly. 'Then I like the Carpenter best—if he didn't eat so many as the Walrus.'

'But he ate as many as he could get,' said Tweedledum.

This was a puzzler. After a pause, Alice began, 'Well! They were *both* very unpleasant characters—' Here she checked herself in some alarm, at hearing something that sounded to her like the puffing of a large steam-engine in the wood near them, though she feared it was more likely to be a wild beast. 'Are there any lions or tigers about here?' she asked timidly.

'It's only the Red King snoring,' said Tweedledee.

'Come and look at him!' the brothers cried, and they each took one of Alice's hands, and led her up to where the King was sleeping.

'Isn't he a *lovely* sight?' said Tweedledum.

Alice couldn't say honestly that he was. He had a tall red night-cap on, with a tassel, and he was lying crumpled up into a sort of untidy heap, and snoring loud —'fit to snore his head off!' as Tweedledum remarked.

'I'm afraid he'll catch cold with lying on the damp grass,' said Alice, who was a very thoughtful little girl.

'He's dreaming now,' said Tweedledee: 'and what do you think he's dreaming about?'

Alice said 'Nobody can guess that.'

'Why, about *you*!' Tweedledee exclaimed, clapping his hands triumphantly. 'And if he left off dreaming about you, where do you suppose you'd be?'

'Where I am now, of course,' said Alice.

'Not you!' Tweedledee retorted contemptuously. 'You'd be nowhere. Why, you're only a sort of thing in his dream!'

'If that there King was to wake,' added Tweedledum, 'you'd go out—bang!—just like a candle!'

'I shouldn't!' Alice exclaimed indignantly. 'Besides, if *I*'m only a sort of thing in his dream, what are *you*, I should like to know?'

'Ditto,' said Tweedledum.

'Ditto, ditto!' cried Tweedledee.

He shouted this so loud that Alice couldn't help saying, 'Hush! You'll be waking him, I'm afraid, if you make so much noise.'

'Well, it's no use *your* talking about waking him,' said Tweedledum, 'when you're only one of the things in his dream. You know very well you're not real.'

'I *am* real!' said Alice, and began to cry.

'You won't make yourself a bit realer by crying,' Tweedledee remarked: 'there's nothing to cry about.'

'If I wasn't real,' Alice said—half laughing through her tears, it all seemed so ridiculous—'I shouldn't be able to cry.'

'I hope you don't suppose those are real tears?' Tweedledum interrupted in a tone of great contempt.

'I know they're talking nonsense,' Alice thought to herself: 'and it's foolish to cry about it.' So she brushed away her tears, and went on as cheerfully as she could, 'At any rate I'd better be getting out of the wood, for really it's coming on very dark. Do you think it's going to rain?'

Tweedledum spread a large umbrella over himself and his brother, and looked up into it. 'No, I don't think it is,' he said: 'at least—not under *here*. Nohow.'

'But it may rain *outside*?'

'It may—if it chooses,' said Tweedledee: 'we've no objection. Contrariwise.'

'Selfish things!' thought Alice, and she was just going to say 'Good night' and leave them, when Tweedledum sprang out from under the umbrella, and seized her by the wrist.

'Do you see *that*?' he said, in a voice choking with passion, and his eyes grew large and yellow all in a moment, as he pointed with a trembling finger at a small white thing lying under the tree.

'It's only a rattle,' Alice said, after a careful examination of the little white thing. 'Not a rattle-*snake*, you know,' she added hastily, thinking that he was frightened: 'only an old rattle—quite old and broken.'

'I knew it was!' cried Tweedledum, beginning to stamp about wildly and tear his hair. 'It's spoilt, of course!' Here he looked at Tweedledee, who immediately sat down on the ground, and tried to hide himself under the umbrella.

Alice laid her hand upon his arm, and said in a soothing tone, 'You needn't be so angry about an old rattle.'

But it isn't old!' Tweedledum cried, in a greater fury

than ever. 'It's new, I tell you—I bought it yesterday
—my nice NEW RATTLE!' and his voice rose to a
perfect scream.

All this time Tweedledee was trying his best to fold
up the umbrella, with himself in it: which was such an
extraordinary thing to do, that it quite took off Alice's
attention from the angry brother.   But he couldn't quite
succeed, and it ended in his rolling over, bundled up in
the umbrella, with only his head out: and there he lay,
opening and shutting his mouth and his large eyes—
'looking more like a fish than anything else,' Alice thought.

'Of course you agree to have a battle?' Tweedledum
said in a calmer tone.

'I suppose so,' the other sulkily replied, as he crawled
out of the umbrella: 'only *she* must help us to dress up,
you know.'

So the two brothers went off hand-in-hand into the
wood, and returned in a minute with their arms full of
things—such as bolsters, blankets, hearth-rugs, table-
cloths, dish-covers, and coal-scuttles.   'I hope you're a
good hand at pinning and tying strings?' Tweedledum

remarked. 'Every one of these things has got to go on, somehow or other.'

Alice said afterwards she had never seen such a fuss made about anything in all her life—the way those two bustled about—and the quantity of things they put on— and the trouble they gave her in tying strings and fastening buttons—'Really they'll be more like bundles of old clothes than anything else, by the time they're ready!' she said to herself, as she arranged a bolster round the neck of Tweedledee, 'to keep his head from being cut off,' as he said.

'You know,' he added very gravely, 'it's one of the most serious things that can possibly happen to one in a battle—to get one's head cut off.'

Alice laughed loud, but managed to turn it into a cough, for fear of hurting his feelings.

'Do I look very pale?' said Tweedledum, coming up to have his helmet tied on. (He *called* it a helmet, though it certainly looked much more like a saucepan.)

'Well—yes—a *little*,' Alice replied gently.

'I'm very brave generally,' he went on in a low voice: 'only to-day I happen to have a headache.'

'And *I*'ve got a toothache!' said Tweedledee, who had overheard the remark. 'I'm far worse than you!'

'Then you'd better not fight to-day,' said Alice, thinking it a good opportunity to make peace.

'We *must* have a bit of a fight, but I don't care about going on long,' said Tweedledum. 'What's the time now?'

Tweedledee looked at his watch, and said 'Half-past four.'

'Let's fight till six, and then have dinner,' said Tweedledum.

'Very well,' the other said, rather sadly: 'and *she* can watch us—only you'd better not come *very* close,' he

'We must have a bit of a fight . . .' said Tweedledum

See page 166

added: 'I generally hit everything I can see—when I get really excited.'

'And *I* hit everything within reach,' cried Tweedledum, 'whether I can see it or not!'

Alice laughed. 'You must hit the *trees* pretty often, I should think,' she said.

Tweedledum looked round him with a satisfied smile. 'I don't suppose,' he said, 'there'll be a tree left standing, for ever so far round, by the time we've finished!'

'And all about a rattle!' said Alice, still hoping to make them a *little* ashamed of fighting for such a trifle.

'I shouldn't have minded it so much,' said Tweedledum, 'if it hadn't been a new one.'

'I wish the monstrous crow would come!' thought Alice.

'There's only one sword, you know,' Tweedledum said to his brother: 'but you can have the umbrella—it's quite as sharp. Only we must begin quick. It's getting as dark as it can.'

'And darker,' said Tweedledee.

It was getting dark so suddenly that Alice thought there must be a thunderstorm coming on. 'What a thick black cloud that is!' she said. 'And how fast it comes! Why, I do believe it's got wings!'

'It's the crow!' Tweedledum cried out in a shrill voice of alarm: and the two brothers took to their heels and were out of sight in a moment.

Alice ran a little way into the wood, and stopped under a large tree. 'It can never get at me *here*,' she thought: 'it's far too large to squeeze itself in among the trees. But I wish it wouldn't flap its wings so—it makes quite a hurricane in the wood—here's somebody's shawl being blown away!'

CHAPTER V

WOOL AND WATER

SHE caught the shawl as she spoke, and looked about for the owner: in another moment the White Queen came running wildly through the wood, with both arms stretched out wide, as if she were flying, and Alice very civilly went to meet her with the shawl.

'I'm very glad I happened to be in the way,' Alice said, as she helped her to put on her shawl again.

The White Queen only looked at her in a helpless frightened sort of way, and kept repeating something in a whisper to herself that sounded like 'Bread and butter, bread and butter,' and Alice felt that if there was to be any conversation at all, she must manage it herself. So she began rather timidly: 'Am I addressing the White Queen?'

'Well, yes, if you call that a-dressing,' the Queen said. 'It isn't *my* notion of the thing, at all.'

Alice thought it would never do to have an argument at the very beginning of their conversation, so she smiled and said 'If your Majesty will only tell me the right way to begin, I'll do it as well as I can.'

'But I don't want it done at all!' groaned the poor Queen. 'I've been a-dressing myself for the last two hours.'

It would have been all the better, as it seemed to Alice, if only she had got someone else to dress her, she was so dreadfully untidy. 'Every single thing's crooked,' Alice thought to herself, 'and she's all over pins!—May I put your shawl a little more straight for you?' she added aloud.

'I don't know what's the matter with it!' the Queen

said, in a melancholy voice. 'It's out of temper, I think.
I've pinned it here, and I've pinned it there, but there's
no pleasing it!'

'It *can't* go straight, you know, if you pin it all on one
side,' Alice said, as she
gently put it right for
her; 'and, dear me, what
a state your hair is in!'

'The hair-brush has
got entangled in it!' the
Queen said with a sigh.
'And I lost the comb
yesterday.'

Alice carefully re-
leased the brush, and
did her best to get the
hair into order. 'Come,
you look rather better
now!' she said, after
altering most of the pins.
'But really you should
have a lady's-maid!'

'I'm sure I'll take you with pleasure!' the Queen said.
'Twopence a week, and jam every other day.'

Alice couldn't help laughing, as she said 'I don't want
you to hire *me*—and I don't care for jam.'

'It's very good jam,' said the Queen.

'Well, I don't want any *to-day*, at any rate.'

'You couldn't have it if you *did* want it,' the Queen
said. 'The rule is, jam to-morrow and jam yesterday—
but never jam to-day.'

'It *must* come sometimes to "jam to-day,"' Alice
objected.

'No, it can't,' said the Queen. 'It's jam every *other*
day: to-day isn't any *other* day, you know.'

'I don't understand you,' said Alice.   'It's dreadfully confusing!'

'That's the effect of living backwards,' the Queen said kindly: 'it always makes one a little giddy at first——'

'Living backwards!' Alice repeated in great astonishment.   'I never heard of such a thing!'

'——but there's one great advantage in it, that one's memory works both ways.'

'I'm sure *mine* only works one way,' Alice remarked. 'I can't remember things before they happen.'

'It's a poor sort of memory that only works backwards,' the Queen remarked.

'What sort of things do *you* remember best?' Alice ventured to ask.

'Oh, things that happened the week after next,' the Queen replied in a careless tone. 'For instance, now,' she went on, sticking a large piece of plaster on her finger as she spoke, 'there's the King's Messenger. He's in prison now, being punished: and the trial doesn't even begin till next Wednesday: and of course the crime comes last of all.'

'Suppose he never commits the crime?' said Alice.

'That would be all the better, wouldn't it?' the Queen said, as she bound the plaster round her finger with a bit of ribbon.

Alice felt there was no denying *that*. 'Of course it would be all the better,' she said: 'but it wouldn't be all the better his being punished.'

'You're wrong *there*, at any rate,' said the Queen: ' were *you* ever punished?'

'Only for faults,' said Alice.

'And you were all the better for it, I know!' the Queen said triumphantly.

'Yes, but then I *had* done the things I was punished for,' said Alice: 'that makes all the difference.'

'But if you *hadn't* done them,' the Queen said, 'that would have been better still; better, and better, and better!' Her voice went higher with each 'better,' till it got quite to a squeak at last.

Alice was just beginning to say 'There's a mistake somewhere——,' when the Queen began screaming, so loud that she had to leave the sentence unfinished. 'Oh, oh, oh!' shouted the Queen, shaking her hand about as if she wanted to shake it off. 'My finger's bleeding! Oh, oh, oh, oh!'

Her screams were so exactly like the whistle of a steam-engine, that Alice had to hold both her hands over her ears.

'What *is* the matter?' she said, as soon as there was a chance of making herself heard. 'Have you pricked your finger?'

'I haven't pricked it *yet*,' the Queen said, 'but I soon shall—oh, oh, oh!'

'When do you expect to do it?' Alice asked, feeling very much inclined to laugh.

'When I fasten my shawl again,' the poor Queen groaned out: 'the brooch will come undone directly. Oh, oh!' As she said the words the brooch flew open, and the Queen clutched wildly at it, and tried to clasp it again.

'Take care!' cried Alice. 'You're holding it all crooked!' And she caught at the brooch; but it was too late: the pin had slipped, and the Queen had pricked her finger.

'That accounts for the bleeding, you see,' she said to

Alice with a smile. 'Now you understand the way things happen here.'

'But why don't you scream now?' Alice asked, holding her hands ready to put over her ears again.

'Why, I've done all the screaming already,' said the Queen. 'What would be the good of having it all over again?'

By this time it was getting light. 'The crow must have flown away, I think,' said Alice: 'I'm so glad it's gone. I thought it was the night coming on.'

'I wish *I* could manage to be glad!' the Queen said. 'Only I never can remember the rule. You must be very happy, living in this wood, and being glad whenever you like!'

'Only it is so *very* lonely here!' Alice said in a melancholy voice; and at the thought of her loneliness two large tears came rolling down her cheeks.

'Oh, don't go on like that!' cried the poor Queen, wringing her hands in despair. 'Consider what a great girl you are. Consider what a long way you've come to-day. Consider what o'clock it is. Consider anything, only don't cry!'

Alice could not help laughing at this, even in the midst of her tears. 'Can *you* keep from crying by considering things?' she asked.

'That's the way it's done,' the Queen said with great decision: 'nobody can do two things at once, you know. Let's consider your age to begin with—how old are you?'

'I'm seven and a half exactly.'

'You needn't say "exactually,"' the Queen remarked: 'I can believe it without that. Now I'll give *you* something to believe. I'm just one hundred and one, five months and a day.'

'I can't believe *that*!" said Alice.

'Can't you?' the Queen said in a pitying tone. 'Try again: draw a long breath, and shut your eyes.'

Alice laughed. 'There's no use trying,' she said: 'one *can't* believe impossible things.'

'I dare say you haven't had much practice,' said the Queen. 'When I was your age, I always did it for half an hour a day. Why, sometimes I've believed as many as six impossible things before breakfast. There goes the shawl again!'

The brooch had come undone as she spoke, and a sudden gust of wind blew her shawl across a little brook. The Queen spread out her arms again, and went flying after it, and this time succeeded in catching it for herself. 'I've got it!' she cried in a triumphant tone. 'Now you shall see me pin it on again, all by myself!'

'Then I hope your finger is better now?' Alice said very politely, as she crossed the little brook after the Queen.

*   *   *   *   *
*   *   *   *
*   *   *   *   *

'Oh, much better!' cried the Queen, her voice rising into a squeak as she went on. 'Much be-etter! Be-etter! Be-e-e-etter! Be-e-ehh!' The last word ended in a long bleat, so like a sheep that Alice quite started.

She looked at the Queen, who seemed to have suddenly wrapped herself up in wool. Alice rubbed her eyes, and looked again. She couldn't make out what had happened at all. Was she in a shop? And was that really —was it really a *sheep* that was sitting on the other side of the counter? Rub as she would, she could make nothing more of it: she was in a little dark shop, leaning with her elbows on the counter, and opposite to her was an old Sheep, sitting in an arm-chair knitting, and every now and then leaving off to look at her through a great pair of spectacles.

'What is it you want to buy?' the Sheep said at last, looking up for a moment from her knitting.

'I don't *quite* know yet' Alice said very gently. 'I should like to look all round me first, if I might.'

'You may look in front of you, and on both sides, if you like,' said the Sheep; 'but you can't look *all* round you—unless you've got eyes at the back of your head.'

But these, as it happened, Alice had *not* got; so she contented herself with turning round, looking at the shelves as she came to them.

The shop seemed to be full of all manner of curious things—but the oddest part of it all was, that whenever she looked hard at any shelf, to make out exactly what it had on it, that particular shelf was always quite empty:

though the others round it were crowded as full as they could hold.

'Things flow about so here!' she said at last in a plaintive tone, after she had spent a minute or so in vainly pursuing a large bright thing, that looked sometimes like a doll and sometimes like a work-box, and was always in the shelf next above the one she was looking at. 'And this one is the most provoking of all—but I'll tell you what——' she added, as a sudden thought struck her, 'I'll follow it up to the very top shelf of all. It'll puzzle it to go through the ceiling, I expect!'

But even this plan failed: the 'thing' went through the ceiling as quietly as possible, as if it were quite used to it.

'Are you a child or a teetotum?' the Sheep said, as she took up another pair of needles. 'You'll make me giddy soon, if you go on turning round like that.' She was now working with fourteen pairs at once, and Alice couldn't help looking at her in great astonishment.

'How *can* she knit with so many?' the puzzled child thought to herself. 'She gets more and more like a porcupine every minute!'

'Can you row?' the Sheep asked, handing her a pair of knitting-needles as she spoke.

'Yes, a little—but not on land—and not with needles——' Alice was beginning to say, when suddenly the needles turned into oars in her hands, and she found they were in a little boat, gliding along between banks: so there was nothing for it but to do her best.

'Feather!' cried the Sheep, as she took up another pair of needles.

This didn't sound like a remark that needed any answer, so Alice said nothing, but pulled away. There was something very queer about the water, she thought, as every now and then the oars got fast in it, and would hardly come out again.

'Feather! Feather!' the Sheep cried again, taking more needles. 'You'll be catching a crab directly.'

'A dear little crab!' thought Alice. 'I should like that.'

'Didn't you hear me say "Feather"?' the Sheep cried angrily, taking up quite a bunch of needles.

'Indeed I did,' said Alice: 'you've said it very often—and very loud. Please, where *are* the crabs?'

'In the water, of course!' said the Sheep, sticking some of the needles into her hair, as her hands were full. 'Feather, I say!'

'*Why* do you say "Feather" so often?' Alice asked at last, rather vexed. 'I'm not a bird!'

'You are,' said the Sheep: 'you're a little goose.'

This offended Alice a little, so there was no more conversation for a minute or two, while the boat glided gently on, sometimes among beds of weeds (which made the oars stick fast in the water, worse than ever), and sometimes under trees, but always with the same tall river-banks frowning over their heads.

'Oh, please! There are some scented rushes!' Alice cried in a sudden transport of delight. 'There really are —and *such* beauties!'

'You needn't say "please" to *me* about 'em,' the Sheep said, without looking up from her knitting: 'I didn't put 'em there, and I'm not going to take 'em away.'

'No, but I meant—please, may we wait and pick some?' Alice pleaded. 'If you don't mind stopping the boat for a minute.'

'How am *I* to stop it?' said the Sheep. 'If you leave off rowing, it'll stop of itself.'

So the boat was left to drift down the stream as it would, till it glided gently in among the waving rushes. And then the little sleeves were carefully rolled up, and the little arms were plunged in elbow-deep, to get hold of the rushes a good long way down before breaking them off—and for a while Alice forgot all about the Sheep and the knitting, as she bent over the side of the boat, with just the ends of her tangled hair dipping into the water —while with bright eager eyes she caught at one bunch after another of the darling scented rushes.

'I only hope the boat won't tipple over!' she said to herself. 'Oh, *what* a lovely one! Only I couldn't quite reach it.' And it certainly *did* seem a little provoking ('almost as if it happened on purpose,' she thought) that, though she managed to pick plenty of beautiful rushes as the boat glided by, there was always a more lovely one that she couldn't reach.

'The prettiest are always further!' she said at last, with a sigh at the obstinacy of the rushes in growing so far off, as, with flushed cheeks and dripping hair and hands, she scrambled back into her place, and began to arrange her new-found treasures.

What mattered it to her just then that the rushes had begun to fade, and to lose all their scent and beauty, from the very moment that she picked them? Even real scented rushes, you know, last only a very little while— and these, being dream-rushes, melted away almost like snow, as they lay in heaps at her feet—but Alice hardly noticed this, there were so many other curious things to think about.

They hadn't gone much further before the blade of one of the oars got fast in the water and *wouldn't* come out again (so Alice explained it afterwards), and the consequence was that the handle of it caught her under the chin, and, in spite of a series of little shrieks of 'Oh, oh, oh!' from poor Alice, it swept her straight off the seat, and down among the heap of rushes.

However, she wasn't a bit hurt, and was soon up again: the Sheep went on with her knitting all the while, just as if nothing had happened. 'That was a nice crab you caught!' she remarked, as Alice got back into her place, very much relieved to find herself still in the boat.

'Was it?   I didn't see it,' said Alice, peeping cautiously over the side of the boat into the dark water.   'I wish it

hadn't let go—I should so like a little crab to take home with me!'   But the Sheep only laughed scornfully, and went on with her knitting.

'Are there many crabs here?' said Alice.

'Crabs, and all sorts of things,' said the Sheep: 'plenty of choice, only make up your mind.   Now, what *do* you want to buy?'

'To buy!' Alice echoed in a tone that was half astonished and half frightened—for the oars, and the boat, and the river, had vanished all in a moment, and she was back again in the little dark shop.

'I should like to buy an egg, please,' she said timidly. 'How do you sell them?'

'Fivepence farthing for one—twopence for two,' the Sheep replied.

'Then two are cheaper than one?' Alice said in a surprised tone, taking out her purse.

'Only you *must* eat them both, if you buy two,' said the Sheep.

'Then I'll have *one*, please,' said Alice, as she put the money down on the counter. For she thought to herself, 'They mightn't be at all nice, you know.'

The Sheep took the money, and put it away in a box: then she said, 'I never put things into people's hands—that would never do—you must get it for yourself.' And so saying, she went off to the other end of the shop, and set the egg upright on a shelf.

'I wonder *why* it wouldn't do?' thought Alice, as she groped her way among the tables and chairs, for the shop was very dark towards the end. 'The egg seems to get further away the more I walk towards it. Let me see, is this a chair? Why, it's got branches, I declare! How very odd to find trees growing here! And actually here's a little brook! Well, this is the very queerest shop I ever saw!'

So she went on, wondering more and more at every step, as everything turned into a tree the moment she came up to it, and she quite expected the egg to do the same.

CHAPTER VI

HUMPTY DUMPTY

HOWEVER, the egg only got larger and larger, and more and more human: when she had come within a few yards of it, she saw that it had eyes and a nose and mouth; and when she had come close to it, she saw clearly that it was HUMPTY DUMPTY himself. 'It can't be anybody else!' she said to herself. 'I'm as certain of it, as if his name were written all over his face!'

It might have been written a hundred times, easily, on that enormous face. Humpty Dumpty was sitting with his legs crossed, like a Turk, on the top of a high wall—such a narrow one that Alice quite wondered how he could keep his balance—and, as his eyes were steadily fixed in the opposite direction, and he didn't take the least notice of her, she thought he must be a stuffed figure.

'And how exactly like an egg he is!' she said aloud, standing with her hands ready to catch him, for she was every moment expecting him to fall.

'It's *very* provoking,' Humpty Dumpty said after a long silence, looking away from Alice as he spoke, 'to be called an egg—*very*!'

'I said you *looked* like an egg, Sir,' Alice gently explained. 'And some eggs are very pretty, you know,' she added, hoping to turn her remark into a sort of compliment.

'Some people,' said Humpty Dumpty, looking away from her as usual, 'have no more sense than a baby!'

Alice didn't know what to say to this: it wasn't at all like conversation, she thought, as he never said anything to *her*; in fact, his last remark was evidently addressed to a tree—so she stood and softly repeated to herself:

'*Humpty Dumpty sat on a wall:*
Humpty Dumpty had a great fall.
All the King's horses and all the King's men
Couldn't put Humpty Dumpty in his place again.'

'That last line is much too long for the poetry,' she added, almost out loud, forgetting that Humpty Dumpty would hear her.

'Don't stand chattering to yourself like that,' Humpty Dumpty said, looking at her for the first time, 'but tell me your name and your business.'

'My *name* is Alice, but——'

'It's a stupid name enough!' Humpty Dumpty interrupted impatiently. 'What does it mean?'

'*Must* a name mean something?' Alice asked doubtfully.

'Of course it must,' Humpty Dumpty said with a short laugh: '*my* name means the shape I am—and a good handsome shape it is, too. With a name like yours, you might be any shape, almost.'

'Why do you sit out here all alone?' said Alice, not wishing to begin an argument.

'Why, because there's nobody with me!' cried Humpty Dumpty. 'Did you think I didn't know the answer to *that*? Ask another.'

'Don't you think you'd be safer down on the ground?' Alice went on, not with any idea of making another riddle, but simply in her good-natured anxiety for the queer creature. 'That wall is so *very* narrow!'

'What tremendously easy riddles you ask!' Humpty Dumpty growled out. 'Of course I don't think so! Why, if ever I *did* fall off—which there's no chance of— but *if* I did——' Here he pursed up his lips, and looked so solemn and grand that Alice could hardly help laughing. '*If* I did fall,' he went on, '*the King has promised me*—ah, you may turn pale, if you like! You didn't think I was going to say that, did you? *The King has promised me—with his own mouth—to—to——*'

'To send all his horses and all his men,' Alice interrupted, rather unwisely.

'Now I declare that's too bad!' Humpty Dumpty cried, breaking into a sudden passion. 'You've been listening at doors—and behind trees—and down chimneys—or you couldn't have known it!'

'I haven't, indeed!' Alice said very gently. 'It's in a book.'

'Ah, well! They may write such things in a *book*,' Humpty Dumpty said in a calmer tone. 'That's what you call a History of England, that is. Now, take a good look at me! I'm one that has spoken to a King, *I* am: mayhap you'll never see such another: and to show you I'm not proud, you may shake hands with me!' And he grinned almost from ear to ear, as he leant forwards (and as nearly as possible fell off the wall in doing so) and offered Alice his hand. She watched him a little anxiously as she took it. 'If he smiled much more, the ends of his mouth might meet behind,' she thought: 'and then I don't know what would happen to his head! I'm afraid it would come off!'

'Yes, all his horses and all his men,' Humpty Dumpty went on. 'They'd pick me up again in a minute, *they* would! However, this conversation is going on a little too fast: let's go back to the last remark but one.'

'I'm afraid I can't quite remember it,' Alice said very politely.

'In that case we may start fresh,' said Humpty Dumpty, 'and it's my turn to choose a subject——' ('He talks about it just as if it was a game!' thought Alice.) 'So here's a question for you. How old did you say you were?'

Alice made a short calculation, and said 'Seven years and six months.'

See page 182

Humpty Dumpty leant forwards and offered Alice his hand

'Wrong!' Humpty Dumpty exclaimed triumphantly.
'You never said a word like it.'

'I thought you meant "How old *are* you?"' Alice
explained.

'If I'd meant that, I'd have said it,' said Humpty
Dumpty.

Alice didn't want to begin another argument, so she
said nothing.

'Seven years and six months!' Humpty Dumpty
repeated thoughtfully. 'An uncomfortable sort of age.
Now if you'd asked *my* advice, I'd have said "Leave off
at seven"—but it's too late now.'

'I never ask advice about growing,' Alice said indignantly.

'Too proud?' the other inquired.

Alice felt even more indignant at this suggestion. 'I
mean,' she said, 'that one can't help growing older.'

'*One* can't, perhaps,' said Humpty Dumpty, 'but *two*
can. With proper assistance, you might have left off
at seven.'

'What a beautiful belt you've got on!' Alice suddenly
remarked. (They had had quite enough of the subject
of age, she thought: and if they were really to take turns
in choosing subjects, it was her turn now.) 'At least,'
she corrected herself on second thoughts, 'a beautiful
cravat, I should have said—no, a belt, I mean—oh, I *beg*
your pardon!' she added in dismay, for Humpty Dumpty
looked thoroughly offended, and she began to wish she
hadn't chosen that subject. 'If only I knew,' she thought
to herself, 'which was neck and which was waist!'

Evidently Humpty Dumpty was very angry, though he
said nothing for a minute or two. When he *did* speak
again, it was in a deep growl.

'It is a—*most*—*provoking*—thing,' he said at last,
'when a person doesn't know a cravat from a belt!'

'I know it's very ignorant of me,' Alice replied, in so humble a tone that Humpty Dumpty relented.

'It's a cravat, child, and a beautiful one, as you say. It's a present from the White King and Queen. There now!'

'Is it really?' said Alice, quite pleased to find she *had* chosen a good subject, after all.

'They gave it me,' Humpty Dumpty continued thoughtfully, as he crossed one knee over the other and clasped his hands round it, '—for an un-birthday present.'

'I beg your pardon?' Alice said with a puzzled air.

'I'm not offended,' said Humpty Dumpty.

'I mean, what *is* an un-birthday present?'

'A present given when it isn't your birthday, of course.'

Alice considered a little. 'I like birthday presents best,' she said at last.

'You don't know what you're talking about!' cried Humpty Dumpty. 'How many days are there in a year?'

'Three hundred and sixty-five,' said Alice.

'And how many birthdays have you?'

'One.'

'And if you take one from three hundred and sixty-five, what remains?'

'Three hundred and sixty-four, of course.'

Humpty Dumpty looked doubtful. 'I'd rather see that done on paper,' he said.

Alice couldn't help smiling as she took out her memorandum-book, and worked the sum for him:

$$\frac{\begin{array}{r}365\\1\end{array}}{364}$$

Humpty Dumpty took the book, and looked at it very carefully. 'That *seems* to be done right——' he began.

'You're holding it upside down!' Alice interrupted.

'To be sure I was!' Humpty Dumpty said gaily, as she

turned it round for him. 'I thought it looked a little queer. As I was saying, that *seems* to be done right—though I haven't time to look it over thoroughly just now—and that shows that there are three hundred and sixty-four days when you might get un-birthday presents——'

'Certainly,' said Alice.

'And only *one* for birthday presents, you know. There's glory for you!'

'I don't know what you mean by "glory,"' Alice said.

Humpty Dumpty smiled contemptuously. 'Of course you don't—till I tell you. I meant "there's a nice knock-down argument for you!"'

'But "glory" doesn't mean "a nice knock-down argument,"' Alice objected.

'When *I* use a word,' Humpty Dumpty said in rather a scornful tone, 'it means just what I choose it to mean—neither more nor less.'

'The question is,' said Alice, 'whether you *can* make words mean different things.'

'The question is,' said Humpty Dumpty, 'which is to be master—that's all.'

Alice was too much puzzled to say anything, so after a minute Humpty Dumpty began again. 'They've a temper, some of them—particularly verbs, they're the proudest—adjectives you can do anything with, but not verbs—however, *I* can manage the whole lot! Impenetrability! That's what *I* say!'

'Would you tell me, please,' said Alice, 'what that means?'

'Now you talk like a reasonable child,' said Humpty Dumpty, looking very much pleased. 'I meant by "impenetrability" that we've had enough of that subject, and it would be just as well if you'd mention what you mean to do next, as I suppose you don't intend to stop here all the rest of your life.'

'That's a great deal to make one word mean,' Alice said in a thoughtful tone.

'When I make a word do a lot of work like that,' said Humpty Dumpty, 'I always pay it extra.'

'Oh!' said Alice.   She was too much puzzled to make any other remark.

'Ah, you should see 'em come round me of a Saturday night,' Humpty Dumpty went on, wagging his head gravely from side to side: 'for to get their wages, you know.'

(Alice didn't venture to ask what he paid them with; and so you see I can't tell *you*.)

'You seem very clever at explaining words, Sir,' said Alice.   'Would you kindly tell me the meaning of the poem "Jabberwocky"?'

'Let's hear it,' said Humpty Dumpty.   'I can explain all the poems that ever were invented—and a good many that haven't been invented just yet.'

This sounded very hopeful, so Alice repeated the first verse:

> *"Twas brillig, and the slithy toves*
> *Did gyre and gimble in the wabe:*
> *All mimsy were the borogoves,*
> *And the mome raths outgrabe.'*

'That's enough to begin with,' Humpty Dumpty interrupted: 'there are plenty of hard words there. "*Brillig*" means four o'clock in the afternoon—the time when you begin *broiling* things for dinner.'

'That'll do very well,' said Alice: 'and "*slithy*"?'

'Well, "*slithy*" means "lithe and slimy." "Lithe" is the same as "active." You see it's like a portmanteau ——there are two meanings packed up into one word.'

'I see it now,' Alice remarked thoughtfully: 'and what are "*toves*"?'

'Well, "*toves*" are something like badgers—they're something like lizards—and they're something like corkscrews.'

'They must be very curious creatures.'

'They are that,' said Humpty Dumpty: 'also they make their nests under sun-dials—also they live on cheese.'

'And what's to "*gyre*" and to "*gimble*"?'

'To "*gyre*" is to go round and round like a gyroscope. To "*gimble*" is to make holes like a gimlet.'

'And "*the wabe*" is the grass plot round a sun-dial, I suppose?' said Alice, surprised at her own ingenuity.

'Of course it is. It's called "*wabe*," you know, because it goes a long way before it, and a long way behind it——'

'And a long way beyond it on each side,' Alice added.

'Exactly so. Well then, "*mimsy*" is "flimsy and miserable" (there's another portmanteau for you). And a "*borogove*" is a thin shabby-looking bird with its feathers sticking out all round—something like a live mop.'

'And then "*mome raths*"?' said Alice. 'If I'm not giving you too much trouble.'

'Well, a "*rath*" is a sort of green pig: but "*mome*" I'm not certain about. I think it's short for "from home"—meaning that they'd lost their way, you know.'

'And what does "*outgrabe*" mean?'

'Well, "*outgribing*" is something between bellowing and whistling, with a kind of sneeze in the middle: however, you'll hear it done, maybe—down in the wood yonder—and when you've once heard it you'll be *quite* content. Who's been repeating all that hard stuff to you?'

'I read it in a book,' said Alice. 'But I had some poetry repeated to me, much easier than that, by— Tweedledee, I think.'

'As to poetry, you know,' said Humpty Dumpty, stretching out one of his great hands, '*I* can repeat poetry as well as other folk if it comes to that——'

'Oh, it needn't come to that!' Alice hastily said, hoping to keep him from beginning.

'The piece I'm going to repeat,' he went on without noticing her remark, 'was written entirely for your amusement.'

Alice felt that in that case she really *ought* to listen to it, so she sat down, and said 'Thank you' rather sadly.

'*In winter, when the fields are white,*
I sing this song for your delight——

only I don't sing it,' he explained.

'I see you don't,' said Alice.

'If you can *see* whether I'm singing or not, you've sharper eyes than most,' Humpty Dumpty remarked severely.   Alice was silent.

'*In spring, when woods are getting green,*
I'll try and tell you what I mean.'

'Thank you very much,' said Alice.

'*In summer, when the days are long,*
Perhaps you'll understand my song :

In autumn, when the leaves are brown,
Take pen and ink and write it down.'

'I will, if I can remember it so long,' said Alice.

'You needn't go on making remarks like that,' Humpty Dumpty said: 'they're not sensible, and they put me out.'

'*I sent a message to the fish:*
I told them " This is what I wish."

The little fishes of the sea,
They sent an answer back to me.

The little fishes' answer was
" We cannot do it, Sir, because——"'

'I'm afraid I don't quite understand,' said Alice.

'It gets easier further on,' Humpty Dumpty replied.

'*I sent to them again to say*
" It will be better to obey."

The fishes answered with a grin,
" Why, what a temper you are in!"

I told them once, I told them twice :
They would not listen to advice.

I took a kettle large and new,
Fit for the deed I had to do.

My heart went hop, my heart went thump ;
I filled the kettle at the pump.

Then someone came to me and said
" The little fishes are in bed."

I said to him, I said it plain,
" Then you must wake them up again."

I said it very loud and clear ;
I went and shouted in his ear.'

Humpty Dumpty raised his voice almost to a scream as

he repeated this verse, and Alice thought with a shudder,
'I wouldn't have been the messenger for *anything*!'

> *'But he was very stiff and proud;*
> *He said "You needn't shout so loud!"*

> *And he was very proud and stiff;*
> *He said "I'd go and wake them, if——"*

> *I took a corkscrew from the shelf:*
> *I went to wake them up myself.*

> *And when I found the door was locked,*
> *I pulled and pushed and kicked and knocked.*

> *And when I found the door was shut,*
> *I tried to turn the handle, but——'*

There was a long pause.

'Is that all?' Alice timidly asked.

'That's all,' said Humpty Dumpty. 'Good-bye.'

This was rather sudden, Alice thought: but, after such
a *very* strong hint that she ought to be going, she felt
that it would hardly be civil to stay.   So she held out her
hand. 'Good-bye, till we meet again!' she said as
cheerfully as she could.

'I shouldn't know you again if we *did* meet,' Humpty
Dumpty replied in a discontented tone, giving her one
of his fingers to shake; 'you're so exactly like other
people.'

'The *face* is what one goes by, generally,' Alice
remarked in a thoughtful tone.

'That's just what I complain of,' said Humpty Dumpty.
'Your face is the same as everybody has—the two eyes,
so——' (marking their places in the air with his thumb)
'nose in the middle, mouth under.   It's always the same.
Now if you had the two eyes on the same side of the

nose, for instance—or the mouth at the top—that would be *some* help.'

'It wouldn't look nice,' Alice objected.   But Humpty Dumpty only shut his eyes and said 'Wait till you've tried.'

Alice waited a minute to see if he would speak again, but as he never opened his eyes or took any further notice of her, she said 'Good-bye!' once more, and, on getting no answer to this, she quietly walked away: but she couldn't help saying to herself as she went, 'Of all the unsatisfactory——' (she repeated this aloud, as it was a great comfort to have such a long word to say) 'of all the unsatisfactory people I *ever* met——' She never finished the sentence, for at this moment a heavy crash shook the forest from end to end.

CHAPTER VII

THE LION AND THE UNICORN

THE next moment soldiers came running through the wood, at first in twos and threes, then ten or twenty together, and at last in such crowds that they seemed to fill the whole forest.   Alice got behind a tree, for fear of being run over, and watched them go by.

She thought that in all her life she had never seen soldiers so uncertain on their feet: they were always tripping over something or other, and whenever one went down, several more always fell over him, so that the ground was soon covered with little heaps of men.

Then came the horses. Having four feet, these managed rather better than the foot-soldiers: but even *they* stumbled now and then; and it seemed to be a regular rule that, whenever a horse stumbled, the rider fell off instantly. The confusion got worse every

moment, and Alice was very glad to get into an open place, where she found the White King seated on the ground, busily writing in his memorandum-book.

'I've sent them all!' the King cried in a tone of delight, on seeing Alice. 'Did you happen to meet any soldiers, my dear, as you came through the wood?'

'Yes, I did,' said Alice: 'several thousand, I should think.'

'Four thousand two hundred and seven, that's the exact number,' the King said, referring to his book. 'I couldn't send all the horses, you know, because two of them are wanted in the game. And I haven't sent the two Messengers, either. They're both gone to the town. Just look along the road, and tell me if you can see either of them.'

'I see nobody on the road,' said Alice.

'I only wish I had such eyes,' the King remarked in a fretful tone. 'To be able to see Nobody! And at that distance too! Why, it's as much as I can do to see real people, by this light!'

All this was lost on Alice, who was still looking intently along the road, shading her eyes with one hand. 'I see somebody now!' she exclaimed at last. 'But he's coming very slowly—and what curious attitudes he goes into!' (For the Messenger kept skipping up and down, and wriggling like an eel, as he came along, with his great hands spread out like fans on each side.)

'Not at all,' said the King. 'He's an Anglo-Saxon Messenger—and those are Anglo-Saxon attitudes. He only does them when he's happy. His name is Haigha.' (He pronounced it so as to rhyme with 'mayor.')

'I love my love with an H,' Alice couldn't help beginning, 'because he is Happy. I hate him with an H, because he is Hideous. I feed him with—with—with Ham-sandwiches and Hay. His name is Haigha, and he lives——'

'He lives on the Hill,' the King remarked simply, without the least idea that he was joining in the game, while Alice was still hesitating for the name of a town beginning with H. 'The other Messenger's called Hatta. I must have two, you know—to come and go. One to come, and one to go.'

'I beg your pardon?' said Alice.

'It isn't respectable to beg,' said the King.

'I only meant that I didn't understand,' said Alice. 'Why one to come and one to go?'

'Don't I tell you?' the King repeated impatiently. 'I must have *two*—to fetch and carry. One to fetch, and one to carry.'

At this moment the Messenger arrived: he was far too much out of breath to say a word, and could only wave his hands about, and make the most fearful faces at the poor King.

'This young lady loves you with an H,' the King said, introducing Alice in the hope of turning off the Messenger's attention from himself—but it was no use—the Anglo-Saxon attitudes only got more extraordinary every moment, while the great eyes rolled wildly from side to side.

'You alarm me!' said the King. 'I feel faint—Give me a ham sandwich!'

On which the Messenger, to Alice's great amusement, opened a bag that hung round his neck, and handed a sandwich to the King, who devoured it greedily.

'Another sandwich!' said the King.

'There's nothing but hay left now,' the Messenger said, peeping into the bag.

'Hay, then,' the King faintly murmured.

Alice was glad to see that it revived him a good deal. 'There's nothing like eating hay when you're faint,' he remarked to her, as he munched away.

'I should think throwing cold water over you would be better,' Alice suggested: '—or some sal-volatile.'

'I didn't say there was nothing *better*,' the King replied. 'I said there was nothing *like* it.' Which Alice did not venture to deny.

'Who did you pass on the road?' the King went on, holding out his hand to the Messenger for some more hay.

'Nobody,' said the Messenger.

'Quite right,' said the King: 'this young lady saw him too. So of course Nobody walks slower than you.'

'I do my best,' the Messenger said in a sullen tone. 'I'm sure nobody walks much faster than I do!'

'He can't do that,' said the King, 'or else he'd have been here first. However, now you've got your breath, you may tell us what's happened in the town.'

'I'll whisper it,' said the Messenger, putting his hands to his mouth in the shape of a trumpet and stooping so as to get close to the King's ear. Alice was sorry for this, as she wanted to hear the news too. However, instead of whispering, he simply shouted at the top of his voice 'They're at it again!'

'Do you call *that* a whisper!' cried the poor King, jumping up and shaking himself. 'If you do such a thing again I'll have you buttered! It went through and through my head like an earthquake!'

'It would have to be a very tiny earthquake!' thought Alice. 'Who are at it again?' she ventured to ask.

'Why, the Lion and the Unicorn, of course,' said the King.

'Fighting for the crown?'

'Yes to be sure,' said the King: 'and the best of the joke is, that's it's *my* crown all the while! Let's run and see them.' And they trotted off, Alice repeating to herself, as she ran, the words of the old song:

'The Lion and the Unicorn were fighting for the crown;
The Lion beat the Unicorn all round the town.
Some gave them white bread and some gave them brown;
Some gave them plum-cake and drummed them out of town.'

'And does—the one—that wins—get the crown?' she asked, as well as she could, for the long run was putting her quite out of breath.

'Dear me, no!' said the King. 'What an idea!'

'Would you—be good enough——' Alice panted out, after running a little further, 'to stop a minute—just to get—one's breath?'

'I'm *good* enough,' the King said, 'only I'm not strong enough. You see, a minute goes by so fearfully quick. You might as well try to stop a Bandersnatch!'

Alice had no more breath for talking, so they trotted on in silence, till they came in sight of a great crowd, in the middle of which the Lion and Unicorn were fighting. They were in such a cloud of dust, that at first Alice could not make out which was which: but she soon managed to distinguish the Unicorn by his horn.

They placed themselves close to where Hatta, the other Messenger, was standing watching the fight, with a cup of tea in one hand and a piece of bread and butter in the other.

'He's only just out of prison, and he hadn't finished his tea when he was sent in,' Haigha whispered to Alice: 'and they only give them oyster-shells in there—so you see he's very hungry and thirsty. How are you, dear child?' he went on, putting his arm affectionately round Hatta's neck.

Hatta looked round and nodded, and went on with his bread and butter.

'Were you happy in prison, dear child?' said Haigha.

Hatta looked round once more, and this time a tear or two trickled down his cheek: but not a word would he say.

'Speak, can't you!' Haigha cried impatiently. But Hatta only munched away, and drank some more tea.

'Speak, won't you!' cried the King. 'How are they getting on with the fight?'

Hatta made a desperate effort, and swallowed a large piece of bread and butter. 'They're getting on very

well,' he said in a choking voice: 'each of them has been
down about eighty-seven times.'

'Then I suppose they'll soon bring the white bread
and the brown?' Alice ventured to remark.

'It's waiting for 'em now,' said Hatta: 'this is a bit of
it as I'm eating.'

There was a pause in the fight just then, and the Lion
and the Unicorn sat down, panting, while the King called
out 'Ten minutes allowed for refreshments!' Haigha
and Hatta set to work at once, carrying round trays of
white and brown bread. Alice took a piece to taste, but
it was *very* dry.

'I don't think they'll fight any more to-day,' the King
said to Hatta: 'go and order the drums to begin.' And
Hatta went bounding away like a grasshopper.

For a minute or two Alice stood silently watching him.
Suddenly she brightened up. 'Look, look!' she cried,
pointing eagerly. 'There's the White Queen running

See page 195

The messenger handed a sandwich to the King

across the country! She came flying out of the wood over yonder—How fast those Queens *can* run!'

'There's some enemy after her, no doubt,' the King said, without even looking round. 'That wood's full of them.'

'But aren't you going to run and help her?' Alice asked, very much surprised at his taking it so quietly.

'No use, no use!' said the King. 'She runs so fearfully quick. You might as well try to catch a Bandersnatch! But I'll make a memorandum about her, if you like—She's a dear good creature,' he repeated softly to himself, as he opened his memorandum-book. 'Do you spell "creature" with a double "e"?'

At this moment the Unicorn sauntered by them, with his hands in his pockets. 'I had the best of it this time!' he said to the King, just glancing at him as he passed.

'A little—a little,' the King replied, rather nervously. 'You shouldn't have run him through with your horn, you know.'

'It didn't hurt him,' the Unicorn said carelessly, and he was going on, when his eye happened to fall upon Alice: he turned round instantly, and stood for some time looking at her with an air of the deepest disgust.

'What—is—this?' he said at last.

'This is a child!' Haigha replied eagerly, coming in front of Alice to introduce her, and spreading out both his hands towards her in an Anglo-Saxon attitude. 'We only found it to-day. It's as large as life, and twice as natural!'

'I always thought they were fabulous monsters!' said the Unicorn. 'Is it alive?'

'It can talk,' said Haigha, solemnly.

The Unicorn looked dreamily at Alice, and said 'Talk, child.'

Alice could not help her lips curling up into a smile
as she began: 'Do you know, I always thought Unicorns
were fabulous monsters, too! I never saw one alive
before!'

'Well, now that we *have* seen each other,' said the
Unicorn, 'if you'll believe in me, I'll believe in you. Is
that a bargain?'

'Yes, if you like,' said Alice.

'Come, fetch out the plum-cake, old man!' the Unicorn
went on, turning from her to the King. 'None of your
brown bread for me!'

'Certainly — certainly!' the King muttered, and
beckoned to Haigha. 'Open the bag!' he whispered.
'Quick! Not that one—that's full of hay!'

Haigha took a large cake out of the bag, and gave it to
Alice to hold, while he got out a dish and carving-knife.
How they all came out of it Alice couldn't guess. It was
just like a conjuring trick, she thought.

The Lion had joined them while this was going on: he
looked very tired and sleepy, and his eyes were half shut.
'What's this!' he said, blinking lazily at Alice, and
speaking in a deep hollow tone that sounded like the
tolling of a great bell.

'Ah, what *is* it, now?' the Unicorn cried eagerly.
'You'll never guess! *I* couldn't.'

The Lion looked at Alice wearily. 'Are you animal—
or vegetable—or mineral?' he said, yawning at every
other word.

'It's a fabulous monster!' the Unicorn cried out, before
Alice could reply.

'Then hand round the plum-cake, Monster,' the Lion
said, lying down and putting his chin on his paws. 'And
sit down, both of you' (to the King and the Unicorn):
'fair play with the cake, you know!'

The King was evidently very uncomfortable at having

to sit down between the two great creatures: but there
was no other place for him.

'What a fight we might have for the crown, *now*!' the
Unicorn said, looking slyly up at the crown, which the
poor King was nearly shaking off his head, he trembled
so much.

'I should win easy,' said the Lion.

'I'm not so sure of that,' said the Unicorn.

'Why, I beat you all round the town, you chicken!'
the Lion replied angrily, half getting up as he spoke.

Here the King interrupted, to prevent the quarrel going
on: he was very nervous, and his voice quite quivered.
'All round the town?' he said. 'That's a good long
way. Did you go by the old bridge, or the market-place?
You get the best view by the old bridge.'

'I'm sure I don't know,' the Lion growled out as he
lay down again. 'There was too much dust to see anything. What a time the Monster is, cutting up that
cake!'

Alice had seated herself on the bank of a little brook, with the great dish on her knees, and was sawing away diligently with the knife. 'It's very provoking!' she said, in reply to the Lion (she was getting quite used to being called "the Monster"). 'I've cut off several slices already, but they will always join on again!'

'You don't know how to manage Looking-glass cakes,' the Unicorn remarked. 'Hand it round first, and cut it afterwards.'

This sounded nonsense, but Alice very obediently got up, and carried the dish round, and the cake divided itself into three pieces as she did so. '*Now* cut it up,' said the Lion, as she returned to her place with the empty dish.

'I say, this isn't fair!' cried the Unicorn, as Alice sat with the knife in her hand, very much puzzled how to begin. 'The Monster has given the Lion twice as much as me!'

'She's kept none for herself, anyhow,' said the Lion. 'Do you like plum-cake, Monster?'

But, before Alice could answer him, the drums began.

Where the noise came from, she couldn't make out: the air seemed full of it, and it rang through and through her head till she felt quite deafened. She started to her feet, and in her terror she sprang across

$$* \quad * \quad * \quad * \quad *$$
$$* \quad * \quad * \quad *$$
$$* \quad * \quad * \quad * \quad *$$

the brook, and had just time to see the Lion and Unicorn rise to their feet, with angry looks at being interrupted in their feast, before she dropped to her knees, and put her hands over her ears, vainly trying to shut out the dreadful uproar.

'If *that* doesn't "drum them out of town,"' she thought to herself, 'nothing ever will!'

CHAPTER VIII

'IT'S MY OWN INVENTION'

AFTER a while the noise seemed gradually to die away, till all was dead silence, and Alice lifted up her head in some alarm. There was no one to be seen, and her first thought was that she must have been dreaming about the Lion and the Unicorn and those queer Anglo-Saxon Messengers. However, there was the great dish still lying at her feet, on which she had tried to cut the plum cake, 'So I wasn't dreaming, after all,' she said to herself, 'unless—unless we're all part of the same dream. Only I do hope it's *my* dream, and not the Red King's! I don't like belonging to another person's dream,' she went on in a rather complaining tone: 'I've a great mind to go and wake him, and see what happens!'

At this moment her thoughts were interrupted by a

loud shouting of 'Ahoy! Ahoy! Check!' and a Knight, dressed in crimson armour, came galloping down upon her, brandishing a great club. Just as he reached her, the horse stopped suddenly: 'You're my prisoner!' the Knight cried, as he tumbled off his horse.

Startled as she was, Alice was more frightened for him than for herself at the moment, and watched him with some anxiety as he mounted again. As soon as he was comfortably in the saddle, he began once more 'You're my——' but here another voice broke in 'Ahoy! Ahoy! Check!' and Alice looked round in some surprise for the new enemy.

This time it was a White Knight. He drew up at Alice's side, and tumbled off his horse just as the Red Knight had done: then he got on again, and the two Knights sat and looked at each other without speaking. Alice looked from one to the other in some bewilderment.

'She's *my* prisoner, you know!' the Red Knight said at last.

'Yes, but then *I* came and rescued her!' the White Knight replied.

'Well, we must fight for her, then,' said the Red Knight, as he took up his helmet (which hung from the saddle, and was something the shape of a horse's head), and put it on.

'You will observe the Rules of Battle, of course?' the White Knight remarked, putting on his helmet too.

'I always do,' said the Red Knight, and they began banging away at each other with such fury that Alice got behind a tree to be out of the way of the blows.

'I wonder, now, what the Rules of Battle are,' she said to herself, as she watched the fight, timidly peeping out from her hiding-place: 'one Rule seems to be that, if one Knight hits the other, he knocks him off his horse, and if he misses, he tumbles off himself—and another Rule

seems to be that they hold their clubs in their arms, as if
they were Punch and Judy.   What a noise they make
when they tumble.   Just like fire-irons falling into the
fender!   And how quiet the horses are!   They let them
get on and off them just as if they were tables!'

Another Rule of Battle, that Alice had not noticed,
seemed to be that they always fell on their heads, and the
battle ended with their both falling off in this way, side
by side: when they got up again, they shook hands, and
then the Red Knight mounted and galloped off.

'It was a glorious victory, wasn't it?' said the White
Knight, as he came up panting.

'I don't know,' Alice said doubtfully.   'I don't want
to be anybody's prisoner.   I want to be a Queen.'

'So you will, when you've crossed the next brook,' said the White Knight. 'I'll see you safe to the end of the wood—and then I must go back, you know. That's the end of my move.'

'Thank you very much,' said Alice. 'May I help you off with your helmet?' It was evidently more than he could manage by himself; however, she managed to shake him out of it at last.

'Now one can breathe more easily,' said the Knight, putting back his shaggy hair with both hands, and turning his gentle face and large mild eyes to Alice. She thought she had never seen such a strange-looking soldier in all her life.

He was dressed in tin armour, which seemed to fit him very badly, and he had a queer little deal box fastened across his shoulders upside-down, and with the lid hanging open. Alice looked at it with great curiosity.

'I see you're admiring my little box,' the Knight said in a friendly tone. 'It's my own invention—to keep clothes and sandwiches in. You see I carry it upside-down, so that the rain can't get in.'

'But the things can get *out*,' Alice gently remarked. 'Do you know the lid's open?'

'I didn't know it,' the Knight said, a shade of vexation passing over his face. 'Then all the things must have fallen out! And the box is no use without them.' He unfastened it as he spoke, and was just going to throw it into the bushes, when a sudden thought seemed to strike him, and he hung it carefully on a tree. 'Can you guess why I did that?' he said to Alice.

Alice shook her head.

'In hopes some bees may make a nest in it—then I should get the honey.'

'But you've got a bee-hive—or something like one—fastened to the saddle,' said Alice.

'Yes, it's a very good bee-hive,' the Knight said in a discontented tone, 'one of the best kind. But not a single bee has come near it yet. And the other thing is a mouse-trap. I suppose the mice keep the bees out—or the bees keep the mice out, I don't know which.'

'I was wondering what the mouse-trap was for,' said Alice. 'It isn't very likely there would be any mice on the horse's back.'

'Not very likely, perhaps,' said the Knight; 'but, if they *do* come, I don't choose to have them running all about.'

'You see,' he went on after a pause, 'it's as well to be provided for *everything*. That's the reason the horse has anklets round his feet.'

'But what are they for?' Alice asked in a tone of great curiosity.

'To guard against the bites of sharks,' the Knight replied. 'It's an invention of my own. And now help me on. I'll go with you to the end of the wood—What's that dish for?'

'It's meant for plum-cake,' said Alice.

'We'd better take it with us,' the Knight said. 'It'll come in handy if we find any plum-cake. Help me to get it into this bag.'

This took a long time to manage, though Alice held the bag open very carefully because the Knight was so *very* awkward in putting in the dish: the first two or three times that he tried he fell in himself instead. 'It's rather a tight fit, you see,' he said, as they got it in at last; 'there are so many candlesticks in the bag.' And he hung it to the saddle, which was already loaded with bunches of carrots, and fire-irons, and many other things.

'I hope you've got your hair well fastened on?' he continued, as they set off.

'Only in the usual way,' Alice said, smiling.

'That's hardly enough,' he said, anxiously. 'You see, the wind is so *very* strong here. It's as strong as soup.'

'Have you invented a plan for keeping one's hair from being blown off?' Alice inquired.

'Not yet,' said the Knight. 'But I've got a plan for keeping it from *falling* off.'

'I should like to hear it very much.'

'First you take an upright stick,' said the Knight. 'Then you make your hair creep up it, like a fruit-tree. Now the reason hair falls off is because it hangs *down*— things never fall *upwards*, you know. It's my own invention. You may try it if you like.'

It didn't sound a comfortable plan, Alice thought, and for a few minutes she walked on in silence, puzzling over the idea, and every now and then stopping to help the poor Knight, who certainly was *not* a good rider.

Whenever the horse stopped (which it did very often), he fell off in front; and whenever it went on again (which it generally did rather suddenly), he fell off behind. Otherwise he kept on pretty well, except that he had a habit of now and then falling off sideways; and as he generally did this on the side on which Alice was walking, she soon found that it was the best plan not to walk *quite* close to the horse.

'I'm afraid you've not had much practice in riding,' she ventured to say, as she was helping him up from his fifth tumble.

The Knight looked very much surprised, and a little offended at the remark. 'What makes you say that?' he asked, as he scrambled back into the saddle, keeping hold of Alice's hair with one hand, to save himself from falling over on the other side.

'Because people don't fall off quite so often, when they've had much practice.'

'I've had plenty of practice,' the Knight said very bravely: 'plenty of practice!'

Alice could think of nothing better to say than 'Indeed?' but she said it as heartily as she could. They went on a little way in silence after this, the Knight with his eyes shut, muttering to himself, and Alice watching anxiously for the next tumble.

'The great art of riding,' the Knight suddenly began in a loud voice, waving his right arm as he spoke, 'is to keep——' Here the sentence ended as suddenly as it had begun, as the Knight fell heavily on the top of his head exactly in the path where Alice was walking. She was quite frightened this time, and said in an anxious tone, as she picked him up, 'I hope no bones are broken?'

'None to speak of,' the Knight said, as if he didn't mind breaking two or three of them. 'The great art of riding, as I was saying, is—to keep your balance. Like this, you know——'

He let go the bridle, and stretched out both his arms to show Alice what he meant, and this time he fell flat on his back, right under the horse's feet.

'Plenty of practice!' he went on repeating, all the time that Alice was getting him on his feet again. 'Plenty of practice!'

'It's too ridiculous!' cried Alice, getting quite out of patience. 'You ought to have a wooden horse on wheels, that you ought!'

'Does that kind go smoothly?' the Knight asked in a tone of great interest, clasping his arms round the horse's neck as he spoke, just in time to save himself from tumbling off again.

'Much more smoothly than a live horse,' Alice said, with a little scream of laughter, in spite of all she could do to prevent it.

'I'll get one,' the Knight said thoughtfully to himself. 'One or two—several.'

There was a short silence after this; then the Knight went on again. 'I'm a great hand at inventing things. Now, I dare say you noticed, the last time you picked me up, that I was looking thoughtful?'

'You *were* a little grave,' said Alice.

'Well, just then I was inventing a new way of getting over a gate—would you like to hear it?'

'Very much indeed,' Alice said politely.

'I'll tell you how I came to think of it,' said the Knight. 'You see, I said to myself, "The only difficulty is with the feet: the *head* is high enough already." Now, first I put my head on the top of the gate—then the head's high enough—then I stand on my head—then the feet are high enough, you see—then I'm over, you see.'

'Yes, I suppose you'd be over when that was done,'

Alice said thoughtfully: 'but don't you think it would be rather hard?'

'I haven't tried it yet,' the Knight said, gravely: 'so I can't tell for certain—but I'm afraid it *would* be a little hard.'

He looked so vexed at the idea, that Alice changed the subject hastily. 'What a curious helmet you've got!' she said cheerfully. 'Is that your invention too?'

The Knight looked down proudly at his helmet, which hung from the saddle. 'Yes,' he said, 'but I've invented a better one than that—like a sugar-loaf. When I used to wear it, if I fell off the horse, it always touched the ground directly. So I had a *very* little way to fall, you see—But there *was* the danger of falling *into* it, to be sure. That happened to me once—and the worst of it was, before I could get out again, the other White Knight came and put it on. He thought it was his own helmet.'

The Knight looked so solemn about it that Alice did not dare to laugh. 'I'm afraid you must have hurt him,' she said in a trembling voice, 'being on the top of his head.'

'I had to kick him, of course,' the Knight said, very seriously. 'And then he took the helmet off again—but it took hours and hours to get me out. I was as fast as— as lightning, you know.'

'But that's a different kind of fastness,' Alice objected.

The Knight shook his head. 'It was all kinds of fastness with me, I can assure you!' he said. He raised his hands in some excitement as he said this, and instantly rolled out of the saddle, and fell headlong into a deep ditch.

Alice ran to the side of the ditch to look for him. She was rather startled by the fall, as for some time he had kept on very well, and she was afraid that he really *was* hurt this time. However, though she could see nothing but the soles of his feet, she was much relieved to hear that he was talking on in his usual tone. 'All kinds of fastness,' he repeated: 'but it was careless of him to put another man's helmet on—with the man in it, too.'

'How *can* you go on talking so quietly, head downwards?' Alice asked, as she dragged him out by the feet, and laid him in a heap on the bank.

The Knight looked surprised at the question. 'What does it matter where my body happens to be?' he said. 'My mind goes on working all the same. In fact, the more head downwards I am, the more I keep inventing new things.

'Now the cleverest thing that I ever did,' he went on after a pause, 'was inventing a new pudding during the meat-course.'

'In time to have it cooked for the next course?' said Alice. 'Well, that *was* quick work, certainly.'

'Well, not the *next* course,' the Knight said in a slow thoughtful tone; 'no, certainly not the next *course*.'

'Then it would have to be the next day. I suppose you wouldn't have two pudding-courses in one dinner?'

'Well, not the *next* day,' the Knight repeated as before:

'not the next *day*. In fact,' he went on, holding his head down, and his voice getting lower and lower, 'I don't believe that pudding ever *was* cooked! In fact, I don't believe that pudding ever *will* be cooked! And yet it was a very clever pudding to invent.'

'What did you mean it to be made of?' Alice asked, hoping to cheer him up, for he seemed quite low-spirited about it.

'It began with blotting-paper,' the Knight answered with a groan.

'That wouldn't be very nice, I'm afraid——'

'Not very nice *alone*,' he interrupted, quite eagerly: 'but you've no idea what a difference it makes, mixing it with other things—such as gunpowder and sealing-wax. And here I must leave you.'

Alice could only look puzzled: she was thinking of the pudding.

'You are sad,' the Knight said in an anxious tone: 'let me sing you a song to comfort you.'

'Is it very long?' Alice asked, for she had heard a good deal of poetry that day.

'It's long,' said the Knight, 'but it's very, *very* beautiful. Everybody that hears me sing it—either it brings the *tears* into their eyes, or else——'

'Or else what?' said Alice, for the Knight had made a sudden pause.

'Or else it doesn't, you know. The name of the song is called "*Haddocks' Eyes*."'

'Oh, that's the name of the song, is it?' Alice said, trying to feel interested.

'No, you don't understand,' the Knight said, looking a little vexed. 'That's what the name is *called*. The name really is "*The Aged Aged Man*."'

'Then I ought to have said "That's what the *song* is called"?' Alice corrected herself.

'No, you oughtn't: that's another thing. The *song* is called "*Ways and Means*": but that's only what it's *called*, you know!'

'Well, what *is* the song, then?' said Alice, who was by this time completely bewildered.

'I was coming to that,' the Knight said. 'The song really is "*A-sitting On a Gate*": and the tune's my own invention.'

So saying, he stopped his horse and let the reins fall on its neck: then, slowly beating time with one hand, and with a faint smile lighting up his gentle, foolish face, he began.

Of all the strange things that Alice saw in her journey Through The Looking-Glass, this was the one that she always remembered most clearly. Years afterwards she could bring the whole scene back again, as if it had been only yesterday—the mild blue eyes and kindly smile of the Knight—the setting sun gleaming through his hair, and shining on his armour in a blaze of light that quite dazzled her—the horse quietly moving about, with the reins hanging loose on his neck, cropping the grass at her feet—and the black shadows of the forest behind—all this she took in like a picture, as, with one hand shading her eyes, she leant against a tree, watching the strange pair, and listening, in a half-dream, to the melancholy music of the song.

'But the tune *isn't* his own invention,' she said to herself: 'it's "*I give thee all, I can no more.*"' She stood and listened very attentively, but no tears came into her eyes.

> *'I'll tell thee everything I can;*
> *There's little to relate.*
> *I saw an aged aged man,*
> *A-sitting on a gate.*

See page 209

. . . Alice watching anxiously for the next tumble

"Who are you, aged man?" I said.
  "And how is it you live?"
And his answer trickled through my head
  Like water through a sieve.

He said "I look for butterflies
  That sleep among the wheat:
I make them into mutton pies,
  And sell them in the street.
I sell them unto men," he said,
  "Who sail on stormy seas;
And that's the way I get my bread—
  A trifle, if you please."

But I was thinking of a plan
  To dye one's whiskers green,
And always use so large a fan
  That they could not be seen.
So, having no reply to give
  To what the old man said,
I cried "Come, tell me how you live!"
  And thumped him on the head.

His accents mild took up the tale:
  He said "I go my ways,
And when I find a mountain-rill,
  I set it in a blaze;
And thence they make a stuff they call
  Rowlands' Macassar Oil—
Yet twopence-halfpenny is all
  They give me for my toil."

But I was thinking of a way
  To feed oneself on batter,
And so go on from day to day
  Getting a little fatter.

I shook him well from side to side,
  Until his face was blue:
"Come, tell me how you live," I cried
  "And what it is you do!"

He said "I hunt for haddocks' eyes
  Among the heather bright,
And work them into waistcoat-buttons
  In the silent night.
And these I do not sell for gold
  Or coin of silvery shine,
But for a copper halfpenny,
  And that will purchase nine.

"I sometimes dig for buttered rolls,
  Or set limed twigs for crabs;
I sometimes search the grassy knolls
  For wheels of Hansom-cabs.
And that's the way" (he gave a wink)
  "By which I get my wealth—
And very gladly will I drink
  Your Honour's noble health."

I heard him then, for I had just
   Completed my design
To keep the Menai bridge from rust
   By boiling it in wine.
I thanked him much for telling me
   The way he got his wealth,
But chiefly for his wish that he
   Might drink my noble health.

And now, if e'er by chance I put
   My fingers into glue,
Or madly squeeze a right-hand foot
   Into a left-hand shoe,
Or if I drop upon my toe
   A very heavy weight,
I weep, for it reminds me so
Of that old man I used to know—
Whose look was mild, whose speech was slow
Whose hair was whiter than the snow,
Whose face was very like a crow,
With eyes, like cinders, all aglow,
Who seemed distracted with his woe,
Who rocked his body to and fro,
And muttered mumblingly and low,
As if his mouth were full of dough,
Who snorted like a buffalo—
That summer evening long ago
   A-sitting on a gate.'

As the Knight sang the last words of the ballad, he gathered up the reins, and turned his horse's head along the road by which they had come. 'You've only a few yards to go,' he said, 'down the hill and over that little brook, and then you'll be a Queen—But you'll stay and see me off first?' he added as Alice turned away with an eager look. 'I shan't be long. You'll wait and wave

your handkerchief when I get to that turn in the road?
I think it 'll encourage me, you see.'

'Of course I 'll wait,' said Alice: 'and thank you very
much for coming so far—and for the song—I liked it
very much.'

'I hope so,' the Knight said doubtfully: 'but you didn't
cry so much as I expected.'

So they shook hands, and then the Knight rode slowly
away into the forest. 'It won't take long to see him *off*,
I expect,' Alice said to herself, as she stood watching him.
'There he goes! Right on his head as usual! However, he gets on again pretty easily—that comes of having
so many things hung round the horse——' So she went
on talking to herself, as she watched the horse walking
leisurely along the road, and the Knight tumbling off,
first on one side and then on the other. After the fourth
or fifth tumble he reached the turn, and then she waved
her handkerchief to him, and waited till he was out of
sight.

'I hope it encouraged him,' she said, as she turned to
run down the hill: 'and now for the last brook, and to be
a Queen! How grand it sounds!' A very few steps
brought her to the edge of the brook. 'The Eighth
Square at last!' she cried, as she bounded over

and threw herself down to rest on a lawn as soft as moss,
with little flower-beds dotted all about it here and there.
'Oh, how glad I am to get here! And what *is* this on
my head?' she exclaimed in a tone of dismay, as she put
her hands up to something very heavy, that fitted tight
round her head.

'But how *can* it have got there without my knowing it?' she said to herself, as she lifted it off, and set it on her lap to make out what it could possibly be.

It was a golden crown.

CHAPTER IX

QUEEN ALICE

'WELL, this *is* grand!' said Alice. 'I never expected I should be a Queen so soon—and I'll tell you what it is, your Majesty,' she went on in a severe tone (she was always rather fond of scolding herself), 'it'll never do to loll about on the grass like that! Queens have to be dignified, you know!'

So she got up and walked about—rather stiffly just at first, as she was afraid that the crown might come off: but she comforted herself with the thought that there was nobody to see her, 'and if I really am a Queen,' she said as she sat down again, 'I shall be able to manage it quite well in time.'

Everything was happening so oddly that she didn't feel a bit surprised at finding the Red Queen and the White Queen sitting close to her, one on each side: she would have liked very much to ask them how they came there, but she feared it would not be quite civil. However, there would be no harm, she thought, in asking if the game was over. 'Please, would you tell me——' she began, looking timidly at the Red Queen.

'Speak when you're spoken to!' the Red Queen sharply interrupted her.

'But if everybody obeyed that rule,' said Alice, who was always ready for a little argument, 'and if you only spoke when you were spoken to, and the other person always waited for *you* to begin, you see nobody would ever say anything, so that——'

'Ridiculous!' cried the Queen. 'Why, don't you see, child——' here she broke off with a frown, and, after thinking for a minute, suddenly changed the subject of the conversation. 'What do you mean by "If you really are a Queen"? What right have you to call yourself so? You can't be a Queen, you know, till you've passed the proper examination. And the sooner we begin it, the better.'

'I only said "if"!' poor Alice pleaded in a piteous tone.

The two Queens looked at each other, and the Red Queen remarked, with a little shudder, 'She *says* she only said "if"——'

'But she said a great deal more than that!' the White

Queen moaned, wringing her hands. 'Oh, ever so much more than that!'

'So you did, you know,' the Red Queen said to Alice. 'Always speak the truth—think before you speak—and write it down afterwards.'

'I'm sure I didn't mean——' Alice was beginning, but the Red Queen interrupted.

'That's just what I complain of! You *should* have meant! What do you suppose is the use of a child without any meaning? Even a joke should have some meaning—and a child's more important than a joke, I hope. You couldn't deny that, even if you tried with both hands.'

'I don't deny things with my *hands*,' Alice objected.

'Nobody said you did,' said the Red Queen, 'I said you couldn't if you tried.'

'She's in that state of mind,' said the White Queen, 'that she wants to deny *something*—only she doesn't know what to deny!'

'A nasty, vicious temper,' the Red Queen remarked; and then there was an uncomfortable silence for a minute or two.

The Red Queen broke the silence by saying to the White Queen, 'I invite you to Alice's dinner-party this afternoon.'

The White Queen smiled feebly, and said 'And I invite *you*.'

'I didn't know I was to have a party at all,' said Alice; 'but if there is to be one, I think *I* ought to invite the guests.'

'We gave you the opportunity of doing it,' the Red Queen remarked: 'but I dare say you've not had many lessons in manners yet?'

'Manners are not taught in lessons,' said Alice. 'Lessons teach you to do sums, and things of that sort.'

'Can you do Addition?' the White Queen asked. 'What's one and one and one and one and one and one and one and one and one and one?'

'I don't know,' said Alice. 'I lost count.'

'She can't do Addition,' the Red Queen interrupted. 'Can you do Subtraction? Take nine from eight.'

'Nine from eight I can't, you know,' Alice replied very readily: 'but——'

'She can't do Substraction,' said the White Queen. 'Can you do Division? Divide a loaf by a knife—what's the answer to that?'

'I suppose——' Alice was beginning, but the Red Queen answered for her. 'Bread and butter, of course. Try another Subtraction sum. Take a bone from a dog. What remains?'

Alice considered. 'The bone wouldn't remain, of course, if I took it—and the dog wouldn't remain; it would come to bite me—and I'm sure *I* shouldn't remain!'

'Then you think nothing would remain?' said the Red Queen.

'I think that's the answer.'

'Wrong, as usual,' said the Red Queen; 'the dog's temper would remain.'

'But I don't see how——'

'Why, look here!' the Red Queen cried. 'The dog would lose its temper, wouldn't it?'

'Perhaps it would,' Alice replied cautiously.

'Then if the dog went away, its temper would remain!' the Queen exclaimed.

Alice said, as gravely as she could, 'They might go different ways.' But she couldn't help thinking to herself, 'What dreadful nonsense we *are* talking!'

'She can't do sums a *bit*!' the Queens said together, with great emphasis.

'Can *you* do sums?' Alice said, turning suddenly on the White Queen, for she didn't like being found fault with so much.

The Queen gasped and shut her eyes. 'I can do Addition,' she said, 'if you give me time—but I can't do Substraction under *any* circumstances!'

'Of course you know your A B C?' said the Red Queen.

'To be sure I do,' said Alice.

'So do I,' the White Queen whispered. 'We'll often say it over together, dear. And I'll tell you a secret—I can read words of one letter! Isn't *that* grand? However, don't be discouraged. You'll come to it in time.'

Here the Red Queen began again. 'Can you answer useful questions?' she said. 'How is bread made?'

'I know *that*!' Alice cried eagerly. 'You take some flour——'

'Where do you pick the flower?' the White Queen asked. 'In a garden, or in the hedges?'

'Well, it isn't *picked* at all,' Alice explained: 'it's *ground*——'

'How many acres of ground?' said the White Queen. 'You mustn't leave out so many things.'

'Fan her head!' the Red Queen anxiously interrupted. 'She'll be feverish after so much thinking.' So they set to work and fanned her with bunches of leaves, till she had to beg them to leave off, it blew her hair about so.

'She's all right again now,' said the Red Queen. 'Do you know Languages? What's the French for fiddle-de-dee?'

'Fiddle-de-dee's not English,' Alice replied gravely.

'Who said it was?' said the Red Queen.

Alice thought she saw a way out of the difficulty this time. 'If you'll tell me what language "fiddle-de-dee" is, I'll tell you the French for it!' she exclaimed triumphantly.

But the Red Queen drew herself up rather stiffly, and said 'Queens never make bargains.'

'I wish Queens never asked questions,' Alice thought to herself.

'Don't let us quarrel,' the White Queen said in an anxious tone. 'What is the cause of lightning?'

'The cause of lightning,' Alice said very decidedly, for she felt quite sure about this, 'is the thunder—no, no!' she hastily corrected herself. 'I meant the other way.'

'It's too late to correct it,' said the Red Queen: 'when you've once said a thing, that fixes it, and you must take the consequences.'

'Which reminds me—' the White Queen said, looking down and nervously clasping and unclasping her hands, 'we had *such* a thunderstorm last Tuesday—I mean one of the last set of Tuesdays, you know.'

'In *our* country,' Alice remarked, 'there's only one day at a time.'

The Red Queen said, 'That's a poor thin way of doing things. Now *here*, we mostly have days and nights two or three at a time, and sometimes in the winter we take as many as five nights together—for warmth, you know.'

'Are five nights warmer than one night, then?' Alice ventured to ask.

'Five times as warm, of course.'

'But they should be five times as *cold*, by the same rule——'

'Just so!' cried the Red Queen. 'Five times as warm, *and* five times as cold—just as I'm five times as rich as you are, *and* five times as clever!'

Alice sighed and gave it up. 'It's exactly like a riddle with no answer!' she thought.

'Humpty Dumpty saw it too,' the White Queen went on in a low voice, more as if she were talking to herself. 'He came to the door with a corkscrew in his hand——'

'What for?' said the Red Queen.

'He said he *would* come in,' the White Queen went on, 'because he was looking for a hippopotamus. Now, as it happened, there wasn't such a thing in the house, that morning.'

'Is there generally?' Alice asked in an astonished tone.

'Well, only on Thursdays,' said the Queen.

'I know what he came for,' said Alice: 'he wanted to punish the fish, because——'

Here the White Queen began again. 'It was *such* a thunderstorm, you can't think!' ('She *never* could, you know,' said the Red Queen.) 'And part of the roof came off, and ever so much thunder got in—and it went rolling round the room in great lumps—and knocking over the tables and things—till I was so frightened, I couldn't remember my own name!'

Alice thought to herself 'I never should *try* to remember my name in the middle of an accident! Where would be the use of it?' But she did not say this aloud, for fear of hurting the poor Queen's feelings.

'Your Majesty must excuse her,' the Red Queen said to Alice, taking one of the White Queen's hands in her own, and gently stroking it: 'she means well, but she can't help saying foolish things, as a general rule.'

The White Queen looked timidly at Alice, who felt she *ought* to say something kind, but really couldn't think of anything.

'She never was really well brought up,' the Red Queen went on: 'but it's amazing how good-tempered she is! Pat her on the head, and see how pleased she'll be!' But this was more than Alice had courage to do.

'A little kindness—and putting her hair in papers—would do wonders with her——'

The White Queen gave a deep sigh, and laid her head on Alice's shoulder. 'I *am* so sleepy!' she moaned.

'She's tired, poor thing!' said the Red Queen. 'Smooth her hair—lend her your nightcap—and sing her a soothing lullaby.'

'I haven't got a nightcap with me,' said Alice, as she tried to obey the first direction: 'and I don't know any soothing lullabies.'

'I must do it myself, then,' said the Red Queen, and she began:

> '*Hush-a-by lady, in Alice's lap!*
> *Till the feast's ready, we've time for a nap:*
> *When the feast's over, we'll go to the ball—*
> *Red Queen, and White Queen, and Alice, and all!*

'And now you know the words,' she added, as she put her head down on Alice's other shoulder, 'just sing it through to *me*. I'm getting sleepy too.' In another moment both Queens were fast asleep, and snoring loud.

'What *am* I to do?' exclaimed Alice, looking about in great perplexity, as first one round head, and then the other, rolled down from her shoulder, and lay like a heavy

lump in her lap. 'I don't think it *ever* happened before,
that anyone had to take care of two Queens asleep at
once! No, not in all the History of England—it couldn't,
you know, because there never was more than one Queen
at a time. Do wake up, you heavy things!' she went on
in an impatient tone; but there was no answer but a
gentle snoring.

The snoring got more distinct every minute, and
sounded more like a tune: at last she could even make out
words, and she listened so eagerly that, when the two
great heads suddenly vanished from her lap, she hardly
missed them.

She was standing before an arched doorway, over
which were the words QUEEN ALICE in large
letters, and on each side of it there was a bell-handle;
one marked 'Visitors' Bell,' and the other 'Servants'
Bell.'

'I'll wait till the song's over,' thought Alice, 'and then
I'll ring the—the—*which* bell must I ring?' she went on,
very much puzzled by the names. 'I'm not a visitor,
and I'm not a servant. There *ought* to be one marked
"Queen," you know——'

Just then the door opened a little way, and a creature with a long beak put its head out for a moment and said 'No admittance till the week after next!' and shut the door again with a bang.

Alice knocked and rang in vain for a long time, but at last a very old Frog, who was sitting under a tree, got up and hobbled slowly towards her: he was dressed in bright yellow, and had enormous boots on.

'What is it, now?' the Frog said in a deep hoarse whisper.

Alice turned round, ready to find fault with anybody. 'Where's the servant whose business it is to answer the door?' she began.

'Which door?' said the Frog.

Alice almost stamped with irritation at the slow drawl in which he spoke. '*This* door, of course!'

The Frog looked at the door with his large dull eyes for a minute: then he went nearer and rubbed it with his thumb, as if he were trying whether the paint would come off; then he looked at Alice.

'To answer the door?' he said. 'What's it been asking of?' He was so hoarse that Alice could scarcely hear him.

'I don't know what you mean,' she said.

'I speaks English, doesn't I?' the Frog went on. 'Or are you deaf? What did it ask you?'

'Nothing!' Alice said impatiently. 'I've been knocking at it!'

'Shouldn't do that—shouldn't do that—' the Frog muttered. 'Wexes it, you know.' Then he went up and gave the door a kick with one of his great feet. 'You let *it* alone,' he panted out, as he hobbled back to his tree, 'and it'll let *you* alone, you know.'

At this moment the door was flung open, and a shrill voice was heard singing:

'*To the Looking-Glass world it was Alice that said*
"*I've a sceptre in hand, I've a crown on my head;*
Let the Looking-Glass creatures, whatever they be,
Come and dine with the Red Queen, the White Queen, and me!"'

And hundreds of voices joined in the chorus:

'*Then fill up the glasses as quick as you can,*
And sprinkle the table with buttons and bran:
Put cats in the coffee, and mice in the tea—
And welcome Queen Alice with thirty-times-three!'

Then followed a confused noise of cheering, and Alice thought to herself, 'Thirty times three makes ninety. I wonder if anyone's counting?' In a minute there was silence again, and the same shrill voice sang another verse:

"O Looking-Glass creatures," quoth Alice, "draw near!
'Tis an honour to see me, a favour to hear:
'Tis a privilege high to have dinner and tea
Along with the Red Queen, the White Queen, and me!"'

Then came the chorus again:

'Then fill up the glasses with treacle and ink,
Or anything else that is pleasant to drink;
Mix sand with the cider, and wool with the wine—
And welcome Queen Alice with ninety-times-nine!'

'Ninety times nine!' Alice repeated in despair. 'Oh, that'll never be done! I'd better go in at once—' and in she went, and there was a dead silence the moment she appeared.

Alice glanced nervously along the table, as she walked up the large hall, and noticed that there were about fifty guests, of all kinds: some were animals, some birds, and there were even a few flowers among them. 'I'm glad they've come without waiting to be asked,' she thought: 'I should never have known who were the right people to invite!'

There were three chairs at the head of the table; the Red and White Queens had taken two of them, but the middle one was empty. Alice sat down, rather uncomfortable at the silence, and longing for someone to speak.

At last the Red Queen began. 'You've missed the soup and fish,' she said. 'Put on the joint!' And the waiters set a leg of mutton before Alice, who looked at it rather anxiously, as she had never had to carve one before.

'You look a little shy; let me introduce you to that leg of mutton,' said the Red Queen. 'Alice—Mutton; Mutton—Alice.' The leg of mutton got up in the dish

and made a little bow to Alice; and she returned the bow,
not knowing whether to be frightened or amused.

'May I give you a slice?' she said, taking up the knife
and fork, and looking from one Queen to the other.

'Certainly not,' the Red
Queen said, very decidedly:
'it isn't etiquette to cut
anyone you've been intro-
duced to. Remove the
joint!' And the waiters
carried it off, and brought
a large plum-pudding in
its place.

'I won't be introduced
to the pudding, please,'
Alice said rather hastily,
'or we shall get no dinner
at all. May I give you
some?'

But the Red Queen
looked sulky, and growled
'Pudding—Alice; Alice—Pudding. Remove the pudding!' and the waiters took it away before Alice could
return its bow.

However, she didn't see why the Red Queen should
be the only one to give orders, so, as an experiment, she
called out 'Waiter! Bring back the pudding!' and there
it was again in a moment like a conjuring trick. It was
so large that she couldn't help feeling a *little* shy with it,
as she had been with the mutton; however, she conquered
her shyness by a great effort, and handed a slice to the
Red Queen.

'What impertinence!' said the Pudding. 'I wonder
how you'd like it, if I were to cut a slice out of *you*, you
creature!'

Alice could only look at it and gasp.

'Make a remark,' said the Red Queen: 'it's ridiculous to leave all the conversation to the pudding!'

'Do you know, I've had such a quantity of poetry repeated to me to-day,' Alice began, a little frightened at finding that, the moment she opened her lips, there was dead silence, and all eyes were fixed upon her; 'and it's a very curious thing, I think—every poem was about fishes in some way.   Do you know why they're so fond of fishes, all about here?'

She spoke to the Red Queen, whose answer was a little wide of the mark.   'As to fishes,' she said, very slowly and solemnly, putting her mouth close to Alice's ear, 'her White Majesty knows a lovely riddle—all in poetry—all about fishes.   Shall she repeat it?'

'Her Red Majesty's very kind to mention it,' the White Queen murmured into Alice's other ear, in a voice like the cooing of a pigeon.   'It would be *such* a treat! May I?'

'Please do,' Alice said very politely.

The White Queen laughed with delight, and stroked Alice's cheek.   Then she began:

> '"*First the fish must be caught.*"
> *That is easy: a baby, I think, could have caught it.*
> "*Next, the fish must be bought.*"
> *That is easy: a penny, I think, would have bought it.*
>
> "*Now cook me the fish!*"
> *That is easy, and will not take more than a minute.*
> "*Let it lie in a dish!*"
> *That is easy, because it already is in it.*
>
> "*Bring it here.   Let me sup!*"
> *It is easy to set such a dish on the table.*
> "*Take the dish-cover up!*"
> *Ah,* that *is so hard that I fear I'm unable!*

For it holds it like glue——
Holds the lid to the dish, while it lies in the middle:
Which is easiest to do,
Un-dish-cover the fish, or dishcover the riddle?'

'Take a minute to think about it, and then guess,' said
the Red Queen. 'Meanwhile, we'll drink your health
—Queen Alice's health!' she screamed at the top of her
voice, and all the guests began drinking it directly, and
very queerly they managed it: some of them put their
glasses upon their heads like extinguishers, and drank
all that trickled down their faces—others upset the
decanters, and drank the wine as it ran off the edges of the
table—and three of them (who looked like kangaroos)
scrambled into the dish of roast mutton, and began to lap
up the gravy, 'just like pigs in a trough!' thought Alice.

'You ought to return thanks in a neat speech,' the Red
Queen said, frowning at Alice as she spoke.

'We must support you, you know,' the White Queen
whispered, as Alice got up to do it, very obediently, but a
little frightened.

'Thank you very much,' she whispered in reply, 'but
I can do quite well without.'

'That wouldn't be at all the thing,' the Red Queen said
very decidedly: so Alice tried to submit to it with a
good grace.

('And they *did* push so!' she said afterwards, when she
was telling her sister the history of the feast. 'You would
have thought they wanted to squeeze me flat!')

In fact it was rather difficult for her to keep in her place
while she made her speech: the two Queens pushed her so,
one on each side, that they nearly lifted her up into the air:
'I rise to return thanks—' Alice began: and she really *did*
rise as she spoke, several inches; but she got hold of the
edge of the table, and managed to pull herself down again.

'Take care of yourself!' screamed the White Queen,

seizing Alice's hair with both her hands. 'Something's going to happen!'

And then (as Alice afterwards described it) all sorts of things happened in a moment. The candles all grew up to the ceiling, looking something like a bed of rushes with fireworks at the top.

As to the bottles, they each took a pair of plates, which they hastily fitted on as wings, and so, with forks for legs, went fluttering about: 'and very like birds they look,' Alice thought to herself, as well as she could in the dreadful confusion that was beginning.

At this moment she heard a hoarse laugh at her side, and turned to see what was the matter with the White Queen; but, instead of the Queen, there was the leg of mutton sitting on the chair. 'Here I am!' cried a voice from the soup-tureen, and Alice turned again, just in time to see the Queen's broad good-natured face grinning at her for a moment over the edge of the tureen, before she disappeared into the soup.

There was not a moment to be lost. Already several of the guests were lying down in the dishes, and the soup-ladle was walking up the table to Alice, and signing to her to get out of its way.

'I can't stand this any longer!' she cried, as she seized the table-cloth with both hands: one good pull, and plates, dishes, guests, and candles came crashing down together in a heap on the floor.

'And as for *you*,' she went on, turning fiercely upon the Red Queen, whom she considered as the cause of all the mischief—but the Queen was no longer at her side—she had suddenly dwindled down to the size of a little doll, and was now on the table, merrily running round and round after her own shawl, which was trailing behind her.

At any other time, Alice would have felt surprised at this, but she was far too much excited to be surprised at anything *now*. 'As for *you*,' she repeated, catching hold of the little creature in the very act of jumping over a bottle which had just lighted upon the table, 'I'll shake you into a kitten, that I will!'

CHAPTER X

SHAKING

SHE took her off the table as she spoke, and shook her backwards and forwards with all her might.

The Red Queen made no resistance whatever; only her face grew very small, and her eyes got large and green: and still, as Alice went on shaking her, she kept on growing shorter—and fatter—and softer—and rounder —and——

CHAPTER XI

WAKING

——and it really *was* a kitten, after all.

CHAPTER XII

WHICH DREAMED IT?

'YOUR Red Majesty shouldn't purr so loud,' Alice said, rubbing her eyes, and addressing the kitten respectfully, yet with some severity. 'You woke me out of— oh! such a nice dream! And you've been along with me, Kitty—all through the Looking-Glass world. Did you know it, dear?'

It is a very inconvenient habit of kittens (Alice had once made the remark) that, whatever you say to them, they *always* purr. 'If they would only purr for "yes," and mew for "no," or any rule of that sort,' she had said, 'so that one could keep up a conversation! But how *can* you talk with a person if they always say the same thing?'

On this occasion the kitten only purred: and it was impossible to guess whether it meant 'yes' or 'no.'

So Alice hunted among the chessmen on the table till she had found the Red Queen: then she went down on her knees on the hearthrug, and put the kitten and the Queen to look at each other. 'Now, Kitty!' she cried, clapping her hands triumphantly. 'You've got to confess that that was what you turned into!'

('But it wouldn't look at it,' she said, when she was explaining the thing afterwards to her sister: 'it turned away its head, and pretended not to see it: but it looked a *little* ashamed of itself, so I think it *must* have been the Red Queen.')

'Sit up a little more stiffly, dear!' Alice cried with a merry laugh. 'And curtsy while you're thinking what to —what to purr. It saves time, remember!' And she caught it up in her arms, and gave it one little kiss 'just in honour of its having been a Red Queen, you know!'

'Snowdrop, my pet!' she went on, looking over her
shoulder at the White Kitten, which was still patiently
undergoing its toilet, 'when *will* Dinah have finished
with your White Majesty, I wonder? That must be the
reason you were so untidy in my dream.—Dinah! Do

you know that you're scrubbing a White Queen? Really,
it's most disrespectful of you, and I'm quite surprised
at you!

'And what did *Dinah* turn to, I wonder?' she prattled
on, as she settled comfortably down, with one elbow on
the rug, and her chin in her hand, to watch the kittens.
'Tell me, Dinah, did you turn to Humpty Dumpty? I
think you did—however, you'd better not mention it to
your friends just yet, for I'm not sure.

'By the way, Kitty, if only you'd been really with me
in my dream, there was one thing you *would* have enjoyed

—I had such a quantity of poetry said to me, all about fishes! To-morrow morning you shall have a real treat. All the time you're eating your breakfast, I'll repeat "The Walrus and the Carpenter" to you; and then you can make believe it's oysters, my dear!

'Now, Kitty, let's consider who it was that dreamed it all. This is a serious question, my dear, and you should *not* go on licking your paw like that—as if Dinah hadn't washed you this morning! You see, Kitty, it *must* have been either me or the Red King. He was part of my dream, of course—but then I was part of his dream, too! *Was* it the Red King, Kitty? You were his wife, my dear, so you ought to know—Oh, Kitty, *do* help to settle it! I'm sure your paw can wait!' But the provoking kitten only began on the other paw, and pretended it hadn't heard the question.

Which do *you* think it was?

A BOAT, beneath a sunny sky,
Lingering onward dreamily
In an evening of July—

Children three that nestle near,
Eager eye and willing ear,
Pleased a simple tale to hear—

Long has paled that sunny sky:
Echoes fade and memories die:
Autumn frosts have slain July.

Still she haunts me, phantomwise,
Alice moving under skies
Never seen by waking eyes.

Children yet, the tale to hear,
Eager eye and willing ear,
Lovingly shall nestle near.

In a Wonderland they lie,
Dreaming as the days go by,
Dreaming as the summers die:

Ever drifting down the stream—
Lingering in the golden gleam—
Life, what is it but a dream?

[TURN OVER

AN EASTER GREETING

TO

EVERY CHILD WHO LOVES

'ALICE'

DEAR CHILD,

Please to fancy, if you can, that you are reading a real letter, from a real friend whom you have seen, and whose voice you can seem to yourself to hear, wishing you, as I do now with all my heart, a happy Easter.

Do you know that delicious dreamy feeling when one first wakes on a summer morning, with the twitter of birds in the air, and the fresh breeze coming in at the open window—when, lying lazily with eyes half shut, one sees as in a dream green boughs waving, or waters rippling in a golden light? It is a pleasure very near to sadness, bringing tears to one's eyes like a beautiful picture or poem. And is not that a Mother's gentle hand that undraws your curtains, and a Mother's sweet voice that summons you to rise? To rise and forget, in the bright sunlight, the ugly dreams that frightened you so when all was dark—to rise and enjoy another happy day, first kneeling to thank that unseen Friend, who sends you the beautiful sun?

Are these strange words from a writer of such tales as 'Alice'? And is this a strange letter to find in a book of nonsense? It may be so. Some perhaps may blame me for thus mixing together things grave and gay: others may smile and think it odd that anyone should speak of solemn things at all, except in church and on a Sunday: but I think—nay, I am sure—that some children will read this gently and lovingly, and in the spirit in which I have written it.

For I do not believe God means us thus to divide life into two halves —to wear a grave face on Sunday, and to think it out of place to even so much as mention Him on a week-day. Do you think He cares to see only kneeling figures, and to hear only tones of prayer— and that He does not also love to see the lambs leaping in the sunlight, and to hear the merry voices of the children, as they roll among the hay? Surely their innocent laughter is as sweet in His ears as the grandest anthem that ever rolled up from the 'dim religious light' of some solemn cathedral?

And if I have written anything to add to those stores of innocent and healthy amusement that are laid up in books for the children I love so well, it is surely something I may hope to look back upon without shame and sorrow (as how much of life must then be recalled!) when my turn comes to walk through the valley of shadows.

This Easter sun will rise on you, dear child, feeling your 'life in every limb,' and eager to rush out into the fresh morning air—and many an Easter-day will come and go, before it finds you feeble and grey-headed, creeping wearily out to bask once more in the sunlight —but it is good, even now, to think sometimes of that great morning when the 'Sun of Righteousness shall arise with healing in his wings.'

Surely your gladness need not be the less for the thought that you will one day see a brighter dawn than this—when lovelier sights will meet your eyes than any waving trees or rippling waters—when angel-hands shall undraw your curtains, and sweeter tones than ever loving Mother breathed shall wake you to a new and glorious day— and when all the sadness, and the sin, that darkened life on this little earth, shall be forgotten like the dreams of a night that is past!

Your affectionate friend,

LEWIS CARROLL.

[TURN OVER

CHRISTMAS GREETINGS

FROM A FAIRY TO A CHILD

LADY dear, if Fairies may
  For a moment lay aside
Cunning tricks and elfish play
  'Tis at happy Christmas-tide.

We have heard the children say—
  Gentle children, whom we love—
Long ago, on Christmas Day,
  Came a message from above.

Still, as Christmas-tide comes round,
  They remember it again—
Echo still the joyful sound,
  'Peace on earth, goodwill to men.'

Yet the hearts must child-like be
  Where such heavenly guests abide:
Unto children, in their glee,
  All the year is Christmas-tide.

Thus, forgetting tricks and play
  For a moment, Lady dear,
We would wish you, if we may,
  Merry Christmas, glad New Year.

Christmas, 1867.